THE FLOWER & THE BLACKBIRD

THE FLOWER & THE BLACKBIRD

Book Two in the Elioud Legacy Series

By Liane Zane

ZEPHON ROMANCE

Boston, Massachusetts

Copyright

Digital Edition AUGUST 2021 ISBN: 978-1-7351318-9-4
Print Edition ISBN: 978-1-7351318-8-7

Cover design by Perla Enrica Giancola

FIRST EDITION

Dedication

To Ashlyn

Thanks for always reading and talking story and character with me

One

*I*n *bocca al lupo. Into the wolf's mouth.* The unknown Italian who coined that phrase wishing performers luck before facing an audience had no idea how accurate it was. Then again, whoever coined that phrase had no idea that inhabiting a cover identity during a covert operation qualified as performing. But Anastasia Fiore, the descendant of opera divas and theater leads, knew better than most what facing the sharp teeth of hostile foreign agents and brutal criminals entailed: fail to convince an audience filled with killers and sociopaths that you were who you said you were and there were no second acts.

Fortunately, Anastasia—known as Stasia to her colleagues in the *Agenzia Informazioni e Sicurezza Esterna*—had inherited her acting chops from some of Italy's finest performers on her mother's side. On her father's side, she'd inherited a moral code to uphold the law and a talent for fighting. She knew in her bones, in fact, that it must have been a Fiore progenitor who had supplied the traditional comeback to the colorful idiom: *Crepi! May it die.* In other words, when your acting fails to convince criminals and enemies, abandon pretense, and take the bastards down. Or out. Whatever was most expedient.

It was her ability to excel at both operational modes that made her such an invaluable asset to her country's intelligence services.

The fact that she could wear a swimsuit and sarong with the enviable allure of a model only added to her usefulness. That and the skill to use any number of weapons hidden in said sarong (and on her body) at a moment's notice.

Yet Stasia preferred to avoid violence. Much better to charm the wolf and keep her blade sharp than to go for the wolf's throat only to find herself surrounded by the pack. Much easier to outmaneuver an enemy than to outfight him. And much more satisfying.

The key to adopting a cover identity was believing that your legend was an alternative you without forgetting who you were in the process. The closer the cover identity to your real life the better. In fact, the closer to your *imagined* life, the life you had dreamed about in your heart of hearts, was the ideal.

This afternoon, as Stasia made her way to the bar pavilion at the Hula Hula Beach Club on the Croatian island of Hvar, she appeared to be nothing more than a beautiful, confident woman who had spent untold hours relaxing on the beach among other beautiful beachgoers. It was easy enough for her to play this role because she was indeed a beautiful woman who had grown up on the coasts of Calabria. No one needed to know that the wealthy, refined woman that she seemed to be came almost entirely from her teenage imagination of being Sophia Loren's granddaughter.

Looking at her, many of the older beach visitors might have been forgiven for thinking that she *was* indeed related to Italy's most famous film star. Stasia did what she could to encourage that perception. She wore her luxurious golden-brown hair held back in soft waves by a silk scarf tied at the side of her neck. Her high, arched brows emphasized large, almond-shaped eyes, which she'd lined with black before brushing black mascara on her naturally long lashes. Other than some sheer coral lip gloss, she wore no makeup. The dimple in her chin, however, she'd been born with, unlike her imaginary grandmother, whose chin was chiseled by shrapnel during World War II.

Her swimsuit, a black one-piece with thick shoulder straps and a square neckline, added to her resemblance to the grand dame of the golden age of Italian cinema. However, Ms. Loren never wore a miniature dagger hidden in a large crystal pendant nor a garrote hidden in a sterling silver snake wrapped around her upper arm.

And Stasia, smiling to herself like the Mona Lisa, thought that it was highly unlikely that the most beautiful woman in the world had ever strapped a Kel-Tec P32 9mm handgun to her thigh or hid a World War II-era BC-41 fighting dagger in her tote bag. Then again, Ms. Loren had never sought to infiltrate an Albanian art theft ring responsible for stealing a Rembrandt and a Renoir. The most dangerous men that Ms. Loren had ever had to face in her career were love-struck leading men such as Peter Sellers, who'd grown so infatuated with his glamorous co-star that he'd left his wife for her.

As Stasia strolled toward the Albanians in question, she felt a tingle on the back of her neck. Her stride never changed, but she glanced around. There was something about this tingle that was familiar. It had the same quality as the sensation that had danced along her spine a few weeks ago when she'd been in Brigittenau, Vienna's Twentieth District, following up on a lead for a personal investigation. Perhaps she had her own romantic stalker.

Stasia frowned at that thought.

Of course she didn't. The irritating *Elioud* couldn't possibly be here at the same time as she was and watching her.

But then, he *was* a Croatian with angel blood.

Although the crowds at the beach club had diminished since the high season of August, there were still plenty of people enjoying what had been deemed Europe's best island vacation. Stasia observed everything with the practiced thoroughness of a trained operative, all while looking as though she hadn't a care in the world beyond finding a seat where she could enjoy her cocktail, a *negroni*. The classic Italian *aperitivo* featured orange-flavored Campari liqueur, gin, and sweet red vermouth, stirred *not* shaken. So basically a lush, dark version of James Bond's martini—appropriate for an Italian spy on a covert mission.

And the current mission required her to channel her inner bombshell to catch the eye of two bold con men who'd brazenly stolen famous paintings worth nearly thirty million euros from an Italian art dealer. They'd run a long con, meeting with the art dealer multiple times to negotiate a price, and then taking the paintings while he sat in a conference room waiting for them to bring him coffee to enjoy as they finalized the sale.

Stasia rather admired the nerve of these criminals—their con was the dark side of her own exploits. That was why she was going to relish sending them to prison and returning the art to Italy. So when the *Carabinieri* Command for the Protection of Cultural Heritage, better known as Italy's Art Squad, contacted her boss and asked for her help, she'd eagerly agreed.

Unfortunately, all of the tables near the Albanians were occupied. Fortunately, the closest, and therefore most prime, table seated four young men wearing unbuttoned short-sleeved shirts, swim trunks, and slide-on sandals. In front of them were four empty glasses. As she approached, one of the young men signaled to a waitress wending her way through the lounge chairs overlooking the Adriatic.

Stasia got to the table first.

"*Ciao*," she said, smiling. She felt genuine warmth for these targets of her attention, and it oozed from her.

They sat up straighter and smiled back. "*Ciao*."

Croatians. Better and better. Though there was a complicated history between her country and theirs, often Stasia could find and exploit a love, especially among younger Croatian men, for Italian culture. She shifted her stance slightly to highlight her curves, holding her *negroni* almost level with her breasts. Her targets' gazes tracked her movement. She smiled to herself. Of course, she defined the epitome of Italian *culture* that Croatian men loved.

At that thought, a vivid image of Miró Kos flashed into her thoughts like lightning. *There* was a Croatian male who hadn't drawn any amount of affection from her, though there had been plenty of heat of the annoyed and impatient kind. True, he hadn't seemed at all duped by her external charm. Perhaps that explained her very strong desire to throttle him. That and the fact that he'd destroyed her *surujin*, a type of martial-arts weapon consisting of a weighted stainless-steel chain. A chain the infuriating *Elioud* had melted on their first meeting. Never mind that she'd wrapped it around his body during a street fight.

Stasia shoved the memory away and focused on the men before her, whose eyes all looked a little glazed already—and not a little scared. She consciously let her irritation go. Perhaps they'd seen something of it in her expression. She aimed her smile at the man at the far side of the table and the closest to the Albanians. In that moment, she imagined that he was her beloved and she bent to kiss him, her fingers sliding through the gray frosting his temple. ...

Reality intruded on her and threatened to break the spell she wove. She felt her smile dim.

The young man did *not* have any gray hairs.

No matter. She was a professional. What mattered whether it was affection or irritation that heated her expression? But her pace was off. She was in danger of losing her opening hook.

"I am meeting a friend. I would prefer to sit out of the sun while I wait." She gestured at the thatched roof shading their table. Her smile grew, warmer than ever. "Would you mind very much that I join you?"

The young man on the other side of the table to whom she spoke swallowed heavily and stood. "Please, sit here. I will stand."

"*Grazie*," she said, infusing that one word with even more warmth and laying her hand briefly on his forearm as she passed him to sit. Most people—those who had empathy anyway—would be bound by a sense of obligation for the gratitude they'd inspired in others. It was a much more effective weapon most of the time than the actual weapons she carried. She wanted to keep it that way.

She made a show of dropping her tote bag at her side and crossing her legs so that her sarong slipped open, revealing smooth skin and shapely thighs and calves. The collective breath intake around her was gratifyingly audible, but Stasia had accomplished more than enthralling her male companions: she'd freed her legs, whose allure owed not a little to hundreds of hours spent kicking the stuffing out of a weight bag. And bad guys. Lots of bad guys. Like the ones at the VIP table next to her.

Keeping said bad guys in her peripheral vision, Stasia lifted her *negroni* in a toast to the Croat who'd given her his seat.

"*Alla nostra*! We have missed the crowds of *turistas*." She emphasized the word *we*, as though she were a native Croat. This spurred a round of comments to which she paid little attention. Instead, she discreetly tapped the almost-invisible earbud in her right ear. She was blessed with acute hearing, but these earbuds from a friend at the American CIA had been programmed to match the speech frequencies of the Albanians while muting those next to her. They also functioned as comms with the Art Squad, whose members waited outside the club for her signal.

While she smiled at her newfound friends and murmured a few comments here and there, Stasia mentally reviewed what she knew about the Albanians in question. Brothers Abdyl and Agron Dervishi had a thick file at Interpol where they were suspected in more than two dozen confidence schemes ranging from selling sub-standard generic prescription medicines manufactured in the Ukraine to unsuspecting clinics in France and Germany to hawking defective pacemakers produced in Poland to small hospitals in Italy and England. Until now, the Dervishi brothers had trafficked in shoddy fakes in the medical industry. Agron had been caught four years ago selling expired prescription contact lenses to an Austrian pharmacy chain and had spent the intervening years in prison. When he got out last April, he and Abdyl had disappeared only to surface two weeks ago in northern Italy negotiating a sham art deal worth a hundred times more than their previous scams—and leaving them with the goods instead of the cash.

It was a perplexing turn of events. Why would these con men switch their game at this stage? They had the contacts and the experience to handle harried hospital administrators and naive retail managers in small metropolitan areas. And the cons were endless, as endless as the variety and demand for all things health related. As long as people got sick or needed help with the vagaries of life, there would be snake-oil salesmen selling them false hope.

The change in *modus operandi* suggested that the brothers had a new partner or partners with the means to move expensive and identifiable artwork stolen by more expendable thieves. The Art Squad believed that Abdyl and Agron had come to Hvar to meet this canny partner and exchange the paintings for cash.

The waitress that the Croats had signaled halted at their table.

"What are you drinking?" The Croat next to her gestured with his chin toward Stasia's untouched cocktail. Unlike James Bond, she never drank alcohol while on a mission, but appearing to drink aided her cover at the moment.

Just then, Agron spoke. "I don't trust this *ropqir*." Stasia almost winced at the crude Albanian slang for *loser* from the mouth of the older, harder-looking brother with the hawk-nosed profile. "He has kept us waiting too long."

Ah ha! The Art Squad was right about the mysterious partner in crime.

Stasia smiled at the Croat and leaned toward him, letting her fingertips touch his where they lay on the table. She held his gaze for a fraction of a second, suggesting that they had a connection. It allowed her to listen to Abdyl's response.

"You worry too much." The younger brother lifted his beer glass and drank. His file said he was something of a strutting peacock who, unlike his brother, wore designer clothes and paid hundreds of euros for his haircuts. As far as Stasia could tell, that assessment was accurate.

"*Negroni Sbagliato, per favore.*" She blinked and looked down, tilting her cocktail glass. Let the Croat who'd asked about her cocktail think that she preferred the 'bungled' version with its bubbly Prosecco. It added to her innocuous image.

Abdyl went on. "Of course he is not trustworthy. Who steals paintings only to have a closer look? It is no matter. We will never let him or them out of our sight." He laughed. "Unlike that idiot art dealer."

As Abdyl finished saying this, his roving gaze intercepted hers. He sat across from his brother on a cushioned bench where he'd been ogling the beachgoers around him as they waited. Now he trained that assessing look on her. Stasia controlled her reaction and returned his frank appraisal, lifting an eyebrow and inclining her head.

As vain as Abdyl appeared to be, she counted on him assuming that her extended regard signaled interest. While it was true that she was interested in him, it wasn't true that she found him at all appealing. He slouched, his shirt open to display a muscular, tattooed chest that seemed more courtesy of hours in a gym than due to hours in honest physical labor. Or honed against a sparring partner or opponent.

Unbidden, an image of Miró dressed in a tight black t-shirt, unshaven and with shadows under his arctic blue eyes, overrode Abdyl Dervishi's smirking, well-groomed image. For a moment, Stasia recalled the muscular strength of the *Elioud* lieutenant's body as he restrained her from assaulting him more than once. She'd seen him fight *bogomili*, minions of a dark angel who killed with a wicked dagger called a *subulam*. Miró had earned every single hard plane and clear definition on his sculpted frame.

Stasia blinked and Abdyl came back into focus. To her amazement, he no longer smirked. Instead, he looked filled with longing. He straightened and stood, his regard locked onto her. *Showtime.* Apparently she'd managed to capture Abdyl's attention without actually performing.

Agron's disbelief bellowed through Stasia's custom-tuned earbud. "What are you doing?" he asked as he swiveled to look at the object of his brother's stare. "We are not here for you to find a woman."

Abdyl ignored his brother and crossed the few meters between him and Stasia. He stopped and openly scrutinized her from head to toe, his bold study lingering on her breasts and exposed thigh before returning to her face. Stasia quelled the irritated nausea his examination had caused and, picking up her cocktail, tilted the glass so that the liquid touched her lips. She smiled and said nothing, again imagining that she was the Mona Lisa, enigmatic and coy—a woman he would be compelled to know.

"*Signora,*" he said, impressing her with his ability to discern her nationality but not with his rough accent, "join me. I will take care of you the way you are meant to be taken care of." As he said this, he let his gaze slide over the Croats, who had stopped talking and bristled at his tone.

Stasia sensed a microcosmic shift in their posture, a spike in their breathing, and an almost measurable rise in temperature. She sighed. She didn't need a fight to ensue to prevent something that she had orchestrated. Her ability to charm her targets had its drawbacks, and one was that sometimes they didn't want to let her go.

She turned and smiled at the young men. The tension eased. They relaxed. "Thank you, my friends, for sharing your table with me. I have enjoyed making your acquaintance." She stood and watched as their gazes devoured the movement. "*Alla prossima.*" An encouraging promise: *until next time.* But there would be no next time.

Then, remembering that she was walking into the wolf's mouth, Stasia bent, lifted her tote, and, tossing her hair, slid it onto her shoulder. She stepped next to Abdyl, whose gleaming eyes and shoulder-length dark hair were definitely *lupine.* Agron glowered behind him.

Crepi, she prayed, raised her chin, and let Abdyl guide her toward the cushioned bench.

Like a warning, the tingle she'd felt earlier returned as a sharp jolt down her spine.

Stasia channeled the frisson of awareness into the smile she aimed at Abdyl when he slipped his fingers under the straps of her tote to carry it the few steps to his table. The man blinked, looking dazed, and his gait hitched. She didn't know if the maddening *Elioud* somewhere in the vicinity meant to throw her off her game, but she welcomed his observation of her performance. Though the inherent danger of most of her missions always added an edge to her delivery, playing to her hidden audience of one electrified her in a way she couldn't remember since her first covert operation.

Unexpectedly, knowing that Miró watched somewhere nearby comforted Stasia as Abdyl sat next to her, dropping a heavy arm across her shoulder. She was used to operating alone, except for when she'd teamed up with Olivia Markham, then a CIA officer, to rescue a group of women held as sex slaves by a Serbian arms dealer. Olivia had already recruited Alžběta Černá, an officer in the VZ, the Czech military intelligence, to help her with other off-the-books rescues. In the succeeding two years, they had grown as close as three women from different countries and in different, sometimes competing, intelligence organizations could. In fact, she counted Liv and Beta as her two closest friends, friends who would come to her aid without stopping to ask questions.

Nevertheless, Stasia relied on herself for her official missions. Now, inhaling the heavy musk Abdyl favored laced with his sweat and favorite Albanian foods, she recalled Miró's complex scent of bergamot and ash, leather and sage. And it hit her: as vexing as the taciturn *Elioud* warrior was, she knew in her bones that he'd have her back—whether or not she'd asked him. For the first time outside of her friends, Stasia felt as though she had a safety net during a dangerous operation.

She shoved that feeling aside and focused on Abdyl.

Twisting toward him (and refusing to inhale through her nose), Stasia put her right hand on his chest and smiled, ignoring the feel of his hot skin. Time to ease out on the tightrope. "*Bello, per favore*, I have left my drink behind with those *pasticcinos*."

She refrained from cringing as Abdyl squeezed her tighter against his side at her flirty usage of Italian endearments. It surely helped that she'd chosen ones that aligned with his views: he was handsome, and her former tablemates were indeed nothing but puppies.

Agron, growing impatient, leaned across the table. His sharp gray gaze speared her. Stasia felt ice slide down her spine. Here was one who wouldn't be charmed not matter how she smiled. "You do not belong here. We are waiting for a business partner."

"What harm can it be for her to have a drink with us while we wait?" Abdyl asked, cajoling. "And what does it matter if the American arrives before we are done? I am sure he appreciates beauty as we do."

To Stasia's surprise, Agron seemed to relent and sat back. So. The hawk-faced criminal could be charmed by his younger brother.

"Besides," Abdyl said, leaning forward as if to conspire with his brother, "she will be a useful distraction."

Agron scowled and said nothing to this, simply lifted his beer and drank.

An American. It wasn't much, but it was more than the Art Squad had managed to discover before this. As Abdyl raised his hand to beckon the waitress, Stasia edged farther out over dangerous territory.

"Americans … they have no culture. They cannot tell a Bellini from a Bernini." She waved her hand dismissively.

A threatening glint lit Agron's gaze, but Abdyl sat back and laughed. "*Signora*, all Italians have art in their blood. It is to be expected with so much of it around you."

"But you speak as if you know more than your typical Italian," Agron said. It sounded like an accusation. After a few minutes with the Dervishi brothers, Stasia had a pretty good idea which brother had pulled off conning the art dealer, and why Agron had gotten caught selling bad contact lenses: his hostile wariness set off internal alarms in anyone dealing with him. He might be paranoid, but he wasn't wrong to be in her case. She would have to tread carefully around him.

"I am guilty," she said, subtly addressing his suspicions head on, and accepted the cocktail that Abdyl had finagled for her from the waitress's tray. *How kind of him*, she thought sarcastically. It looked like it tasted blandly sweet. "I teach art history and Italian culture at the *Università Cattolica del Sacro Cuore* in Milan. Many of my students are exchange students from the United States."

The gleam in Agron's eyes turned speculative. "Perhaps you are right," he said to Abdyl. "And our American friend will appreciate your little Italian beauty and her art knowledge."

Abdyl nodded and sipped from his beer. Looking at Stasia, he asked, "*Signora*, what do you know about Rembrandt and Renoir?"

Stasia's heart began to beat faster. No turning back to a safe perch now. "Rembrandt was a prolific Dutch artist of the Seventeenth Century. He never studied in Italy, but the Italian

Renaissance painter Caravaggio influenced him indirectly. Renoir was a French Impressionist painter who celebrated beauty and feminine sensuality. Both these artists are known for how they paint the quality of light and their interest in ordinary subjects. Their paintings are worth millions of euros." She paused. Surely that was enough to establish her bona fides with these two. "But I am far from an expert on these artists."

The brothers shared a look. Abdyl grinned. "See? You worry too much. Every man is the smith of his own fortune. She is going to help us negotiate a better deal."

Two

Miró watched Anastasia Fiore, the woman who'd tormented his dreams for the past six weeks, play the two dark-haired rogues across from her like a virtuoso. He blinked, his eyes narrowed. Otherwise, he allowed himself no reaction.

Despite her swimwear, it had been clear from the moment that he'd watched Ms. Fiore enter the beach bar on this island off the coast of his home country that she had a mission here that had nothing to do with vacationing and everything to do with these two men. Their harmonic signatures, individual vibrations on an invisible sound scale, jangled his *Elioud* nerves like the discordant screech of demons.

Knowing Ms. Fiore as he did, he hadn't been at all surprised that it took a matter of minutes for her to succeed in charming them. She was about the best he'd ever seen—and that was saying something given that she'd had no idea she had any angel blood until six weeks ago and hadn't had any training in how to use her special gifts.

Miró studied Ms. Fiore's profile as she stood next to the younger of the two men. In the dimmer setting under the bar's thatched roof, her faint nimbus shone to his penetrating vision. It did not, however, identify her weapons, which were a given for the full-time covert operative and part-time, self-appointed protector of the vulnerable. Nor did it give him a better read on the infrared signatures of the two men, which he didn't need to see to know had a telltale sickly cast.

What was she after? It could be no coincidence that she'd appeared on Hvar at the same time that he was here surveilling an enemy in the age-old battle among angelic forces. What were the odds that the men Ms. Fiore had targeted had a connection to Joseph Fagan, chief of the Central Intelligence Agency's Vienna substation and acolyte to the Dark *Irim* Asmodeus?

Miró lifted his smartphone and snapped a photo of the object of Ms. Fiore's charm offensive, the one who resembled a sleazy nightclub owner conditioned by outdated American movies smuggled into his Eastern European country. And who draped an overly familiar arm around Ms. Fiore's petite shoulders as he sat, pinning her to his side. Miró's jaw tightened, but he forced it to relax. Ms. Fiore's backup waited outside the club.

He focused on the younger man, to apply what he knew about humanity from a long life fighting against its worst impulses. Concentrating, he slowed his breathing and heartrate so that he could harness his *Elioud* gifts to extract as much underlying angelic data from the man's demeanor and countenance as he could. He might not have the same gifts as Mihàil and András, his *Elioud* comrades, but he'd long honed the ones he did have until he was extremely good at reading people. He often knew where a person with any angel blood stood on the angelic spectrum between Light and Dark, faithful and unfaithful. And he could usually guess what their particular gifts tended to be.

Sleazy Nightclub Owner had a trace of angel blood. So technically an *Elioud*—a human-angel hybrid descended from the mating of *Irim*, or Watcher Angels, and humans in humanity's prehistory—but so garden-variety in his levels that he hardly registered on the spectrum as Grey. The man more often than not used his innate ability to manipulate the people around him for his own selfish benefit.

Stasia turned at that moment and set a light hand on the Sleazy Nightclub Owner's bare chest, smiling. The man drew her closer to his side, and his body temperature spiked. His groin radiated like a star. Miró wondered idly if any of the jewelry Ms. Fiore wore concealed a dagger.

The other man, whose features resembled a coarser version of the younger with an unfortunate hawk nose pinned onto them, leaned toward her, his gaze sharp and predatory. He had no angel blood. That didn't prevent Miró from identifying him as someone squarely on the side of wrong.

He would bear watching.

Miró considered the trio. An Italian covert operative targeting two shady Eastern Europeans on an island known for its party life and the attendant hapless tourists suggested an operation to infiltrate a human trafficking ring. Add in Ms. Fiore's propensity for rashly risking her own safety and life to free young women from sex slavery, and he could guess her willingness to serve as bait.

He shifted to ease the sudden tightness in the muscles in his upper back but resisted sending any heat to them. He needed to stay alert and cool with his *Elioud* energy feeding his mental faculties and not to indulge in soothing his human limitations.

He continued his impartial assessment of the situation and ignored the theatrics as Ms. Fiore punctuated a remark with a hand wave.

Now factor in Ms. Fiore's *Elioud* heritage and the fact that her operation took place at the same bar that Fagan, a known agent of a fallen Watcher Angel, had arranged to meet someone. Fagan, who had arrived in Vienna only two months ago from a station in the Balkans and could have intelligence on Ms. Fiore.

Miró answered his own earlier question: the odds that the men Ms. Fiore had gotten so cozy with were connected to Fagan were excellent.

He sped up his harmonics until he was invisible to the naked human eye and moved closer to Ms. Fiore and the strangers. He needed to take extreme care. Though Ms. Fiore had no training in using her *Elioud* senses, she'd shown in the past a striking sensitivity to his presence. But his own *Elioud* hearing was exceptional. It was worth the risk to overhear what the trio was discussing.

Was there more danger here to Ms. Fiore than having her real identity exposed or her person harmed? Though Ms. Fiore clearly chose to use her *Elioud* gifts for good in this murky human world, she had also chosen to return to her career as an Italian intelligence officer after learning about her *Elioud* status. And despite the fact that her close friend Olivia Markham, also newly identified as *Elioud* and the ex-leader of their trio of rescuers, had left the CIA to marry a *drangùe*, an *Elioud* general. That made the former Ms. Markham a *zonjë*, the *drangùe*'s lady, and bound to his duty to protect humanity from dark angelic forces.

Unfortunately, Ms. Fiore's decision to return to her previous life made her a Grey *Elioud*, someone who knew his or her hybrid bloodline and knowingly took no side. It also left Ms. Fiore open to angelic persuasion—she could be manipulated into believing that she was acting justly when in fact she supported the Dark *Irim* and all their followers in their efforts to sever humanity permanently from the Lord Most High. If she fell into the life of a Dark *Elioud*, then she also risked the Archangel Michael's wrath. That meant that any contact with Fagan could be used to recruit Ms. Fiore to a life she might have cause to regret for eternity.

As if on cue, Ms. Fiore said, "I am guilty" as she accepted the cocktail that the Sleazy Nightclub Owner cajoled from a waitress who fell for his maneuvering.

Those words threw cold water on Miró's speculation about Ms. Fiore's immortal soul. He focused on what she was saying, which was that she was an Italian art professor. He frowned. It was an odd ploy for catching the interest of two men who seemed most unlikely to be art lovers. But there was no denying the lustful spark that lit the older brother's gaze. Or the smug expression that the younger man wore as a result.

This was something more than a honeypot to entrap sex traffickers.

"Perhaps you are right," the older brother said to the younger. "And our American friend will appreciate your little Italian beauty and her art knowledge."

Miró's battle senses stirred. American friend? Fagan?

Sleazy Nightclub Owner nodded and sipped from his beer. Looking at Ms. Fiore, he asked, "*Signora*, what do you know about Rembrandt and Renoir?"

Ms. Fiore's heart beat faster at his question. Miró's eyes narrowed. *Interesting. And puzzling.* She was seducing these men for artwork?

In answer, she delivered an expert, casual summary of the two famous artists that led the brothers to share a pointed look.

Then the younger man grinned in a way that made Miró's jaw ache and said to his brother, "See? You worry too much. Every man is the smith of his own fortune. She is going to help us negotiate a better deal."

Just then Miró's cellphone vibrated. He tapped his earwig.

"Abdyl Dervishi," Olivia Kastrioti said in answer to his earlier text with the photo of the younger brother appended. "That looks like Stasia with him."

"It is." Miró snapped a photo of the older brother and sent it to her. "What is his brother's name?"

"Agron. But don't think to avoid talking about Stasia. I thought you were trailing Fagan. Get a little distracted and lose your way?"

Miró ignored the question. "Fagan has failed to show for a meet at this location. The Dervishi brothers stand out as likely candidates as his disappointed contacts."

"Your Spidey sense tingling?" his lady asked. "Or did Agron's lack of proper attire clue you in that he doesn't belong at a beach club among scantily clad swimmers?"

Miró knew that the former American spy still grappled with the reality of being an *Elioud*, but he had his own adjustment to make for *her*, including her propensity to make superhero jokes. "You could say that."

"The Dervishis are Albanian con men who like to sell faulty ventilators to hospitals among other things. Interpol has quite the file on them going back a dozen years when Lover Boy was barely 15. Agron got out of an Austrian prison four months ago. Do you think Fagan plans another move against Mihàil?" Her voice sharpened on this question. Miró knew from experience that she could be as fierce as a dragon when her mate was threatened—and as deadly.

Six weeks ago, Olivia and Mihàil Kastrioti, the Albanian *drangùe*, had attracted Fagan and Asmodeus's notice in Vienna. The American spymaster, a narcissistic, power-hungry human, had foolishly gone off on his own after the couple with a team of *bogomili*, humans controlled by Asmodeus. The *bogomili* never stood a chance. While it took Mihàil and Olivia some time to acknowledge their feelings for one another, they had stood shoulder-to-shoulder from the start against the brainless thugs. Miró suspected that it was this aspect of the power couple's romance that had found a crack in his formidable leader's emotional armor.

The 570-year old *drangùe* had lost his first wife, Luljeta, to a Dark *Irim* near the end of the Middle Ages and perversely had gone straight into Asmodeus's arms as his greatest acolyte. Mihàil had never truly been Dark, however. In the early seventeenth century, the *drangùe* had rescued Miró from a horrific life and death, and the Archangel Michael had freed Mihàil from his bond with the Dark *Irim* and given him penance. Suffice it to say, the *Elioud* general had been reluctant to make himself vulnerable that way again.

In the end, Fagan had been taken by Mihàil and the other *Elioud* fighting with him and charmed into amnesia to forget his failed operation against them. The *drangùe* had released the acolyte back into his former life while keeping him under surveillance. Fagan had so far shown no signs of consciously acting on Asmodeus's behalf.

"Unlikely, though not impossible," Miró answered the *zonjë*. "Albanian criminals steer clear of him as a rule." Miró saw Abdyl finish his beer in a single gulp and then throw some cash on the table. The two brothers stood. Ms. Fiore also stood. "Ms. Fiore appears to be working an operation involving stolen artwork, if I am to guess from her cover and the conversation."

"Stolen artwork? Two men who make money off of someone's grandma dying from pneumonia? *That* seems unlikely."

"Unless Rembrandt and Renoir are codenames for other players or clever names for the latest party drugs, the Dervishis have moved into a new arena."

"Artwork at that level suggests non-cash funding for all kinds of illicit activities. Certain arms dealers are known to accept high-value items in trade, for example. Fagan may be working a legitimate CIA operation that the Italians haven't been read in on."

"The Dervishis are leaving with Ms. Fiore."

"Fagan must have made Stasia's team outside and moved the location."

It wasn't unusual for meetings to be moved at the last minute, especially if one party suspected that the original site was compromised. Had Fagan also guessed that the Italians had someone inside? Whether he had or not, as soon as he saw an Italian woman leaving with his contact, he'd suspect her of being an undercover agent, and Ms. Fiore's operation would be blown—not to mention her life at risk.

"Not to worry, my lady. I will provide Ms. Fiore with backup."

"I never doubted that you would."

Miró waited as the trio left their table and headed toward the club's exit. Ms. Fiore had deftly made sure to keep her tote bag slung over her shoulder when it appeared that Abdyl would try to carry it. He suspected that she had her BC-41 in that bag, but he knew that she definitely had a 9mm. She'd flashed just enough skin on her inner leg when sliding out of the bench for him to glimpse the black band of her holster. Thank the Archangel she was strapped.

As she passed within a meter of his position, Ms. Fiore glanced his way. Her gaze caught his, though he was certain that she couldn't see him, sending an unexpectedly wild oscillation through his tightly controlled harmonics. Miró, caught off guard, flailed for a moment until he'd gotten his harmonics back in proper rhythm before turning to follow the group. Behind him, he heard an amazed woman's voice asking her companions if they'd seen the angel in their midst. Fortunately, her friends laughed and asked what she was drinking.

He would have to be more careful around Ms. Fiore. There was something about her *Elioud* nature that had a profound and unpleasant effect on his. It could prove deadly for both of them.

He followed at a discreet distance.

There was another possibility that Miró hadn't mentioned to the *zonjë*: Fagan might be fully aware of Ms. Fiore's presence on Hvar—in fact he might have lured her here. Mihàil and Miró had both charmed the CIA officer so that he'd forgotten what had transpired in Budapest when he'd tried to capture the Kastriotis, but that was weeks ago. Anastasia Fiore, a secondary player in the action, might have lodged in Fagan's memory where his subconscious may have identified her as *Elioud* and a valuable prize for his master.

Miró had no way of knowing whether Fagan had come on CIA business or not. Although he'd tapped into the acolyte's personal email and phones, he'd refrained from hacking the CIA's servers to gain access to the man's work email and phone. Though he could do so without leaving a trace, he knew that Fagan had treated his relationship with Asmodeus as he would have treated a foreign handler if he were a double agent—meaning off book.

However, Fagan's relationship with Asmodeus was a bit of an enigma at the moment. Normally the Dark *Irim* was a formidable opponent who would stop at nothing to gain control of a Grey *Elioud* of Ms. Fiore's obvious talents. In fact, he would prefer having her as his right hand over the lesser human, Fagan. But six weeks ago, the former Ms. Markham had taken them all by surprise when she'd unconsciously used an angelic power move against the fallen angel. The Dark *Irim* had entered a human vessel to confront her, and she'd jabbed heated fingertips into the vessel's eyes, sending the temporarily vulnerable Asmodeus into an angelic coma. Their best guess was that Asmodeus had not yet awoken from it.

But what if he had?

What if Fagan had created a false-flag operation so that the Dervishis could separate Ms. Fiore from her Italian team? The seducer could become the seduced?

What if Ms. Fiore were the target?

Miró tapped his earwig again as he sped up to get through the exit ahead of new arrivals. The Dervishis and Ms. Fiore walked inland against the tide of people heading into the Hula Hula Beach Club for the evening. "Can you identify any chatter around Rembrandt and Renoir? How about the Italians? Is there some way to confirm Ms. Fiore's mission with the Dervishis?"

"I can try a backchannel for some information, but it'll take time. What're you thinking?" Olivia was too quick to miss the implication of his questions. "That Fagan is playing the Italians for some reason?"

Miró didn't respond as he maneuvered through the unsuspecting throng fast enough to be in touching distance of Ms. Fiore. The two Italian agents stationed outside the beach club, pretending to be a couple returning from a stroll to the shore, began following the trio, but the crowd was large enough here that Stasia could be whisked away or mortally injured before they could stop it.

"Or are you worried about Stasia specifically?" his lady asked as the subject of her question turned north onto Vlad Avelini Street. There were no sidewalks on the narrow street, and only a handful of people walking in either direction. The Italian agents had to drop back or risk calling attention to their tail.

"Does Ms. Fiore make it a habit to accompany dangerous men to unknown destinations without adequate backup?" Miró asked instead of answering Olivia. "Besides her 9mm, does she wear any other weapons?"

"She always has options. Is she wearing any jewelry?"

"Some."

"Then she's got other weapons. If all else fails, she can fight as I'm sure you're aware."

A memory of his first meeting with Ms. Fiore flooded Miró. She'd thrown her *surujin*—a Japanese weighted chain—around his legs. After he'd melted it, she'd thrown herself at him in a fury, striking him over and over before trying to choke him. Not an hour later, she'd launched herself at him again, this time slashing his arm with her BC-41 and not doing more injury simply because he'd managed to move in time. Less than twelve hours later, he'd watched her efficiently and expertly strike and kick a sandbag in Mihàil's Vienna gym. They'd ended up fighting side-by-side against the *bogomili* in Budapest.

"Indeed" was all he said.

The Dervishis escorted Ms. Fiore right onto Red Paul Street and uphill. Ahead, Bishop Jurja Dubokovica Street led east towards the main part of the port town of Hvar. There were also a couple of four-star hotels in that direction. In his experience, con men like the Dervishi brothers generally sought out the best accommodations—and got someone else to pay for them.

"We can be there in a couple of hours," Olivia reminded him.

"Not necessary." Miró scanned the darkening street. The two Italian agents strolled hand-in-hand thirty meters behind them, but he sensed no other individuals tracking or watching Ms. Fiore and the Dervishis. "You and Mihàil are more secure where you are."

After their wedding a month ago, the Kastriotis had honeymooned on Mihàil's estate outside Shkodër in his home country of Albania. As long as they didn't know Asmodeus's status, it was better if the *Elioud* couple remained there where the very land boosted Mihàil's power.

"I could send András."

Abdyl Dervishi, his hand on Ms. Fiore's elbow, turned at a set of stairs next to a market situated at the intersection of the two streets. The setting sun outlined Ms. Fiore's warm brown hair in golden light for a moment, and a slight air current carried her sweet anise-laced vanilla scent to him. In that instant, Miró was catapulted back in time to his childhood in Split, before he'd learned that the world held some very dark corners and dark forces toyed with humanity—especially young, pretty children.

Shaking his head to clear it, Miró responded to Olivia. "Should the need arise for all out mayhem and loss of subterfuge, I will let you know."

András Nagy, the third *Elioud* in their chorus of demi-angelic fighters, deserved his assigned Hungarian surname meaning *large*. Over two meters tall, he excelled at combat, though not at less-direct forms of engagement. Subtlety was lost on the man.

"Okay, then. I'll see what I can learn about the Italians and any stolen artwork by Rembrandt and Renoir."

Abdyl's hand dropped from Ms. Fiore's elbow before curving around to rest on her hip. Ms. Fiore laughed up at him and tried to sidestep his grip, but the creep only pulled her closer.

Miró, his harmonics thrumming, slipped next to them. He tapped Abdyl's hand, emitting a sharp harmonic burst that would have felt like an intense buzzing along the man's nerves.

Abdyl yelped and pulled his hand away, stumbling up the last step before falling to the pavement. Agron, who'd been looking through narrowed eyes at the Italian couple behind them, growled and bent to pull his brother to his feet.

"What is the matter with you? Stop playing around. We need to get back to the hotel. I think we are being followed."

Stasia, who'd halted at the top of the stairs, stared wide eyed at the spot where Miró had passed them before crossing herself. He hadn't seen that type of reflexive behavior in decades and only then in elderly faithful women in small Italian and Croatian villages. Compressing his lips together, he held his harmonics steady with an iron will.

Wearing a sour frown, Abdyl shook his hand as if flinging off something nasty before gesturing for Agron to lead the way. He reached for Ms. Fiore but stopped himself, instead leaning close to say, "Whatever you did to me, I will find out when we get to our hotel room."

So the Dervishis weren't working for Fagan or they would have been better informed about the Italian team. Unfortunately, Agron's natural paranoia made the situation more volatile.

And now Abdyl suspected Ms. Fiore of assaulting him.

She put a hand on the Albanian's forearm. He flinched, but she succeeded in keeping it there. "I did nothing. It was the angel following us." Her voice rang with impassioned truth. She even looked in Miró's direction. He felt the force of her gaze and wondered if she really could see him. It was an odd, unexpected feeling.

Or perhaps she just saw a way to keep Abdyl off balance, perchance drive a tiny wedge between him and Agron.

Clever woman. Miró could run with her improvisation. Angelic beings loved music—the language of Heaven—but it was the *Elioud*, with their human genetics, who had learned to play jazz.

Abdyl blinked several times and then, grumbling, pulled his arm from Ms. Fiore's hand. "Whatever." He followed Agron, who walked briskly down the sidewalk, his head swiveling as he scanned the sun-washed street. "Come or not, I do not care."

Ms. Fiore waited until he'd gone five meters before she said in a low voice, "Thank you," and then set off after the brothers, her graceful steps unhurried.

Behind them at the intersection, the Italian couple turned north and went uphill. Ms. Fiore must have signaled them to back off.

Miró stayed on her heels, though by now he could see where the Dervishis were headed. Five minutes later, they'd reached the backside of the Amfora Grand Beach Resort, one of the best hotels on the island of Hvar. Guests typically entered the hotel from the private bay, as often as not arriving on their own private yachts. Mihàil had stayed here several times during his playboy days, escorting beautiful women by day and battling demons and Dark *Elioud* by night.

There were always demons and Dark *Elioud* to battle.

With that in mind, Miró's battle senses sharpened as they entered the hotel grounds.

Three

Olivia Kastrioti, former CIA field agent and harlequin-masked superhero, melted as her husband's warm fingers found the base of her neck and began massaging. She let out a soft groan as gentle heat began radiating through her.

"You should pay attention to your muscles, *dashuria ime*," Mihàil said. "There is no need for you to grow so tight while sitting in a chair."

He bent and kissed the delicate skin just beneath her left ear and electric fire raced straight down her spine to her groin.

Olivia sucked in breath as sweat dampened her skin and banked desire roared to life. It took her by shock. *Every. Time.* Swiveling in her chair, she grabbed Mihàil's shoulders and kissed him. His large hands came up to cradle her face and the back of her head. The music of the heavenly spheres sang through her as their harmonics synced. At the same time, the glow of their conjoined auras seeped under her lowered eyelids, adding to her sense of wonder. She could have sworn that time stopped.

She pulled back a few centimeters, deliriously happy to see the glazed look in his eyes and the flush on his cheekbones. The room was several degrees hotter and a smoky scent lingered.

"Then you shouldn't make me grow so tight, my love,' she whispered against his lips before laughing at his stunned look at her double meaning. Sitting back, she sighed. "Miró identified Fagan's likely contact at the beach club. I ran their images through a few databases and came back with two brothers named Abdyl and Agron Dervishi. But it's gotten complicated, fast."

Mihàil stood, his demeanor transformed from besotted newlywed to hardened battle commander. "Tell me."

It sounded like an order, but Olivia knew it was more style and habit than attitude.

"While he waited for Fagan to show, someone else made contact. Any guesses?" She tilted her head and held his gaze.

"I take it that it is someone we both know."

"Stasia. Apparently, she's running an op against these guys. From what Miró overheard, it has something to do with Rembrandt and Renoir. I'm going through some backchannels for more intel. But what I'm hearing so far doesn't make any sense."

Mihàil sat on the leather sofa under the windows in her office. His sharp gaze reminded her of an eagle, the symbol of his country, renowned Land of Eagles. Behind him in the distance rose the Albanian Alps, otherwise known as the Accursed Mountains. But it was in Krujë, southwest of them about an hour as the crow flies, that his father, Gjergj Kastrioti, had given his life defending Albania from the Ottoman Turks almost 600 years ago. At that thought, she touched the St. Michael medal on a chain around her neck.

Mihàil brought her back to the present day and their present conflict, which was much more clandestine and obscure but no less epic.

"Rembrandt and Renoir? Italian and American intelligence? Albanian criminals?" He listed the key points of the situation. "And that is before you add in a Dark *Irim*'s acolyte and a Grey *Elioud*. 'Complicated' is an understatement. What exactly does not make sense?"

Olivia flinched at the term Grey *Elioud*. She was well aware, now that she was the wife of a *drangùe*, what that meant. It was a sore subject between them, but she didn't have time to revisit the troubling status of her two best friends. Putting it aside for the moment, she continued with the most pressing issue.

"The Dervishis are con men whose area of expertise—for lack of a better description—is selling faulty medical devices and drugs to healthcare providers. Yet the *Carabinieri* suspect them of having conned an Italian art dealer out of a Rembrandt and a Renoir worth almost thirty million euros. That's the first aspect that doesn't make any sense."

"The second is why is Anastasia Fiore, an officer in the *Agenzia Informazioni e Sicurezza Esterna*, on a mission for the Art Squad?"

"My guess is that she was loaned to the Art Squad once they tracked the Dervishis out of country. As far as I can tell, the *Carabinieri* have no leads on any potential buyers nor does Interpol. Their most hopeful course of action is to recover the stolen paintings before they disappear, assuming the Dervishis are looking for a fence or a buyer."

Olivia paused before shaking her head. "No, what I can't quite get my head around is what interest Fagan has in the Dervishis and their stolen artwork. It just doesn't seem to be his style. I've got a call in to another contact at AISE about any chatter surrounding the paintings, but when I called Murphy, he was unaware of an op using stolen artwork. Then I called Stenson, who is also unaware of such an op. If Fagan's running something, he's doing it way off book."

Cameron Murphy and Paul Stenson were former CIA colleagues at the Vienna substation where she'd been stationed until six weeks ago. Olivia maintained contact with them even though she'd technically gone out into the cold as far as the Agency was concerned.

Mihàil, who'd listened with an unsettling raptness, leaned forward. His deep-blue gaze pinned her. "*Dashuria ime*, do not overlook the obvious. Fagan is very likely targeting Stasia on Asmodeus's behalf. This could be the first sign that the Dark *Irim* has awakened from his angelic coma."

There. It was out in the open now. Olivia turned back toward the meter-wide monitor on the carved antique rosewood desk that Mihàil had gifted her just a week ago. He waited.

"Does Miró think the same thing?" she asked at last, turning to face him. "That Stasia is in danger, not because she is risking her life on a dangerous undercover operation but because Fagan intends to recruit her for his evil master?"

"Undoubtedly." He didn't bother expounding on the reasons why. As he'd said, it was a pretty obvious conclusion even if she hadn't found the link yet.

"Will Miró protect her?" Olivia's voice had turned husky, but she kept her eyes wide. Getting emotional about something she had no power to affect was something she no longer had the luxury to indulge in. The *drangùe*'s lady had no tears to spare on potential tragedy, even for a close friend.

Mihàil didn't indulge his new wife either. Neither did he waiver in his convictions. "Miró will protect her with his life."

***

Joseph Fagan stood inside the deluxe penthouse at the Amfora Hvar Grand Resort gazing at the object of his current quest: a stolen Rembrandt painting titled *Judgment of the Watcher Angels*. It depicted the ancient Hebrew apocalyptic vision shown to Enoch, the great-grandfather of Noah. Looking skyward, the prophet stood among boulders and bare ground in the lower left of the composition, illuminated by brilliant white light. Above him rose two massive angelic figures wrestling in a stormy sky. Over the muscular snowy wings of the higher angel on the left, golden light streamed through a break in the clouds. Though his stern face looked down in shadow, it glowed. The lower angel, whose dark angry face shone with a fiery internal light, grimaced as he was bound with a gleaming golden rope. In the bottom right of the painting a group of winged serpents writhed in seething darkness next to a deeper shadow in the ground, their golden bindings glinting.

It was classic Rembrandt: a vivid use of light and dark to capture a dramatic scene from the flow of a longer narrative.

And the world didn't know that it existed.

Fagan stayed still, mesmerized. He had no idea why he'd been compelled to seek out the Dervishi brothers in Vienna and send them to con the Italian art dealer in order to steal the paintings. But now that he stood in front of *Judgment of the Watcher Angels*, Fagan recognized its figures from the recurrent and intense dreams that had plagued his sleep since his failed mission to capture Mihàil Kastrioti.

The alarm on his smartphone sounded, alerting him to the passing seconds. He needed to act before the Dervishis returned to the penthouse.

Fagan went into motion, his movements efficient and precise. He placed the painting inside the special padded case that he'd had made to transport it. Zipping the case shut, he turned for a last look at the reproduction of the Rembrandt that he'd brought. It lay on the suite's dining table next to the Renoir where the Dervishi brothers had left the two priceless paintings. Satisfied that the fake looked just like the real one, he chuckled to himself. It would take time for the switch to be discovered, time in which he and the original painting would disappear.

He knew that the Dervishis intended to extort him for more money once they'd discovered the value of the paintings. But he had no intention of paying them. Anything at all. In fact, he'd planned for them to get caught redhanded. That's why he'd sent the *Carabinieri* an anonymous tip about the Albanian criminals. The irony was that the Dervishis had thrived on selling fakes. Now they would be caught with one.

Fagan gripped the case and exited the penthouse via the the sliding door to the terrace. The sun, low in the sky, blazed across the blue waters of the Adriatic. Although it was September, tourism had crept up in recent years and the hotel was almost at capacity. Guests lounged in and around the large cascading pool, many sitting on cushioned sofas under lighted pergolas or under the sail-covered terrace of the poolside restaurant.

The trick to getting out unobserved, Fagan knew, was just to walk out. He'd dressed as a wealthy vacationer in a polo with a sweater draped over his shoulders. The padded case, though large and rectangular, was made from fine leather and sporting a luggage tag. Once he'd stripped off the leather gloves he wore and slipped on the expensive sunglasses, he'd be hard to describe even if someone did notice him. To compound the deception, he'd worn a blond hairpiece styled with fashionable short hair on top. Blond hair automatically lowered his age a decade or more for any casual observer.

Skirting the pool, Fagan walked with purpose to the broad cement walkway that led down to the hotel's private bay where a dinghy waited to take him out to the yacht that he'd chartered for this mission.

He'd reached the dock and was lowering the case to the dinghy operator when his smartphone chimed again. This time it alerted him that the door to the penthouse had been opened.

After he'd descended and seated himself in the dinghy, he pulled his smartphone out and watched the video streaming from the small camera he'd installed in an air conditioning vent near the dining table.

The older Dervishi brother, Agron, entered the frame first. As he moved toward the paintings, his gaze darted around the space, his nostrils flaring and his hand on the gun inside his waistband. Though he had little imagination and less intelligence, he had a brute instinct that led him to suspect that something had occurred in their absence.

Fagan laughed. The man would never figure out what had happened to him, though he'd probably suspect that the Italians had set him up when later they questioned him about the painting. Either the art dealer or the *Carabinieri*, Agron would rage, or both together.

A moment later, Abdyl came into view with a beautiful woman. She looked Italian, almost stereotypically so. Fagan laughed again. The Italians had clearly profiled this preening peacock, who'd brought the enemy inside the gates.

Fagan's gaze fixed on her. She also looked very familar.

The dinghy reached the yacht where it idled in the mouth of the bay. Fagan had set the video program to record the incoming video for a minute and thirty seconds, so he pocketed his smartphone and handed the painting up to the crewman waiting at the top of the ladder hanging from the yacht's side.

By the time he was seated in the cabin and the painting safe next to him, whatever was about to happen with the Dervishis and the *Carabinieri* team had already gone down. He looked back through high-powered binoculars toward the Amfora resort. Lights blazed on the penthouse terrace where the Italian woman stood gazing toward the Adriatic.

He couldn't resist. He waved.

To his great surprise, she waved back. Her eyesight must be extraordinary. Something niggled in the back of his mind, but he let it go for now. Long experience told him that his diligent subconscious would work on the puzzle and then present him with an answer much faster if he focused on the present reality.

A figure materialized on the broad walkway around the bay seemingly from thin air.

Fagan blinked and, leaning forward, turned the binoculars on the man standing there.

The man also looked familiar. In the magnifying lens of the binoculars, his narrow-eyed gaze gleamed icy blue—even at the increasing distance and growing darkness. There was something infinitely threatening about him. Threatening, but graceful too, like a dancer. Light on his feet and ready to move in an instant.

Fagan watched this figure observing the yacht until it had sailed out of the bay and headed north. It was no matter. In an hour and a half, he would be in Split. From there, he would fly back to Vienna with his prize.

Nevertheless, despite his better judgment, he sat brooding over the Italian woman and the menacing man on the walkway. Somehow he believed that they were together, but he didn't know why he thought that. He glanced toward the package sitting on the seat next to him. His fingers itched to open the case so that he could study the oddly compelling painting, but his willpower was strong enough to deny this compulsion. Under no circumstances would he allow anyone else to gaze upon the mysterious wonder emanating from the canvas.

Instead he pulled out his smartphone and reviewed the video of the Dervishis meeting their doom.

Ten seconds after Abdyl and the Italian woman came into view, another figure appeared behind them. Fagan frowned. The figure was strangely warped and fuzzy as though something interfered with the video capture, but the rest of the image remained perfectly clear. The figure laid a hand on Agron's upper back and he turned slightly, collapsing as he did into the arms of his attacker.

Abdyl yelled and lunged toward his brother and the mysterious figure. The Italian woman followed him, a gun in her hand and speaking. Even as Abdyl turned to confront her, the wavering figure clarified into the man from the walkway. Dropping Agron's body, he stepped toward Abdyl and grabbed the other man by the upper arm, pulling him around and away from the woman. Fagan caught a glimpse of the man's face with a shock: the stern features, the icy blue eyes. They were familiar because he'd seen them on the face of the highest angel in Rembrandt's painting, the one with the snowy white wings who glowed with a heavenly internal light. Saint Michael the

Archangel, commander of the Angelic Hosts and primal Defender of the Faith.

Had he captured video of the most powerful supernatural being under God?

An electric thrill of terror shot through his chest and pierced him in the very root of his being—and he was watching the playback of events. Fagan's heart pounded. There was a rushing in his ears.

Abdyl's own reaction in the next five seconds of video mirrored Fagan's. And then he appeared to faint, whereby St. Michael's doppelganger let him drop to the floor. The being stepped over his body and reached for the woman but pulled back before touching her. For a moment, the sternness of his expression wavered.

Something inside Fagan smirked. *That flash of vulnerability came from no archangel.*

Then the man turned and looked into the hidden camera. The iciness in his gaze intensified and a moment later the recording abruptly stopped.

Fagan read the time signature on the video file. Forty-five seconds had elapsed. Letting his hand holding the smartphone relax, he considered the timing of his exit and the appearance of the mysterious man on the walkway around the bay.

How had this man so quickly subdued two men? Let alone made it down to the bay in the time that it had taken Fagan to sail from the dock and be seated in the yacht cabin?

More importantly, how did he know about Fagan?

Fagan replayed the video several more times before stopping on the last frame with the man's visage frozen in mid-stare.

He'd seen him before in Budapest. But that made no sense. That operation had been to bring in Kastrioti, suspected head of an Albanian crime syndicate. Fagan had been holed up in a flat for the better part of a week following leads on The Dragon of Albania, Kastrioti's moniker, and the renegade CIA agent who had joined his operation, a cool blonde disdainful of Fagan's authority.

At the memory, a sharp pain stabbed Fagan's head and embedded itself in his right eye. Massaging his temple with two fingers, he closed his eyes and let the headache take over. Whoever this asshole was, it didn't matter. Fagan had the painting.

***

Stasia watched in satisfaction as Rossi and Buonocore secured the Dervishi brothers before turning to study the paintings that the two Albanian con men had stolen. She didn't recognize either painting, but that didn't mean much, since both artists had been exceptionally prolific. The Renoir didn't appeal to her after more than a cursory glance. Its saturated color and vibrant light, depicting fuzzy female sensuality, owed a great deal to earlier masters like Rembrandt, who had used these ephemeral qualities to such effect. But the Renoir lacked emotional depth and drama, instead focusing on an intimate and mundane scene, pleasant but not memorable, in sharp contrast to the Rembrandt next to it.

She'd just turned to study the Rembrandt when she heard a whisper, a disturbance in the air pressure really, behind her. Her fingers tightened on the grip of her P32, which she still held (a habit she'd gained after an inexperienced field agent lost control of a prisoner before his restraints had been fully engaged), but otherwise she didn't move. Rossi and Buonocore, with thirty-five years in law enforcement between them, made no such potentially deadly mistake, however. They yanked the two prisoners to their feet and prodded them to the hotel room door. Rossi turned to Stasia as they passed, a rare grin lighting his saturnine features.

"I owe you a drink, Fiore. We will return home as heroes now."

Buonocore laughed as she maneuvered Abdyl through the door. "You owe her several drinks given how soon you can go home to your wife."

That wiped the grin from Rossi's face, but Stasia knew him from other operations and didn't misinterpret his somber expression. The man adored his wife of twenty-five years and didn't talk about her on the job.

"In Rome, after they are processed," she said, gesturing with her chin at the Dervishis.

He nodded and pushed a heavy-footed Agron, who was babbling about an angel patting his back, forward. Stasia couldn't blame Agron. *She* knew what Miró was yet was spooked to see his luminous winged form as he touched Abdyl on their walk here.

After the two art-squad agents hustled the con men into the hall, the door shut with a firm click. Stasia moved her index finger from the trigger but squeezed the grip so hard her knuckles hurt. Silence filled the room along with tension.

Finally she couldn't stand it anymore and whirled, bringing the P32 up to aim at Miró, who stood five meters away now, his face inscrutable.

"Why are you here?" Hostility thrummed in her voice, but she didn't care.

He didn't answer. Instead, his eyes narrowed as he looked at her. His gaze should have been cold, but she burned. Despite the fact that her heart beat faster, she didn't flinch or budge. All at once, she felt exposed in her swimsuit and sarong.

She dropped the P32 to her side and swore. "*Azz!*"

Miró said nothing about the common Neopolitan idiom for certain male body parts or the clear frustration that prompted her outburst. "The Rembrandt is a forgery."

"What?" Stasia said, confused. She'd forgotten why she was there, which made her angrier when she recalled the reason.

He tipped his head toward the paintings next to her. "*Judgment of the Watcher Angels.* The acolyte came to this room and took it before we arrived. He sailed out of the bay a few minutes ago."

Stasia took the time to replace her P32 in its thigh holster. When she looked up, Miró's gaze had grown frostier if possible. She suspected that he disdained guns as an *Elioud*, someone who could disorient with a flash of angelic white noise or incinerate to ash with a heated touch. *Good for him. She* needed to use weapons. "Joseph Fagan is their American partner?"

At his nod, Stasia thanked her extensive training and long experience for helping her to cover her lapse in mental agility. Even so, she was nonplussed at her internal struggle to process the details of her situation. If she lost her focus this way while on a mission, she'd risk failure or worse, death. She'd be happier when the irritating demi-angel had gone so that she could think.

She frowned. "He must plan to fund an operation with something untraceable."

Miró shrugged. Stasia couldn't help herself. She noticed how his broad shoulders moved inside his tailored suit. The jacket splayed open, and though his shirt covered him, she could tell that his waist was lean and his chest was well muscled. "Perhaps" was all he said.

Sighing, Stasia turned to her tote bag. She didn't know what Miró's game was. He should have gone after Fagan or returned to Mihàil's Albanian estate or wherever it was that he did his *Elioud* intelligence work. She had her own work to do, and it involved getting a team in to recover and transport the paintings back to Rome where someone else would verify Miró's claim of forgery. Whatever the *Elioud* was up to didn't matter one whit to her even if he did wear a suit better than most men she knew, including and especially that sleazy Albanian con man she'd just spent the better part of two days pursuing.

She pulled the secure cellphone that the *Carabinieri* had given her from a hidden inner pocket of the tote bag. "Thank you," she said, turning back toward Miró, "for help—" but he was gone.

"*Ha le guallera!*" Throwing up her hands, Stasia looked around the hotel room, wondering if the damn *Elioud* lingered out of sight just to eavesdrop on her angry, crude language. So what if she said he had balls? She'd grown up among a family of law enforcement officers who didn't soften their speech for polite society. And everyone knew that an excess of testosterone drove men to daring and outrageous behavior. If any male had an excess of testosterone, it was Miró Kos.

But the room lacked the energy that Miró exuded when present, whether he himself was visible or not. The *Elioud* had left while she was still speaking to him, damn him.

Then Stasia recalled that she'd only moments before thought that she'd be happier when he'd gone. Had the infuriating man read her mind?

Letting out a frustrated roar, she launched a throw pillow at the sideboard, sending a glass bowl spinning to the floor where it broke into a dozen large shards and for which the *Carabinieri* would be billed.

Four

S tasia drove her rented Range Rover slowly through the northern Albanian town of Fushë-Arrëz. It had been six months since she'd last been here for Olivia's wedding, and she still found it rather remarkable that her glamorous American friend had ended up in such a sleepy backwater, or as Olivia put it, one-stop-light town.

Not that Stasia was unfamiliar with life in a small town among the mountains. Her hometown of Spezzànu nestled among mountains just like Fushë-Arrëz. In fact, Olivia's new home looked remarkably like Spezzànu. Perhaps those Albanian mercenaries who came to fight for Naples and Venice after the Ottomans conquered their country assuaged their homesickness by settling in the province of Cosenza. They'd certainly recreated the Albanian villages they'd left behind, forming enclaves throughout Calabria that preserved their language and customs.

Stasia's best friend as a child, Doruntina, had taught her to speak *Arbëresh*, the dialect of medieval Albanian preserved in these transplanted villages. It was related to the modern Albanian language as Church Latin was to the dead Latin of the Romans. Meaning not very closely. Then again, one could say the same thing about Stasia's Cosentian dialect and its relationship to Italian.

That's because Calabria, the toe of the Italian boot wedged between the city of Naples and the island of Sicily, had a long history of being settled by outsiders. From the Greeks who colonized the Magna Grecia in ancient times to the Byzantines, Normans, Angevins, Aragonese, and Spaniards through the Middle Ages, a veritable melting pot of people had left their mark on Stasia's Italian dialect. Besides Doruntina, she'd also had a friend who spoke Occitan, a Romance-language spoken mostly in Provence that was more like Spanish than French. Thanks to her birthplace and almost supernatural hearing, Stasia had grown up a polyglot, capable of reading, writing, and speaking almost any language that she encountered. No wonder she'd ended up in the foreign intelligence service instead of local law enforcement with her family.

At the eastern end of the main street running through Fushë-Arrëz, Stasia turned left and drove up the small mountain overlooking the town. Most of the houses and municipal buildings hugged the main street, which was really a bypass of the local highway through a valley big enough for twenty-five hundred souls to live. But Mihàil had chosen to remake the mountaintop into a plateau so that he could build a compound, a surprisingly moderate one for the leader of the Kastrioti clan.

Even so, the recent snow had been cleared from the winding private drive, which was lit with custom steel bollards featuring the double-eagle of the Kastrioti crest—the same double-eagle on the Albanian flag. Though Mihàil might keep a relatively low profile here in this remote place, he certainly wasn't hiding. The medieval chapel at the far side of the plateau, moved with great expense from the Kastrioti lands farther south, only served to clarify his relationship to the legendary Albanian hero. If memory served, everyone in Fushë-Arrëz knew exactly who and what lived above them.

Stasia pulled into the circular driveway that fronted the main residence, a stone mansion that would be called a large house in most European cities, and under the portico on the left side of the front door. Mihàil's steward, Pjëter, waited on the lanai for her to park before coming to open her car door for her.

"*Grazie*, Pjëter," she said, holding his gaze before handing him her keys. On impulse, she squeezed his upper arm before he could turn away. "You are always right where you are needed, *sì?* Mihàil is very fortunate to have such a loyal retainer."

He smiled, the corners of his eyes crinkling in genuine pleasure, and tipped his head. "*Grazie mille, mia signorina,*" he said. At the sound of his low, mellifluous voice, Stasia found herself wondering if Mihàil's steward had *Elioud* blood. Then he slid into the driver's seat to park her car in the smaller garage connected to the portico.

Stasia didn't wait for Pjëter before entering the house. She knew that he would be unhappy, if not vocal about it, if she stood in the cold. So she walked along the lanai toward the brightly lit glass door at the far end that led into the kitchen. As she expected, the door was unlocked even though no one was in sight. Nothing brought home Mihàil's authority quite like the fact that his home was unguarded and left accessible, and yet no one would dare to enter without his permission. That and the *Elioud* general had enacted some angelic safeguards to make the house seem undesirable to anyone not welcome.

Once inside Stasia stood, shivering a little, in the warmth. The scent of freshly baked bread permeated the air, and a round loaf waited on a wooden cutting board on the island. A small bowl of coarse salt sat next to it. As with many other cultures, Albanians had an ancient tradition of hospitality that involved welcoming guests with bread and salt, formerly an expensive commodity. Unfortunately, it was an uncommon practice in this day and age, but Olivia had taken on her new duties as an Albanian wife with enthusiasm and her usual drive to excel.

Which was why Olivia was the *zonjë*, and not someone like Stasia, who preferred to sleep late on her day off and drink espresso and eat croissants in bed.

Her friend appeared almost as soon as Stasia thought of her. Olivia wore white jeans and a soft, rose-colored sweater, but her feet were bare. Her long, straight blond hair was pulled back with a clip, with strands falling loose around her face. She looked radiant, but it was more than happiness that added a glow to her skin: her *drangùe*'s native land fed her angelic spirit, sending energy into her *Elioud* nimbus.

Of course, it probably didn't hurt that she was still a newlywed married to a demi-angel with smoldering good looks and exuding a raw sexuality that promised purely carnal delight— one who looked at her as if she were the most precious thing under Heaven.

Stasia sighed and shook herself, ignoring the ache that pierced her at her friend's happy state. Olivia deserved to be loved and cherished and had gone through a harrowing trial before she'd gotten married. If she, Stasia, were still spending more time conning criminals than in wooing and loving her mate, well then, so be it.

Out of nowhere the thought came: *How does Miró feel about it?*

Before Stasia could evaluate the source of this thought, Olivia gave an excited shout and rushed toward her, arms extended. "Staz! You're here!" And then Stasia was enfolded in a warm American-style hug. As usual, Olivia smelled of roses, but now the scent was a custom one blended just for her. Mihàil's mother, an angel, had gifted Olivia with her own white rose cultivar named *The Harlequin* after her chosen disguise as a protector. A small conservatory behind the main house supported several of the delicate shrubs even in February.

Olivia stepped back. "How was the drive from Shkodër? Had the snow been plowed from the highway? Here, let Besjana take your hat and coat."

The Albanian teenager stood behind Olivia's right shoulder, waiting for her employer to hand her Stasia's outerwear. Olivia had confided to Stasia the last time she'd visited that she felt awkward directing the teen in daily tasks, but now she seemed more comfortable having staff.

She waited until Besjana had disappeared from the kitchen into the cavernous front hall. Then she turned. "Her parents finally agreed to let her stay in the spare bedroom. Now I'm able to help her with her schoolwork and give her a little self-defense training."

Stasia sat on a barstool and reached for the bread, cutting several small squares from the still warm loaf. "I am sure that her antagonizers are also wary of Mihàil's wrath."

Olivia grabbed some wine glasses and set them on the counter along with a bottle of dry red wine and a dish of olive oil with herbs and parmesan, something that she'd told Stasia was a common practice in Italian-style restaurants in America.

She poured a generous amount of wine in their glasses and sat. "They're learning to be wary of *my* wrath."

Stasia dabbed a bit of bread in the oil and popped it into her mouth. She finished chewing and swallowing before saying, *"Cara, O peggio surdo è chillo ca nun vo' senti."*

Olivia tilted her head as she translated the Neapolitan proverb. "None is more deaf who doesn't want to hear?"

Stasia sipped her wine. "Italian men are often unable to hear the words women speak. I suspect that Albanian men are unaware that they are even speaking."

"Indeed." Olivia nodded. "Mihàil has little patience for their behavior, but he's been able to ignore it because he's been a bachelor businessman trying to bring industry to his country. Now that we're spending more time here, he's taking a more active role in guiding local customs—including inviting a few to his gym for a little one-on-one grappling. And head banging. Whatever works."

Stasia tilted her head and studied her friend. "And you have found a way to fulfill your duty as the *drangùe*'s lady on your own terms." At Olivia's surprised look, Stasia decided to change the subject. Her friend wasn't one for discussing her inner state, preferring instead to tackle problems head on. Best not to dwell on her unasked-for insight. "This bread dipped in oil is good but not Italian. We do not waste extra virgin olive oil by pouring it in a bowl to dip. I will show you how true Italians eat bread and oil."

Standing, she went to the sink on the other side of the island and washed her hands before turning the broiler in the top oven on and sliding several slices of bread under it. Then, after rummaging through a large bowl on Olivia's counter for a head of garlic, she quickly peeled and halved a clove. By now, the bread had toasted to a light golden brown, so she pulled it out and lay the pieces on the cutting board where she rubbed the cut garlic over them. Next she drizzled some of the verdant green oil on the toast, finishing with a sprinkle of salt from Olivia's welcome bowl.

"This is *fettunta*. Eat," she said with a flourish, holding a piece out to Olivia. "It is a simple meal, not something you eat in distraction while waiting for your dinner only to find that your stomach is full."

Seeing Besjana standing in the corner of the kitchen, Stasia motioned her over with a warm smile. "*Per favore*, eat."

Besjana, looking not a little overwhelmed and a lot surprised at herself, nevertheless came forward and accepted the *fettunta*.

Stasia took that opportunity to speak to the teen, infusing her words with warmth to cushion her bluntness. "*Bella*, you must carry yourself as if you are the Queen of Heaven and no one is worthy to touch the hem of your robe, *sì?* How does the Queen of Heaven stand? That is right, stand straight and smile with serenity. And always carry a weapon that you know how to use as if it were a part of yourself. *Më kuptoni?*" She switched to Albanian at the end, sharpening her tone to set the hook.

Besjana had stopped chewing, eyes wide, and nodded.

"But remember: the Queen of Heaven is not a *bushtër*. Do all that you can to avoid the necessity of a weapon," Stasia said.

Suddenly Miró spoke. "Did you know that the primary definition of *bushtër* is not *bitch*? It is *dragoness*."

He stood on the far side of the kitchen, leaning against the cabinets with his arms folded. Instead of the suit that he'd worn the last few times that she'd seen him, he wore a wine-colored button-down shirt, cream-colored chinos, and Italian leather shoes without socks. He didn't look happy to see her, but then again, his face showed as little emotion as ever. Only his eyes hinted at some emotion. She was sure that whatever it was, it wasn't particularly good. The Albanian word that he'd repeated and its translation certainly sounded wrong coming from his mouth. He was not a man who indulged in profanity or crude language. She flushed.

As Stasia turned to face him, Besjana fled, avoiding the intimidating *Elioud* as much as possible by walking along the opposite wall toward the doorway. Before Stasia could speak, however, Olivia stood. She went to the wall cabinet where crystal goblets sparkled behind glass doors.

"Would you like a glass of wine, Miró?" She didn't wait for an answer but took a goblet out, poured a generous serving of the wine, and carried it to him. "Join us." Even Stasia could hear that it was a command.

Something flashed in Miró's gaze, but he accepted the goblet without a word and followed her to the far end of the island, where he remained standing.

"You will be happy to learn that the *Carabinieri* have confirmed that the Rembrandt we recovered is a forgery," Stasia said, slinging her words at the silent *Elioud* lieutenant as if they were the weights at the end of her *surujin*. She almost wished that it wasn't packed away in her duffel.

Olivia sat back on her barstool and sipped her wine but said nothing.

"Why would you think that would make me happy?" Miró asked. His quiet voice made Stasia angry.

It also made her stop and count to ten before answering. She could see Olivia from the corner of her eye. Her friend was watching the two of them in a manner that made Stasia remember that she was behaving badly...in a way, in fact, that she had always prided herself on *not* behaving. What was it about the taciturn *Elioud* that made her want to talk too much, gesticulate too much, *emote* too much? He also made her self conscious in a way that nobody and nothing else ever did. No, she might be an actress, a con artist, a performer while on a mission, but she was never anything other than coldly rational. And she was always on a mission.

As she was now. She must not forget that.

Slowing her breathing, she slowed her heartrate and clamped down on her irritation. As she'd just instructed the hapless Besjana, she needed to act as if she were the Queen of Heaven.

Not as a *bushtër*. And remember what she already knew: it was much better to charm the wolf and keep her blade sharp than risk getting more hurt than she was prepared to handle. Miró Kos was certainly a wolf if she ever saw one walking on two legs, predatory and alert.

In bocca al lupo then.

Stasia willed herself to smile wide into the tense air, imagining that she was in the midst of dear friends. It was easy enough to do because of her deep love and affection for Olivia. Ignoring Miró's question, she turned to the cabinet behind her and found a small china plate. She slid a few slices of the *fettunta* onto the plate and offered it to her intimidating adversary.

"*Per favore,* would you like to have some bread with your wine?" Stasia deliberately held his arctic gaze, imagining that the warmth of her smile and the heat of her own gaze would melt his coldness. Eventually.

Miró blinked.

For an instant, his gaze unshuttered enough that she saw surprise before it closed again. Maybe he thought she was crazy to pivot so quickly from angry to attentive.

Regardless, Stasia felt a brief surge of triumph. The aloof angel-man could be affected. *She* could affect him. In that moment she determined that she would do all in her considerable power to charm him. She had never failed before to win over anyone that she'd set her will to charming, and she would be damned if the *Elioud* lieutenant would be her first failure. He was just perhaps her most challenging target to date.

Miró inclined his head and accepted the plate from her. "*Grazie.*" He lifted a slice of bread before adding, "Perhaps you have some advice for me as well? How should I stand? *Come un lupo?*"

Che bastardo! Could he read her mind? Wasn't it enough for him to eavesdrop? Stasia's ire spiked again. She narrowed her eyes.

Olivia intervened. "*Dashuria ime,* would you like some *fettunta?* Stasia insists that dipping bread in olive oil is for unsophisticated people like me."

Stasia realized with alarm that Mihàil stood next to Olivia's stool, one hand on its back and the other stroking her hair. She couldn't recall the last time someone had entered a room without her awareness. Then, with a shock, she immediately realized that Miró had done it only five minutes before.

"*Fettunta?* I love *fettunta,*" Mihàil said, his baritone exuding geniality, and took the last slice from the cutting board.

Stasia grew calmer despite herself. She glared at the *drangùe,* no longer intimidated by a man who was massaging his wife's scalp and neck and using his fingers to comb her hair.

"Enough," Mihàil said. There was a slight edge of warning in his tone.

Stasia blinked and let his charm wash over her. She turned to Olivia. "You are fortunate, *cara*, that you have married a man who will be able to tame your children with a word."

"Hmm," Olivia said, sipping. She turned toward Mihàil, and placing a palm on his cheek, gazed at him. "One day, *dashuria ime*."

They shared a private look before Mihàil turned back to Stasia and Miró.

"We were unaware that the acolyte intended to meet the Dervishis about stolen artwork. If we had discovered his plans, you can be assured that one of us would have contacted the *Carabinieri*."

Stasia felt chastened. Until Mihàil said this, she'd been certain that Miró had deliberately withheld information that would have helped her to recover the Rembrandt.

Miró finished chewing his *fettunta*. As always he was hard to read, but she thought that his eyes looked less frosty and his posture less ready for combat.

"Ms. Fiore," he said, setting his empty plate on the counter. "The truth is that I only surmised what had happened once I returned to the hotel suite. It was clear when looking at the painting that Rembrandt had not painted it. It was equally clear that the acolyte had been in the suite. I just put two and two together as the Americans say."

"How did you know that Rembrandt had not painted it? It took experts six months to be sure." Stasia let skepticism color her statement.

Miró shrugged. "Rembrandt was a Grey *Elioud* for most of his life. It is why he is considered an Old Master who excelled at multiple media, why his treatment of light and dark revolutionized Western art. He infused his paintings with his angelic essence."

"His brushstrokes are lustrous," Olivia said. "They have a soft but distinct shine. I noticed this quality a long time ago but only realized why when Miró debriefed us after returning from Hvar."

Stasia looked at the three *Elioud* warriors. "Is that why you think that Fagan stole a previously unknown Rembrandt? Because Rembrandt was a Grey *Elioud*?" Puzzled, she shook her head. "Why?"

Miró glanced at Mihàil, who gave a slight nod. He looked back at Stasia. "The *zonjë* has been working with former CIA colleagues for the past six months to track the acolyte's Agency business. There is no official record of his trip to Hvar, nor is there any current program that would necessitate using a stolen Rembrandt—or any valuable artwork for that matter—in lieu of cash funding."

"There is also a legend, a rumor really, that a Dark *Irim* took a series of Grey *Elioud* painters as apprentices," Mihàil said when Miró had finished. "No one knows for sure why, but some speculate that this Dark *Irim* was able to motivate or influence these susceptible artists in some way that is preserved in their art."

Stasia leaned back against the counter and folded an arm around her waist while the other hand held her wineglass. Sipping, she adopted a firm nonchalance as if she were at a

cocktail party. Discussing the metaphysical realities of angels—
let alone angels marrying and mating with people—made her
more than a little uneasy. She might see the world as a stage
and herself as an actor on it, but she was very practical. She
didn't indulge in flights of fancy. Watching Miró stun and then
incinerate braindead *bogomili* six months ago had been almost
too much for her to take.

But they expected her to ask questions, and she was here to get
answers. "You speak as if this rumored Dark *Irim* is someone
other than Asmodeus."

Miró's astute gaze never strayed from her face. She doubted
that he bought her detachment. "Despite being a long-
standing thorn in St. Michael's side, Asmodeus is a lesser *Irim*.
In the past, he has lacked the patience and subtlety for
unpredictable Grey *Elioud* of Rembrandt's stature. He prefers
easy satisfaction."

"What my lieutenant is trying to say is that his *modus operandi* is
lust," Mihàil said, "which bypasses an *Elioud*'s angelic nature
and targets the human one instead." He shared a look with
Miró that set Stasia's antennae twitching. There was something
more to that comment.

Miró's gaze slid back to Stasia. "It is an effective strategy and
works even better on ordinary humans. Grey *Elioud* can be a
lot of work to woo and win. In fact, targeting Grey *Elioud* can
perversely have the opposite effect than the one a Dark *Irim*
intends. The target may commit to fighting against the dark
angelic forces."

Stasia found herself intrigued despite her wariness. "So do you think that Fagan stole the Rembrandt because his master knows what Rembrandt preserved in his painting? Is Asmodeus out of his angelic coma?"

Mihàil shook his head. "We do not think so."

At that moment, András came into the kitchen, which suddenly shrank in size by a third and rose a degree in temperature. He wore a black t-shirt, black tactical pants, and black combat boots. Upon seeing Stasia, a big grin lit his face.

"*Kis virág*! Have you returned to teach this one"—here he slapped Miró on the back—"some manners? He's grown soft, and I'm tired of trying to train some vigor into him."

Miró frowned. His gaze had frosted over again.

Stasia grinned back at the big Hungarian, whose smile and sunny disposition elicited an uninhibited response from almost everyone he met. Everyone, that is, who wasn't engaged in combat with him because then he became a hard-faced, hard-eyed, implacable fighting machine.

"'Little flower'! Do you think that I am so delicate and pretty that I cannot teach you some manners too, *bello*?" Stasia asked, laughing.

"No," András said, shaking his head, "I think you have briars and a very sharp thorn hidden beneath your petals. I suspect you also have poisonous leaves and other sharp edges."

He came to stand next to what was left of the bread on the cutting board. Tearing a chunk, he stuffed it into his mouth before beaming over his shoulder at Olivia, who sat watching him with a smile playing at the corners of her mouth.

Chewing, he said, "This is the best one yet, my lady." He swallowed. "Well, the best one after the *kalács* that you made last week."

"Which you ate the entire loaf of, leaving none for Mihàil," Olivia said, rising on her stool to smack the back of his head. She sounded pleased nonetheless. "I'll make you some more braided bread during Stasia's visit."

Everyone turned to Stasia to see what she said to this.

And for the first time since she'd met Olivia that night in Venice when they took one look at the half-dressed teen girls tied to rusty cots and wordlessly agreed to save them, Stasia lied to her friend.

"I am on leave and have no plans. I would like to stay and train with you, *cara*." She started with the falsehood and followed with her genuine wishes, forcing herself to smile and look into Olivia's eyes to gloss over the difference.

"Of course, *cara*!" Olivia slid off her barstool and came around the island to hug Stasia. "It's been forever since we trained together. The Jolly Green Giant there might be tired of beating up on Miró, but I'm tired of sparring with partners who are afraid to hurt me. I'll be run over by the next *bogomili* mob that Fagan sends."

After that, chaos reigned as András vowed to squash any runty *bogomili* that came anywhere near her while Mihàil assured her that he wouldn't restrain himself in the gym the next day. Miró said nothing about Stasia's proposed visit, but she felt his gaze on her as the cook came into the kitchen. She shooed them all out so that she and Besjana could make dinner. András grabbed the last of the bread and a bottle of Czech ale from the refrigerator before following his general and his lady from the room.

As Stasia bent to pick up her purse, Miró was there before her. His warm hand slid under her fingers and around the straps, and he snared her with his gaze. All at once Stasia couldn't breathe. His scent of bergamot, sage, and leather underscored by a distinct hint of ash enveloped her in its bracing masculinity. His face dominated her field of vision so completely he might have been the whole world. She saw now that his pale-blue eyes had creamy threads in a halo around their pupils and the irises were rimmed in a darker blue-gray. There were small lines at the corners of his eyes—she wondered if they were from smiling or squinting—and a dusting of gray at his temples. Not enough to convey his age of nearly 400 years.

She hadn't been this close to Miró since the morning after she met him when she'd been kicking a punching bag in Mihàil's gym because it was the only thing that made sense after learning that angels and demons walked among them. And that she, Anastasia Fiore, Italian foreign intelligence officer and private defender of the weak and vulnerable, had their blood in her veins.

As she watched, Miró's pupils dilated and his stare grazed her mouth before returning to her eyes. Her heartbeat kicked her ribs and ringing sounded in her ears.

"Why did you lie to the *zonjë*, Ms. Fiore?"

"Lie?" She sounded breathless even to herself. "About what?" But she knew what he was referring to. She could see it in his eyes.

"Your plans."

And for the first time ever on a mission, when Anastasia Fiore needed to dissemble, she told the bald truth.

"Because I had to."

Miró nodded as if unsurprised. He stood, lifting her purse and sliding it onto her shoulder, letting his hand rest there. It was warm and heavy and sent a shiver down her spine. "Then I should warn you, Ms. Fiore. As long as you remain here with the *drangùe* and the *zonjë*, I will be monitoring your movements."

That's when Stasia knew that she was in serious trouble.

***

Besjana watched the Croatian and the Italian woman from the doorway to the dining room. Even to her less sensitive eyes, these two radiated an unearthly magnetism. Unlike the *drangùe* and his American wife, whose individual charisma had united in harmony, however, they fairly crackled and popped together as they were now. Some of that energy she could see came from their mutual attraction to each other. But some of it came from antagonism: they didn't trust one another. Or perhaps more to the point, they didn't like being attracted to each other.

Which was too bad because they made a very intriguing and balanced pair, he with his cold eyes and she with her warm smile. They both had enviable poise. Somehow Besjana doubted that they'd ever stumbled or walked into anyone or dropped anything that they didn't mean to drop. Unlike her, they seemed to know exactly where they were in space and in relation to everyone and everything around them. And their timing was always impeccable, though after observing them earlier, Besjana guessed that their gifts here were different, if complementary: the Italian woman had a gift for knowing when to speak and how to direct the conversation while Miró, the *drangùe*'s right hand and spymaster, choreographed all of his actions in a complex ballet.

Yet they threw each other off balance and out of time.

Besjana saw the exact moment when the Italian woman blushed, when the pulse in her throat tapped a fast, uneven rhythm, like a rabbit frozen under an wolf's stare. When she spoke, it was clear that whatever she said surprised her, as though she hadn't intended to say it. And when she stood up, she was a little wobbly and unsure. To underscore the affect that Miró had on her, the sophisticated Italian woman seemed lost in the clouds as she walked away.

Interesting. Not so poised after all.

As for Miró, he remained where he was, his focus solely on the Italian woman. He was so absorbed, in fact, that he didn't notice Besjana as she worked near him, even when she deliberately bumped into him.

And that was even more interesting. The *Elioud* whose eyes saw everything went blind around the Italian woman.

Besjana was going to find her work here a gratifying challenge.

Five

After a sleepless night, Miró rose before dawn and went to the media room, his domain, with its workstations and surveillance equipment, so that he could puzzle over Anastasia Fiore's visit. As soon as she had driven into Fushë-Arrëz, he'd known it. It was like a beacon had appeared on his internal angelic intrusion-detection system. He'd stayed away from the kitchen as long as he could, but that beacon called to him. It had kept him awake and now glowed in the periphery of his awareness where it was likely to drive him mad. After all, he was certain that he would be conscious of Ms. Fiore in the guest room without it.

Sighing, he rubbed his temple with heated fingertips. After Hvar, he'd gone back over all of Fagan's communications and spotted an anonymous email to the *Carabinieri* that had gotten flagged as spam. Perhaps if he'd seen it, he would have anticipated that Ms. Fiore would be involved. At the very least, he would have contacted Officer Rossi, a long-time collaborator, who would have read him in on the operation. Then they—*he*—would have chosen a different course. One that avoided the *Carabinieri* and Ms. Fiore.

She would still come to visit Olivia regardless. They were friends.

But would she still feel the necessity to lie about her purpose?

He couldn't know for sure, but he suspected that Ms. Fiore had done what any good intelligence officer would do if an operation had gone pear shaped on her watch: get back into play and gather more intel. She'd likely already interrogated the Dervishis in prison about the American who had commissioned them to steal the *Judgment of the Watcher Angels*. Now she was here to learn what the *Elioud* warriors knew. And she hadn't come openly.

She was treating them as if they were foreign agents. Which, in all honesty, they were.

Miró let his head drop to stretch his neck before abandoning all attempts at working. No sleep, no work. That meant it was time to hit the gym.

Returning to the bedroom that he used when not staying at the apartment he'd rented in town, he changed into a t-shirt and shorts and put on training shoes. The gym was over the three-car garage attached to the main house, on the other side of the stairs from his room. When the mansion was built, Mihàil had the dimensions of the garage resized to accommodate a gym above it large enough for their style of mixed-martial arts training. It wasn't as large as some of the gyms in Mihàil's foreign residences, but it had plenty of room for the three *Elioud* warriors, some free weights and weight bench, a small and long bag, a jump rope, and pullup bar. Lockers held shared sparring gear while the center of the room was designated as a sparring ring.

Today was Muay Thai day.

Today he'd stand a better than even chance against Mihàil, and even Andràs wouldn't knock him down.

He slipped Bluetooth earbuds in and brought along his smartphone to stream music. The best instructor that he'd had, a Thai champion named Vut Kamnark, had told him how important music was to Muay Thai. That and the martial art should be approached as if it were dancing, loose and rhythmic. Little did Vut know how much that inspired Miró, a dancer who'd long ago foregone dancing and a singer who never felt like singing. No, listening to music while training in Muay Thai set Miró free. Indeed, Vut might be shocked to see what his lesson had done for Miró's capacity for *martial* art.

Miró entered the dark gym, leaving the lights off while he performed the *wai khru ram muay*, the Thai ritual that showed respect for the boxer's teacher and tradition. Although the room was dark, the skylights in the roof showed the warm gray of early dawn. Miró didn't need more light than that. He focused on his *Elioud* senses, using his harmonics as angelic sonar to navigate. At each corner of the ring, he bowed three times, praying not to the Eastern deities of Thailand but to *Elohim*, St. Michael, and Zophiel, his guardian angel. Then he danced the *ram muay* portion of the ritual, American band Lionheart in his ears. The hardcore punk was most definitely *not* angelic music, but then again angry, aggressive sound suited this most personal ritual: his *ram muay* contained clues about how he'd been formed as a warrior.

He'd been formed by sacrifice and loss. All the more reason to train against violent, clashing dissonance.

Besides, it was the perfect soundtrack: when it came to mixed martial arts, he was what was known as a "striker." That was how he survived. Big guys like Mihàil and András, who outweighed him as well as had a longer reach, dominated in grappling submissions. Miró couldn't afford to let them take the fight to the ground.

He spent the next half an hour warming up and stretching, making sure that his joints and movements were supple. After he'd taped his hands and put on ankle wraps, he moved to the long bag to practice his kicks, elbow strikes, and punches. Though Muay Thai also included clinches and blocks, its true power lay in how well a fighter could absorb a strike without reeling. In competitions, Muay Thai fighters won points for balance and composure. It wasn't just an aesthetic judgment: they knew that staggering from a blow made a counterattack ineffective and signaled to your opponent that you can be defeated.

He'd worked up a sweat and likely some bruises on his shins when he stopped, panting. The morning sun had risen, washing the gym in a pale, eggshell light. Turning from the bag, he meant to get water from the dispenser in the corner but halted when he saw Ms. Fiore standing just inside the gym door. *That* was like a punch to the gut. He'd been so focused on training, so sure that he was alone, even more sure in his ability to sense another person—especially Ms. Fiore—that his shock at seeing her tested his poise more than any physical hit.

But he'd had four hundred years to work on his self control. It would take more than this unexpected appearance to send him reeling. Nevertheless, he shunted some of the heat that spiked at seeing her to his skin, lowering his core temperature by several degrees.

He pulled an earbud out before speaking. Nodding, he acknowledged her, "Ms. Fiore," and headed for the water cooler.

She blinked and quite literally shook herself. "Do you mind if I join you?"

"You are already here." He swept his hand around the gym before filling his water bottle. "Feel free to use whatever equipment suits you."

When he finished, he saw that she'd moved to drop her bag on a bench against the wall and was now wrapping her hands. Suddenly, he wished that András, who liked to sleep later, had already shown up for sparring.

"Why do you train so hard if you can use your *Elioud* magic to take out opponents?" Ms. Fiore asked, not looking at him.

It took Miró a moment to process what she'd said. He'd been rather distracted watching the movement of her arm as it deftly twined the long strip of elastic cloth around her wrist and between her thumb and fingers. She was, if possible, more attractive in a simple black tank top and leggings than the dressier sweater and slacks that she'd worn yesterday. Everything about her was sculpted and muscular. She radiated confident energy.

"'*Elioud* magic'?" he asked, incredulous, when her words finally clarified in his thoughts.

She turned toward him. Her face was bare of makeup, allowing him to see her luminous skin and wide hazel eyes unadorned. In a word, she was beautiful.

Shrugging, she said, "What else would you call it?"

Miró tilted his head. "What do you call your ability to manipulate others with a smile or touch?"

Something flitted across her face. Guilt? Surprise?

Whatever it was, it disappeared behind a calm exterior. She turned toward her duffel as she answered. "Tradecraft. It allows me to accomplish my goals without resorting to violence."

Miró dropped his water bottle next to his smartphone before grabbing his towel and drying his neck. The temperature in the gym had risen several degrees, and he could smell ash. He scowled. Why in the name of all that was holy did he always smell like the bottom of a fireplace when she was around?

Flinging the towel to the bench, he faced her. "How about we call it what it is, Ms. Fiore? *Elioud* charisma, which is an exceptional amount of *Elioud* charm. Because you and I both know that you are especially gifted at convincing others to do as you wish, and that it is because of your *Elioud* blood." He walked back to the long bag before continuing, "And you should know that not all of our opponents are willing puppets of Dark *Irim* or ordinary humans. Sometimes we face other *Elioud*, and then our own gifts are less decisive."

Almost like hitting the leather of this bag, he thought. What good would harmonics do? Make it swing more wildly?

"And not all of his opponents are *tutyimutyi* men," András said as he came through the gym door, grinning, "who are charmed by him." He set his duffel down on an open space on the bench. "I'm sure that's hard for you to comprehend, *Kis virág*, as everyone finds you unbelievably lovely and would jump to do your least bidding."

"If only that were true," Ms. Fiore said, securing the end of her second hand wrap. She pulled a pair of fingerless MMA gloves out of her bag and donned them as she spoke. "Then I would have no need to train harder than you both. Unfortunately, some see my small stature as proof that I am easily overcome, either to satisfy their desire or a need to control me. In either instance, I must fight."

Though she didn't look at Miró as she spoke, he nevertheless felt that she directed her words at him. He ignored the implied warning. Pressing his earbud back into his ear, he struck the bag again in a flurry of elbows, fists, and knees, except that this time he chose to modulate his harmonics to control the bag's swing. It wouldn't help him against another *Elioud*, who would adjust his own harmonics in response to Miró, but it did give Miró some added satisfaction when his strikes connected more solidly. Despite herself, Ms. Fiore had inspired a useful technique for training alone.

He'd finished a particularly challenging sequence of knee and elbow strikes when he realized that Ms. Fiore was hanging from the small bag by her legs, doing crunches.

He couldn't help himself. He halted to watch until she jumped off to begin shadow boxing on the sparring mat away from the bag. Periodically she stopped to test and reset her balance. Then she did something totally unexpected. She backed and took a running leap to stride up the wall next to the bag before twisting and lunging at it, striking it with an elbow near the top. Even as the bag swung away, she let gravity take her into it. Latching on with both arms and legs, she delivered a head butt before pushing off into a back handspring.

A memory of a dark, tumultuous evening the previous August came to him: Ms. Fiore and her friend Ms. Černá had executed just such fearless acrobatic maneuvers in a coordinated attack to rescue Olivia. Though they wouldn't be able to go toe-to-toe with larger, stronger male fighters, their agility, speed, and training—not to mention their team tactics—made them formidable opponents. That and they didn't hesitate. At. All. At that thought, Miró rubbed the back of his upper arm where Ms. Fiore had sliced him last summer.

This morning Ms. Fiore looked determined, her gaze focused on something internal as she came to stand in the middle of the mat with her hands guarding her face. A light sheen of sweat covered her skin, but her breathing held steady.

András, who'd been warming up doing burpees interspersed with plyometrics, began cheering and clapping. Miró shot his friend a look, but the big Hungarian didn't see it.

"That's the way to take that bag down! You've got mad skills! Have you ever considered parkour?" András sounded very serious. He probably thought that if he wasn't joking that he was being respectful.

Miró closed his eyes and pressed his lips together, shaking his head.

Ms. Fiore stared at András. Her expression was inscrutable, but Miró found himself sensing her gathering herself for an attack. She was likely running through the most effective scenarios in her arsenal. Miró dropped his own hands and removed his earbuds. This should be interesting. Ms. Fiore came to the middle of András's chest and weighed less than half his weight. It was extremely unlikely that she would be more than a nuisance to the big man.

Ms. Fiore smiled suddenly. It was warm and generous, as if András were a dear friend whom she hadn't seen in much too long. Miró recognized that smile. He'd had it aimed at him yesterday. Folding his arms, he leaned back against the wall to watch. András might be a fighter beyond compare, but no one charmed like the inestimable Ms. Fiore, and András was particularly vulnerable to beautiful women.

"You would not spar with me, would you? You are as tall as that bag"—she gestured toward the small bag that she'd just so expertly jumped on and struck—"but you stand firm, like an oak with deep roots. You would be good practice for me." Miró especially liked the little deprecating way that Ms. Fiore indicated herself.

András, who'd taken a drink while she spoke, wiped the back of his mouth and tossed the empty bottle toward his gear. He tilted his head, studying her. "That's easy, *Kis virág*. Of course, I'll be your punching bag."

Ms. Fiore smiled and dipped her chin. "Thank you, *bello*."

She began dancing around András, who raised his hands in a relaxed guard, and for the next several minutes, he deftly met her punches. The fierce look had returned to Ms. Fiore's face, and she appeared to strike his hands as hard as she could. Then she began kicking András in the thigh and calf. Miró recognized the Muay Thai style of low kicks. Those would hurt, but they wouldn't be painful enough to cause András to strike Ms. Fiore. The man took more hurt daily sparring Mihàil and Miró and even more during his own training regimen.

But Ms. Fiore wasn't using András as a punching bag any more than he was sparring with her. Miró could see her watching András and timing her movements to her bigger opponent, testing his reactions to her tactics. He recognized when she began to lead András in an intricate dance.

It was mesmerizing.

Miró realized with a start that she had an instinctual control over her harmonics and had gained a modicum of control over András's. In seeming contradiction to safety, she moved closer as she punched and kicked. Their movements had all the grace of a tango, intimate and familiar.

Miró's temperature began to rise as he saw Ms. Fiore's small form brush against András again and again.

Then she struck, whip fast.

She hammered her forehead into András's solar plexus, immediately doubling him over only to smash the top of her head into his chin. It wasn't enough to topple the big Hungarian, but he let out a pained yell and staggered. Ms.

Fiore, instead of scurrying away from danger, followed up with two alternating forearm strikes to András's neck, now in reach. Miró again recognized Muay Thai in her technique. She didn't weigh much, but she leveraged every gram in her strikes against his friend's arteries.

Still András didn't fall. But he looked like a massive drunk.

Ms. Fiore moved beneath his arm as he reached for her and around behind him to stomp on the back of his knee, driving her slight weight into this weak point with her heel. András fell to his knees where Ms. Fiore delivered a vicious side kick to his lower back but not to his kidney, Miró noted. He knew that she was quite capable of injuring her opponent in that way but had chosen not to do so.

András was far from beaten. In fact, he was roused by this time.

Unfortunately, he turned into Ms. Fiore's elbows, which she put to brutal effect. She might not be willing to hurt András seriously, but she had no problem "cutting" his forehead—an MMA technique that caused a lot of harmless bleeding and won competition points.

András roared and rose up from the mat, spilling Ms. Fiore onto her back.

And in time to meet Miró's extremely effective Muay Thai front teep—a push kick—to the chest. András, who hadn't yet regained his balance, flew backwards. But now his warrior instincts had been engaged. He stumbled to a halt, catching himself and bringing his own hands up in the guard position while his stance widened. Blood sheeted his face. The familiar grin was gone. The temperature in the gym rose dangerously.

Miró waited. Ms. Fiore scooted out of the way.

And then it happened. András flared. His angelic nature rose in blinding white around him. The blood evaporated from his superheated skin. He locked in on Miró. An instant later he stood within arms' length.

All hell broke loose.

András threw superfast punching combos, his elbows and knees joining in. Miró kept Ms. Fiore behind him as he countered his friend's furious onslaught, repeatedly *teep*ing to keep András at a safe distance and tracking the big man's rhythm and tactics. It was the most devastatingly real sparring that they'd ever engaged in. András had gone into battle mode. When that happened, a switch flipped in the good-natured Hungarian. He became as cold and pitiless and efficient as an automaton.

"András." Ms. Fiore's voice cut into Miró's focus. "*Per favore*, I am so sorry! *Per favore*, András!"

Miró never took his gaze from András, but he sensed her rising panic, her unhappiness—her *fear*.

His own battle senses flared.

The next time that András let a series of punches fly, Miró was ready. He blocked the first, but instead of *teep*ing, he pressed forward. András backed in surprise at the savageness of Miró's blows, trading punches and throwing an occasional front *teep* at Miró, who took them all without losing his balance or halting his advance. He forced András across the mat and away from Ms. Fiore. Then he threw a rapid right-left-right at András's jaw before the taller man managed to push him back, breaking his rhythm.

What happened next took less than two seconds.

Miró threw a left, absorbed András's answering left, and then swung with his right, following the punch all the way through this time. At the same instant, András ducked away from the anticipated left that never came.

He was off balance and his right flank exposed.

Miró took the opening.

He lifted his right forearm under András's right elbow and pushed. András fell back sideways, rolling over onto his stomach. Before he could get his hands under him, Ms. Fiore was on his back, choking him using a short-arm hold, her thighs pressing his elbows. He rose up anyway, growling, but she drove his head into her wrist using her shoulder and clasped her hands together. András collapsed, unconscious for the moment.

Into the silence that followed, Olivia said behind them, "I can see why you won't let me spar with you." Her dry tone underscored her ironic observation.

"And I can see that Miró has found a battle partner," Mihàil said. "He and Stasia fight together almost as well as we do, *dashuria ime.*"

Miró, startled, looked at his *Elioud* general and his *zonjë.* They'd clearly been there for some time and had seen more than Ms. Fiore's fight-ending submission.

Ms. Fiore stood. She ignored him to speak to Mihàil. "I fight alone or with my friends."

"I don't know, Staz," Olivia said, "we stood shoulder-to-shoulder with these guys against the *bogomili* and held our own." She threw Mihàil an affectionate, pointed look. "I'm pretty sure that they could use our help."

Mihàil walked over to András and nudged him—none too gently—with his toe. "Awake, Sleeping Beauty." As the big Hungarian groaned and started to come around, Mihàil continued, "Sweet merciful St. Zophiel! How in the world did someone Stasia's size manage to choke you out?"

"I truly adore the sound of that. Say it again."

At the sound of Zophiel's voice, they all looked at the long bag. She hung upside down from it, her legs wrapped around the top. Spiky strands of her pale hair floated in the air as if static electricity levitated them.

As Mihàil clasped András's hand and hauled him to his feet, he asked her, "Say what again exactly?"

"Saint."

She unfolded her legs from the bag and slid toward the floor where she put her palms on the ground. Balancing a moment in a graceful handstand, she dropped first one leg and then the other, sliding into a split.

"Michael likes to remind me that I am not a saint, not in Heaven or on Earth. Perhaps one day." She seemed unconcerned with her fate.

Miró watched Ms. Fiore, who stood frozen, a look close to horror on her lovely face. Why the horror? Then he realized that she'd never met Zophie before, only seen her for a brief moment at Olivia and Mihàil's wedding. Grey *Elioud* were distinctly uncomfortable around angels.

"You're a saint in my book," Olivia said, "putting up with these three." She gestured at the male *Elioud* warriors. András leaned over, hands on knees, a bloody hand towel on the floor between his feet. Looking up, he smiled through a flush not entirely due to exertion or *Elioud* temper. Miró himself felt bemused. He couldn't remember a time when his friend had had the grace to be embarrassed. Or a time when his own battle senses had flared against another faithful *Elioud*.

"Indeed." Zophie shook her head before brightening. "But I remain ever optimistic. Look how far I have come: you are Mihàil's *zonjë*. The others cannot be so far behind." She smiled, looking from the corner of her eyes at Miró and András before moving to Ms. Fiore, who had been easing toward the door. The angel's shocking blue gaze lost its humor, pinning Ms. Fiore to the spot.

"You are free to leave the gift your grandfather bequeathed you in its velvet bag, but make no mistake, little flower, that is a choice as much as wielding his fighting knife. You cannot in good conscience accept the one without the other. And a time is rapidly approaching when it will be exceedingly clear to you what the stakes are for choosing wrongly."

Ms. Fiore's mouth opened and shut several times. Nothing came out.

Miró felt compelled to defend her. "The wisest choices are made in full knowledge." And he stood his ground when Zophie turned that penetrating angelic gaze on him, holding it even though it seared him to his soul.

After a moment, Zophie nodded and a small smile softened her sternness. "You will do, Miró Kos. You will do." Then she looked up, her gaze distant and unfocused. "Yes, my lord, I will leave the chastising to you from now on. You cannot fault me, however, for speaking out on my ward's behalf. You assigned me to him after all."

An instant later, she stood at the gym door, her hand on the lever. Her sly smile lent an almost demonic edge to her ethereal features. "Oh, yes, my mute blackbird. Your fight songs are *so* edgy and rebellious. I approve." Then she opened the door and stepped into a flash of angelic white light.

And like that, the thick miasma of tension that had enveloped them lifted as the mid-morning sun brightened the room. More than that, wellbeing soaked into the very marrow of Miró's bones. Despite Zophie's words, her gift of peace left no doubt that his choice of training music left its mark on his spirit. It was an implicit warning not to wallow in bitterness and toy with despair.

Miró looked at Ms. Fiore, who remained rooted. Whatever conflicting emotions she evoked in him, right now concern dominated.

He was at her side instantly.

"Ms. Fiore," he said, touching her forearm. She turned unfocused eyes to him. "Please, come and sit. Zophiel can be a bit much for those unaccustomed to her style."

She let Miró lead her to a bench. Though he kept only his fingertips on her elbow, electricity coursed all the way to his soles. She smelled of clean sweat and of smoky-sweet vanilla with notes of sharp anise and rich iris. Her sensual, complex perfume reminded him of another era, one in which beautiful women sang romantic songs in cafés where lovers stared into each other's eyes and promised eternal faithfulness.

Promises no more enduring than the gaslights under which the lovers sat.

"*La Sciantosa,*" he murmured to himself, the memory bittersweet.

Ms. Fiore looked up at him, her hazel eyes haunted and haunting. "*Cosa hai detto?*"

Miró shook his head. "*Non è niente.*" But it *was* something. At one time, *la sciantosa* had been everything.

He sat next to Ms. Fiore, telling himself that it was because she needed reassurance. A brush with the divine took time to absorb. Drawing on the serenity that Zophiel had granted him, Miró modified his harmonics into a gentle current that soothed her own wildly oscillating ones. She shifted almost imperceptibly closer, her thigh brushing his. He wanted to put an arm around her but didn't.

Mihàil and Olivia had gone to the far end of the bench to deposit their bags. While Mihàil wrapped his wrists and hands, Olivia watched them. Miró sensed that she wanted to comfort her friend but refrained from doing so. András came over to them wearing a somber expression. There was a bruise on his neck, likely from Ms. Fiore's wrist. He waited until she looked at him. Then he knelt and took her hands in his large ones.

"Forgive me. I underestimated your skill and your heart. And then I lost control. If Miró hadn't intervened, I might have done something I would regret forever."

Ms. Fiore blinked and seemed to shake herself. Leaning forward, she said, "I forgive you." Then she stood, sending a wave roiling through Miró's harmonics. He'd gotten more in sync with her than he'd intended. Pulling her hands from András's, she gestured at the group and raised her voice. "*Per favore*, excuse me. It has been some time since I trained so intensely. I–I would like to take a break."

And she dashed for the door, leaving Miró more confused and unhappy than he had been in a long time.

Six

After her encounter with Zophiel, Stasia considered her options for recovering the missing Rembrandt painting. Preferably anything that would justify leaving before the midday meal. Between her increasing awareness of Miró and the shocking and sudden appearance of an actual angel, she felt off balance in a way that she'd never felt before. It spooked her.

But missions always threw up unanticipated hurdles, no matter how farsighted or thorough she'd been. Anyone involved in planning complex operations knew the famous saying from the nineteenth-century Prussian field marshal, Helmuth Von Moltke: no battle plan ever survives contact with the enemy. And in this case, she'd failed to account for the supernatural in a situation defined by the supernatural. She had to be honest. If she had any hope of succeeding in getting the stolen artwork back for her countryman, then she couldn't overlook this factor.

Or her own reaction to it.

And if she were honest, she'd have to admit that the thought of seducing Joseph Fagan paled in comparison to seducing Miró Kos.

Because that's what her options looked like right now: either travel to Vienna and surveil the American spymaster to determine his sexual proclivities so that she could exploit them to recoup the priceless artwork or stay here and ostensibly help Olivia and the other *Elioud* as they kept eyes on the target, looking for an opportunity to retrieve the painting on her own and return to Italy. And leveraging the chemistry already burgeoning between her and the taciturn Croatian had a certain poetry to it. It would absolutely be more pleasant for her, and therefore easier to pull off.

Maybe she'd known all along that was what she was here to do.

It would also likely end the attraction, dispelling the mystery and excitement of being around Miró. Sex had always spelled the beginning of the end in all of Stasia's previous infatuations. Having it as part of a mission crossed a line that she'd never crossed before, and she knew that once she did, it would be a breach for which she'd never forgive herself. Neither would he, she suspected, because he clearly didn't indulge his baser, human instincts.

Perhaps he needs to have sex.

Stasia laughed at the wicked thought. *She* was the one who needed sex. She'd do well to avoid projecting that onto the current object of her desire. Just because he exuded an intoxicating scent and virility that seemed designed especially for her didn't mean that he viewed her the same way.

Unfortunately, Miró knew that she'd lied to Olivia. He'd be even more on his guard around her than he already was. Worse, given their verbal sparring and her prickliness toward him, his suspicions would be roused if she switched to an all-out charisma offensive. Plus, she wasn't sure that she *could* charm him well enough to distract him from learning her true motive.

But she couldn't risk telling the *Elioud* team what she was up to because they wouldn't be inclined to let her bring the painting back to its rightful owner, not when it had "lustrous" brushstrokes.

So she spent the next few days training in the Kastrioti gym, sparring with Olivia and observing the way the male *Elioud* warriors trained. It didn't take long before she realized that she'd been extremely fortunate that Miró had stepped in and fought András. The Hungarian never lost his composure again. While his intensity equaled the other *Elioud* warriors, his fighting skill was unmatched. He reminded Stasia of the legendary Achilles. She wondered what—or who—his vulnerable point was. She'd often wondered the same thing about Beta, who was the most intense of their trio.

On the third morning, Stasia knew that it was time to make a move.

When she arrived at the gym, however, Miró wasn't alone. Mihàil and Olivia stood talking with him and András near the bench where everyone tended to drop their personal gear. Something about their expressions made Stasia think that whatever they spoke about might not be something that they wanted to share with her. Tension swirled around them.

She halted in the doorway, uncertain.

A moment later, Miró's face turned towards her, his penetrating blue gaze pinning her. She saw wariness and distrust there. Before she could speculate about the current reason for his suspicion or whether it was truly directed at her, Olivia seemed to realize where Miró's gaze had gone. Turning, she gave a happy shout and trotted to Stasia.

"Staz!" She clasped Stasia around the shoulders and pressed quick kisses to her cheeks in the Italian manner. "Come here and join us. Mihàil and I are just about to demonstrate some new techniques that we've been working on."

Stasia hid her unease behind a warm smile. "I do not wish to intrude, *cara*." She lifted her chin toward the group of male *Elioud* watching them. "They are not so happy to see me."

Olivia looked back. Something passed between her and her husband. Stasia suspected that the *Elioud* couple had the ability to speak to each other without words. Olivia had certainly shown an almost-mystical connection to Mihàil last summer after he'd been captured and tortured by Fagan. It seemed the natural outgrowth of their preternatural awareness of each other.

As she seemed to be of Miró.

Stasia shot a glance at him. He still watched her. She shivered.

Olivia shook her head. "Never mind them. We're finished with our discussion." She spoke with an air of finality.

Stasia followed Olivia back, halting at her friend's side. Miró stood on her left. She raised her chin and squared her shoulders, narrowing her eyes at him before turning her attention back to the others. Nevertheless, heated electricity vibrated along her skin where it was exposed to him. She had the strangest sensation of melting on that side of her body. Almost as if her body wanted to merge with his.

Mihàil nodded once at Stasia. Then he addressed the group.

"As you all know, Olivia and I stopped in Bratislava last July." Everyone nodded. On the run from the authorities at the time, the couple had adopted the identities of newlyweds who honeymooned on a river cruise from Vienna to Budapest. "While there Olivia told me a story about what had spurred her desire to save innocents. Suffice it to say, it was a difficult story." Here he took his wife's hand and kissed it. "As she spoke, she made a version of this."

He lifted his palm to reveal an origami eagle that appeared to be folded from black paper and lacquered. It made Stasia think of the Albanian eagle.

"This is a replica of the eagle that she folded that day. I left that eagle on the altar of the Blue Church. Later Zophiel brought it to me in the slaughterhouse just after you arrived. I gave it back to Olivia when she met me."

Now Olivia spoke. "At this point, we didn't know exactly where Fagan was although we'd identified the most likely quadrant. Mihàil had the idea that he could fly the eagle as a kind of angelic drone to find Fagan's location. However, he needed my familiarity with Fagan's signatures to target him." The others nodded, clearly understanding what Olivia referred to.

Stasia focused on Olivia's description, ignoring her body's disconcerting reaction to Miró as best she could. She'd always wondered how the couple had found Fagan so quickly. It had seemed lucky—and she didn't believe in luck. The man had parked an escape vehicle right next to the box truck that he'd used as his control room. Without pinpointing his precise location, the *Elioud* team wouldn't have found him before he'd driven away. At that point, even though they had a helicopter, they would have been hard pressed to keep Fagan from disappearing.

"Frankly, I was rather surprised at how well it worked," Mihàil said. "As a Wild *Elioud*, she had angelic talents that she used instinctively that would not have prepared her to work with mine."

"Such as charisma?" Miró asked. Stasia turned to him. He looked at her, a small smile curling his mouth and warming his gaze, and for a moment every molecule in her body wanted to be subsumed into his.

All at once, she knew what he was doing.

"*Smettila!*" *Stop it.*

Of course, he flashed.

Stasia froze, blinking. Had she just heard Miró's voice in her head?

The urge to burrow into his protective embrace, to press against his hard chest and nuzzle his neck and jaw eased but didn't entirely disappear. She felt bereft and exposed. Gritting her teeth and clenching her hands, she shifted toward Olivia.

Mihàil appeared not to have heard either of them. He nodded. "A powerful, seductive appeal is the most common gift the

Irim bequeathed the *Elioud*, especially those of us descended from Yeqon the Seducer."

"Who?" Stasia asked. She'd only ever heard of the archangels Michael, Gabriel, and Raphael.

András, who slouched against the wall, one knee bent while he opened and closed a steel grip trainer, answered. "The Watcher Angel who convinced two hundred of his mates to come down to Earth and seduce human women. Some say Yeqon was the one who convinced Eve to take a bite out of the apple, but that was pretty clearly Sêmîazâz, the leader of the Fallen *Irim*."

"You know him as Satan, the Adversary," said Miró, his expression somber now. "Though some foolishly call him Lucifer, which feeds his insatiable ego."

Stasia tilted her head and studied Olivia. "Olivia is charismatic indeed. But I would have said that she has other qualities that make her equal to a *drangùe*. *É nata per comandare.* Beta and I both would follow her against any foe."

"I agree. She was born to command. As a Wild *Elioud,* she put together a team of Wild *Elioud* with a mission to aid innocents. That alone distinguishes her."

Stasia heard the pride in Mihàil's voice and felt a pang. What would it feel like to have the man you love speak about you that way? She refrained from looking at Miró, but her heartrate sped up a notch at the thought.

Mihàil continued. "Even so, without knowing who or what she is, Olivia should have had more difficulty using thermogenesis and harmonics without some training. Instead she grasped them intuitively. I realized later that her quick mastery stemmed in no small measure from her foundation in martial arts. That made me curious, so I asked her about her training."

Stasia felt Miró shift next to her. Stealing a glance, she saw that his lips had compressed. He'd also folded his arms across his chest. He disapproved. Why? Was it her presence? Or something more?

Olivia fingered the small silver pendant that she wore. Stasia recognized it as the St. Michael's medal that Mihàil had quizzed her about last summer. Suddenly Zophiel's words echoed in her thoughts: *You are free to leave the gift your grandfather bequeathed you in its velvet bag.* Her grandfather had given her a St. Michael's medal when he died. Unlike Olivia's medal her grandfather's was an antique bronze oval. It and its velvet bag rested inside an inner pocket in her duffel.

Olivia let the pendant drop and looked around the group. "If you recall, I told you that I got my St. Michael's medal because I had a friend who had one and that I felt I had to get one. What I didn't say was that this friend was my *sensei*. I'd started taking karate classes during my freshman year in college."

She paused to clear her throat. Mihàil slipped his hand around hers. "After my cousin was murdered the summer before."

Stasia was shocked. She'd had no idea that Olivia had suffered such a terrible loss. She wanted to put her arms around her friend, who suddenly looked young and vulnerable.

"I'd been a student for more than a year when the trial of Emily's murderer was held. I testified. Afterwards I found that I couldn't focus on my studies. I couldn't concentrate on anything. I even had trouble writing. My hands would shake too much. Finally, I took a leave of absence from college.

"But I kept going to karate even though I really struggled. *Sensei* Mark was very patient, encouraging me to study privately. He kept bringing me back to the present moment. He became my anchor. Long story short, he became a mentor beyond martial arts. I got the medal as a reminder of who he was, what he meant to me, and what he valued. He suggested that I get the medal blessed, but I laughed and said that he could do it. I believed more in his teaching than the teaching of a church I didn't attend. So he blessed it."

Silence descended on the group. Stasia blinked several times, confused. Mihàil had said last summer that the *Elioud* could see the blessing. What did it mean that they saw a karate teacher's blessing?

Miró looked shocked. "That means that her *sensei* was an angel."

"Not just any angel." Mihàil paused, holding first András's gaze and then Miró's. "St. Michael. As I said last summer, he chose her."

"What? That's fantastic!" András sounded excited. He came to Olivia and folded her in a hug, lifting her off her feet and causing her to squeak.

"That fits." Miró acknowledged with a reluctant nod when András had set Olivia down. "The name 'Mark' comes from the Latin god of war, Mars. St. Michael commands the Heavenly Hosts." He turned to study Olivia, his icy blue eyes holding new respect. "St. Michael does not appear often among humanity. He sends messengers like Zophiel instead."

"And when he does come, it is often in visions or dreams," Stasia said. Everyone looked at her. She shrugged. "My grandfather told me that when I was a girl. He claimed that he had seen the Archangel more than once."

She felt Miró's gaze on her, but he said nothing.

"It seemed to me that I should take advantage of this great gift from my commander." Mihàil raised the origami eagle. "For this reason, Olivia and I have spent the past few months training as a unit using the weapons that she brought with her, such as this eagle."

Stasia cocked her head. "You have been perfecting flying your angelic drone?"

"Among other things," Olivia said, smiling. "We'd like to demonstrate. Just give us a few minutes to warm up a bit before we get started."

Stasia sat on the bench, folding her hands in her lap and leaning back against the wall. Miró still stood next to her, his heat and solid presence enticing even though his folded arms warned against getting any closer. András came and sat on her other side, leaning forward with his hands clasped between his knees and his gaze keen on the *Elioud* couple. Together they watched as Mihàil wrapped his hands with black cotton before jumping rope to warm up. Olivia had already wrapped her hands and began shadow boxing, alternating with sets of tucked squat jumps, an exercise designed to build explosive power.

The zonjë's power has increased rapidly over the past six months. Miró's voice came in Stasia's thoughts again. *It is because she has gained fine control over her harmonics. And vice versa. The more she trains using plyometrics, the better her control.*

Stasia looked up at him, but he kept his gaze on Olivia and Mihàil.

Well okay then. She'd try this speaking using only her thoughts. Who knew if it would work? And for all she knew, her thoughts would broadcast to the room at large. Best to keep her language mild.

What are these 'harmonics' that you speak of? It sounds like music.

He clearly heard her. András didn't look her way, so perhaps she'd succeeded in targeting Miró's mental ears only.

Because it is. Music is the fundamental language and energy of Creation all the way to the atomic level. Everything in Creation vibrates in relationship to everything else.

Capisco. Angels sing. Ergo they can control the underlying vibrations. Elioud inherited this gift.

Yes, if you listen you will hear the hum of this musica universalis.

Perhaps it was because Miró stood next to her and spoke in her thoughts or perhaps it was because she found the idea of everything vibrating in some celestial symphony appealing, but Stasia found the gym sounds receding into white noise as she listened.

And then it happened.

She heard it. And now that she heard it, she couldn't unhear it.

Stasia's eyes widened and a shiver tore down her spine. She looked up at Miró, who watched her with sharp curiosity.

Olivia stopped on the mat across from them. "That's enough for me. I'm ready to go. How 'bout you?" She grinned over at Mihàil.

Mihàil, a fine sheen of sweat on his face, nodded. "Of course, my lady."

He pulled what looked like a fencing mask from a bag and tossed it to his wife. She deftly caught it. Stasia saw that the mesh face had been replaced with solid polymer with a breathing filter. Olivia wouldn't be able to see through it. It wasn't even clear that she would be able to hear. Stasia leaned forward, her curiosity piqued. Olivia went to the far corner of the mat and tugged the mask on.

Everything disappeared from Stasia's awareness as she watched her friend. What was Olivia planning?

Mihàil tossed the origami eagle into the air where an air draft appeared to catch it and send it gliding across the gym. Then he came to stand and watch with them as Olivia pivoted slowly to follow the origami eagle's flight around the gym's perimeter.

"Is she guiding it?" Stasia couldn't help asking. An incredulous note lifted her voice. She kept her gaze glued to the scene unfolding before her.

"Yes." Mihàil said shortly, sounding distracted.

"Using harmonics?"

Miró looked at her. "It is difficult to explain, but Olivia is using her angelic senses along with harmonics." *She can 'see' the eagle just as you can 'hear' me now.*

"Ever see Star Wars?" Olivia called cheerfully. She stood now with the mask under an arm. "It's like the angelic force, and I'm a Jedi knight. Mihàil acts as my harmonic amplifier."

"Let us see if this knight can find a target, shall we?"

Olivia tugged the mask back on. The origami eagle glided around her head like a baby's mobile.

Can you hear the eagle? Miró asked.

It sent long, slow vibrations in wide arcs like ripples in a pond after a stone had been tossed.

Yes. Stasia's unwilling belief colored even her mental voice. She had the urge to cross herself but didn't.

Mihàil tipped his chin toward the door where Besjana now stood, watching the origami eagle with an odd look on her face. Stasia's gaze narrowed. She didn't know why, but her intuition told her that something was off about the young woman's reaction. Mihàil waved Besjana toward a far corner away from Olivia.

Olivia stood motionless, relaxed but alert. And then her head swiveled toward Besjana. The origami eagle darted across the gym until it reached the teen, kissing her on the cheek before settling on her hair.

At that, Stasia rose, and before anyone could stop her, sprinted toward Olivia.

Who apparently sensed her coming.

Pulling her extensible *bō* from its hidden sheath on her back and flicking it open as she did, Olivia swung it at the front of Stasia's thigh.

Stasia sensed the move a beat before Olivia made it. She swerved a step.

Unfortunately, Olivia veered a beat ahead of Stasia. She pulled her strike short, swiping the other end of the *bō* around to catch Stasia on her hamstring instead.

That stung.

"Point!" András cried.

Stasia stumbled and went down on her right knee. She popped up again even as Olivia reversed the motion of the *bō* to strike Stasia's upper thigh.

But Stasia anticipated that move and clamped onto the *bō* before it could tag her again.

Only to have the origami eagle land on the back of her hand.

"Match!" András whooped.

Stasia glared at him. He didn't seem to notice. Miró watched her closely, though. He smiled when she looked at him. It made her breathless. He looked happy *and* proud.

You relied on harmonics. It wasn't a question.

Yes.

Olivia collapsed her *bō* and slid it into its sheath. The origami eagle flew up to her outstretched hand. Mihàil, Miró, and András came to join them. Stasia, who'd twisted to rub at her aching thigh, caught a glimpse of Besjana, still in the corner. Naked avarice and dislike gleamed on the young woman's face as she stared at their group. Then she noticed Stasia's gaze, and her expression cleared as if wiped.

She would bear watching.

Mihàil wrapped an arm around Olivia's shoulders and kissed her.

Nodding at the origami eagle, Miró asked, "How far can you send one of these?"

Olivia shrugged. "We've only tested it around Fushë-Arrëz. The wind resistance and sightlines make it hard to know. Plus paper isn't the most durable material. That's why we lacquered this one after I folded it. Fortunately, it's cheap and easy to replace. We've already lost a few dozen."

Ah. That is how Besjana knows.

"Farther than I can see or sense now," said Mihàil, answering Miró.

Miró looked thoughtful. "May I?" he asked Olivia, who handed him the origami. He studied it. "Would you mind if I tried to optimize your design?"

Olivia shook her head and smiled. "Not at all." She turned to Stasia. "I'd like to say that I didn't know that was you, but I did. Sorry about the bruise you're going to have."

Stasia shrugged. "*Prego.* It is to be expected when sparring. After all, I would have left a few bruises if your harmonics had failed to warn you in time."

Mihàil turned and called to the waiting teen. "Besjana, thank you for your help. Please ask Pjëter to have a full breakfast for us this morning. Olivia and I are quite ravenous." He turned to the others. "Will you join us?" At their nods, he turned back and said, "Tell Pjëter that we will all have breakfast together."

"Make sure that the *kalács* is put out," Olivia added. "Both loaves. I'm sure András has worked up a hearty appetite watching us." She winked at him. He smiled and rubbed his midsection.

Besjana nodded and hurried past them but not before Stasia saw the flash of resentment.

Miró put a hand on her upper arm as she started to follow the others out of the gym. His warm fingers brought goosebumps to her skin and a shiver ran down her spine. Her gaze was drawn to his. His eyes had turned icy again.

"It is time, Ms. Fiore, that you and I had a private conversation about your future, and whether you can remain here any longer."

The goosebumps intensified, but she controlled the corresponding shiver with a tight rein on her willpower.

Yes, it was past time that she made progress on her mission.

"*Prego.*" She tipped her chin toward the door. "After breakfast you can demonstrate harmonics using your own origami outside of Fushë-Arrëz. Perhaps a blackbird this time, *sì?*"

Miró's eyes narrowed at the reference to Zophiel's endearment. "What more you learn about your *Elioud* gifts remains to be seen."

Seven

Fifteen hundred kilometers away, Beta Černá stalked three *bogomili* along the snowy early-morning streets of Prague District 3. A ten-minute drive from the Danube River, the western side of the district housed a number of brothels, strip clubs, and cheap bars. The district also housed a refugee center in a former clinic, although many young refugees found shelter where they could and with whomever they could for drugs or for sex. Often both. In other words, the district was the perfect hunting ground for the soulless thugs.

The three *bogomili* headed south and away from Vitkov Hill where the giant bronze equestrian statue of Jan Žižka, fifteenth-century Czech general, stood guard over the Old Town. They walked in a loose wedge, dominating the sidewalk on the narrow cobblestone street. Ahead the Žižkov Television Tower, the 216-meter hypodermic needle built in the late 1980s on the literal bones of the Old Jewish Cemetery, loomed over the rooftops of the modest three- and four-story apartment buildings.

Beta, who always grew excessively hot whenever she tracked criminals and predators, wore only a light jacket, t-shirt, and jeans. Her breath steamed the frigid air. Dragon's breath, she called it, amusing herself. Ever since she'd been a child and heard some of the old Slavic tales about benevolent dragons falling in love with men and women, she'd imagined that she was the daughter of a dragon. A *dcera draka.*

She was fatherless, after all. What better way to soothe her childish longings? It was certainly much better than the reality that she came to learn later: that she was the product of her mother's rape.

Maybe her long fascination with dragon progenitors had primed her eyesight. She'd known what Mihàil Kastrioti was as soon as she saw him with her friend Olivia Markham. Seeing the old tales embodied made her wish that the Albanian *drangùe* had been her father so fiercely that she could still taste the sharp tang of it.

But Mihàil Kastrioti wasn't her father. And she wasn't a *dcera draka,* just a woman who had an angel ancestor and an implacable need to rid the world of predators like her unknown father.

A woman whose latent *Elioud* blood now stirred.

How else to explain the fact that she could read the infrared signatures for the *bogomili* ahead of her without thermal goggles?

Beta slipped her fingers into her pocket where the folded length of her chain whip lay. It was the reason that she wore a jacket. Light as it was, it certainly offered no warmth. She palmed the cold metal dart, its weight comforting. It warmed in her hand, feeling alive and restless now. That sensation always began moments before she unleashed the dart, sending it toward prey. A cold smile flitted across her face. She may not be a *zmeitsa,* but she had a dragon's tongue.

And a subcompact SIG Sauer P365 9mm handgun concealed in an ankle holster to deliver a dragon's fiery kisses.

The three *bogomili* passed Prokopova Square just as dawn made the milky February sky blush. They joked and shared a cigarette, the smoke heavy in the frigid air. Beta squinted, studying their physiques in the growing light. All three had broad shoulders inside black fleece jackets and short haircuts. Though there were no other distinguishing traits, her gut told her that they were former military or law enforcement of some kind.

Most likely mercenaries.

So not the typical *bogomili* recruited from among the refugees. Which meant that they were likely to have some of their higher-level cognitive functions intact. The last time she'd encountered *bogomili* of this caliber, they had worked in tactical teams at the behest of the American spymaster Fagan. The one who had come after Mihàil, leaving Olivia for dead.

Rage, long banked, detonated in Beta's chest. Now the breath she exhaled smelled as smoky hot as the lingering puffs of the *bogomili* ahead of her on the other side of the street. Her nostrils flared at the scent, and for a moment all thought cleared from her mind and her eyesight sharpened. She saw the pulse in each man's throat, heard his heartbeat, smelled his individual scent. She knew exactly where to tear and rend the soft flesh to maim and kill.

No one targeted Olivia without consequences.

Olivia had found her when she was lost and given her a purpose beyond brutal revenge. She'd shown Beta how to contain her dragon nature so that her humanity could rise to the fore. For the first time in almost a decade, Beta had actually been able to interact with other people, albeit awkwardly. Moreover Olivia and Stasia were the only two friends she'd ever had.

Beta's pace picked up until she was sprinting doubled over so that the cars parked along both sides of the street blocked view of her approach. As she came abreast of the trio, she reached into her ankle holster for the SIG. No need to play with her prey.

The lead *bogomili*'s cellphone chirped. He answered. "Sir?"

And then Beta's conscience asserted itself, and cold thought clamped onto her dragon mind. She wouldn't kill these bastards. Yet.

She slowed, dropping back a car's length. On the deserted street, her acute hearing caught the *bogomili*'s speech as if he stood next to her.

"Yes, sir, I recced the museum yesterday. As advertised the target is on the ground floor of the Schwarzenberg Palace." He spoke with an Australian accent, both surprising and not surprising Beta. Often built like the actor who played Thor in the superhero franchise, Aussies were tough, brutal soldiers. If she had to recruit a deadly hit squad, she'd start with them or the Americans. "Security measures are minimal. *L'Amante* arrives this afternoon, so there shouldn't be any problems acquiring it."

Schwarzenberg Palace? The 16th century Renaissance castle, the largest of its kind in the world, was one of the buildings of the National Gallery Prague. It housed the Czech Republic's Old Masters Collection. What was the target? She'd seen posters announcing a traveling exhibition featuring a "lost" painting that opened this week. It seemed unlikely that *bogomili* would be sent to steal a Baroque painting.

The mercenary's next words snapped Beta back to the present.

"No, sir, we've been keeping a low profile. We kept our fun off the streets." His companions hooted. "But don't worry. She's not going to say anything."

Beta had gotten close enough that she heard Fagan's reply via the cellphone's speaker. "No body, McIntyre."

"Copy that." McIntyre ended the call and slid the phone into his pocket. "Okay, mates, one last round before we disappear the woman."

And like that Beta's dragon roared, breaking the chains of her restraint.

Peering out from behind a car, she sighted on the right *bogomili*. A moment later he went down, blood spraying from his neck. Her next bullet hit the leader in the shoulder before he and the third *bogomili* dropped for cover. At the same time, Beta raced across the street to the car in front of the *bogomili* position, diving to the ground to crouch next to the rear tire. The hot scent of blood mixed with her own smoky breath, driving her half mad with battle lust.

"Ya got Buckley's chance, mate, of makin' it out o' here alive," the lead *bogomili* yelled.

Unfortunately for him, Beta could see the displacement of heat as he directed the third *bogomili* to circle around the back of the car they hid behind. Leaning over on one knee, she aimed under the car next to the tire and shot at the third *bogomili*'s leg. He yelped and tumbled to the street.

His head was a clear target that Beta didn't miss.

By this time, the lead *bogomili* had circled around the front of the car against which Beta knelt. She managed to get off a shot before he launched himself at her. Rolling, she ended up next to him on the pavement instead of under him. He roared and reached for her, but Beta got a leg over him, straddling his chest and punching his head with the butt of the SIG—repeatedly, even as he struck at her face and ribs with his good hand.

She shot his other shoulder.

"Enough," she said, not shocked to hear the power in her voice.

His eyes widened. There was enough rational thought in that gaze that whatever he saw made him go still.

"Where is she?"

"Get stuffed."

She shoved the 9mm's muzzle into his wound. He screamed.

"Where is she?"

"You stupid cunt!" he gasped.

She leaned into the gun. He screamed again. "I can do this all morning, bogan."

"So can I," he said through gritted teeth.

Bogan was accurate: he really was an idiot who would let her torture him on a public street that was starting to waken. The sounds of traffic on the nearby Prokopova Avenue had started to increase. The shops would open soon. A few pedestrians crossed the intersection at the bottom of the hill, but none looked their way.

She held the *bogomili*'s gaze a moment, slipping the lead back onto her dragon. "On second thought, I have better things to do."

She stood. He twisted, intending to rise. Before he could, she kicked him under his chin, snapping his head back into the pavement. He lost consciousness.

Reaching into his pocket, she pulled his cellphone out. Locked. Kneeling, she pressed his forefinger to the screen. It sprang to life.

She didn't need him to tell her where he'd been. His cellphone would do that. Quickly she dialed a colleague in the VZ and asked him to trace the last twelve hours of the *bogomili*'s GPS history. As she waited, she went through his cellphone's photos. There were dozens taken inside the National Gallery Prague.

Then a painting filled the screen.

Beta stood transfixed.

Perhaps it was her newly awakened dragon sight, but the painting luminesced. The velvety blacks, ethereal whites and rich reds called to her. Beta touched a light fingertip to the screen. She wanted to see this painting in person.

She stood there until her cellphone alerted her to an incoming message. Blinking, she pulled her focus under tight control, sucking frigid air into her lungs and exhaling the rest of the heated, smoky air. Her head cleared. She immediately found Olivia's cellphone number and called before the painting could lure her back into its field of influence.

Olivia answered on the second ring.

"Liv, Fagan plans to steal a Caravaggio called *Infatuation of the Watcher Angels.*"

***

Miró watched Ms. Fiore through breakfast. He knew her well enough to read the fine alterations in her harmonics, and he could tell that she was both nervous and uneasy. She had good reason to be. Still he was impressed at how well she hid it. He watched as she flirted with András, who sat next to her eating the sweet braided bread that Olivia had baked for him as though he had hollow limbs. Miró noted every time Ms. Fiore placed a small hand on the big Hungarian's arm or smiled at him. She seemed to draw some energy from the contact, and the nervous rhythm vibrating through her harmonics smoothed.

Miró observed all of this. Her actions were almost a tic.

Almost.

But he'd stripped Ms. Fiore of her willful blindness about her charisma—what she'd so blithely termed 'tradecraft.' Even if she had no ulterior motives in flirting with András but simply wanted the comfort that it provided, she had to be conscious of its direct effect on her harmonics now that she was aware of them.

What he didn't know was whether she could see how her harmonics affected *his*. Ever since he'd comforted her following Zophiel's visit, he'd been in sync with the diminutive Italian spy in a way that he couldn't explain and had trouble controlling. As a result, he'd spent the past few days avoiding her as much as possible.

Unfortunately, he hadn't been able to avoid this congenial breakfast, not without drawing unwanted attention. András might be oblivious, but Mihàil would certainly notice something odd in Miró's demeanor, and once that happened, he'd identify the reason.

The truth was that Miró didn't just read the nervous rhythm of Ms. Fiore's harmonics or see how they smoothed at her flirty touches of another *Elioud*. He and she were in tune. His harmonics resonated with hers.

As he left the gym, he'd tamped down on his own harmonics, reining them in until he felt so tightly wound that he feared something would snap. Now his head ached.

Breakfast had just ended when Olivia's cellphone rang. The look on her face caused Miró to halt as he gathered up his breakfast dishes. András, Mihàil, and Ms. Fiore had already left the dining room. Only Besjana, the young Albanian woman that Olivia had hired, remained clearing the table.

"My lady, is something wrong?" he asked when she'd ended the call and slid the cellphone into her back pocket.

Olivia looked at him, worry shading her eyes. Miró was struck again at how young she was. *Elioud* blood often kept the limits of human nature at bay, and living according to St. Michael's dictates further enhanced their angelic nature. Even so, all of the other *Elioud* that he knew were much older, even András, the baby, who was almost a hundred. The three of them—Mihàil, András, and he—had all been born into cultures and times marked by war and widespread suffering, when the Dark *Irim* made the world their playground. Olivia and her friends, despite facing crime and violence, had not.

She glanced at Besjana, waiting until the young woman gathered her stack of plates and left. "Beta just called. She's taken out a small *bogomili* team sent to Prague by Fagan."

Miró's battle senses went on alert. "She is sure that Fagan sent these *bogomili*?"

Olivia nodded. "She heard one *bogomili* speaking to Fagan about an operation. She recovered his cellphone and is going through its contents now."

"You do not think that this is a CIA operation."

"This was a team of Australian mercenaries. Fagan has access to black ops teams and untraceable funding if he needs to go off book." She shook her head. "No, he'd send mercs only on business that he doesn't want the Company to know about." She paused. "The *bogomili*'s target appears to be a recently discovered Caravaggio painting called *Infatuation of the Watcher Angels*."

No wonder she was troubled. Despite recruiting old colleagues at the Agency to keep an eye on Fagan's activities, bugging his flat, and hacking into his email, they'd had no indication of his next steps as Asmodeus's acolyte. It was sheer good fortune that Beta had stumbled across his team.

Miró studied her. "There is more."

She sighed. "Miró, I kept Beta out of the loop on the Rembrandt."

Which meant that Beta should have no idea about Fagan's motives.

"But she guessed that the Caravaggio was more than just an old painting by a Baroque Master?"

Olivia nodded. "It seems that Beta's eyesight has been altered since our last operation against Fagan. She says that she tracked the *bogomili* using their infrared signatures, so when she saw the painting, she recognized the *Elioud* nature with which it was imbued. She's planning to wait for the final team member to arrive to see if she can get more information out of him."

"We need to tell Mihàil and András. This presents an opportunity to learn more about Asmodeus and whether he has awakened fully."

"I agree." She hesitated, appearing to weigh her next words. "I know that you're opposed to including Stasia because she's a Grey *Elioud*, but, Miró, you also said that the wisest choices are made in full knowledge. I think that we need to give her a chance to do the right thing."

Miró stiffened, pain shooting down his neck and to his upper back. Instead of sending soothing heat to his tight muscles, he contained it in his core. Olivia, watching him, widened her eyes and took a step back. Then, as if remembering who she was, she planted her feet and lifted her chin, holding his gaze in clear command.

He dropped his own chin in acknowledgment. "Of course, my lady." He paused. "I had already intended to speak with her. I will do so now."

***

Stasia's head ached so fiercely she had trouble seeing. It had started to hurt almost as soon as she sat down to breakfast. To make matters worse, the spot where Olivia's *bō* had struck her hamstring throbbed and kept her from sitting still even on the padded dining chair.

It hadn't helped that Miró, sitting as far from her as possible, watched her throughout the meal, his expression closed again after the unbelievable smile directed at her only moments before in the gym. Maybe she'd gotten whiplash from his swift change in demeanor. Whatever it was, she'd instinctively sat next to the sunny András, who didn't take himself seriously and who made her laugh, not always on purpose.

She'd touched András out of a genuine need to feel close to him. And it had worked. It wasn't until the third or fourth time that she noticed how her headache had abated each time. Then she'd paid closer attention. She realized that her personal harmonics didn't seem very harmonious. In fact, she vibrated in a jittery manner that settled whenever she touched the remarkably even *Elioud* next to her. But every time she moved her hand away, her harmonics oscillated dramatically. Either she'd lost control of them in the interim or some other external source affected her harmonics as the moon's gravitational pull affected the tides.

Now she sat in the easy chair in the guest suite, her eyes closed, rubbing her temples with her fingertips. She'd left the lights off and the shades drawn. She tried humming and found it soothing. As she hummed, she imagined that she could see the way that she vibrated. Each vibration appeared as a jewel-colored band starting at her skin that expanded into the dark atmosphere around her. They came in regular waves, floating away as ripples in a pond: magenta, deep purple, electric blue, grass green, butter yellow, candy red.

Stasia let her hands drop, flicking her fingers in front of her. The vibrations skittered. Inhaling slowly and evenly as she motioned towards herself, she saw the concentric waves return to her, their common axis.

Her harmonics normalized into a confident, steady hum of braided colors dominated by golden white and navy blue. Her headache had vanished.

A knock came at the suite door.

Perhaps it was because she'd just concentrated so intently on her own harmonics, but she recognized the tightly controlled harmonics in the hallway outside her room.

Miró.

Stasia hurried to the door and flung it open. The *Elioud* loomed dark, outlined in bright sunlight from the window behind him. His predatory gaze traveled over her from the top of her head to her feet. When it returned to her face, he regarded her as if he would devour her whole.

She stared back at him, for once lost for words.

Her mind went completely blank.

No internal voice evaluated her situation or ran through her options. Nothing directed her actions toward some goal or outcome. Her harmonics, under control only moments before, jolted and then became erratic.

She panted in the heated air, heady with his scent.

Miró took a step forward, his gaze burning, forcing her to look up at him. She couldn't have looked away if she'd tried.

He took another step. She stepped backward into the suite. His hands came up to brace the doorframe. His gaze slid over her face, resting on her mouth. It tingled in expectation. Stasia could have sworn that feathery caresses smoothed over her lips and along her jaw.

They stood that way for an excruciating moment.

"How is your leg?" he asked. His chocolatey-smooth voice had gravel in it now.

"Wh—" She licked her lip, but her mouth had gone dry. "What?"

He leaned closer until his chest skimmed her breasts. Her hardened nipples tightened further. "Where the *zonjë*'s *bō* landed."

Before she could attempt to form a response, he placed a large, warm hand on her injured thigh. It felt so good that she arched up closer to him, pressing her breasts into his chest. She let out a little moan, willing him to pick her up and carry her to the large bed not five meters away.

He didn't.

Instead his fingers grew warmer, sending heat into the aching bruise. Stasia's eyelids drifted down. She rubbed the top of her head under his chin, but when she raised her hands to wrap around his neck, he pulled away.

"No." The gentle delivery stung nevertheless.

Stasia opened her eyes. Miró stood out in the hallway, his features in shadow.

Confused, she dropped her arms, her heart flailing inside her ribcage in a disorienting mix of desire and rejection. She wanted to hide. She wanted to *cry*. And on that thought, painful prickles danced in the corners of her eyes. She turned back into her room and moved blindly toward the chair that she'd sat in earlier.

Then she remembered that Miró had come here, to her. Not the other way around.

When she looked up at him, her eyes were dry. All of her was dry. Her skin radiated.

Before she could say anything, Miró shut the door to the guest suite and studied her. He didn't look aloof. Neither did he look predatory. Instead, he looked a little sad.

"I am sorry, Ms. Fiore. I should not have behaved that way. I should not have touched you or led you to believe that the desire we both obviously share can be acted upon. Please forgive me."

Although Stasia's confusion didn't disappear, Miró's genuine regret took the heat from her anger. She sat down and looked at him, gathering her composure. She couldn't remember the last time that she'd been so uncalculating and lost in the visceral grip of sexual craving—if she ever had been. Some part of her always held back a little, judging the performance, hers and his. Perhaps she should be grateful that Miró had halted the proceedings because she had no idea where her emotions and her body might have taken her.

It was a sobering thought. She had forgotten her mission.

Tilting her head, she asked, "Why not? As you said, we both want it."

He shook his head. "It has not been my experience that it works out well for anyone to satisfy physical urges untethered from emotional, intellectual, and spiritual concerns."

"Is that why you have avoided me for the past three days?"

He nodded. "Partly. And partly because you are not one of us. You are a Grey *Elioud*, one who has her own agenda and does not fight on either side in our angelic war."

"Like Rembrandt?" She shrugged. "That does not seem to be such a bad thing, seeing the light and dark in the world."

Miró studied her for a moment. His light blue eyes looked haunted now. Stasia wondered what he was seeing when he looked at her. She felt gooseflesh crawl up the back of her arms, ending in a slight shiver. His harmonics were so even and low pitched that they disappeared into his form. For a moment she saw the bright outline of his angelic nature. And a great chasm seemed to open between them.

"Despite his *Elioud* gifts, his life ended alone, in bankruptcy and destitution. When you have walked into the light from the dark, you can appreciate how dim Rembrandt's vision really was."

She had the feeling that Miró spoke about himself. What had he lived through to be so cynical that even the art of an Old Master was a cautionary tale to him? She wanted to put her hand on his jaw and comfort him, but of course she couldn't.

"What would you have me do?" she asked instead. "Leave?"

"Start by being honest with Olivia." He looked hopeful, and Stasia found herself not wanting to disappoint him. She had no idea how this would work, especially once she admitted to Olivia that she needed to get the Rembrandt back, for her pride, but also because it was her job. Foreign agents couldn't be allowed to steal Italian cultural artifacts from Italian citizens regardless of her personal conflict of interest. It would have been better if she could have kept the conflict to herself.

As the seconds passed while she thought about his request, she sensed Miró withdrawing farther into himself. The bright outline around him winked out, and the light in his eyes frosted over. Stasia knew that she'd pay for dithering about her mission objective, but she couldn't stand to be shut out from Miró. She wanted to know more about what—or who—had hurt him.

At that thought, a small, ugly part of her suggested that she might need to know to seduce him. It brought to mind the Neapolitan proverb *quanno 'o diavulo t'accarezza, vo' ll'anem. When the devil caresses you, he wants your soul.*

A wry laugh threatened. Would that make her the devil?

She shoved that away. Sighing, she said, "*Molto bene.* I will tell Olivia."

"*Grazie.*" The warmth in his voice sent a thrill of pleasure through her. She refused to consider why.

Instead, she said, "But I doubt that will resolve the problem. I will still be a Grey *Elioud* with my own agenda. I lied to Olivia to avoid creating an intractable situation between us."

Miró acknowledged her admission with a head tilt. "Because you intend to recover the *Judgment of the Watcher Angels*, and you suspect doing so is at cross purposes with our objectives." It was a statement.

Stasia sucked in a surprised breath. *Naturalmente.* Miró had seen through her.

Letting the breath out, she nodded. "*Sí.*"

"That is a bit premature. We are unclear about what should happen to the painting because we are unsure about its genesis or how Fagan intends to use it." He paused. "So despite my misgivings about your status as a Grey *Elioud* and your intentions, the *zonjë* wishes to include you in a briefing about new developments regarding Fagan."

Remembering her earlier ugly thought about seducing him, Stasia asked, "Are you sure that you can trust me?"

Miró's unwavering gaze pinned her. "No." The bluntness of his answer underscored his honesty. "But as the *zonjë* has reminded me, we need to give you the opportunity to do the right thing."

Stasia felt a prickle of premonition. "And if I end up choosing the wrong course?"

"*Doće maca na vratanca.*" *The cat will come to the tiny door.* It was a Croatian saying about consequences. "In other words, there will be an intractable situation between *us.*"

Eight

Fagan sat in one of three easy chairs in the tiny wood-paneled lobby of the two-star International Hotel in Fushë-Arrëz, Albania. It was about what one could expect from a hotel that charged twenty American dollars. The gauzy red curtains appeared to be the same as the ones in his single room. He suspected that most of the hotel had the same curtains, though the dining room had heavy red-patterned drapes and coffered ceilings. And the travel Web site showed a new "resort"—a euphemism for a recent addition with a red-brick patio featuring a fountain and lighted canopies over tables.

He was heartily glad that he'd risen to station chief for the Company and now had a spacious luxury flat in Vienna. He'd done his time through the past two decades in shitty little places like this poverty-stricken town in the middle of bumfuck Albania. In researching Fushë-Arrëz, he'd discovered a defunct blog from an American Peace Corps volunteer who'd arrived five years ago to teach English. If her blog entries were anything to go by, she'd lasted six months. It seemed that the attractive young woman didn't like having nothing better to do than watch another teacher all day at the high school or trudging through the barrage of lewd comments the local men aimed at her whenever she stepped outside her apartment.

Which was why it was extremely interesting to note that Olivia Kastrioti, formerly Markham, a highly trained, highly skilled intelligence officer for the CIA, now lived here as the wife of an Albanian mafia lord.

Fagan frowned. No, that wasn't right. There was definitely something off about Mihàil Kastrioti, but he wasn't the garden-variety Eastern European crime don that his sparse CIA file suggested. That file, filled with innuendo and thin facts on the ground, implied something more subtle and far-reaching. Perhaps that was why Kastrioti was able to attain an accomplished American wife who'd burned herself as a field agent for him.

It had to be. Something about his moniker The Dragon of Albania niggled....

Fagan had apparently written the file, but for the life of him, he couldn't recall doing so except in the most fuzzy, maddening way. He might not have taken a second look at it, in fact, if he hadn't recognized the man in Hvar as an associate of Kastrioti's. He still didn't know why the female Italian agent looked familiar, but his gut told him that she'd been in Budapest too. Whatever the reason behind his memory lapse, Fagan knew that Kastrioti represented a dangerous mystery that he needed to solve.

It was the peculiar combination of circumstances around the couple—the boring, sexist, impoverished mountain town and the appearance of a beautiful outsider married to the local *de facto* ruler—that had allowed Fagan to recruit a mole in Kastrioti's household. Besjana, jealous of the new Kastrioti bride and wanting more than her scraps, provided him the best source of intelligence: human. Otherwise known as HUMINT.

Fagan pulled his smartphone from his pocket and tapped its screen. It sprang to life and there, in vivid color, shone the Rembrandt painting he'd stolen from the Albanians last fall.

He stared at the image.

It was a cold reflection of the real thing, like the moon shining on still water. Nevertheless, it evoked a response in him. It was as if his spirit only needed reminding about how it felt to gaze on the actual painting.

What would it be like to possess the other one, the Caravaggio?

As soon as the news story mentioning it showed up in his email, Fagan had felt a compulsion for it. The art journalist had mentioned in passing that another painting on the apocryphal Biblical tale by Rembrandt had been found two years before only to be stolen last fall after its authentication. Then the article had described the art lineage that linked Caravaggio and Rembrandt despite the fact that they'd lived apart in time and place. Rembrandt, in fact, had never left The Netherlands and likely never saw a Caravaggio painting.

Fagan had set an Internet alert for all mentions of the Rembrandt. It had been sheer luck that he'd learned about the *Infatuation of the Watcher Angels*, but it felt like destiny. Already a hunger to hold it, to stare at its luminous canvas alone and safe from ignorant eyes, gnawed at him.

The door to the hotel's lobby opened and Besjana entered, carrying a packet.

He pressed the power button to turn the smartphone's screen off and slipped it into his pocket. He ignored the young woman, tapping instead on his laptop keyboard. The screen showed a complex spreadsheet that purported to itemize data on deposits of copper, gold, silver, and cobalt in the surrounding district. Albania might be a poor country, but that was almost entirely due to its history, first as a province of the Ottoman Empire and then as a communist country. It was only a matter of time before Albania's natural resources brought foreign investors and a new standard of living.

It also provided him with a cover.

Besjana walked to the front desk and spoke to the woman working there. In this country optimal tradecraft when meeting with a single woman required a cutout—an unaware intermediary. Too, Besjana had no idea what he looked like. She thought that he was a fellow northern Albanian who, like her, loathed an American having such intimate control over their beloved ruler.

After a few minutes, she left, but Fagan didn't watch. Instead, he let the hotel employee come over and leave the packet next to his laptop without even a nod of acknowledgement. The Kastrioti Venture Partners logo—the Albanian double-eagle the man seemed to think belonged to him—filled the upper left corner. In the center of the heavy envelope the name of his cover identity, Joseph Eagan, Director, Arian Resources, had been typed. He slipped the packet into his briefcase for perusing later in his room.

Once he'd pulled the CIA's file on Kastrioti, Fagan had realized that there was a black hole surrounding the former Olivia Markham and her husband The Dragon of Albania, an absence of surveillance where there should have been at least OSINT, that is, data collection from public records. That fact, along with his strange amnesia, made him keep his little trip here quiet. He began, however, to build a new file on Kastrioti's ties with Russian investors in Albania's mining industry. Someone very wise had once told him that the best evidence should be collected in person and kept on paper, so here he was.

It may be that someday he would need to backstop a decision to take out the Kastriotis for personal reasons.

***

Five minutes after Miró left her room, Stasia heard a knock on her door. She scanned the room, but nothing looked different. It just felt different without Miró's vital harmonic energy. And that was her problem. Her overly sensitive nerves only made her *think* that the room resonated from his departure.

Breathing deeply, she pulled her door open and smiled at Olivia.

For once Olivia looked grave. She didn't return Stasia's smile. Stasia's heart threatened to jump, but she'd had long practice in keeping her breathing even and her smile easy in the face of tense, uncertain situations.

"Please come in, *cara*, I need to speak with you as I am sure you are aware."

Olivia came in, her eyes narrowed as she looked around the room. She turned a suddenly sharp gaze on Stasia. "Is everything all right, Staz? Did you and Miró argue?"

Stasia blinked. Perhaps her nerves weren't overly sensitive after all. "Everything is fine. We did not argue, although we did have a very blunt conversation."

Olivia studied her a moment before nodding. "Okay, but you'll tell me if you two do argue, won't you? It's not just that I want my friends to get along. If we're going to work together, I need to know about any problems among our team members."

Stasia sighed, closing her eyes briefly to reset her focus. And her courage. "Whether we are going to work together is the question. Miró told me that I am a Grey *Elioud*, that I am not one of you. He also knows that I lied to you about why I am here."

At her confession, Olivia blinked, shock washing over her face to be replaced by a surprisingly cool expression.

Stasia hurried on. "The truth is that I came to get more information about the Rembrandt painting."

"I see." Olivia's eyes narrowed slightly, but she waited. Clearly she suspected more.

"Once I learned that it had *Elioud* qualities, I determined to recover it without informing you, using whatever means available to me." Stasia lifted her chin and straightened her shoulders. "Miró realized this. You should know that if he had not confronted me, I would not have told you."

Olivia blinked. In that moment, Stasia realized that she cared very much what Olivia thought about her transgression. It didn't matter that she hadn't set out to do it. It was a betrayal nevertheless.

At last her friend spoke, appearing to choose her words with care. "We all make mistakes, Stasia, though I certainly understand that you have a duty to your country that made you believe that you had no choice. Whether Miró forced your hand is irrelevant. What matters is that you have told me."

She paused and seemed to gather herself. "And now I have my own dilemma. Mihàil and I have discussed your status as a Grey *Elioud* before this. Like Miró, he's concerned about including you and Beta in any of our missions for obvious reasons."

"Then do not." Stasia wanted to cross her arms to feel less exposed. Instead, she flexed her fingers, imagining sending energy into the room. It was an old trick that she'd developed to bolster her confidence. "Miró said that you have no information about Fagan's plans for the painting. Surely you can let me recover it without reading me in on your operation."

Olivia nodded, biting her lower lip. She crossed her arms, her gaze inward as she considered. "We could. Or rather, we could have before Beta called me twenty minutes ago."

"Beta?" Stasia scented Olivia's discreet maneuvering. She smiled to herself. Her friend was a skilled operative, after all. "What has Beta to do with Fagan's plans?"

Olivia looked at her, her eyes only a fraction wider. She shook her head. "That I cannot tell you without reading you in. I'd planned to invite you to a briefing upstairs in the media room before I knew that you'd lied about the reason for your visit."

Stasia cocked her head. "Let me see if I understand. Your dilemma is how to get me to agree to abide by your *Elioud* objectives. Otherwise you will be forced to keep me out? Perhaps wipe my memory as Mihàil did with Fagan?"

Olivia pressed her lips together, nodding. "Yes, that's it in a nutshell. If you'd been truthful before, I could've brought you into the meeting. I'm afraid my hands are tied now."

Anger threatened, but Stasia refused to let that emotion develop. She'd treated Olivia and the other *Elioud* as foreign agents, so she deserved this ultimatum. "What guarantee will you accept if I agree to your terms?" She kept her voice level, cool. Professional.

"That's easy." Olivia's gaze hardened on her, all dragon fire and no softness. "Just your word. Miró will know if you lie. But it won't matter because I'll trust but verify your commitment."

Stasia nodded. "That is fair. I give you my word that I will abide by whatever objectives the *Elioud* team identifies." She put her hand on Olivia's forearm. "I *am* sorry."

Olivia glanced at Stasia's hand and then leaned forward, hugging her hard. "I know. I forgive you." She stood back. "You must believe that I'll do all that I can to make sure that you recover the Rembrandt. But, Staz, please don't lie to me again."

Stasia swallowed against the thickness clogging her throat. After a moment, she nodded. "I will not lie to you again, *cara.*"

***

Fifteen minutes later, Stasia sat in the media room wondering how she'd gotten to the point where she'd ceded control of her choices regarding the stolen Rembrandt to the *Elioud* sitting around her. In the end, she realized that it came down to friendship and trust that it would all work out. Neither of these had ever driven her official mission priorities before.

That and she was really curious about how Beta figured into all of this. Beta, a loner who'd disappeared once Olivia had gotten married.

Stasia shook her head and focused on her surroundings.

A massive curved monitor, its screen blank, dominated the wall in front of her. Around her three personal computers sat on individual desks, screensavers dancing on their monitors. In the far corner a large monitor mounted on an adjustable swing arm displayed live video from the estate's security cameras. The furniture was comfortable but utilitarian. There were no pictures or other personal items.

It could have been a tactical operations center in any small intelligence operation.

Miró, his arms crossed, stood near a closed set of double doors, a shadowy figure in the dim room. András sat staring at his smartphone, alternately muttering and humming.

One of the double doors opened with a click. Olivia entered, followed by Mihàil, whose closed features told Stasia all she needed to know. His eyes gleamed, a dragon in his lair. She felt a frisson of unease race along her limbs and down her spine.

It is only the reflection from the displays, she assured herself.

Olivia stopped at the front of the room and nodded toward Miró, who stepped toward a stand in the rear corner and raced his fingers across a keyboard. An image of a painting filled the massive screen.

Stasia sat upright, her senses tingling. Especially those she now recognized as *Elioud.* Even as a digital facsimile, the painting emanated an unearthly light.

She wasn't a student of art history, but one could hardly be Italian without knowing the work of Michele Angelo Amerighi da Caravaggio. Or simply *Caravaggio.* This particular painting was one that she'd never seen before, although the composition reminded her of his later works. As with all of Caravaggio's paintings, the subject had been captured *in medias res,* that is, in the middle of action as if spot lit on stage. It was his defining genius, this intense fascination with the raw human condition.

A terrible genius that also led him to consort with prostitutes and gamblers, brawl repeatedly, commit murder, and die too soon from a violent wound, alone and exiled.

The performer in her admired Caravaggio's art, but the professional in her decried his life.

"This is *Infatuation of the Watcher Angels*," Olivia said, drawing Stasia back to the present. "It was found two years ago in Aix-en-Provence and is now on exhibit at the National Gallery Prague. This morning Beta came across a group of Australian mercenaries that she identified as *bogomili* who planned to steal it for Fagan."

András, now standing, his phone forgotten at his side, said, "It's another one."

"'Another one'?" Stasia stood as well.

"Do you remember that legend I told you about?" Mihàil asked. At her nod, he gestured toward the digital painting with his chin. "We already knew that Caravaggio was a Grey *Elioud*, but given the subject matter, he clearly worked with a Dark *Irim*, just as Rembrandt did."

Stasia tilted her head, narrowing her eyes. "He is hardly unique in his choice of subject. Many others painted scenes from the Bible during the Renaissance and Baroque periods."

"True," Mihàil said, "but the *First Book of Enoch* was not in their artistic canon because it was not in their religious canon. The Church rejected it as authentic in the fourth century, and it survived only in Ethiopia. The first known copies of the *First Book of Enoch* written in Ge'ez were brought to Europe by Scottish explorer James Bruce in 1773, long after Caravaggio and Rembrandt died."

"Fagan has the Rembrandt, and now he wants the Caravaggio." Stasia turned to Olivia. "But he cannot con the museum out of it."

"And his *bogomili* were no match for *én vézna fejsze fogantyú*," András said, sounding satisfied. "She handled them on her own."

My scrawny axe handle? Stasia stared at the big Hungarian. *Does he mean Beta?*

Olivia continued, "Beta overheard the *bogomili* team leader telling Fagan that someone named *L'Amante* arrives this afternoon to acquire the painting. Interpol wants *L'Amante* in connection with two dozen art thefts in Italy and France."

"*L'Amante* works alone." Everyone looked at Stasia. She shrugged. "*L'Amante* is well known to the *Carabinieri*, who suspect him in a great many more thefts in Western Europe. He is called The Lover because he has an obsession for art, stealing only those items that call to him and never selling them. But he usually steals smaller items, not large canvases."

Olivia appeared to consider Stasia's statement before continuing. "That supports my working theory. I believe that Fagan hired this mysterious figure to steal the Caravaggio, but the *bogomili* were supposed to ensure that *L'Amante* didn't actually keep the painting."

"You three will go to Prague," Mihàil said, looking at Stasia and the two male *Elioud* warriors, "where you will work with Ms. Černá to identify *L'Amante*." He paused. "And then pretend to be Fagan's team."

Stasia blinked. "You mean that we should allow *L'Amante* to steal the Caravaggio and then take it from him?"

The banked dragon fire in Mihàil's gaze flickered. "That is exactly what I mean, Ms. Fiore."

Nine

"It would seem you are in the days of the *ledoví muži*." Beta sat in the car's front passenger seat, opening and closing a folding karambit tactical knife with one hand, first the left and then the right. Its red hawkbill blade made Stasia think of a dragon's talon.

Why do I keep thinking of dragons?

She turned to stare at her Czech friend. Although the sun reflecting from the snow on the sidewalk blinded her, it shed no warmth. And yet here sat Beta—*scrawny-axe-handle* Beta—coatless in a parked car. A parked car that should have been frigid inside yet was moderately warm.

Beta's words finally hit her. "'The ice men'?" Stasia frowned. She was beginning to doubt her linguistic abilities given all the strange language she was translating these days.

Beta stopped manipulating the karambit and held Stasia's gaze. As usual, her dark eyes reflected nothing. "Or perhaps I should say *ledový muž*, the ice man, hm?" She turned her gaze toward the front again, watching the entrance to the Michelangelo Grand Hotel Prague. "You are from the south. The ice men are nothing but saints there. No wonder you are so perplexed."

Stasia's ire rose. It didn't help that her fingers and toes had grown cold despite the inexplicably warm car interior. She wanted an espresso and a slice of *medovnik*, the unique Czech honey cake popular in Prague. "*Dio santo*, what are you talking about Beta?"

It figured that the Czech military intelligence officer, normally laconic, would choose to speak in riddles when she did say more than a few words.

Beta looked again at Stasia, a smile quirking her lips. "Here, where it is cold, gardeners wait until after the feast days of St. Pancras, St. Servatius, and St. Boniface of Tarsus in the second week of May to plant their most delicate plants."

She swung her gaze back to the hotel, the vicious hooked blade of her defensive knife again swinging open and closed at her shoulder. "However, the wisest wait until after St. Sophia's feast day on the fifteenth of May, the coldest night of spring." She shot a glance at Stasia and pointed the tip of the karambit at her. "Žofie, *ledová žena*. You could learn from her."

Stasia sighed and rolled her head around on her neck. They'd been sitting outside the hotel where *L'Amante* had taken a room, but no one who'd entered over the two hours they'd been watching seemed remotely like an international art thief. She should just play along with Beta, who clearly enjoyed being opaque.

"The moniker 'ice woman' suits you better," she said, baiting the cool Czech.

"The Croatian is not interested in me."

Shocked, Stasia stared at Beta. Who knew that Beta noticed anything that didn't involve her chain whip, her gun, or her knife? Unless it was drinking her favorite Czech *slivovice*, a potent plum brandy, or throwing darts while drinking said *slivovice*.

Stasia cleared her throat and composed her thoughts. "Are you advising me to act as you do? Toward Miró Kos specifically? Why?"

Beta turned that dark, unfathomable gaze on her again. Not for the first time, Stasia sensed a powerful current beneath the other woman's controlled expression. And then she realized that she heard a distinct harmonic signature emanating from Beta. It was so tight and low that it disappeared in the harmonic noise around them unless she focused on it. It was as if Beta was piano wire: exceptionally light, strong, and flexible, capable of performing under high tension, and designed to produce music under repeated blows.

"Because you risk whatever it is you most want to cultivate."

"And that is?" Stasia asked, distracted.

A very handsome man pulling a rolling briefcase walked toward the Michelangelo hotel. He resembled the Roman actor Giulio Benetti, whose older brother Gian Luca, a lieutenant colonel with the *Guardia di Finanza*, had worked with her a number of times on joint operations. Gian Luca had introduced them. She and Guilio had slept together more than once. He was an exceptional lover, but it had never been more than a casual affair for either of them.

Beta snapped a photo of the stranger with her cellphone before sending it to Olivia, who waited to identify any promising candidates for *L'Amante*. "Something sturdy with roots. Or do you always want something shallow and short lived?" She gestured with her chin toward the stranger as he entered the hotel.

"Miró Kos is not interested in me in the way that you think."

Beta's sideways look said she begged to differ, but she said nothing. They waited in silence until Olivia contacted them.

"His name is Zaccaria Angelli. He's an independent *sommelier* who sells Italian wines from the Veneto region to high-end restaurants and hotels in Central Europe. There's nothing flagged in his records. However, I don't need to remind you two that a traveling wine salesman makes an excellent cover for an international art thief. I'm still digging into his life to see if his travels coincide with any reported thefts."

"No one else suitable has appeared today," Stasia said. "My intuition tells me that this Zaccaria Angelli is *L'Amante*."

"You mean your libido," murmured Beta.

Stasia ignored her.

"That's good enough for me," Olivia said. "You two take the first shift. I'll send Angelli's photo to Miró and András and put them on standby."

Beta slipped the karambit into her jeans pocket, and they both got out of the car. While Beta put on a non-descript winter jacket and dark woolen cap so that she wouldn't stand out, Stasia went around to the trunk and got her overnight bag. She would check into the hotel, finagling a room close to Angelli's so that she could orchestrate a meeting. It was her job to keep the sommelier busy so that Beta could slip into his room, go through his things, and plant bugs. Stasia herself would need to put a micro-sized GPS tracker on Angelli's person.

Twenty minutes later, Stasia stood in front of Angelli's hotel door and inserted her key card into his door lock. It didn't work, of course. She re-inserted it and began muttering in Italian about annoying technology, incompetent staff, and other travel frustrations.

It took only sixty seconds for Angelli to open the door.

Stasia stared at him, carefully openmouthed, her keycard held in front of her. She threaded just enough surprised outrage into her voice to sell the question of who was in *her* room. *"Chi sei?"*

Angelli took her in with a comprehensive—and appreciative— glance. Stasia's body responded. The man was devilishly handsome, even more so than Giulio. He was tall, taller than Miró, but not as tall as András. And his glossy black hair, long enough to cover his ears, was brushed back in carefree waves from his strong face, which was covered in masculine stubble and long sideburns. Straight black eyebrows drew her gaze to his intelligent blue-gray eyes, though it was his full mouth that snagged her attention. This man oozed sexual magnetism.

Suddenly the name *L'Amante* took on another meaning.

Stasia felt her face grow warm under Angelli's thorough perusal. Realizing it, she blushed even more. Her rational brain said that it was time to go on the offense, to charm and wheedle, but her ability to do so had been swamped under his gaze.

"*Signorina*, I am afraid you are mistaken. This is my room," he said at last in Italian, his voice low and sexy. "However, if you would like to share, I am willing." He smiled to underscore his invitation.

Stasia's heart fluttered and her breathing sped. She'd never felt this way before so quickly. Was this how it felt when she charmed her targets? At that thought, Miró's icy blue eyes filled her mind. Her breathing evened out. She smiled, compelling herself to exert her own warmth, leaning into the pleasure of standing in front of a handsome man whose attention focused on her without letting it engulf her.

Angelli blinked, looking startled.

Stasia's smile grew. It would seem that he was unused to being the object of another's charisma. This could be fun.

"This is not room six-forty-one?" she asked.

"No." He shook his head from side to side, slowly, a curious smile on his face. "It is *five*-forty-one."

"What a happy accident." She slipped her keycard into her pocket. "Perhaps it was fate that we met."

"Indeed." He cocked his head. "I have only just arrived in Prague. Would you care to join me for a coffee or perhaps a glass of wine?"

Stasia dipped her chin coyly and took a step back. "I must take my bag to my room first."

Angelli took the bait and stepped forward. Of course, his step was bigger than hers. He now stood closer than before. Warmth and masculine cologne wafted around her. And a low, seductive harmonic hum that made her think of hot kisses and sweaty skin vibrated through her.

"Let me help you." His hand came down on hers clutching the handle of her suitcase.

Stasia sucked in a breath. This was the most dangerous target she'd ever had. She would be walking a high wire every second that she was with him.

She forced herself to laugh, a little shaken to hear the strain in the sound. Again, the memory of Miró's icy gaze and aloof demeanor bolstered her. She leaned into her nerves, fluttering her eyelashes at Angelli.

"Of course," she said.

Let him think that he overwhelmed her. It would make him less cautious, more certain of himself.

She would need to finish this quickly, however, and get far from temptation.

***

Miró's neck and upper back hurt. He was honest enough to know it was because of Ms. Fiore's presence on this mission.

That and because of his increasing sexual frustration.

He'd come very close—so close he knew exactly how it would be—to picking her up and carrying her to her bed. He hadn't. Instead, he'd held off by touching her harmonically, running invisible fingers along her lips and jaw. That had only sent his harmonics fluctuating like a kite in a hurricane. And then he'd done something that he hadn't done in almost a hundred years: he put a hand on a woman in desire.

He could still feel her small, firm breasts pressing against his chest through two layers of clothing. He could still hear the soft moan. And he'd sent some of the heat she'd stirred in him into her injured thigh, so perfect beneath his fingers.

Then he'd glimpsed their auras melding together, and the shock had been like plunging into icy water.

No, he'd suffer through the physical hunger plaguing him. It would eventually abate. But he wasn't about to put himself through the agony of getting any more involved with a Grey *Elioud*. That way laid madness and despair.

And apparently anger and jealousy.

Because he was forced to watch as their target seduced the woman that he couldn't allow himself to have. He, András, and Ms. Černá—was there ever a name more fake than *Ms.*

Black?—followed as Ms. Fiore and Angelli strolled through Schwarzenberg Palace, which was practically deserted this late February afternoon. The three of them managed to operate as a team despite Ms. Černá's lack of experience with them and need to use an earwig to communicate. Her tradecraft was impeccable.

It had to be. Angelli was a consummate professional. Nothing he did as he walked and talked with Ms. Fiore suggested that he surveyed the gallery in anything more than a casual manner, but Miró saw the pointed glances Angelli made at exits and security guards. He saw how Angelli carefully navigated the entire palace even though the Caravaggio exhibit was in the main hall on the first floor.

Nevertheless, Angelli didn't linger, and he seemed to enjoy Ms. Fiore's presence at his side. He touched her often, in small but intimate gestures—a hand on the small of her back to guide her through a passage, a chance brushing of his hand along her upper arm, a gentle tap to get her attention.

And every time he did, Ms. Fiore's harmonics thrummed in pleasure. Which of course redounded on Miró's harmonics, increasing his sour mood.

Narrowing his eyes, Miró studied the tall stranger. Something about his infrared and harmonic signatures bothered him.

Olivia had already correlated Angelli's travels with suspected *L'Amante* thefts. Given the ease with which Angelli had included Ms. Fiore in his planning, Miró had an epiphany: *L'Amante* used unwitting female companions to aid him. Each theft came after a seduction and the act of stealing merged with the sex act such that the successful theft represented a kind of climax and the actual artwork a token of *L'Amante's* sexual conquest.

If his intuition was correct, *L'Amante* would only take the Caravaggio after taking Ms. Fiore.

Miró's gaze flew to her. In that instant—perhaps feeling the turbulence in his harmonics—she looked in his direction. For a heartbeat the intensity of the connection between them made everything else recede.

And then Ms. Fiore looked up at Angelli, who'd started to turn toward Miró, and brought his gaze back to hers with a sinuous turn into his arms and a proprietary hand on his chest. She said something; Angelli laughed and bent to kiss her.

Miró, who'd frozen at the certainty of being made, sped his harmonics until no human could see him and hurried into the next gallery.

What was that? András asked. Irritation and confusion colored his tone. *You two lit the spectrum like a phosphorous flare. Any* Irim *or* Elioud *for fifty klicks will know we're here.*

"Sitrep," Mihàil, who monitored the op along with Olivia, said into their earwigs at that moment. The *Elioud* general had a preternatural sixth sense for when things were about to go sideways.

"Target has left Schwarzenberg Palace with Stasia," Ms. Černá said. Her cool voice gave nothing away. "She left intel about the next location. Target is headed to the Sternberg Palace. The National Gallery displays its main collection of Old Master paintings there."

Miró fell into step next to her. She might be newly aware of the angelic world, but she'd seen and understood what had happened. Yet she said nothing.

"Copy that," Mihàil said. "Stay on target. History shows that *L'Amante* acts within seventy-two hours of arrival."

***

Stasia walked arm-in-arm with Angelli the hundred meters north across **Hradčanské Square** to the Sternberg Palace, still stunned from the electric jolt that had passed between her and Miró. She shivered in the icy twilight.

"You are cold, *mia cara amica*," Angelli murmured and drew her closer to his side, wrapping his arm around her waist. Even through his heavy wool coat he radiated soothing warmth. Stasia's teeth chattered. She pressed against him.

"You seemed drawn to the lost Caravaggio in the special exhibit," she said, trying to keep working him. It was just *so* hard to focus. Her head was beginning to hurt.

"Ah, yes, the Caravaggio," he said. He looked down at her, his gaze thoughtful and a little inward. "How perceptive of you, Signorina Crea. Seeing the *Infatuation of the Watcher Angels* again is the main purpose of my visit to Prague."

"Again?" Her shivers abated as they reached the entrance to Sternberg Palace, a High Baroque structure tucked behind other palaces on the square. "I thought that it was lost until two years ago."

Angelli waited until they'd entered the palace, and he'd shown his museum pass at the desk before answering. "I was in Aix-en-Provence when *Infatuation of the Watcher Angels* was discovered in the attic of a mansion in the Mazarin Quarter. Such an elegant district. It was of course the work of an Italian, an archbishop. Have you visited?"

"No." Stasia shook her head, which hurt so much now that she winced. She wondered whether this was casual conversation or if there was more significance to Angelli's question. Why hadn't *L'Amante* stolen the painting when it was unknown and less carefully guarded?

Perhaps that was the whole point.

Angelli smiled at her. Stasia loved the color of his eyes. They were such a changeable blue. Right now they were a vivid cerulean. "There is much there for a lover of art." He led her to the stairs.

They climbed until they reached the top floor. Angelli took Stasia's cold hand in his large warm one. She was grateful. She felt a little wobbly, and the edges of her vision had a blurry, dreamy quality. Had Angelli drugged her? She should feel alarmed but didn't.

"You *must* travel to Aix-en-Provence," he said to her, his voice immensely alluring. It sounded more like music than human speech. As he spoke, her headache faded. "At one time, it was the capital of Provence. *Le Cours Mirabeau* with its terraced cafes is fondly known as the southern *Champs-Elysées*. I myself am partial to the entire Old Town with its innumerable Roman fountains. And of course it is the birthplace of Cézanne, whose studio is there. Mont Sainte Victoire, Cézanne's favorite subject, rises above the city."

He stopped in front of the National Gallery Prague's sole Rembrandt, *Scholar in His Study*. "1634. That is a year after he painted *Judgment of the Watcher Angels*, another recently discovered masterpiece. Perhaps you know of it?"

"It was stolen." Stasia slurred the words. "And I let the thief get away with it."

On the wall almost directly across from her, Rembrandt's scholar sat before a large open book on a table covered in rich brocade. He looked over his shoulder at her, his expression solemn and a little sad, as if he knew the internal battle she waged. Who knew that such a sedate subject could dredge up such tumultuous emotions?

Miró.... She tried to call him, but her voice stayed inside her head.

Angelli made a soothing noise as he pulled her close. He wrapped an arm around her shoulders. "Never fear, *mia cara* Stasia. You will recover the Rembrandt. Just as you will keep the Caravaggio safe and find the third painting for the triptych."

Stasia believed him. The trouble was, his speech sounded as if she were underwater. What had she been looking at only a moment ago? It was crucial that she find it again. Dropping her gaze, she fixated on the scholar's luxurious black-velvet robe. It looked warm and soft....

And then she either fell into the black-velvet robe or it rose up and swallowed her.

Ten

Stasia awoke to the buzzing of her cellphone. Weak February sunlight streamed through the sheer curtains of her hotel room. She lay on her bed under a heavy white duvet and crisp white sheets. Sitting up, she groaned. Her head pounded. Cotton stuffed her mouth and throat. Her stomach hurt.

Her cellphone stopped buzzing.

She massaged her temple with shaking fingers and looked down at herself. She wore the cropped t-shirt and shorts that she'd packed yesterday to sleep in.

Awareness flooded her, and she swiftly surveyed the room. She was alone. The slacks and blouse that she'd been wearing were folded neatly in a chair next to a small round table. Her bra and purse were on the tabletop. Her boots stood under it. Her cellphone was on the nightstand next to her. And across from the foot of the bed was a folding easel displaying Caravaggio's *Infatuation of the Watcher Angels*.

Or an excellent fake.

It featured a group scene that reminded her of Caravaggio's *The Martyrdom of St. Ursula*, long thought to be his final painting. The framing of the group before her was such that the viewer seemed to be just outside of it, no more than a couple of meters away. When hung at the usual height on a wall, the figures would be at the viewer's eye level. In the brightly lit foreground, an ethereal man whose beauty radiated from him reached toward a spellbound woman. Behind the ethereal man stood other ethereal men, though not all were beautiful. Their forms were lost in shadow. Caravaggio's uplifted face, lit from above and visible over the primary angel's shoulder, beseeched heaven. After her gaze went back to the Watcher Angel in the foreground, she knew exactly how Caravaggio felt.

Because he'd painted Angelli as the Watcher Angel. And the woman Angelli stood gazing on with desire was *her*.

Shock cleared Stasia's thoughts. All she could do was stare at the painting.

Her cellphone buzzed again.

The door to the room flew open. Ten seconds later, Miró appeared as if stepping out of thin air and halted next to the Caravaggio. He looked toward Stasia and then at the painting before looking at her again.

Beta came in behind him, her 9mm in a two-handed grip. She glanced around the room and into the bathroom.

The cellphone stopped buzzing. Silence reigned.

After fifteen long seconds, Beta dropped the 9mm to her side. "The Italian thief is not hiding in the bathroom."

Stasia was surprised. And strangely disappointed.

Shoving those feelings aside, she cleared her throat. Even so, when she spoke, her voice was hoarse. "He must have drugged me last night, though I do not know how he managed it. I do not recall anything after the Sternberg Palace."

"That was twelve hours ago, Ms. Fiore." Miró's voice was raspy as if he'd been screaming. Or as if currently restraining strong emotion. "We have been searching all night for you."

She suddenly *hated* that he still called her 'Ms. Fiore.' As if they were strangers. Or must maintain a formal distance.

"Stasia! Call me Stasia!" She flung the duvet back, swung her legs off the bed, and stood. She didn't know why she was so irritated, but she didn't have time to figure it out. "None of this makes any sense, least of all why Angelli and I appear in a painting that resembles *Infatuation of the Watcher Angels*."

Miró blinked hard. He looked at Beta and then at the painting next to him. Beta didn't bother looking at anything but Stasia.

"That *is* the *Infatuation of the Watcher Angels*," she said. "It was stolen last night. No one knows how. We lost you and Angelli after you entered the Sternberg Palace."

Stasia looked at the painting again. The Watcher Angel clearly had Angelli's face. And the spellbound woman had *her* features, including the dimpled chin.

Was her mind playing tricks on her?

"I think that I can explain, at least partially," Miró said. Stasia and Beta both looked at him. "Zaccaria Angelli is a Dark *Irim*. He charmed you and wiped your memory."

***

It turned out that it had been Olivia who kept calling Stasia's cellphone. Its coordinates had popped up again on Olivia's system twenty minutes before Miró and Beta had burst into the hotel room. She'd sent them to find Stasia.

The GPS tracker that Stasia had slipped onto Angelli hadn't reappeared, however. Nor had the bugs that Beta had hidden in his luggage. Even András, who was an exceptional *Elioud* tracker, could find no trace of the Dark *Irim* beyond the Sternberg. It was as if the angel had never been in Prague.

Beta had arranged for the VZ to secure the Caravaggio painting prior to their arrival yesterday, so she left Miró and Stasia alone while she called her colleagues. Stasia needed to check in with her own case officer. Despite this, she stood in her pajamas waiting for an explosion.

It didn't happen. Instead Miró took a bottle of water from the room's refrigerator and holding it out to her asked, "How are you feeling?"

Stasia, uncomfortable in her belly-baring t-shirt and shorts, wished that he raged at her or acted intimidating or even icy—anything except polite and calm. For the first time that she could remember, she felt self-conscious standing in front of him, and she didn't know why. Her earlier irritation returned.

"Hungover, if you must know." Grabbing the water bottle, she raised her chin and stared, willing him to respond in some overtly emotional manner—as if she mattered to him.

Still he didn't. "I will order room service while you shower. You have a long day ahead of you." His voice was mild, and his eyes were opaque.

Stasia squinted, trying to ascertain what he wasn't saying, but she came up blank. Her personal emotional radar had been shorted during the op. She might as well have lost an eye.

Folding her arms across her chest, she asked, "Does this mean you have plans for me?"

He studied her for a moment. She had no idea what he was thinking.

"We need to debrief Mihàil and Olivia. It will be up to them to determine whether and how we continue to work with you."

Stasia could find nothing wrong with this statement. Yet all she wanted to do was leave Prague and return to Italy as soon as possible. She wanted to get back to her former life. This line of investigation hadn't netted anything useful. If anything, she was farther from her goal of recovering the Rembrandt.

She opened the water and drank deeply before responding. "Fine, but I can get ready on my own. I will meet you in the lobby in thirty minutes."

He shook his head. "That would not be wise, Ms. Fiore, while the Caravaggio is unsecured, and Angelli's motivations remain hidden. Until we can make arrangements, both you and the painting are vulnerable, especially while you remain here."

"Stasia. Call me Stasia."

Miró ignored her and picked up the room's phone. Hearing him place an order for breakfast, she threw up her free hand and whirled to grab clean clothes from her suitcase before stomping into the bathroom.

She came out later, hair damp and toiletries packed, to find András and Miró studying the painting. Something about their expressions told her that they were conferring. She tried reaching Miró that way, but her mental voice stayed locked in her skull. She was mute. The realization stung. She'd only just tasted that particular *Elioud* gift.

While she finished packing, a knock on the door preceded Beta's entrance along with two dark-haired VZ officers dressed in street clothes. They looked like business professionals. They spoke for several minutes with Miró, who confirmed that they'd taken precautions to shield the painting from surveillance normally reserved for sensitive audio and data equipment, presumably to prevent a Dark *Irim* from tracking it.

Beta watched as the VZ officers placed the painting inside a specially designed box. She glanced at Stasia, her dark eyes enigmatic as always. "He was frantic to find you," she said, her voice low. "He would not stop looking for you."

"He was frantic about the Caravaggio."

Beta shook her head. "No. He never once mentioned the Caravaggio."

Stasia shrugged. "I doubt he said very much about anything."

She felt Beta's penetrating gaze. "On the contrary, he called Kastrioti as soon as we lost sight of you and requested him to alert local assets to help search for you."

That caught Stasia by surprise. "He did?"

Beta nodded. "He was on the verge of calling someone he knows in Italian intelligence when we got Olivia's call."

Stasia stole a glance at Miró, who felt her gaze and looked at her. She saw nothing in his expression to confirm Beta's story, but she knew that Beta would never lie to her.

The VZ officers finished securing the Caravaggio and with a nod at Beta filed out of the room.

Beta turned to Stasia. "*Vaše záda jsou zakryta.*" As the Americans would say, Beta had her back.

Then she left Stasia alone with Miró and her disquiet.

Thirty minutes later, they were flying out of Prague in Mihàil's private helicopter. András had remained behind to scour the city for traces of Angelli and to try to piece together what had happened during Stasia's lost twelve hours, including how the Caravaggio had been stolen, though it was unlikely that they'd ever know exactly what transpired. Despite being locked out of the Celestial realm, Dark *Irim* had abilities beyond their *Elioud* kin, and not all of them were known or fully understood.

Stasia slipped her cold hands into her pockets. The fingers of her right hand brushed against what felt like a business card. Puzzled, she pulled it out. It read Emilio Gregori, Esperto di Caravaggio, Galleria Borghese.

Miró, sitting next to her, noticed her holding the card. "You look surprised."

She slid the card back without looking at it again. "I had forgotten that was in my pocket."

He didn't question her answer, though she suspected that he knew that she'd lied. She didn't know why she had; it had been reflexive given the situation. Now she wondered if the *Elioud* had read what it said or guessed, as she had, that Angelli had put it there.

The debriefing with Mihàil and Olivia went about as well as she expected. It seemed rather surreal that a scant twenty-fours ago she'd confessed to one of her closest friends that she'd intended to use her for a mission. Now she found herself leaving under a cloud while the inscrutable *Elioud* who'd haunted her dreams for months treated her like an untrustworthy stranger. It was almost more than she could take.

Olivia came to the guest room after the briefing and watched while Stasia gathered her belongings and gave the room a final look. Then she turned to face Olivia, whose concerned expression added to her uneasiness.

"You don't have to go, Staz."

"*Sì, cara*, I do." Her tongue tripped over the previously effortless endearment. Was it dishonest of her to use it?

"At least stay the night and get a fresh start in the morning."

Shaking her head, Stasia said, "I doubt that I will sleep much tonight regardless. I will keep trying to understand what happened during those lost twelve hours in Prague."

Olivia touched Stasia on the upper arm. "Mihàil said the disorientation and feeling out of sorts will fade with time."

"But my memory may never come back." Stasia tried to say it matter-of-factly. It came out as a whisper instead. She swallowed. "Nevertheless, I need to return to Rome and debrief my handler. I have already gathered enough intel to justify further surveillance on Fagan in Vienna."

"You can choose to stay here and become one of us," Olivia said. "Mihàil, Miró, and András may not be *Irim*, but they can do a lot to restore your *Elioud* wellbeing. Zophiel may even decide to appear and give you a kiss of peace. Then you can find another way to return the Rembrandt to its rightful owner."

Stasia held her friend's gaze. How had she never seen the unearthly light that shone from Olivia's eyes before?

"Perhaps once I know what I did or did not do with a Dark *Irim* I will feel free to stay."

Olivia held her gaze a few moments longer, and then, sighing, leaned forward and hugged Stasia hard. "Take care, *carissima*. I will be here when you're ready."

Stasia hugged her back before heading out to the portico where Pjëter had parked the Range Rover and left it running. He stood by the front of the vehicle waiting for her.

"*Grazie*, Pjëter," she said as he opened the driver's door and turned to take her duffel bag. On impulse, she leaned in to hug him. He looked shocked when she stepped back. She turned quickly and got into her seat, tears pricking her eyes. Why did she suddenly feel as though she might never see the dear man's generous smile again?

Stasia took her time pulling her leather driving gloves on and adjusting the Range Rover's seat before fussing with the review mirror and the heater's vents. After dawdling long enough, she sighed and put the vehicle into gear. She was about to turn out onto the circular driveway in front of the house when she saw Miró standing at the end of the lanai watching her. The last view she had of him was lost in the glare of the sun on her review mirror.

Six hours later, Stasia found herself in The Eternal City. She took a taxi straight to the Palazzo Sant'Ignazio where her Carabinieri case officer had an office. It was not a fun or quick meeting. Between the interview with the Dervishi brothers and the intel that the VZ had recovered from the *bogomili* cellphone, the evidence clearly pointed to Fagan, an American CIA officer. They would need to move carefully as well as work through backchannels to confirm that he'd stolen Italian cultural property without his agency's approval.

Major Andriano Costa, his fingers steepled together and his dark gaze trained on Stasia, listened as she finished describing the recovery of the Caravaggio. Despite still being tired and less than confident about her ability to sway an audience, Stasia thought that she'd kept detail of her own role at a convincing minimum.

"I do not relish sending someone to Vienna," he said when she was done. "But I do not have much choice. However, it will not be you."

Stasia sat straighter, shocked. "*Scusi, signore?* I should be the one to go to Vienna. I have contacts and experience there."

He shook his head. "I have been in communication with General Caravelli. There are some inconsistencies in your account concerning *L'Amante* and the Caravaggio. As a result, I have asked for a new officer to be assigned to surveil Fagan."

Stasia's stomach clenched. She'd never before faced a reprimand let alone been reassigned for performance reasons. She needed to know more if she had to face the Deputy Director of AISE, who was known to be a stickler for details and outcomes. And who didn't like to clean up messes with his colleagues in other security agencies.

"'Inconsistencies'? May I ask to what you are referring, *signore?*"

Major Costa sighed and rubbed his forehead before looking at her. "Fiore, you are a good operative, dedicated, thorough, and passionate. But I think perhaps you lost your focus on this operation. The VZ found the Caravaggio in your hotel room but not *L'Amante*. Before that you spent several days in Albania with a disavowed CIA operative. Now there are questions about your loyalties."

Stasia swallowed against the sudden thickness in her throat. This couldn't be happening. "I am as loyal as I have ever been." Her voice was husky.

He leaned toward her, his gaze intense. "I have no doubt, Fiore. But you will sit this one out. In fact, General Caravelli has asked that you submit a written report to his office by the end of the day tomorrow. He suggests that you take some personal time while it is being reviewed."

"For how long, *signore*?" Stasia asked. Something burned behind her eyes.

Major Costa sat back. "Indefinitely. You will be contacted when it is time for you to meet with him."

"I see." Stasia's face had become stone.

Major Costa stood, and she followed on reflex. "Thank you, Fiore. That is all for now."

"*Signore*." She nodded, but he was already sitting back down and returning to his work.

Stasia made her way to her apartment in the Pigneto neighborhood in a daze. Fortunately the Manzoni metro station was only a five-minute walk from the Palazzo Sant'Ignazio. She was exhausted. It had been a long twelve hours. No, make that a long twenty-four hours. Actually the past *thirty-six* hours had been draining, ever since Miró came to her room and rejected her.

She managed to make the connection at San Giovanni and five minutes later exited the metro and headed east onto Via di Pigneto. The eclectic working-class neighborhood had seen a resurgence in recent years, and even though it was a cold February evening, there were numerous people out on the sidewalks searching for a place to dine in one of its many restaurants or heading to one of its indie cinemas. Stasia ignored them, but something inside eased at the familiar sight of the small two-family houses and three-storey buildings.

As she turned right onto Via Braccio da Montone, she caught sight of a shop whose windows were still adorned with paper hearts.

St. Valentine's Day.

It had been more than a week ago, and she'd never paid attention before. So why did it make her chest ache to see that flimsy red paper curling away from the glass?

Her studio apartment was in one of the low-rise buildings on the second floor. It was cold and dark, but she sighed when she shut and locked the door behind her. She pulled her duffel on its wheels into the small sitting area and returned to the kitchen to pour a glass of Vino Nobile di Montepulciano then collapsed on her small sectional. She'd order some *salsiccio al sugo* from Necci, a landmark Italian restaurant down the block after she'd taken her shoes off and enjoyed her red wine.

Her cellphone rang just as she recalled the business card in her pocket. Groaning, she stood and walked to the only table in her apartment to set her wineglass down. She pulled the cellphone and business card out.

It was Beta. That was unexpected.

She held the phone to her ear and studied the business card. "*Come va?*"

"The Caravaggio's been taken." Beta wasn't one for unnecessary preliminaries.

"*L'Amante?*" Stasia asked, pulling out a chair and sitting. This day just kept getting better and better.

"Not his style. One officer was killed, the other wounded as they transported the painting to a secure site. I have been grilled all day about what I know."

"That explains much."

"I gather that you have also had some questions?" Beta's dry voice underscored the gravity of the situation.

"*Sì*. In fact, I am on indefinite leave."

"Ah."

Stasia waited. She didn't know what to say. Even her sense of Beta, limited as it had been, had disappeared. Perhaps she should thank her friend and say good luck and good bye....

"I was not put on leave, but it was made clear to me that my association with you and Olivia has tarnished my standing. It would seem that it is easier to blame me than to pursue an American intelligence officer."

Stasia shut her eyes. A sharp pain had started behind the right one. She leaned her forehead into her hand. *"Perdonami."*

"There is nothing to forgive, Staz." Beta sounded implacable. "I wanted you to know that I am going after the team that killed Andrej and left Eliska almost dead. Tell Olivia that I will contact her."

So Beta hadn't called Olivia. That was telling. Beta, a true lone wolf, had bonded with Olivia before she'd met Stasia. It seemed that their little pack had fallen apart, and it was her fault.

Swallowing, she said, "Stay safe."

"Ci rivediamo." *We* will *see each other again*. And Beta was gone.

Stasia held the business card up. Now that she was unemployed, she had time to devote to her art studies.

Eleven

Miró avoided Rome as much as he could, though that was nearly impossible given how drawn to the ancient city (the whole Italian peninsula, really) the Dark Angelic forces were and how often they led Mihàil and his lieutenants there.

He'd not always lived in Mihàil's sphere, close at hand to the *drangùe*, however. There was a time during the early decades of the twentieth century that he'd actually lived in Italy. Italy drew him as well, though his own fascination centered on the southern provinces, especially those in the foot of Italy's boot. Maybe that said something about his *Elioud* nature.

Of course it does. He knew full well that dark currents ran through him.

After that brief and unhappy episode on his own, Miró had returned to live in closer proximity to his lord. But now he found himself in Italy again on his own, again drawn by a woman who had been converted to the Dark Angelic side.

Or had she?

Miró didn't know if it was his heart or his intuition telling him that Stasia couldn't have become Angelli's pawn, whoever that devilish art thief really was. But his gut and his emotions were all that he had to go on. Given that he was an *Elioud* truthseeker, his inability to interpret the complex interplay among her harmonics, breathing, and temperature chilled him.

He'd been blind to another woman's nature once before and it had nearly cost him everything. *La Sciantosa* had been merely a woman with only a trace of *Elioud* blood, though even that was enough to charm him, he who had fallen in love for the first time in his long life. How would he fare against a woman whose charisma had caught a Dark *Irim* off guard? If Mihàil's suspicion about the Dark *Irim*'s identity was correct, that would make Stasia's achievement all the more remarkable.

And it would mean that Miró had no chance of withstanding her manipulation unless he never let his guard down.

So he wouldn't.

Regardless of how much it cost him, Miró had to discover the truth about what happened to Stasia after she disappeared with *L'Amante*. Because if she was still free to choose the right path, it was his duty to do all he could to encourage her to choose it.

And it has nothing to do with your own desire for Stasia, does it?

Clenching his jaw, Miró slipped into the Pigneto neighborhood where Stasia's apartment was located. He walked past the building and took up a post farther down the block to observe who came and went. It was evening and many students from the University of La Sapienza mixed on the sidewalks with permanent residents, Romans as well as immigrants from Peru, Egypt, Romania, and the Philippines, as they searched for restaurants and clubs.

"Not exactly what you envisioned for Stasia, my dear blackbird?" Zophie leaned against the wall of the building behind him. Il Pigneto was known for its street art, and the wall featured a mural by the international graffiti duo known as Sten and Lex. Her shadow hovered protectively over the half-shade stencil of a couple embracing.

Miró said nothing. He found it best to let the guardian angel talk unimpeded.

"You must admit that it is rather astonishing that she lives in this neighborhood even if it is becoming gentrified with hipsters."

Miró squinted at the woman wearing the black leather jacket with motorcycle gloves, half a shaved head, and a nose piercing who came out of Stasia's apartment building. Despite her edgy appearance, she carried herself with a crisp precision that suggested military or law enforcement training. She was too old to be a university student. He would bet a week's worth of covering for András on reconnaissance missions that she was American.

"Of course, if Stasia lived in a luxury apartment in either the Piazza di Spagna or on Via Veneto instead of a modest studio here, then you would find her easier to dismiss."

Miró glanced at the angel, who now stood next to him. "There is vitality here that is lacking in those neighborhoods," he said as he turned back to make sure that the other operative headed away from Stasia's building. "Here there are artists and intellectuals, students—people who are curious and creative like her."

He looked at his watch. It was getting late. He needed to get into Stasia's apartment and have a look around before she returned. He started walking knowing that Zophiel would keep pace.

"She missed a traditional university career," he said, as much to himself as to her. "Her gift with languages and her quickness at martial arts and weapons training caught the eye of Italian intelligence long before she had a chance to choose her own path. It was something her family wanted and expected for her."

"Ah, so you *have* read your Italian flower's file." Zophie slid a hand through his arm, easily matching his stride. "You should know that she could have been an opera diva. Her *Elioud* gifts include a very fine, very powerful mezzo-soprano voice. But she is too pragmatic and too devoted to justice. Singing seems so frivolous to her."

Miró ignored the gibe. What could he say? That after having been forced to sing and dance as an Ottoman *köçek*, a boy made to cross dress and entertain the men who raped him, he agreed wholeheartedly with Stasia? If he never had to sing again, it would be too soon. He reached Stasia's apartment and slipped through the entrance behind another resident.

Zophie met him at the second landing. She reached out and held his face in her hands.

"Dear, dear man, you must learn to have a little faith."

"I do have faith," he said through tight lips.

"Do you really? Faith is just another word for trust. You must trust that your heart is strong enough to love."

Zophiel's brilliant gaze gleamed like a beacon in the warm light from the overhead fixture. Miró couldn't have looked away if he'd tried.

For once the guardian angel's touch didn't soothe, it didn't bring profound peace.

"I trust my judgment," he said at last, his voice harsh in his ears, "I trust myself to do what must be done."

Sadness radiated from Zophiel's eyes. She kissed him on the forehead. In the air a hint of hardcore punk, an echo of his *ram muay* ritual, sounded.

"You may speak with the tongue of angels," she said and left the rest of the admonition unspoken.

Then with a clang she disappeared, leaving dissonance to mar his harmonics.

***

András Nagy ended his futile efforts to track the Dark *Irim* who called himself Angelli at the Captain's Club in the Admiral Botel, a uniquely Czech floating hotel designed to look like a boat. András snorted and swigged his Pilsner Urquell. The Admiral had never sailed. And despite the dark wood and brass décor suggesting that it had been in service for decades, the botel had been permanently anchored on the left bank of the Vitava River since 1971.

As he sat there stewing over his failure, the club's lights dimmed and 1990s dance music replaced the 1930s period music. Swiveling, he scowled at the bright round dance floor revealed where an oriental rug had lain in the center of the club. A large round fixture on the ceiling glowed above it. Outside the Admiral Botel would be lit up from stem to stern, its neon green marquee visible on the far river bank. Light from dozens of windows gilded the dark water of the river. Local Prague residents filled the small club, creating a veritable cloud of cigarette smoke and babble.

András sighed and stood to pull his wallet from his jeans. And then he sensed her.

Gomba. His mushroom.

Before he could consider why she was there or pinpoint her position, a young woman laid her hand on his arm. She smiled up at him.

"Walk me home. You are so big and so warm! And it is so cold outside." She rubbed her heavy breasts against his side. "I promise I will be hot in bed."

András tugged his arm from her grasp. In the hazy club, heavy cigarette smoke clung to her long dark tresses. Why did all the Czech women have to style their hair like a supermodel from twenty years ago? All those hair products did was filter and trap unsavory smells from the surrounding air.

"He would burn you to a crisp," Beta said, suddenly standing on András's other side. She picked up his Pilsner Urquell and, quirking an eyebrow at him, drank the last of it in a single swallow. "Though perhaps you would enjoy the experience?"

She let her gaze travel over the young woman, her expression never changing.

The young woman stood her ground. András ignored her.

"So you found me," he said to Beta as she set the empty bottle on the bar. He grinned. "Miss me, Gomba?"

Beta gestured with her chin toward the bartender, who came over. "Trebitsch."

He nodded and poured her a shot of the single-malt whisky. She narrowed her eyes. He poured another shot.

"No," she answered András and lifted the tumbler to her mouth.

He watched as she sipped the whisky, muscles in her delicate throat moving. He wanted to trace them with his fingertip but refrained.

Beta looked over her shoulder at the young woman. "You are still here?"

She turned and leaned against the bar, pulling a karambit from her jeans as she did so. The red hooked blade gleamed dully under the neon lights. She folded and unfolded the karambit one handed.

Impressive. He didn't recognize the knife's folding mechanism, but it was smooth like a cat's claw retracting.

The young woman squawked and fled.

András gestured for another Pilsner Urquell, never taking his eyes from Beta. Her glossy black curls brushed her narrow shoulders, and her black eyes laughed at him. She folded the karambit with a flick and slid it into her pocket.

He leaned forward and inhaled.

Even in the smoke-filled club, her complex scent teased him: orchid, incense, and gardenia. But more than that. He could taste vanilla, chocolate, black currant, and mandarin orange on his tongue. And anchoring it all, a fecund trace of vetiver like rain on earth. She smelled sweet, rich, dark, and wild. He wondered what she would smell like in clean air.

What her bare skin would smell like.

He sat back, blinking and dazed.

Beta brought the whisky to her mouth with long, graceful fingers. She finished it and then picked up his fresh beer and handed it to him. The corners of her mouth curled. "You look like you can use this." She tilted her head, studying him. "For an *Elioud* warrior, you do not seem to have much tolerance for smoke."

András shook his head vigorously, like a dog emerging from a pond. He grabbed the beer from Beta, his fingers brushing hers. A jolt ran through him. He tipped the bottle and gulped half without breathing.

Wiping the back of his hand across his mouth, he let his mind clear. "So, Gomba, how did you find me?"

"Coincidence?" she leaned forward and took his beer back.

He watched as she drank. Her lips looked soft and pink. Until this moment, he hadn't realized that any part of her was soft. But he'd been wrong. Her lips, her skin, her hair. They were all soft.

It was his turn to deny her. "No."

His hand encircled hers holding the bottle. He held her dark, fathomless gaze and wondered where the humor had gone.

She shrugged but didn't try to pull her hand away. "You have a distinct scent."

András grinned and sat back. "Something so delicious you couldn't help yourself. You had to get closer."

Now she did pull her hand back. The bottle fell, but he caught it without looking and set it onto the bar. "*Jsi smradlavá velká kráva.*"

András leaned close, almost nudging her. *She* smelled delicious. "So I'm a stinking big cow, hm?" he said, his lips brushing her ear. A tremor ran through her.

An instant later, he felt the warning prick of the karambit's blade on his neck. Without moving, he gazed up at Beta's glittering black eyes.

"You would do well to move away," she said in a low hiss.

Keeping his gaze trained on her, he sat upright. He touched his neck. His fingers came back tipped in blood.

"It always goes well until a karambit comes to play." He reached for his wallet. "I wondered if you had any defenses inside your chain whip."

"Now you know." Beta stood. She slipped the karambit back into her pocket but kept her hands loose at her sides.

"That is a particularly clever design." He pulled out some *koruna* notes, enough to pay for her Trebitsch. He dropped the cash on the bar. "Small talk is over. You found me. Your wordplay doesn't hide the fact that no spy technology on Earth has yet been made that can track my whereabouts unless I intend to be found. Your *Elioud* senses are astonishing. But that doesn't answer the real question. Why are you here?"

Beta shifted and looked away. András got the distinct impression that she was uncomfortable.

Interesting.

"The Caravaggio has been taken. Whoever did it killed one of the team members and gravely injured the other. I need help tracking them."

András tipped his head and studied her. Was that a faint blush?

His *Elioud* vision read her infrared signature. She had the densest blue-white core he'd ever seen with cooler bands of orange and red in her extremities. But delicate wisps of heat wafted from her face as she stood under his scrutiny.

"Ah! You're not an exceptional *Elioud* tracker after all! You can track *me*." He threw his head back and laughed. "Do you know what this means, Gomba? Hm? It means you like me."

Beta moved so fast András hadn't finished laughing. She got inside his reach and had her chain whip unfolded enough to wrap around his neck before he knew what had happened. She didn't have to tighten the links to make her point.

He'd tired of her prickliness, however. He raised his temperature until the steel links grew hot. Beta yelped and tried to move away, but he grabbed her wrists to keep her close.

"Will you help me or not?" she said between her teeth.

"Yes, of course," he said. "All you had to do is ask." He let her wrists go.

She stepped back, her chain whip disappearing inside her jacket and her face once again impassive. "I have not told Olivia."

"Do you plan to recover the Caravaggio?"

She tipped her chin. "Yes."

András felt the weight of her dark gaze. "Then I have no problem."

"Good." She paused. "I do not promise to recover the *bogomili*, however."

András grinned. He didn't let it reach his eyes. "Then I have no problem," he said again.

Beta rewarded him with the first smile she'd ever given him. It was like the sunrise over a mountain.

***

He followed Ms. Fiore as she left her apartment and headed to the Ponte Casilino bus stop. Despite her training and instincts, she seemed unaware of him. More alarmingly, she seemed completely unaware of the others shadowing her. They joined the edge of the crowd at the bus stop, separating so that each covered a flank. He maneuvered so that he was near enough to touch her, his senses attuned to her shadowers. She made her way to the back half of the bus and sat reading her cellphone. He hurried and took the open seat behind hers. The shadowers sat, one in the rear of the bus opposite her and the other in the third row on the same side.

At Termini, Ms. Fiore exited and headed to Bar Fondi, a bustling café not far from the station. She spoke to the two employees behind the counter as if she knew them, laughing and chatting until they gave her a cappuccino and a croissant. Then she squeezed into an open seat next to a small table where another customer still ate breakfast. One shadower remained outside the café while the second ordered an espresso and sat on a black leather bench under a large sign that said "Sofa" along the back wall.

He waited among a group of tourists ordering pastries and coffee. He was good at blending in and no one noticed that he never ordered.

He studied the shadowers. The shadower seated on the bench had shoulder-length wavy hair, dark-framed glasses, and scrubby facial hair. This shadower pretended to read a paperback book, but his gaze remained on Ms. Fiore. There was also a 9mm handgun at the small of his back, hidden by his down jacket. Added to his choice of seating whereby he faced the exit with his back covered, and it was clear that he had training.

The other shadower stood across the street, pacing and talking on his cellphone. He kept the door to Bar Fondi in sight. He too had a 9mm handgun, kept in a shoulder holster under his camel-colored wool overcoat.

When Ms. Fiore left the cafe, both shadowers followed. So did he.

She returned to Termini and took the bus to the Victor Hugo/Museo Bilotti stop. Her shadowers got off the bus after her, though there were fewer people doing so. The wool-overcoat shadower hurried his pace and passed Ms. Fiore as if he were late for a meeting. He turned off into the Carlo Bilotti Museum on the grounds of the Villa Borghese, the third largest park in Rome. Ms. Fiore glanced at this shadower's back but didn't linger. Instead she continued another six hundred meters to the Galleria Borghese, the former main house of the villa.

He watched her enter the grounds of the Galleria Borghese, an imposing 17th Century building surrounded by lavish gardens, now dormant in the February cold. The second man continued on the sidewalk past the Galleria as Ms. Fiore reached the museum, where Baroque artwork filled galleries on both floors. She would be safe inside.

The second man doubled back and came to stand next to one of the two plinths guarding the entrance where he could watch for Ms. Fiore to exit the Galleria. Whatever the ultimate intentions of this trained team, for now they observed.

He, however, didn't need to observe any longer.

The second man didn't see or sense him coming. Rendering the man unconscious, he dragged his deadweight to one of the stone benches just inside the stone balustrade demarcating the Galleria's grounds. Then he disabled the man's 9mm and pocketed the magazine. That done he searched the man's pockets and emptied his wallet. As expected, there was no revealing intelligence such as photo identification or hotel room key.

The man's cellphone buzzed. He took the cellphone, using the man's finger to unlock it. An incoming text popped on the dark screen. It read, "Orders from Mother. Grab package on exit. Exfil details follow at rendezvous point." An attached text file contained a map with a marked location northwest of the Galleria.

The team's ultimate intentions had just become a little clearer.

Swiping through the text app, he saw no texts. Self-deleting. But the phone gallery had photos of Ms. Fiore, and the contacts had another number besides that of the text sender. He responded using his cellphone and spoofing the unconscious man's number.

"Copy that. Will signal when package leaves."

No response. He'd attached a hidden file that would allow him to track the other man's cellphone even if he removed the SIM card. Once the other man read the text, he got a notification. His code had ferreted out the cellphone's unique IMEI number.

It would make it easier to prevent the team from succeeding in their mission. It would also make *his* job easier when the time came.

One of the team members was going to tell him who he worked for and what he wanted from Ms. Fiore.

Twelve

Emilio Gregori, renowned Caravaggio expert, met Stasia inside the entrance to the Galleria Borghese. She'd called ahead and mentioned her relationship with the Art Squad (leaving out her current status, of course). She'd also let slip that she'd helped prevent the theft of the *Infatuation of the Watcher Angels,* which Gregori had authenticated and negotiated with the Catholic Church to lend to the National Gallery Prague. In fact, the Galleria Borghese sought to position itself as the leading authority on Caravaggio through its planned Caravaggio Research Institute, funded by the luxury brand Fendi.

"It is very critical that we take control of Caravaggio's legacy," Gregori said as he escorted her to his office. "Or these paintings will continue to multiply, and no one will be able to tell the real from the imposters like that other French discovery, *Judith Beheading Holofernes.*"

"An imposter? You do not agree with Monsieur Turquin?" Eric Turquin was France's top authority on paintings by the Old Masters. "He is staking his reputation that it is a true Caravaggio."

"It is clearly a copy by Finson." Gregori dismissed his rival's claim as he gestured for her to sit at a chair facing his desk. Even though he worked in a museum dedicated to Baroque art, his office was furnished in modern Italian style and almost sterile in its neatness.

"Finson?"

The name sounded familiar to Stasia. Fortunately, she remembered why. A member of the Art Squad wouldn't be ignorant of the Flemish painter who followed Caravaggio, especially one instrumental in bringing the Italian master's arresting new style to northern Europe.

"His copy of *Judith Beheading Holofernes* already hangs in the Palazzo Zevallos in Naples."

"True, but Finson spent many years in France where he was more successful than in Naples. It is only logical that the Toulouse painting is another, better copy by his hand."

Stasia nodded and refrained from pointing out that Gregori's colleague Nicola Spinosa had pronounced the Toulouse version authentic last April after seeing it in person. It was time to move to the real subject of her visit.

"If that is true, how can you be so certain that Caravaggio painted *Infatuation of the Watcher Angels*?"

The Italian art expert leaned toward her, excitement sparking in his gaze. "One has only to see it to feel its power, Ms. Fiore. The Watcher Angels in the painting practically glow. Their leader, Yeqon, emanates a magnificent otherworldly desire for the human woman he is in the act of seducing. We, the viewers, feel the pull of that seduction because of Caravaggio's great genius. There are very few artists whose dramatic handling of light compare."

He sat back looking immensely satisfied.

"Is Rembrandt one of these artists?"

Gregori nodded. "Indeed. Though they lived far apart and in different times, Caravaggio and Rembrandt are artistic soulmates."

Stasia pursed her lips. "The subject that Caravaggio painted is rather unusual, no? The *First Book of Enoch* was expunged from the religious canon in late antiquity."

Gregori's excitement dimmed. He studied her. "If you mean by that question to impugn the origin of the painting, nothing can be farther from the truth. The story of the Watcher Angels was known regardless. It is summarized in the book of *Genesis*, which tells of the sons of God falling in love with the daughters of man. Many early Church Fathers believed that 'sons of God' refers to angels set to watch over humanity."

Stasia kept her expression carefully cool. "Rembrandt also painted a scene featuring the Watcher Angels, a painting found only two years ago. Does it not strike you odd that both of these Old Masters painted scenes from a disavowed book from the Bible? Paintings that were lost and then found a year apart?"

Gregori didn't answer right away. Instead, he seemed to consider something before sighing and swiveling in his chair to look at the wall of bookcases behind his desk. After a long moment in which Stasia felt her patience ebb, he stood and pulled a thin volume from a top shelf. He turned to Stasia, started to hand her the book, and then drew it back.

"Signorina, what do you know of the discovery of *Infatuation of the Watcher Angels*?"

Stasia took a small breath and eased into a response. She shrugged a shoulder. "Not much, Signor Gregori. Until my trip to Prague, I had only read about it in the news. You must forgive me. I have spent months trying to recover the Rembrandt stolen last fall from a Milan art dealer."

"*Judgment of the Watcher Angels*?" Now Gregori's gaze could have cut glass. At her nod, he went on. "I see now why you are so fixated on the connection to Caravaggio. In the case of Caravaggio's lost painting, it was found hidden under another painting by a lesser artist. Can you guess why it was hidden?"

At Stasia's head shake, he said, "In all probability for the same reason the *First Book of Enoch* was declared untrue."

"*Perché?*"

Gregori shrugged. "Why else? Because it would reduce the Church's power. *Ma nessuno può tenere un ceci in bocca.* Secrets never stay unspoken. Not long after Caravaggio painted his scene of angelic seduction, the great English explorer Sir Walter Raleigh wrote about the *First Book of Enoch* in his *History of the World*. This"—he wiggled the book that he held— "analyzes the iconography of the Garden of Eden story. The author speculates about the Watcher Angel mythology in a manner not approved by the Magisterium."

"I doubt the Church cares to keep the story about the Watcher Angels hidden any longer," Stasia said. "No, there is something else about the Watcher story that makes the Rembrandt and Caravaggio paintings so desirable. The Caravaggio has been stolen."

"*Santo cielo!*" exclaimed Gregori, sitting upright and crossing himself. "I thought you said that the theft had been foiled."

"It was stolen after I left Prague, likely by the same party who stole the Rembrandt. Signor Gregori, do you have any idea why someone would want both of them?"

Gregori frowned. "Perhaps the legend is true."

"Legend?" Stasia blinked, confused.

"*Sì,* lore says that Caravaggio and Rembrandt were members of a secret society devoted to a divine mystery. Each is said to have painted a scene for a triptych. No one knows what the subject of the triptych is or who painted the third painting."

Triptych. A tingle of recognition began at the base of Stasia's skull.

She leaned forward, intent. "Let us agree that this legend is indeed fact. How did these two Old Masters collaborate on a triptych?"

Gregori sighed, shrugged, and looked away. "Ah, now we are back to Finson." He sounded unhappy.

"Finson?"

"*Sì*. Finson shared his studio in Naples with Caravaggio, who left unfinished works there. This same legend says that Finson took more than Caravaggio's revolutionary techniques to France."

Stasia almost gibed *Judith Beheading Holofernes?* but didn't. No need to remind Gregori that Finson was an art dealer known to have taken several Caravaggio paintings to France.

Instead, she asked, "*Che?*"

Gregori shrugged again. "Finson travelled to Aix-en-Provence where he stayed with Peiresc, the savant and collector. Peiresc was a great admirer of Caravaggio." He paused, his gaze thoughtful. "Perhaps that is it. …"

"*Sì?*" Stasia's sharp tone brought the art expert's wandering attention back.

"Peiresc is known to have owned a copy of *The First Book of Enoch*. In fact, he asked a great Ethiopian scholar to authenticate his copy, but the scholar said that it was a fake. Peiresc was a great scholar in his own right and wrote countless letters to other intellectuals, including the Dutch mathematician Huygens. Huygens met Rembrandt, who was also a collector, in Amsterdam."

Stasia sat back. It was tenuous, but the bare facts suggested a physical link between the two Old Masters.

"You guess that Caravaggio and Rembrandt shared a copy of the *First Book of Enoch*."

He nodded. "And a secret hidden in their paintings."

***

As Stasia stepped out into the weak February sunshine, painful prickles blossomed in her chest and spread through her whole body. She halted, catching her breath. A sharp crystalline edge clarified details in her surroundings. A complex medley of scents blanketed her. A harsh cacophony assaulted her ears.

Dizzy now, she stood blinking and panting. Then an invisible chisel hammered a hairline crack at her temples and over the arch of her forehead. She managed to stumble to the corner of the building before vomiting her breakfast into the piled snow.

Her *Elioud* senses had awakened all at once.

As the wild profusion of stimuli settled down, she became aware of a warm hand rubbing her upper back. Gentle vibrations pulsed through her, soothing her overwrought nerves. She arched against the hand, sighing. The headache eased away. Unlikely as it seemed, she felt almost as good as she did after a week's vacation, lazing in bed after long hours of deep sleep.

"You followed me," she said as she turned.

For a moment Miró's pale gaze burned. And then he reached out and tucked a strand of hair behind her ear. She turned her face into his palm.

"It is not safe here." His low voice stroked her from the base of her neck to her hips. Then he tugged her around the corner of the building and pulled her into a sprint beside him.

A fraction of a second later, the unmistakable sound of bullets hitting stone reached her ears.

"Fagan?" she asked. The windows of the Galleria Borghese sped impossibly past.

Yes, he sent a team for you. I dealt with two of them already.

I can hear you. A jolt of relief caused her to stumble.

Slowing, Miró looked back at her. He squeezed her hand, and she recovered her stride. Then he cut across the *piazzale* toward the trees on the east. Once they'd gotten on the other side of a large trunk, Miró halted and turned toward the museum. Across the *piazzale* a man wearing casual clothes that did nothing to disguise his athletic, muscular build ran around the corner of the building. He held a weapon in a two-handed grip and scanned the area to the front and side.

Wait here.

Miró didn't wait for her response. Instead, he circled around the tree to come back to the *piazzale* from behind their pursuer.

I can distract him.

Of course you can. Stasia heard humor in his tone. More than that, she recognized Miró's certainty. It bolstered her.

She stepped away from the tree. "Are you looking for me?"

The man spun, the muzzle of his handgun aimed at her. He didn't approach, however. Whoever he was, he was well trained.

"Where's your partner?" His accent was American.

Palms up, Stasia shrugged and smiled. "He does not like guns," she said, injecting the truth into her words and not a little *Elioud* charisma.

The operative relaxed his stance, letting his handgun point lower. She took a step toward him. He only watched as she stopped a couple of meters in front of him. A moment later, Miró materialized behind the operative and clapped a hand on his upper back as if greeting an old friend. The operative slid to the ground, unconscious.

"I hope that you show me that trick someday," she said as he knelt to zip-tie the operative's wrists together.

"Someday."

It wasn't much of a promise, but Stasia would take it.

Miró stood, jerking the operative to his feet. The man's head lolled. It looked like Miró held him upright by another *Elioud* technique. Or force of will. Her money was on Miró's willpower. The *Elioud* male was indomitable.

As if he heard her, Miró smiled at her. As that morning in Mihàil's gym, it reached his eyes, dispelling the ever present, if subtle, shadow in his gaze.

Her breath caught. If she'd thought Angelli devilishly handsome, she found Miró's imperfect beauty more compelling.

"Come, Stasia. Let us take our new friend for a chat somewhere more private."

He'd turned before his words registered. He'd used her first name.

Snapping her jaw shut, Stasia hurried to fall in step on the other side of their captive.

"Why are you here?" she asked.

Ahead, a black sedan slid next to the curb on the Viale dell'Uccelliera, which ran past the Galleria Borghese. Miró walked toward it, the operative's smooth gait matching his.

Miró glanced at her. "For you."

Stasia wanted to be irritated, but instead she felt something warm and solid in her breast. Still, she couldn't help asking, "*Per che?* You do not work with Grey *Elioud* such as I am."

Miró opened the rear passenger door and guided the operative into the back seat. Then he opened the front passenger door and gestured for her to get in. "*Per favore.*" She did as he asked. He reached for the seatbelt before she could, his fingers brushing her jacket as he pulled it to the latch. She felt his warm breath on her cheek.

He held her gaze. "We are connected, Stasia. I must keep you safe."

He stepped back and shut the car door before she could speak. While he went around the sedan to the far rear passenger door, she studied the driver, who never looked at her. He appeared to be Italian and wore non-descript clothing. Miró had cultivated many contacts throughout Europe, both *Elioud* and human. The driver was likely someone he'd worked with before and trusted. She wondered if he was in Italian intelligence.

Miró got in beside their prisoner. The driver pulled away as he shut his door.

Stasia looked back at him. *Do Mihàil and Olivia know that you are here?*

Yes.

Stasia shut her eyes and huffed. She needed to get herself under control. *Is that all?*

What else is there?

She clinched her jaw. *Are you here with their permission?*

You misunderstand. I do not need Mihàil's permission, only his blessing, which he has given. As for the zonjë, she asked me what I was waiting for.

I see. Stasia turned to the front before almost immediately turning back. Miró was watching her. *No, I do not see.*

Mihàil and Olivia want you to join us.

And you? Do you want me? She tried to convey what she really meant with her question.

He ignored it. *We no longer have the luxury of waiting for you to come to your senses.*

So this is only a recruiting mission?

Asmodeus's minions are getting restive. There are scattered reports of bogomili *attacking innocents in Austria and Hungary. Some of their activity appears directed.*

That means Asmodeus is no longer in a coma.

Correct. And now there is an unknown Dark Irim *in play.*

Do you know who he is?

We have our suspicions.

Is he an ally of Asmodeus?

Dark Irim *are unpredictable and chaotic. They work together at times but rarely choose to remain in a partnership. They are just as likely to impede one another for sport. We think that is the reason you were charmed and your memory wiped. It also explains why* L'Amante *left the painting with you.*

To impede Asmodeus?

Yes.

So this Dark Irim *may still take the Caravaggio?*

Perhaps.

Then I should tell you that the Caravaggio was stolen shortly after the VZ took it.

He swore so softly that she couldn't decipher the words. *That would explain why András chose to remain in Prague.*

He has not checked in?

When he is tracking, he becomes single minded. He was quite annoyed that L'Amante *slipped our perimeter.*

Or perhaps he realized that Beta was going after the thief, who killed one of her VZ colleagues and seriously injured the other.

Miró looked at her. Understanding passed between them. *Does she know?*

Stasia shook her head. *If she did, András would need to call on all his gifts to track her. And if he found her, she would make my sparring skills look weak.*

In that case I hope that she remains unaware. Miró's eyes laughed. The humor died quickly. *Whoever stole the Caravaggio is human then.* Irim *are forbidden to kill* Elohim*'s creatures.*

That never prevented Cain from killing Abel.

True. But Irim *are quite literally incapable of slaughter by their own hands.*

But not incapable of motivating humans to murder.

Yes.

Miró's gaze moved beyond her to the scene outside the windshield, which showed an older rundown apartment building. Stasia recognized Castel Giubileo, a tiny suburb north of Rome. "Ah, we have arrived. It is time to find out what our companion knows about why Fagan wants you."

***

Signor Gregori had only managed to regain his composure after the disturbingly beautiful Art Squad officer had left when another visitor intruded. This time it was a balding, middle-aged man, soft around the middle but hard around the eyes.

"I am unavailable," he said, irritated that his assistant had allowed the man to enter his office.

The man ignored him. He shut the office door and sat in the same chair that Signorina Fiore had occupied only minutes before. He stared at Gregori without blinking. Gregori's hackles began to rise.

"This will only take a moment," the man said. Though he spoke Italian, his accent was American. "Tell me what you and Signorina Fiore discussed."

Gregori wet his suddenly dry lips. He was smart enough to know that anyone following after an Italian Art Squad officer asking about stolen priceless artwork had questionable motives. Worse, his senses told him that more than broken laws were at stake.

"We discussed a Caravaggio painting," he said, his thoughts frantically searching for insight into how to answer without betraying Signorina Fiore or himself.

"Of course," the man said. "You are an expert on Caravaggio after all." He raised his hands and clasped them before his chin. As he did, his suit jacket shifted momentarily to reveal the cold matte black of a handgun.

Gregori's heart began to tap at the base of his throat like a scared sparrow beating against a closed window.

"She"—he cleared his dry throat—"she wanted to know if there was any connection between Caravaggio and Rembrandt because two of their paintings were recently stolen."

The man leaned forward. His gaze pinned Gregori to his chair. "Is there?" he asked.

"They are, of course, two Old Masters," Gregori said in a faint voice. "Rembrandt knew of Caravaggio certainly." He felt a tic start in his right eyeball.

The man watched him.

Gregori felt hot and cold simultaneously. Something itched on his spine. "I suggested that the Flemish painter Finson perhaps acted as an intermediary. Perhaps."

"Perhaps?" The man's cold, unwavering gaze made Gregori's skin crawl.

"Th-there is n-no record that Finson did."

"Is that all?"

"All?" Gregori's mind had shut down. He honestly had no idea what that word meant.

"Yes, Signor Gregori, is that all that you shared with Signorina Fiore? You did not perhaps have a theory about the stolen paintings?"

The man had leaned forward. His gaze bore into Gregori's skull. Gregori shivered.

"I did." He nodded.

"What was this theory?"

"That they were part of a triptych." The words came out in a heated rush.

Gregori realized that he was still nodding and stopped. He had the urge to keep nodding, so he gripped the arms of his office chair to remain still.

The man sat back. "A triptych? Yes, that fits."

His gaze turned inward as he pondered Gregori's suggestion. Gregori felt immediate relief.

It didn't last long. The man's gaze latched onto Gregori again.

"You also have a theory about the subject of the triptych." It was a statement delivered in a silky low voice.

Gregori cleared his throat. He tried to speak. He cleared it again. "It is only wild conjecture," he whispered.

"Tell me."

"I think—that is, I wondered—if the triptych hid a secret about the Watcher Angels."

His interrogator's gaze brightened. "Do you have any idea what this secret is?"

At this question, Gregori's thoughts buzzed in confusion, overwhelming his fear. Puzzled, he sat up and tried to recall what he and Signorina Fiore had talked about. Had they discussed what the secret hidden in the paintings was?

Slowly shaking his head, he said, "That is very strange. I cannot recall any more of our conversation. It is as if my memory has been wiped clean."

The other man sighed. It was an angry, frustrated sound. He did not, however, ask any more questions. He simply stood and walked from Gregori's office without another word.

Gregori watched him go. He sat staring at the open door, his limbic system on high alert for several long minutes. At last he admitted to himself that he wouldn't be able to focus on work any time soon. As he stood to leave, he glimpsed disorder above him. Frowning, he peered at the row of books on his top shelf before straightening them into their respectable upright position.

Thirteen

Stasia and Miró interrogated the young American mercenary in a grim little apartment whose windows faced the Tiber River in the west. It didn't take long. The mercenary knew little other than that he had been assigned to a three-man team to snatch Stasia and take her to Santa Marinella on the west coast where an extraction team awaited them. They'd been ordered to ensure her "viability" as the operative termed it, but everything else had been on the table, including killing anyone who aided her or otherwise got in the way. He didn't know the name of the client, but he knew that his team leader had called this a black-ops mission for an American spook.

"He is not *bogomili*," Miró said as they stood in the kitchen discussing their options. "Simply a gun for hire. I imagine that your intelligence colleagues would be interested in knowing that the Americans tried to grab you on Italian soil."

"Perhaps." Stasia liked standing so close to Miró, feeling his heat and the genuine openness that she read in his demeanor. "You should know that my superior at AISE has put me on indefinite leave due to the events in Prague. Someone else will surveil Fagan in Vienna." She left out that Major Costa had mentioned her time with Olivia in Albania. "I am required to submit a report to General Caravelli by the end of the day."

"Presumably to review whether you will be reinstated at all." Miró's dry tone pricked her.

She turned to face the window next to her but saw nothing. "Presumably."

His hand on the back of her arm made her look up at him. She wanted him to pull her into his arms, but he didn't. "We should have our American friend deliver your report for you."

She was shocked to see the spark of mischief in his gaze. "Why would you help me with General Caravelli?"

"To win you over, of course." Now Miró was grinning. If his earlier smile had transformed him into an angel, this grin made him more human. Stasia wasn't sure which she preferred.

"Are you not concerned that I aided *L'Amante*?" she asked.

He shrugged, an unhappy expression replacing the grin. At the same time, Stasia couldn't help noticing his powerful muscles flexing under his dress shirt. An image of his bare shoulders with her hands caressing them flashed in her thoughts.

Oh, santo cielo! Why would she think of that *now*?

As if underscoring her impulse, Miró said, "I read your harmonics at the National Gallery. *L'Amante* affected you, yes, but you had them under control. At least until you looked at me."

She latched onto her indignation with both hands, metaphorically and literally. Bringing her fingers to her thumbs, she waved them up and down. "*Ma che stai a di?* That I lost my self-control around you?"

"Rather that I lost control around you." He said it slowly and with his gaze unfocused, as if he'd only just realized the truth.

He turned away.

Stasia's lower jaw slipped down.

Miró turned back. "I said that we are connected, Stasia. More precisely, we are in tune. What happened in the National Galleria could be described as a feedback loop whereby I amplified your conflicted attraction to *L'Amante* and to me, adding in my own desire for you. And my jealousy. It damped your harmonics so much that it likely affected your *Elioud* senses. Tell me: were you sick outside the National Galleria because you suddenly sensed everything too much?"

Stasia shut her mouth, frowning. Her harmonics.... She'd all but forgotten them in the midst of everything else, but now that she focused on them again, she realized that her own personal hum had returned. Along with a thin strand of Miró's harmonics vibrating within its braid. His was a rich ruby color. She wondered if he was aware that they weren't simply 'in tune.' Even more, she wondered what exactly it signified that their harmonics had entwined even a little.

Then she recalled what he'd said. "Your jealousy?"

Now Miró had the grace to look discomfited. "Yes."

Stasia sighed dramatically, rolled her eyes, and crossed her arms. "*I frutti proibiti sono.*"

"That is not quite right." All the humor had evaporated from his expression. "You are not 'forbidden fruit.' You are not 'sweeter' because you are a Grey *Elioud*."

She ignored him. "*Dimmelo chiaro e tondo*, Miró Kos," she said, poking him in the chest, "are you certain that you came to recruit me? Because I cannot afford any more of your jealousy." Her accent had thickened into her childhood Cosentian dialect, making her angrier.

Miró's gaze frosted over. "My personal feelings have no bearing on my duty."

"But how you control them may affect my ability to do *my* duty. Or worse. Next time I may not survive your so-called feedback loop."

He'd stiffened as she spoke. "Rest assured, Ms. Fiore, I have my harmonics well in hand. I have acknowledged my attraction for you and our harmonic connection. They will not interfere in our working relationship going forward."

"Ah, now we have arrived at the heart of the matter! What exactly do you believe will happen after we deliver G.I. Joe in there to General Caravelli?"

Stasia had practically shouted this question at Miró, who stood looking at her through hooded eyes. Their icy blue glittered in a way that made her imagine that she was walking along a precipice in a glacier. She didn't care. She was so hot with longing and dread that she knew that if he touched her, she'd combust. *Good for him!* He would continue feigning indifference to her because of his 'duty.'

"I think," he said slowly, enunciating each word carefully, "that General Caravelli is a busy man, who will focus on the response to the Americans. Eventually he will reinstate you. In the meantime, you will continue to try to recover the Rembrandt on your own, putting you directly on a course for Fagan, who seems to think that you know something useful about it and will go to great lengths to get you. And there is a new player, the Dark *Irim* who calls himself *L'Amante*. He is definitely interested in you."

By the end of Miró's summary, Stasia had gotten her emotions back under control. She folded her arms, soothing the angry buzz of her harmonics into a low hum as she did. So she asked dispassionately, "As more than an obstacle for Asmodeus?"

She watched Miró closely. That was why she caught the slight reverberation and tightening in the ruby filament when he answered. His voice was cool, but his harmonics suggested that he wasn't.

"Yes. He knows what you are, and you not only resisted his considerable *Irim* charisma, *you* charmed *him*. In fact, I believe that *L'Amante* would have taken the Caravaggio if he had seduced you. I suspect that aiding or hindering Asmodeus has become the least of *L'Amante*'s motivations."

Stasia pondered Miró's assessment. She could face all of this alone or she could pretend to let Miró recruit her while she followed up on some leads that niggled at her. Just because she was certain that he would fail didn't mean that she was misleading him. He was likely to learn valuable information about Fagan's plans whether she joined the *Elioud* team or not. They had the same goal short term, anyway: outmaneuver Fagan.

Finally, she asked, "How do you feel about accompanying me to Aix-en-Provence?"

***

They'd reached Viareggio, a seaside resort in northern Tuscany halfway along their route to Aix-en-Provence, before Stasia knew for certain that they were being followed. Whoever Fagan had hired was good: the tail changed cars and their drivers at odd, frequent intervals. The problem for anyone following them, however, was that it was late in the evening on the third week of February, not tourist season inland. She had no trouble tracking the traffic around them in the waning sunlight.

Even so, *Carnivale di Viareggio*, a 40-day event second only in size behind that of Venice, had packed the highways leading into the resort city. She was unable to pick up the newest tail when the previous Fiat headed south on E80 as she drove toward the center of Viareggio.

"We are not alone," she said, looking into the rearview mirror. Was the vehicle with the flicker in the right headlight following them?

Miró looked at her. "How many?"

She shrugged. "It varies from one to two, usually men. The last car turned south toward Pisa."

"It will be challenging to spot a new tail in the midst of this crowd." He nodded at the traffic ahead clogging the streets around La Passeggiata, the long promenade along the beach north of the port.

They'd missed the earlier parade featuring the massive allegorical *papier-mâché* floats that made the century-old carnival famous, but now the spectators thronged the boardwalk, filling ristorantes, bars, and gelaterias. As it was the last weekend before Ash Wednesday with a final parade on *Martedì Grasso*, or Fat Tuesday, tens of thousands of people had swollen Viareggio's population from its normal 60,000.

"*Sì*, but anyone who is not Italian will be obvious." At the last moment, she took a right at a car park. "Besides we will be hard to find, too, especially once we abandon this car."

Miró acknowledged her observation with a slight grunt. Stasia watched as the car with the shaky headlight continued on toward the beach. There were two men in the front, neither of whom turned to look in their direction. But trained operatives wouldn't.

No car followed her as she drove past the car park. Yet her gut told her to stay vigilant. She turned right onto the next street and then a quick left, driving farther away from the promenade and the densest crowds. Five blocks up, she turned right again. As she'd remembered, there was another car park inland closer to the highway. She wedged the car into an illegal spot at the end of a row and parked.

They'd both been careful to wear gloves, so beyond grabbing their bags from the trunk and leaving the keys under the floor mat there was nothing more to do to erase their presence from the rental car. Another car would be left for them in a different car park by an asset of Miró's.

They walked two blocks east to a Japanese restaurant where Stasia ordered takeout while Miró hailed a ride share using an app on his smartphone. Twenty minutes later, they arrived at a bed and breakfast southeast of the port that Stasia had booked earlier in the day. It was still early by carnival standards. After eating, they would need to spend some time in Viareggio appearing to celebrate in order to blend in.

And of course they needed to share a bedroom.

Stasia dropped her bag onto the bed and looked around the room. Miró had remained in the dining room with their takeout while she used the toilet and washed up. It had been difficult enough sharing the ride here, but it would be downright excruciating lying next to him on the double bed. The more time she spent with him, the harder it was to remember that she wanted General Caravelli to reinstate her.

Then again, what did she think would happen if she joined the *Elioud* team permanently?

"If you think that you are burning now, only imagine the conflagration if you choose to work alongside that *allocco*. Then you will be an *allocco* too," she announced to the room.

She didn't feel better calling Miró a stupid jerk.

Sighing, she pulled her 9mm from its holster at her waist and set it on the nightstand. Then she stretched her arms as high as she could before changing into a warm sweater. She grabbed her cosmetic bag and headed to the bathroom across the hall. After washing her face and hands, she applied some makeup and then twisted her hair into a knot that she could hide under a knit cap later. She returned to the bedroom where she changed her comfortable shoes into warm boots and tucked her 9mm again at her waist. Almost as an afterthought, she dabbed some perfume onto the pulse points behind her earlobes, her inner wrists, and the base of her throat. Then she grimaced at her own audacity and left the bedroom.

When she entered the dining room, Miró appeared to be engrossed in his smartphone. She knew better. He sat facing out from the corner where he could see anyone who entered from the hall.

Sitting down, she placed the business card that *L'Amante* had left in her coat pocket on the table. Next to it she laid the book that she'd taken from Gregori's office.

Miró looked at her, a question in his expression, and picked up the book. "*Divine Mystery: Reimagining the Garden of Eden from the Point of View of the Serpent.* A little light reading to help you fall asleep later?"

As if anything will help me fall asleep lying next to you. Stasia was careful not to project that thought where Miró would hear it.

Instead, she said, "*L'Amante* left Gregori's card in my coat pocket. He also told me that he'd seen the Caravaggio while it was in Aix-en-Provence."

Miró's gaze sharpened. "He baited you." His posture became more alert. He scanned the room. "Perhaps he is still working with Fagan."

Stasia placed a hand over Miró's. He brought his gaze back to her. "You may be a battle-hardened *Elioud* warrior who can go without food for hours. *I* am hungry. Let us eat as we talk."

Without waiting for him to agree, she went to the sideboard in the dining room and gathered plates and utensils. The B&B proprietor had already left a carafe of mineral water and a half carafe of a good Tuscan *Chianti* on their table. Miró waited as she sat, but when she reached for the container of *udon*, he stopped her.

"Allow me." He held her gaze.

Stasia swallowed and nodded. As Miró began serving her from the various takeout containers, she picked up the wine carafe and poured them each a glass.

"I had the distinct impression that *L'Amante* was trying to help me," she said after she'd taken a fortifying gulp. "In fact I remembered after my visit with Gregori that *L'Amante* assured me that I would recover the Rembrandt and keep the Caravaggio safe."

Miró stared hard at her before gesturing toward her plate of food. "Eat."

When she took a bite, she was surprised to find that the food was hot. She shot him a coy smile.

"If I am to join your *Elioud* team, you must promise unending hot food while on surveillance," she teased.

"Done."

For a moment their gazes remained magnetized. A tremor sent Stasia's harmonics humming. Across the short distance between them, Miró's own harmonics hummed in sync. She saw the ruby filament thicken and weave itself deeper within her hum. Miró made no move to pull away.

Stasia broke the connection at last by glancing toward the book. She picked it up.

"Gregori mentioned a legend in art circles about a secret society devoted to a divine mystery. Caravaggio and Rembrandt are said to have been members."

"And you think that the divine mystery written about in this book"—he touched the cover, brushing her fingers as he did and sending a shiver through her—"is the same divine mystery? A mystery related to the Watcher Angels?"

She nodded. "Each supposedly painted a subject from this mystery for a triptych. *L'Amante* explicitly linked the stolen paintings with the triptych." She paused before asking, "Miró, is it not likely that Gregori's legend is the same one that Mihàil described?"

"As likely as it is that *L'Amante* is the Dark *Irim* who inspired Caravaggio and Rembrandt to paint his own history."

That observation surprised Stasia. She sat back. "He said that I would find the third painting."

Now it was Miró's turn to sit back. He looked grim. "Then it is exactly as I suspected. *L'Amante* wants more than to seduce you. I fear that he wants to make you his acolyte."

***

Stasia and Miró left the B&B da Luisa after they'd eaten to head north towards the *Cittadella del Carnevale*, where the giant parade floats were displayed. The floats, inspired by international politics and other current events, were both art form and satire. As such, their creators competed for recognition as the best of both. The grand prize winner wouldn't be announced until *Martedì Grasso*, but the front runners included a float dedicated to migrants, one mocking the "jungle of laws" described as "burocrazy," and one representing China's newfound role as superpower.

Fortune had smiled on the festivities. It had been a sunny day, unusual for Viareggio at this time of year, and the night was mild. When they arrived at the open air "citadel," there was a crowd in the elliptical square bounded by the warehouses. Low mesh barriers had been erected around the floats, which sat in front of the open doors of their workshop bays. Some floats were lit from within with neon brightness; others were up lit.

Everywhere there were costumed performers dancing and musicians playing. Confetti and beads littered the pavement.

People of all ages wore masks and makeup, wigs and hats, though most of the colorful clothing was hidden under black jackets. Some danced, some took photos. Many held drinks.

As they walked together, Miró took Stasia's hand. She looked at him, but he didn't look back. Stasia wondered at the change. She felt Miró's harmonics through her own. They were increasingly tense, like the string of a bow slowly being drawn. And her harmonics responded in kind. For the first time she understood the recent spate of headaches that she'd been having.

She recalled how Miró had soothed her headache following the awakening of her *Elioud* senses. Perhaps she could do the same for him. She began humming as they threaded through the teeming square, envisioning as she did that strands of calming vibrations wound around Miró's fingers and wrist and then began coursing up his arm.

He looked down at her in surprise as they halted in front of the "Burocrazy" float that featured chimpanzees hanging from palm trees whose trunks resembled stacked books. The "Burocrazy" band performed a rock tune filled with heavy bass and drum.

How did you learn to do that?

Even though they were surrounded by raucous cheer, the intimacy of his voice in her thoughts made her feel as if they were alone.

Humming eases my head when it aches. I thought it might help you as you have done for me.

He squeezed her hand, sending vibrations careening back into her. In the vivid light of the nearby float, his pale blue eyes gleamed. Stasia had just realized that Miró's harmonics clanged along with the cymbals of the music when deep pain and anger reverberated within their conjoined harmonics. It was like a violent wind battering her on an exposed mountaintop.

Stasia swayed, planting her feet.

Before she could form a thought, he bent his head and kissed her.

Stasia's eyelids closed of their own accord, and she leaned into this beautiful and tortured man who made her breathless and furious all at once. He wrapped his free hand behind her head, pressing her against his chest as if he could inhale her. Raising her free hand to his jaw, she opened her mouth, her tongue flirting and teasing with his.

Somewhere nearby fireworks hissed and screamed into the sky before exploding. Stasia was scarcely aware of this soundtrack to the riotous harmonics trembling through her, gold and navy and ruby bands pulsing with her heartbeat.

A breath later, Miró's weight sagged. She stumbled and would have fallen except two hard arms caught her.

Her eyelids flew up. A myriad of fractured images pinged on her sight.

Miró, staggering as a large male pulled him away into the throng, which closed behind them.

A glimpse of a hard-looking female, rainbow wig and a diamond stud in one nostril. Another large male, oversized fuchsia beret and a black star painted around one eye.

She struggled, trying to kick, managing to connect with the female's thigh.

The crowd shifted away from them. Complaining voices questioned why drunks spoiled everything.

And then she felt a cold prick followed by an excruciating shock to her bare neck.

She collapsed, paralyzed, as the male flung her over his shoulder before carrying her from the square.

Fourteen

Seven minutes after the stun gun overloaded Miró's *Elioud* senses, they roared back—including his battle senses.

In fact, Miró flared.

His angelic nature emanated from him in a blinding white cloud that sent the people nearby into a stupor. All sound and movement ceased except for the periodic crash or thud as someone's numb grip let loose of a musical instrument or dropped whatever they were holding. Just beyond the radius of Miró's aura, people scattered, some shrieking. A few came closer, a look of wonder on their faces. Three or four elderly individuals sank to their knees and began to pray.

Miró had only a slight awareness of this human response to his angelic flare. The mercenary who gripped his upper arm wore earbuds and dark-tinted glasses. He didn't flinch or stumble. He kept towing Miró away from Stasia.

No.

Miró jerked his arm from the man's grip, sending him reeling. By the time his attacker recovered his balance, the superheated skin of Miró's face and hands steamed in the cool air.

The mercenary lunged at Miró, jabbing the stun gun at him. It was a heavy-duty law enforcement model with two sharp prongs designed to send electric current through clothing. The jolt punched Miró's chest and squeezed his heart, but he'd been ready for it this time. Instead of letting it shut down his senses or overwhelm thought, he shunted the electricity through his arms and into his hands.

And then clamped onto the mercenary's head.

The man screamed. The scent of ozone and burnt flesh saturated the air. Miró let go and yanked the stun gun from the mercenary's limp grip, flinging it to the side so hard that it shattered against the wall of the nearest warehouse.

The mercenary dropped to his knees, gasping. Raw red burns in the shape of fingers gave him a new, permanent Carnivale mask.

Pivoting Miró sped toward the spot that he and Stasia had stood kissing only minutes before.

She was gone. Even her harmonic signature had disappeared. Whoever had taken her had cloaked her in something like Fagan's anti-angelic armor.

Miró stalked back to the groaning mercenary, pulling him to his feet. He tugged an earbud out of the man's ear.

"Where are they taking her?"

The man glared at him and said nothing.

He didn't have time for the delicate art of reading the man's signatures while asking him carefully phrased questions. No, there was only time for brute force. Miró let his fingers grow hot again. The mercenary's jacket began to smoke.

The man looked at his arms one at a time. When he looked back at Miró, he sneered. "There's a small *bagno* south of here that's closed for the season."

"That narrows it down," Miró said. Savage irritation dried his tone. There were a couple dozen of the beach clubs on Viareggio's north beach. His fingers charred the layers of the jacket's sleeves. A few more seconds, and then he'd touch skin.

"*Bagno Pido,*" the mercenary said through clenched teeth.

"*Grazie.*" Miró let his radiant fingertips burn the man's flesh anyway, sending a disruptive burst of harmonics to silence the man's hoarse scream in response.

The mercenary fell unconscious to the pavement.

Miró took the time to go through the man's pockets, grabbing a smartphone, a wallet, and a key. Then, speeding up his harmonics so that he was invisible to the human eye, he gave his map app a voice command for directions to *Bagno Pido.*

It was just over three kilometers away.

Or about a minute if he ran.

***

The big male mercenary carrying Stasia dumped her into a hard-backed chair under the covered dining patio of a *bagno* that was closed for the season. He bent and pulled her hands behind the chair back, zip tying them together. A small groan escaped before she could stifle it. At the same time, the female wearing the rainbow wig knelt and zip tied her calves to the chair legs. She took Stasia's 9mm from her waist and handed it to the other mercenary. The effects of the stun gun were already starting to wear off, but whatever he'd injected her with had started to work.

And it felt wonderful.

Oh, santo cielo.

If she had to guess, the feeling of euphoria washing over her came from MDMA, better known in nightclubs the world over as Ecstasy.

But no version of Molly as it was also known was ever injected.

"Ah, it looks like the drug is taking effect." The speaker's Italian was accented. American, she thought.

Fagan.

Stasia tried to focus on the balding man standing three meters away, but the drug had altered her vision so that the bright light behind him hurt. She winced and looked down at the floor.

"Indeed," said the female, still kneeling next to her. She slid a hand down Stasia's calf and removed the smaller gun there. This she stuck at the back of her waist. Then she pulled the rainbow wig from her head and tossed it into the shadows. She had long, glossy dark hair that was shaved high on one side.

Somewhere in the darkness behind Stasia the male mercenary waited. She could feel him.

"And you're sure that she's more malleable now?"

Instead of answering, the female began massaging Stasia's thighs. Stasia looked at her, stunned to find that the caresses felt so good. She wanted to lean into those warm, strong fingers. The female smiled at her, delight lighting her gaze.

"You like that, yes?" The fingers moved up to her hip, kneading and sliding under her sweater to caress her bare skin.

Stasia began panting a little. She felt so warm.

The bald man addressed her again. "As a fellow intelligence officer, I'm sure you're aware that there's no such thing as truth serum. So put that out of your mind. I don't expect to compel the truth from you."

The female's daring fingers traced a delicate path along Stasia's midsection while she watched Stasia as closely as a hawk. Her gaze held a primeval lust. Stasia shut her eyes, willing her body to…what, she didn't honestly know. It felt so good sitting here in the dim, deserted restaurant while the female knelt before her, touching her with such familiar and sensual caresses.

"You see the Company has been experimenting with another formulation, one that induces trust and cooperation in the subject. Feelings of empathy and closeness, love even."

The female knelt up, her hands on Stasia's breasts now, palming them before rubbing her thumbs across both of Stasia's nipples. Stasia arched against the sensation.

"Of course, this version has been reformulated to address your unique biology, which can withstand higher temperatures than an ordinary human."

The female moved between Stasia's knees. "And which is more susceptible to sensory perceptions," she said, leaning in to lick Stasia's jaw.

Stasia swallowed hard. The female smelled enticing, a complex musk that immediately called up visions of naked, warm skin pressing against naked, warm skin among soft furs. She struggled against the zip ties, but even the bite of the plastic in her skin aroused her. As she moved, the female's perfume separated out into notes of caraway seed, dried rosebuds, amber, and patchouli, and a hint of sweat. Behind her closed eyelids, Stasia saw each of these scents as dimensional colors. As she watched, they began to play along her harmonics as skillfully as a concert harpist, sending her throbbing pleasure that pooled between her legs.

She slouched down, no longer fighting the intimate cocoon growing around her and the female, who now ran her hands through Stasia's hair.

"Your response is exquisite," the female said, humming. Her smoky voice had an edge. "Then again, you've been burning for someone for a long time. I'm only leveraging what already simmers inside you."

Stasia opened her eyes languorously. On her tongue now were the tastes of honey, burnt sugar, and a tang of bitter citrus. She felt both energized and relaxed.

Fagan spoke again. "My friend here has tweaked the drug with her own special prowess so that its effects are more potent and longer lasting."

Deep inside Stasia's mind, a voice, muffled as if behind a thick layer of glass, warned her. *It's not real. Don't trust Fagan. Don't trust her.*

But the female grasped her head and kissed her. Stasia's heart leapt, knocking into her ribcage. She scarcely noticed that her breath puffed from her in shallow gasps. The drug had sent her temperature soaring, and now the female's lips and fingers made her harmonics sing. The female sat back but continued stroking her fingertips along Stasia's bare arms.

Somewhere in the recesses of her thoughts, Stasia noted that sensation. She didn't recall what had happened to her coat, but it felt so, *so* good to have the cold air on her overheated flesh.

"She's ready," said the female, never taking her ravenous gaze from Stasia, who felt devoured and full of longing at the same time.

Fagan stepped closer. There was sharp avarice on his face that should have quelled Stasia's fever pitch, but it only stoked it higher. Steam rose around her.

Why had she thought that she burned for Miró?

"Stasia, I'm going to let my friend make you come. Over and over again. How would you like that?"

A guttural sound tore from Stasia's throat. She thrashed against the zip ties. Hot blood coated her wrists, tainting the air with copper. Even the sting of torn flesh sent a bolt of pleasure to her core.

And when I do, you won't be able to get enough of me, the female said inside her head. *You'll do and say anything that I want you to. You'll be mine forever.*

Stasia felt despair and exultation as the female leaned over her, her leather jacket pressed into Stasia's breasts. She wrapped one hand in Stasia's hair and tugged her head back before running the other hand up the inside of Stasia's thigh.

Stasia focused on the lascivious gaze.

Quando gli asini voleranno. When asses fly.

Then she head-butted the female.

***

Miró ignored the shock he felt as he came upon the tableau before him at the *Bagno Pido*. Stasia, naked from the waist up and with her arms and legs bound, sat transfixed while the woman he'd first seen leaving her apartment in Rome knelt next to her caressing her arms. Behind them stood the large male mercenary who'd dared to put hands on Stasia.

And three meters away stood Fagan, looking as though he had a front row seat to a sex act being performed just for him.

Miró's temperature spiked.

"She's ready," said the woman, whose husky voice set off an alarm.

If only he could see her eyes....

Instead, Stasia's infrared signature blazed white to his *Elioud* vision. She was becoming dangerously hot. If she'd been simply human, her organs would fail. As it was, she'd never been taught how to manipulate her temperature. She could still suffer permanent damage.

Fagan stepped closer. "Stasia, I'm going to let my friend make you come. Over and over again. How would you like that?"

A guttural sound tore from Stasia's throat. She thrashed against the zip ties. He could smell blood. Miró's muscles clenched, ready to act. Yet he withheld himself. It would not do to put Stasia in greater danger.

The woman leaned over Stasia as she grabbed her hair and ran another hand on the inside of Stasia's thigh.

Stasia locked gazes with her tormenter.

Quando gli asini voleranno, she flashed. Then she smashed her forehead into the other woman's face.

A beat later Miró leapt at Fagan as Stasia stood, the zip ties falling from her heated wrists and calves. She swung a vicious right uppercut at the reeling woman's torso.

In the next moment, he lost track of the battle between the two women. All of his senses locked onto Fagan, who turned as Miró tackled him. They crashed into a nearby table, the intelligence officer squirming like a fish to keep from being pinned under Miró.

Crashes of tables and chairs testified to the mayhem that followed. Infrared signatures and volatile harmonics roiled Miró as he managed to sit on Fagan's chest. Even as Fagan sought to dislodge him by bucking and twisting, Miró shoved his knees under the other man's arms.

A shot rang out.

Miró absorbed the sound but ignored it. He leaned into the high mount and delivered back-to-back reverse elbow strikes to Fagan's head. Fagan collapsed to the ground, unconscious. Miró jumped up and pivoted into a fighting stance. Stasia, beneath and partially entangled with the woman, managed to pull her pistol free and squeeze off a shot at the mercenary.

Miró lunged at him, taking the wounded man to the ground. He wrapped his arms and legs around the man, rolling to bring them both onto their sides. Blood smeared the floor. Miró slid, trying to bring a hand to the man's chin and another to his shoulder. Wounded though he was, the mercenary fought, placing a palm on the floor and levering them both up. Miró swung around onto the mercenary's back and managed to disrupt his harmonics enough that the mercenary wavered and collapsed. Like lightning, Miró hooked an arm under the man's neck and grabbed his chin. Pressing down on the man's shoulder, he yanked on his chin.

The mercenary stopped moving. His breath sighed from him. Miró didn't have to scan him to know that his infrared signature declined from white hot at its core to cool red.

Miró freed his arm and climbed from the body. He got up and went to Stasia, who still held the pistol in one hand, though she'd turned her head to the side and closed her eyes. He lifted the dead woman from her before pulling her into his arms.

Stasia's beautiful hazel eyes opened. The irises were huge. How she'd ever managed to shoot either of her kidnappers Miró could only guess. If he was right, she'd adapted to her harmonic senses incredibly swiftly.

"Miró," she said. She was unbearably hot.

Miró kissed her, siphoning heat from her and letting it dissipate from his skin. She raised a hand to his jaw, kissing him with a fervor that met the fire already burning in his blood.

He welcomed it.

***

Olivia Kastrioti woke into the silent dark, alert and alarmed. Something felt wrong, but Mihàil's warm bulk reassured her. She waited a moment to see if some sound or movement confirmed her instincts, but she heard nothing. She touched

Mihàil, running a light finger along his shoulder to his elbow before palming his massive upper arm. They had been married six months, yet it still hadn't quite sunk in. This gorgeous man was real, and he was all hers.

He sighed and draped a heavy, hot hand onto her hip. She wiggled a little, considering whether she should wake him up to show him that he was all hers when a faint *snick* from the hall reached her ears. If she hadn't been fine-tuning her *Elioud* senses for the past few weeks, she might not have caught it.

She carefully slid away from his hand.

"Where are you going, *dashuria ime?*" Mihàil's voice was rough with sleep.

Olivia leaned over and kissed him. "Nowhere." Then she kissed him again, whispering, "Go back to sleep."

He exhaled deeply and let her roll away. Though her senses still warned her that something was amiss, she suspected that it wasn't really anything much or the *drangùe*, whose battle senses had been honed over almost 600 hundred years, would have already been up and prowling around their house. It was more likely that her anxiousness about her new duties primed her to worry that she'd forgotten to check the security cameras or that the scripts running the system had updated with the latest routines. Although she could certainly handle the role of security chief while Miró was away, she would be relieved when he returned.

After getting out of bed, Olivia slipped her feet into fleece-lined mules and grabbed her robe from the chair next to her nightstand. Her eyes had adjusted to the dark now, enhanced by her newly trained *Elioud* vision. Besides reading the unique infrared signature of her sleeping husband, she could see a wider spectrum of colors and well in low light. She no longer needed the special goggles she'd used as a CIA officer to move freely at night.

Pulling the door closed gently, she left the master suite and stood on the landing outside scanning the family room to her right before turning toward the foyer on her left. Although she'd lived in this mansion for weeks and knew its interior as well as she'd known her one-bedroom flat in Vienna, she had yet to grow used to its size. It wasn't huge as some American homes were, but its sixty-five hundred square feet felt extravagant, especially in as poor a country as Albania. It didn't help that there were only three adults living here at the moment.

Some day that will change.

Olivia shoved the desire to start a family down and returned to the immediate concern.

The first floor was silent except for the hum of the refrigerator in the kitchen. Besjana hadn't come downstairs for a snack. No intruder moved around.

She hesitated. Perhaps she should just go back to bed. Now that she had more responsibilities toward a more meaningful mission and her *Elioud* team, she thrummed with tension. Her anxieties were playing tricks on her.

No. She needed to do a full security sweep even if she thought she was imagining things. It was her job, and she knew what it required.

Adjusting her harmonics so that she wouldn't be visible to the human eye, Olivia strode swiftly through the first floor checking the perimeter, even the ballistic windows. Nothing was out of place.

She arrived upstairs five minutes later. It only took a moment to identify what was wrong.

Besjana's room lacked her infrared signature.

Oh, there was something warm in her bed, but it wasn't her.

Olivia focused on Mihàil's office. It was empty, but an odd trace reverberation gave it an echo that no other empty room had. Someone had just been in there.

Pivoting, she scanned the media room, Miró's domain and home of their security system and servers.

Bingo.

Someone was inside, someone who was wearing something that hid her signatures. Unfortunately, whatever cloaked those left a black hole in the harmonic spectrum. Fagan's *bogomili* armor, which he'd used last summer, had been designed to reflect the harmonic vibrations around it, though it did so imperfectly. In a room filled with inanimate objects whose molecular vibrations were minimal and slowly degrading, such a garment would have nothing to reflect.

Olivia's anxiety melted into anger.

A moment later she stood behind Besjana, who leaned unaware over the keyboard to their main server, a USB drive inserted into the tower. The young Albanian woman wore a hooded cloak and gloves.

"Rather daring, don't you think? Trying to steal information from the *drangùe* while he sleeps?" Olivia kept her voice even, but she'd sent the extra heat from her anger into her fingertips.

Besjana whirled, a squeaky gasp coming from within the deep hood.

Olivia stared at her until Besjana pushed the hood back. She looked defiant, angry, and scared.

"I am doing this for the *drangùe* and for my country. You do not belong here."

"No," Olivia said, shaking her head, "you are doing it for *you*. And Joseph Fagan, who has no interest in helping Albania and certainly not the *drangùe*."

She looked over Besjana's shoulder at the server's monitor. The screen showed a utility window and a status bar. She recognized it. The traitorous servant had managed to copy an access card, which stored the private encryption key to the server, and had given access to Fagan's hacking toolkit on the thumb drive. Of course, the server's file system was also encrypted. But once the toolkit cracked that, the server and its valuable data would be open for plundering.

"Though perhaps you will end up helping your country after all," she said, smiling, as she reached for Besjana, who yelped as Olivia's heated fingers gripped her. "Let me show you how an *Elioud zonjë* gets the information that *she* needs."

Fifteen

By the time Miró had finished lowering Stasia's elevated body temperature from the drug that they'd injected into her, the CIA substation chief had recovered from the head blows he'd received and made it out of the *bagno*, leaving the bodies of his team behind. They had little time to lose getting out of Viareggio before Fagan tried again, no easy task given how late it was. And Stasia was still a long way from getting the drug out of her system, *Elioud* metabolism or no.

But first, he needed to clothe her.

Miró stripped the dead woman's shirt from her, avoiding touching the bullet entrance wound on her head. There was no exit wound, so very little blood. He helped Stasia to dress, allowing himself to notice the shape and size of her beautiful breasts before covering them. She sat shivering even after he found her coat and tugged it onto her. A powdery black ring of ash surrounded her on the planks of the wooden floor. He guessed that it was her sweater and bra.

He scanned the area for any telltale items, scooping up Stasia's backup gun from the floor and her main 9mm from the dead male mercenary's inside jacket pocket. Her small purse with its over-the-shoulder strap sat on a table. He slung the purse over her neck but stashed the guns in his own inner pocket. There was no reason to test their good luck further by having her try to wield either.

The B&B da Luisa was a fifteen-minute car ride to the south. If he'd been alone, he would have simply run it and been there before Fagan could even locate his other team member at the *Cittadella*. Instead he needed to find someone offering a ride share. So he took a few precious seconds to swipe open the app on his smartphone. On impulse he requested a ride to Marseille, which was an hour south of Aix-en-Provence. If his guardian angel was looking out for them, surely someone was headed that way.

Kneeling, he stroked the hair from her face and tucked it behind her ears. "We need to go now, *dušo*."

She looked at him. Her irises were still huge, making her look like some subterranean creature. "Soul?" She sounded confused at his use of the Croatian endearment for sweetheart.

Ignoring her question, Miró bent and lifted her into his arms. Her own came around his neck. It felt so right holding her this way. Her perfume wafted to his nose. He wanted to bury his face in her hair and inhale, but she shivered again. She'd lost the ability to regulate her temperature. Clenching his jaw, he adjusted her weight to bring her closer and modulated his temperature so that hers followed. He'd have to keep her as close as possible until the drug was gone, and he had no idea when that would be.

His cellphone chimed. The ride-share app had sent a text notification that there was a ride available to Marseille.

Thank you, he said to Zophiel.

Then he exited the *bagno* and headed for a busy restaurant that he'd passed on his way from the *Cittadella del Carnevale*. It wouldn't do for the driver to pick them up at a business closed for the season. One with two bodies and a chaotic mess.

An Audi sedan pulled up a couple of minutes after they arrived outside the restaurant with the ride-share sticker in the front window.

Please let me handle this, he said to Stasia.

She tightened her hold on his neck and nuzzled his jaw. *Are you taking me to bed finally?*

Miró ran a hand down her back, pressing her close. *I am taking you to safety. Trust me, dušo.*

Always.

Miró acknowledged the driver and confirmed the destination before opening the back door to set Stasia on the seat. He buckled her in and then went around to the other side to get in.

"Too much carnival?" the driver asked in a French accent as he pulled away. He appeared to be of Algerian descent, a common ethnic background in Marseille, home to waves of immigrants from North Africa, especially Algeria, a former French colony.

"*Oui*," Miró said, shifting to French and a carefully cultivated accent that matched someone from Provence, specifically from Toulon, a port on the Mediterranean coast sixty-five kilometers east of Marseille. His *Elioud* charm helped with the deception. "My wife does not normally drink anything but wine, but you know how it goes. So many people, the music and dancing. It is easy to go beyond the everyday, yes?"

"Ah," the man said, nodding. "Why do you not stay in Viareggio then?"

"That would be ideal. Sadly, we must return for work tomorrow, but our friends"—here he gestured toward the restaurant—"they have decided to stay. Can you drive us to the B&B da Luisa so that we can gather our bags? There is an extra 50 euros in it for you." He laced his request with a little more *Elioud* charm.

"Of course, *monsieur*." The driver sounded downright happy to drive an extra half an hour out of his way.

Miró gave him the address and then slid closer to Stasia, who sat looking out of the side window with unseeing eyes. He put an arm around her and pressed close, adjusting his temperature again so that she again cooled down. It was like sitting next to a brick oven.

When they approached the bed and breakfast, Miró asked the driver to go to their room and get their bags, which neither of them, as seasoned operatives, had unpacked. He only had to feed a little more *Elioud* charm and another 20 euros into the request. While the driver left the Audi to idle next to the golden-yellow building, Miró scanned the dark for infrared signatures in case Fagan had set someone to watch.

In fact, there was a single infrared signature in a car just across and down the narrow residential street from the bed and breakfast's gated driveway. He debated whether he should leave Stasia and handle the threat. On the one hand, anyone observing wouldn't be certain that the vague forms in the backseat were the target. On the other hand, the longer the operative sat there watching the longer it would take Fagan to learn more about their movements.

Perhaps he could split the difference....

"I will be back momentarily," he said to Stasia, who'd turned unfocused eyes on him.

She laid a hand on his arm. *Promise?*

"Never doubt it."

Opening the door, he slid out and shut it gently behind him.

Speeding his harmonics he moved toward the occupied car faster than human sight could follow. When he reached it, he knelt and unscrewed the front tire's air valve, pocketing the cap before pressing the valve stem to release air until the tire was flat. Then he moved around to the other side and did the same to a back tire. Two flat tires would slow any pursuit.

Miró returned to the waiting Audi only moments before their driver, whistling, popped the trunk and dropped their bags inside. Stasia was again shivering despite the heated car and her warm coat. He unbuckled her seatbelt and pulled her onto his lap where he could wrap both arms around her. She turned and burrowed into his coat, sighing. After fifteen minutes or so, she eased into sleep, her temperature stable as he held her. Perhaps she would sleep away the rest of the drug's effects.

Or perhaps not. Fagan would have accounted for her *Elioud* metabolism in dosing her.

Miró looked down at Stasia. In sleep her features seemed delicate, almost fragile. He smiled and touched the dimple in her chin with a light fingertip. She was so fierce and confident much of the time that he forgot how small and vulnerable she actually was.

They made good time on the dark, nearly empty highway that ran along the Italian coast. Miró chatted with the driver for part of the drive, aware that the man likely accepted the ride-share request as a way to keep himself awake. It would be best to use that to their advantage by crafting a spontaneous legend. So he kept his talk to pleasantries and vagueness, weaving a myth about him and Stasia as a married couple. They had, he said, met last summer during a work event between their respective employers. It had been love at first sight. Despite that, this was their first trip alone.

"Ah, *monsieur*, you should have stayed in Viareggio then," the driver said. "You need time alone to make love to your wife, to stay late in bed telling each other secrets."

Miró looked out the side window as he answered. It was dark and moonless, but his *Elioud* vision enabled him to see the Mediterranean, cold and gray and unfathomable. They would reach Genoa soon. "Ah, but you see, we have not yet told our employers that we have married. And we are in the middle of a very important project."

The man shook his head. "No work is more important than the work of the heart. That is the trouble with modern society! Too many put work ahead of their marriage. You each serve another master when together you could serve a greater cause."

Miró dropped his gaze to the sleeping Stasia. Her mouth had parted slightly. He wanted to kiss her. "Perhaps," he murmured. He closed his eyes and dropped his head back onto the seat behind him. He didn't want to be lectured anymore by a stranger. A stranger who had no idea about the angelic warfare going on around him.

When they reached Genoa about midnight, the driver pulled into a 24-hour Esso station. As he was pumping gas, Miró's cellphone rang. He pressed his Bluetooth earbud to answer. It was Olivia.

"Miró, thank God! I tracked your cellphone to Genoa. Please tell me you're with Stasia and she's safe."

"I am, and she is." Miró shifted Stasia from his lap onto the seat next to him. "What has happened?"

"Fagan recruited Besjana. He used her to plant a tracker on Stasia."

"That explains much." Though not what the female mercenary had been doing in Stasia's Rome apartment. "He has tried twice to take her, once in Rome and once in Viareggio. Did Besjana tell you where she put it?"

"On Stasia's St. Michael medal, the one she never wears but always brings with her."

"Wait a moment."

Miró opened his door and got out. He nodded at the driver, who eyed him, and gestured toward the trunk. The man nodded and clicked the trunk remote on his keychain. Miró waved and ducked under the lid to rummage through Stasia's bag. He found the small velvet pouch in an inner pocket. He opened the pouch and shook the medal into his palm. Turning it over, he saw the micro GPS tracker attached to its back. He pulled it off and was about to drop it onto the pavement to step on it when another thought struck him.

Slamming the trunk lid shut, he said to the driver as he walked toward the Esso market, "I will get us two strong black coffees."

The man's large white teeth split his face. "*Un gran merci!*"

Miró nodded and headed toward the Esso market.

"Please continue, my lady."

"Besjana told Fagan about you and Stasia."

Miró frowned. "Told him what exactly?"

He pushed open the door to the market, scanning the interior for a suitable target.

Olivia sighed. "That you and Stasia are fighting an attraction for one another. I suspect that Fagan intends to exploit that knowledge somehow."

There. A couple of young men studying the snack aisle would do nicely.

"In Viareggio, his team managed to grab her and bring her to him. He drugged her with something before I could get her back. It raised her body temperature."

Miró walked by the young men, slipping the GPS tracker into one man's coat pocket as he did. He continued on to the small coffee bar.

"That sounds like Ecstasy. The Agency has been using it during interrogations, though it hasn't proven to be any more reliable than other psychoactive drugs except in treating field operatives who suffer post-traumatic stress."

Miró ordered two black coffees and turned away from the bar so that the attendant couldn't overhear.

"When I came upon them, Stasia was half naked and an operative was ... physically manipulating her. Fagan threatened her with repeated sexual release." He delivered this statement dispassionately, but a tic started behind his left eye and his core temperature spiked.

There was a long silence on the call. Miró paid for the coffees and was at the door to the market before Olivia finally spoke.

"That vile excuse for a human being."

"Do not expect me to allow him to live once we determine what Asmodeus plans for the paintings."

"Copy that."

"Has András or Beta checked in?"

"No. Mihàil wants to give András as much leeway as necessary to show Beta that he can be trusted. You and Stasia keep Fagan busy while they recover the Caravaggio."

"He has to guess that we are headed for France."

"Has she told you yet why she wants to go there?"

"She thinks that there is a third painting that forms a secret triptych. She hopes to find more information in Aix-en-Provence where the Caravaggio was found."

"Keep me updated. We can be in Aix-en-Provence in eight hours if you need us."

"Copy that."

Miró had gotten into the Audi after handing the driver his coffee when Olivia said, "And Miró? Don't let Fagan get near Stasia again or you'll have me to answer to."

***

From Genoa they drove another four hours before arriving in Toulon around 6 a.m. It was *L'heure bleue*, "the blue hour," whose ambient light inspired painters, poets, and photographers. The twilight of *L'heure bleue*, whether at dawn or dusk, had always been Miró's favorite time of day. He remembered his childhood in Split with something approaching tranquility then. Today the magic of *L'heure bleue* transformed their drive along the French Riviera, lulling him. He let himself pretend that he and Stasia were a couple traveling on a romantic holiday. A stolen honeymoon.

He looked down at her as she leaned against him, the gleaming warm brown of her hair slipping in waves over her profile. Sweet *Elohim*, she was beautiful.

Mihàil had agents all over Europe, some of whom had more than a trace of *Elioud* blood. He'd contacted one of his French agents, who left a car for Miró and Stasia in Toulon, adding some misdirection in case Fagan identified their ride-share driver, whose account logged them as going to Marseille. Unless he went so far as to track down the driver, he would never know that they'd been dropped off without reaching the second largest city in France.

Mihàil's agent had also arranged a place for them to stay in Saint-Cyr-sur-Mer, a small city half an hour west of Toulon, where they could rest, eat, and plan their next steps. Though it was too early in the year for tourists or swimming, the agent had rented a two-bedroom villa a short walk from the beach. Fagan would have a nearly impossible time tracking their location, while any operatives who might come sniffing around would stand out. It was the modern equivalent to cutting down all the trees within an arrow's distance of castle walls: no enemy could sneak up on them.

The ride-share driver transferred their bags while Miró woke Stasia, whose irises were still larger than normal, in order to get her into their car. He handed her a drink with electrolytes and told her to drink it. Then he tipped the ride-share driver well but not exorbitantly, using his *Elioud* charm to leave the man with a vague memory of a pleasant overnight drive with a married French couple.

As they drove toward Saint-Cyr-sur-Mer, Stasia yawned and ran fingers through her hair. Miró suddenly had an image of her waking up next to him in bed. She looked at him.

"Last night is a blur of colors and scents and textures. I cannot recall what happened after you kissed me at the *Cittadella.*" Her voice was husky and strained. Good. She was coming out of the drug-induced trance, fighting it in fact.

"You were kidnapped and drugged with Ecstasy by a team that Fagan led. I managed to extract you before much happened. We drove all night and are about an hour from Marseille now."

Stasia frowned.

"*Ma naturalmente,*" she said to herself. She looked at him again. "You have been helping me to cool down. You are still helping me to control my temperature."

"Yes." He looked straight ahead. "Olivia had our asset pick up some things for you to take to help you recover from the Ecstasy. But she checked with a contact at the CIA, who told her that the Americans have modified the MDMA structure to exacerbate memory loss during interrogations of hostile agents."

He felt her hand on his gripping the steering wheel. He glanced at her.

"*Grazie.*"

"*Ma naturalmente,*" he said, echoing her earlier 'but of course.' He looked ahead again. "I suspect that Fagan tweaked the formula even more to target your *Elioud* biology. And I believe that the woman interrogating you was in fact Asmodeus's vessel."

"Asmodeus's vessel?" Stasia sounded confused.

"Asmodeus inhabited the woman's body, overriding her will. It allows him more direct physical interaction with humanity, but it comes at a great cost. He will need some time to recover."

"But that suggests that he is already close to full strength now," she said slowly.

"Or very motivated to take the risk."

"Or both."

"Or both," he agreed. "Of course Ecstasy boosted his natural talents, shall we say."

"Are we driving on to Aix-en-Provence now?"

Miró shook his head. "No. We have a villa where we can eat and change and clear the rest of the Ecstasy from your system."

"And discuss the divine mystery written about in the book."

He nodded. "And discuss the divine mystery written about in the book."

The sun was still an hour from rising when they reached the villa in Saint-Cyr-sur-Mer within walking distance of Lecques Beach. A white fence enclosed the small grounds with a double gate barring entrance to the paver driveway. The grounds were small and the landscaping minimal so that no one could enter and approach without being seen.

Miró walked through the entire villa while Stasia used the toilet and washed her face. He liked what he saw. Aix-en-Provence was only an hour by car, so they would remain here while they learned more about the mysterious triptych and why Asmodeus and Fagan wanted the paintings. Through it all he would try to convince Stasia to join their *Elioud* team, even though he wasn't sure what that meant for him personally.

If the last day had done nothing else, it had confirmed that Stasia was in great danger from two Dark *Irim*: Asmodeus and Yeqon, an *Irim* so seductive that he'd convinced other angels to disobey God.

And he was beginning to suspect that preventing Fagan from taking Stasia had far greater consequences than winning yet another skirmish against dark angelic forces.

Stasia joined him in the main room, which included a sofa and a small table next to a wide opening to the kitchen. She looked a little more alert and her hair was brushed, but her temperature was still above normal and her harmonics had an odd thrum in them.

"There is only a single double bed."

Miró frowned. "There are two bedrooms."

"The other bedroom has bunkbeds."

He shrugged and turned toward the kitchen.

"I will sleep on a bunkbed. Or better still, I will sleep out here on the sofa where I am close to the front door."

"No."

Stasia stood right behind him.

Miró turned, his heart beating fast. The temperature in the villa had risen fifteen degrees.

"Do you know how I resisted Asmodeus's vessel?" she asked, standing so close that her harmonics hummed along his skin, causing his aura to jump and spark.

She placed her palm on his chest, and his harmonics sung at the touch. This time the smoky vanilla that rose from her warm skin made him think only of her and no ghosts from the past.

He swallowed hard. "No."

"When she spoke in my thoughts and told me that I would not be able to get enough of her, I knew that she was wrong. Because I had no desire for her. I desire only you, Miró Kos."

Stasia stood on her toes and pulled his mouth down to hers. The banked fire in his blood combusted.

When at last she pulled away, she said in a husky voice, "And I am not at all sure that I will get enough of you."

Sixteen

Miró's glacial eyes burned Stasia at her declaration of intent. His irises dilated and for a heartbeat she wondered if she'd gone too far.

And then he bent down and lifted her into his arms, where she'd never felt more safe.

He didn't take his gaze from her, somehow navigating the few meters through the kitchen and down the hallway to the one bedroom with a bed large enough for two. He carried her to the bed and laid her on it. Standing back, he looked at her, his gaze roving over every centimeter of her, devouring her. The remnants of Ecstasy in her blood burned away.

He knelt beside the bed and laid his head on her chest, his breathing harsh. She ran her hand through his hair. When he raised his head to look at her, she saw their harmonics braided and moving in time with their heartbeats. A warm glow emanated from him, slowly enveloping her. She had the strangest sensation of that glow seeping into her skin, drawing her closer.

Everything else in the room faded into nothing before the intensity of his gaze. Stasia welcomed it. She placed her palm on his jaw moments before he kissed her, filling her nostrils with the heated scent of him: bergamot, leather and sage dominated by ash. If she'd been hot before, she burned deep in her chest now. A shimmer of heat rose from Miró, dancing with her own heat. When he pulled her shirt from her, her bare nipples tightened almost painfully.

Miró tugged his shirt over his head, revealing a well-formed chest with dark hair. Stasia touched it reverently, tracing gentle fingertips over his collarbone, pectoral muscles, and flat abdomen. He watched her face, his gaze predatory now. Reaching his waist, she brought her hand back to his chest and smoothed her palm over his heart. It beat hard and fast under her touch. The early morning sun caught the light sheen of sweat on his skin, intensifying her desire.

Miró touched her breast as reverently as she'd touched his chest. She watched as he traced light fingertips over her, leaving gooseflesh in their wake. He cupped her breast, gently rubbing her nipple with his thumb. She arched into his palm, moaning a little. Need stabbed deep in her groin and her core became so swollen and wet that her panties constricted her flesh. Still Miró took his time, savoring and memorizing every square centimeter of her, his gaze absorbed and worshipful. Stasia basked in its warmth, holding her desire at bay.

"We are meant to be one," he said at last, his hand trailing over to cup her other breast, "both physically and spiritually. As part of our calling, the Archangel Michael enjoined the *Elioud* to remain chaste. When we make love, we will be subverting that charge."

Withdrawing his hand, he looked up at her, his intense gaze both enthralling and electrifying. How had she ever thought it cold and distant?

"I will not make you follow the Archangel's mandate, but know this: there will be no other for me whether we make love or not."

Stasia swallowed hard. Her heart danced in her ribcage, both joyful and tremulous. Tears pricked her eyes. She raised her hand to his face, holding his gaze so that he could see the truth there.

He leaned down and kissed her, his tongue encouraging her lips to open. A moment later she felt his chest pressing against hers, the wiry hair abrading her bare skin and stoking the fire in her. She sighed into his mouth as she raised her arms around his neck. He groaned and slipped his arms around her, pulling her close while he stroked her flank before cupping her breast again. A moment later he dragged his mouth from hers and kissed her jaw, along the line of her neck to her collarbone, and farther down until he reached her breast. Stasia sucked her breath in, her hands twisting in his hair and holding his head to her.

After a long, sweetly tortuous moment, he leaned back and stood, unbuttoning his slacks and sliding them and his briefs to the floor. He stepped out of them without breaking his gaze on hers and stood upright.

The breath rushed from her at the sight. Miró had the sculpted proportions and ethereal air of a warrior seraph: perfect and deadly. The earlier warm glow flared into a brilliant nimbus around him.

"You are so beautiful," she said, suddenly fearful of the magnitude of their joining.

He dropped to his knees, taking her hands in his and kissing them before capturing her mouth again with his, one hand tangled in her hair. The other hand found the button at her waist. When she would have broken the kiss, he gripped her head and plunged his tongue into her mouth. Stasia met his ardor with her own, scarcely aware of her pants skimming down her legs.

After that Miró's weight blanketed her. His harmonics hummed along her skin, slowly and gently at first. They paused in anticipation, and then as he moved inside her, they merged with her harmonics until she didn't know where she ended and he began. The humming became a liquid melody, both familiar and wholly new.

And Miró was the maestro conducting it.

He led her in a slow rhythm, his fingers entwined with hers and his mouth possessing hers. She breathed in and it was his breath. She breathed out, and he breathed her in. And then when she had the rhythm, he began to speed the tempo, his harmonics playing along her skin as if she were a harp and he a virtuoso.

Her body sang. It reached for a high, pure note that she only just now sensed was possible.

Stasia broke free of Miró's kiss to meet him, to challenge him, to take the lead in their unfolding duet. To reach that sweet, high note. She pulled her hands from his to grip his shoulders. She clasped her legs around his waist. She panted, and he panted in sync. Miró's haunting blue gaze never left her face.

Their conjoined harmonics thickened the heated air around and between them.

And still she urged him to strive for that resounding high note, until their urgent duet reached a crescendo.

For a piercing, sweet moment their harmonics resonated a pure, unadulterated tone as if an angelic tuning fork had been struck.

And the axis of Stasia's entire existence shifted.

***

They lay entwined, damp and breathless, as the morning sun filled the villa's bedroom.

Stasia smoothed the gray hair at Miró's temple. How had he, an *Elioud*, earned it? Beyond the tiny lines at the corners of his eyes, it was his one visible imperfection.

"You have not always been chaste."

Miró's eyes opened. His irises, rimmed in dark blue-gray, drew her. She couldn't look away.

"No. There was a time when I resented the Archangel's command."

Olivia had told her once that Miró had been abducted by the Ottoman Turks when he was a young boy, forced to dress as a girl and dance seductively, and fought over by pederasts.

"Because you had already had your innocence violated. You wanted control over your body and the right to make your own choices."

He nodded but didn't look away. There was deep, old pain in the depths of his gaze.

Sorrow filled her. She'd wrongly assumed that it was ancient history, that it had nothing to do with them.

"After Mihàil bought me from the *köçek* troupe and released me from service, I felt safe at first because of the Archangel's requirements. But eventually I found them too restrictive. What did it matter whether I indulged my body's urges? I was damaged goods anyway."

Stasia said nothing but traced his side with her fingernails. There was a raised scar under his arm that suggested a perilous wound, perhaps from a *subulam*, the wicked pointed dagger wielded by *bogomili*. She'd seen Miró fight many times. He was an intense, laser-focused warrior whose graceful movements echoed his history as a trained dancer. His syncopated style kept him away from most danger.

Of course, that hadn't stopped *her* from wrapping her *surujin* around him or slicing her dagger across his arm. And there was that time she'd had to rescue him from a *bogomili* trying to choke him to death.

Miró was neither invulnerable nor aloof.

He sighed and linked his fingers through hers, looking at their joined hands. "About a hundred years ago, I left Mihàil to return to Croatia, just in time for the start of World War I as it happens."

He hummed a tune. She recognized *'O surdato 'nnammurato*, the famous Neapolitan love song from the First World War in which a soldier on the front lines pines for his sweetheart. It was often sung to a rather upbeat orchestration with lots of audience clapping during the chorus, but after a moment Miró began to sing in a slow, heartfelt tenor:

> *You are far from this heart,*
> *To you I fly with my thought:*
> *I want nothing and nothing I hope*
> *But to always keep you next to me!*
> *Be sure of this love*
> *As I am sure of you....*

He trailed off, leaving a wistful note lingering on the air. Stasia wondered about the woman who'd broken his heart, this ice man of hers.

"It was not as jauntily romantic then as they sing it for the Napoli football team now," Stasia said, remembering the soccer games she'd attended as a young woman.

Miró shook his head. "Perhaps at first it seemed that way, when the song was written. Young men went off to war dreaming of heroics."

"Not so heroic to march against a former ally simply to claim land because some of the inhabitants speak your language."

Stasia had been a student of history, especially the early twentieth century, which had such a direct impact on her own family history. Her great-grandfather had served as an officer on the Italian Front during World War I. If he hadn't, he would never have met her great-grandmother in Treviso when he was wounded.

Miró shrugged. "What did the soldiers know of backroom diplomatic deals? They only knew that they fought for their country."

"Is that what happened to you? Did you fight to free your countrymen from the grip of the evil Austro-Hungarian Empire?"

"More to keep my countrymen from exchanging one foreign master with yet another."

Early in the war, Italy had seized on its chance to take some of Austria's land along the Adriatic, including land that now belonged to Croatia. As happened at the Western Front, instead of winning decisive battles against the Austrians, the Italians ended up fighting in trenches, their overwhelming numbers and professional officer corps unable to make up for a lack of arms and supplies. In the Alps that meant tunneling into mountainsides at high altitudes and facing very cold winters. Thousands of soldiers died in avalanches, some natural, many not. Thousands of displaced civilians died from starvation and illness in refugee camps.

In the end, the Italians won. In addition to the land taken in battle, they seized control of northern Dalmatia, which was ethnically Croatian but long fought over by outside empires — despite the fact that Croatia had declared independence from

Austria-Hungary, and its troops had started deserting, disobeying orders, and retreating. It was after World War II before Dalmatia was reunited with the rest of Croatia.

Had Miró been one of those faithless troops? She didn't think so.

"I was in Trieste before the Italians declared war on Austria-Hungary in May 1915, infiltrating the local irredentists, who often met in cafés to talk politics and plot their escape to Italy. At that time, it was very popular for female singers to perform arias in cafés."

"*Si*, Trieste remains the city of coffee with many historic cafés. My great-grandmother sang there before the Fourth War of Independence. The café is still there in the Piazza Unitá d'Italia."

"The Café degli Specchi." *The Coffee Shop of Mirrors*. "Franz Lehár directed concerts there."

Stasia pulled her hand from Miró's and sat up, moving away from his warm embrace as she did. How did he know?

Miró held her gaze. There was sadness and resignation. "I fell in love for the first time with the soprano who sang his *Vilja* from 'The Merry Widow.'"

"*La Sciantosa*." Stasia heard the dawning horror in her voice. Miró had used that word at the Kastrioti compound. He'd been referring to her great-grandmother.

"Yes."

"*You* are the Croatian officer who courted her on the eve of the war."

He nodded, watching her closely. Stasia suddenly felt as though she couldn't breathe. Her heartrate and harmonics sped up. She closed her eyes, raising fingers to massage her temples.

"How long have you known?" she whispered.

"I have only known for sure since last night when I found your St. Michael medal, but I suspected it last summer when I recognized your dagger."

"*Non capisco.*" Her accent thickened.

She was a highly skilled operative, used to sudden revelations and shifting situations, but her mind had shut down.

"Olivia called. Fagan had a mole in the Kastrioti household, the servant girl Besjana. She put a micro tracker on your St. Michael medal. When I removed it, I realized that the medal is the same one that I gave to your great-grandmother."

Stasia shivered. Standing, she began dressing.

Miró didn't say anything. He swung his legs over the bed and began to dress also.

Stasia bent to unzip her bag. She couldn't put the sweater that Asmodeus's vessel had worn back on. And she needed a bra. She needed to be fully dressed. In fact, she needed a weapon. Pulling out a bra and a blouse, she donned them before shoving her feet into walking shoes. When she turned, Miró wore a clean shirt and dark pants. His impassive gaze told her nothing.

"That does not explain Nonno's dagger."

"British commandos used the BC-41 for only a short time at the start of World War Two. It was replaced with a different combat knife. But your grandfather was an officer in the Royal Italian Army who hated the fascists. When Mussolini was arrested, he managed to escape the Germans and join a partisan guerrilla band that included Britons. That's how he got the BC-41."

A wave of dizziness washed over Stasia. Before she knew it, Miró had a hand under her elbow.

"*Dušo*, please. Come to the kitchen. You can be upset with me all you want there, but let me make you some breakfast."

"I am not hungry."

Miró tipped her chin so that she was looking at him. She felt warmth and steadying harmonics play along her skin.

"You need hydration, specific supplements, and food. And then you need to rest. You may have the metabolism of an *Elioud*, but Fagan designed his drug to account for that. Please let me take care of you."

Stasia let Miró's harmonics ease her tension and emerging headache. He slipped his hand down to take hers. She followed as he led her to a barstool at the counter facing the small galley kitchen.

She watched as he gathered items to feed her. There was something appealing about his untucked button-down shirt and bare feet. For a moment, she was ravenous, and it had nothing to do with food. She wanted *this*. She wanted to wake up next to Miró, make breakfast together in their kitchen, and then spend their days together in domestic routine.

But he'd known her great-grandmother Beatrix, whose stage name was Serafina.

In fact, if family legend were true, Miró was in actuality her great-grandfather.

He put a glass of orange juice and a small pile of pills in front of her. "MDMA depletes your body of nutrients. These will help you recover. That and water and rest."

Stasia poked at the pills. "What are they?"

She took a sip of juice and found that it tasted exceptionally good. She drained the glass. Miró brought the juice bottle and poured another full glass.

"Vitamin C"—he waggled the bottle—"and here"—he picked up a tablet and handed it to her.

Stasia popped it into her mouth and chased it with some juice.

"Vitamin E and something called 5-HTP to help your brain make serotonin."

After identifying each pill, he handed it to her. She dutifully took each and swallowed it with juice.

Miró returned to the kitchen and removed eggs, milk, and butter from the refrigerator. She watched as he broke several eggs, whipping them with a little milk before scrambling them in butter. While the eggs were cooking, he brought her a glass of milk, a banana, and dark chocolate. Then he toasted bread and layered it with smoked salmon on a plate next to a large serving of eggs.

"Let me guess," she said, watching every movement, longing for his hands to touch her. "A meal high in tryptophan?"

"Yes." He set a plate in front of her before making a plate for himself. He sat next to her. "All things considered, I would rather you were angry at me than sad and depressed."

"That can be arranged." She took a bite of her eggs and toast. For such a simple meal, it tasted delicious. "But my feelings will take some time to sort out and are not the primary reason we are here."

"Olivia has asked us to keep Fagan occupied while András and Beta recover the Caravaggio."

"Ah. We must play a little cat-and-mouse with Fagan."

Miró nodded. "The trick will be remaining the cat. Asmodeus has had his hands on you now, even if through the intermediary of a vessel. He has identified your harmonic signature. We will need to work together to hide it from him."

He took her hand and held her gaze. "So in fact your feelings may be the most important factor in the success of our mission."

***

Asmodeus felt hollow, like a pale, enervated shadow. His head ached. At least this time the *Elioud* cunt hadn't poked his vessel in the eyes. He'd expended a great deal of hard-won energy on possessing the human female only to have his hold broken abruptly, but he wasn't in a coma.

His acolyte had brought him to Marseille to recover. It hadn't been hard to guess that the *Elioud* couple was headed to France where the two Watcher Angel paintings had been found. More than likely they would show up in Aix-en-Provence, the City of Art. Even if Yeqon's third painter had never set foot in Aix-en-Provence, it would be just like his brother *Irim* to leave gleeful clues about the triptych there.

Now Asmodeus waited in the waning hours of nightlife at a club outside the city center, watching the increasingly wild dancing, fueled by drugs and desperation. Soon predators would snatch their prey. Already he could see the dangerous glint in their eyes as they circled their marks.

European Capital of Culture indeed.

It had been a long time since he'd had to identify and stalk targets to satisfy his lust. But the casual wanton milieu of this international port city presented him with a veritable buffet.

What was the French idiom? Ah. *Le faire les doigts dans le nez.* As easy as doing it with your fingers in your nose.

The loud, thumping dance music and flashing lights only added to his anticipation.

Asmodeus's radar alerted him when a male left his mates and approached two females dancing together. He read their harmonic and heat signatures so well it was as if he could read their minds. After several minutes, the group moved to the entrance. The male's pack mates followed with the Dark *Irim* gliding in their wake.

He laughed to himself when the startled females realized that there were four males who wanted sex instead of one. He loved plot twists.

Especially when *he* was the plot twist.

But the females found the prospect titillating. No matter, he could supply the *je ne sais quoi* that made the encounter something truly exciting. For him.

There was, after all, a special room for game play with all sorts of toys at the first male's apartment.

And with the right encouragement and some of that wonderful Ecstasy his acolyte had gifted him, Asmodeus would ensure that it went farther than any but he and the first male intended.

Seventeen

The Hungarian ate copious amounts of food constantly. He was eating right now while they sat in a vehicle watching the *bogomili* compound in Skopje. Beta inhaled slowly and deeply. The scent of warm *burek*, a Macedonian pastry filled with ground meat, wove through András's own scent of black currant, smoky balsam, and magnolia. It made her feel hollow. Ravenous.

It irritated the hell out of her.

She slid the karambit open and closed. The glide and soft *snick* as it did eased her irritation.

"If you're hungry, I'll share."

Beta looked over her shoulder at the giant *Elioud*. His hair needed a cut. It fell in waves across his forehead and curled against his neck.

Perhaps the edge of the karambit blade could trim it for him....

She snorted and looked out the passenger window again.

"I can hear your stomach grumble, Gomba."

"That is not my stomach you hear grumbling."

He laughed. She sensed him wiping his fingers on his jeans before he drank from a water bottle, the plastic bottle crackling as it collapsed. He burped and gave a sigh of satisfaction.

Beta looked back against her better judgment and caught him looking at her. He winked.

"I am perplexed as to how you manage to track anyone given your devotion to eating."

"Ah, but it's exactly because I'm such an excellent tracker that I need to eat. How else would you know that the *bogomili* bastard is here with the Caravaggio?"

He was right, but Beta couldn't resist poking his inflated sense of self.

"The tracking tag that the VZ put on the frame?"

András scowled. "You know full well that tag was disabled before the *bogomili* crossed the Czech border."

"Hm," she said. "But not before Czech security pinpointed the vehicle carrying it. It was a simple operation from there to correlate that with toll cameras, which led to the license plate …"

"And your colleagues are still trying to identify the operator of the stolen vehicle that was abandoned in Budapest while I brought us here, right outside the very building where the *bogomili* scum is *currently*."

Beta shrugged her shoulder and waved her hand, which held the karambit. It sailed under his nose, but he didn't flinch. "Details. It is only a matter of time before the VZ gets here."

"But you don't want to wait for the VZ, do you?" he asked, his voice soft. "Where would be the fun in that?"

Beta narrowed her eyes and refused to answer. She turned back to the compound where armed guards were visible.

"Does Kastrioti have any influence here?" she asked instead.

The Čair district of Macedonia's capital city where the *bogomili* compound was located had an Albanian majority. In fact, a statue honoring Gjergj Kastrioti stood in Skanderbeg Square facing Albania. Many thought that showed a desire for a unified Albanian state.

"Some." She sensed his shrug. "It's complicated."

"Of course it is. It is unlikely that they would submit to the current Kastrioti's leadership style."

That was an understatement. It had been little more than fifteen years since the local Albanian population had created an Albanian National Liberation Army and rose up in armed conflict against the Macedonian government. More recently Macedonian anti-terrorist law enforcement had busted a cell for recruiting people to fight in Iraq and Syria or join other foreign paramilitary forces. Recruits tended to come from Albanian enclaves in the north and west. And no one was under the illusion that the Macedonian authorities had shut the spigot off. Not when some of the poorest areas of a very poor country were also Albanian Muslim and primed for radicalization. It was no wonder that Fagan and Asmodeus had created a *bogomili* cell here.

So, yes, Mihàil Kastrioti would find his reception in Skopje *complicated*.

And the ramshackle houses in this neighborhood in northwest Čair were only a *compound* in the loosest sense of that word. Beta wasn't even sure how many separate residences there were since each house butted up against its neighbor in the entire block. Given that the streets would be better called alleys, she'd resorted to counting entrance doors and address markers. But one thing she had determined was that the nicest house at the intersection of two streets, the one with the small green side yard that was also connected to the market on the next block, *that* was the main *bogomili* house.

Which was why she and András had gone into the market to get food and drinks and why they still sat parked in the next block watching. They couldn't sit here much longer, however, because someone would notice.

"Perhaps you should get another snack."

She looked at András, this time holding his gaze. It was a dangerous proposition. His deep blue eyes made her lose focus, something she absolutely hated. She'd prefer that they were dark brown like hers, opaque and unreadable. And anti-magnetic, if that was an actual quality of eyes.

András's eyes made her think of the mysteries of space, the grandeur and awe of constellations situated inside an incongruous human form.

There, you see? The big *spratek* was doing it again. She held back her sigh.

He smiled at her, a dimple in his left cheek, as if he knew what he did to her thoughts.

"I can always eat something sweet. You think they have any *fanurija?*" There was the sound of teasing in his tone.

"How should I know?" As an officer in the Czech military intelligence, she'd had little reason to visit this Balkan nation.

"*Fanurija* is sweet bread not unlike *panettone*. It's customarily baked in early September to honor St. Fanurij, who grants wishes."

Beta sniffed and glanced back at the market. Somehow she didn't think that he was referring to her wish to gain vengeance on the *bogomili* who'd killed Andrej and gravely wounded Eliska.

"No, you're right," András said as if she'd answered. "I'll have to make do with some Fanta and *baklava*."

Beta wrinkled her nose and transferred the karambit to her right hand. "The *bogomili* is inside the house attached to the market."

"Yes."

"Then that is where the Caravaggio most likely is. He would not want to let it out of his sight."

"Agreed."

Now András appeared to study the armed guards. One slouched against a brick wall across from the market door. Another stood against a red gate around the corner that led into the house next to the market. A third leaned against the late-model sedan parked at the corner. None of their weapons were visible, but even Beta, who didn't have any special *Elioud* ability to see through walls or clothes, knew they wore them.

It was Macedonia, after all, ranked twelfth in the world for small-arms ownership.

"If I had to guess, I'd say the guards carry Zastava M70s, maybe an EZ9 on the team leader." András had switched to all business.

"And the *bogomili* are former NLA soldiers." At András's wordless nod, Beta said, "Fagan may be a *darebák*, but he knows where to recruit his evil thugs."

"Time for Fanta and *baklava*?" He smiled at her.

The smile didn't reach his eyes. She'd been wrong to think that dark blue eyes couldn't look hard and flat. Though she would sooner dig out her own eye with her hawkbilled knife than admit it, this aspect of András sent a chill down her spine. She was glad that he was on her side.

She nodded. "I am sure that you can handle the guards. I will take care of the guy behind the counter."

She slipped the karambit into her jeans pocket. Despite the sun it was chilly. But not so chilly that her dragon's breath wouldn't seem odd. It would be less odd, however, than the smoky scent she now exuded. Perhaps she should carry cigarettes to hide her growing likeness to a mythical fire-breathing creature.

She popped the car's door and slipped out into the space next to it. András followed suit a moment later. The guards looked toward them as they came around the front of the car together. She scented the guards' adrenaline surge from here. Her spine stiffened.

András took her hand, breaking the spell. Beta glanced up at him, eyes narrowed. She felt a strange vibration along her skin at his touch. It made her a little breathless, and then calm washed over her as invisible fingers stroked her spine. She relaxed despite herself.

He began walking as he said in a voice that carried, "*Drágaságom*, forgive me. I'm nothing but a big brat. I shouldn't have eaten everything when you need to eat for two now."

Beta lost a step at his declaration. How did he manage to divert her focus so easily? Everything that came out of his mouth had to be designed to distract her. His false endearment, *my darling*, sounded plausible and sincere. It even sounded like he was calling her a dragon, though she knew that wasn't the word for it in Hungarian. As for big 'brat,' *spratek*, that was what she'd taken to referring to him in her thoughts.

And who could overlook the insinuation that he'd *impregnated* her?

She snatched her hand from his and stomped to the market door, swinging it wide as the guard across from her guffawed. András sauntered in behind her.

The market was tiny. There was also a second *bogomili* there now, standing unsmiling in the corner with his hands crossed in front of him. *His* handgun was obvious in a holster at his waist.

András stopped in front of the cooler. "*Angyalom*, there is milk here."

Beta couldn't believe how it felt for him to call her 'my angel.' She circled around the space, appearing to study the rack with the Macedonian pastries, hoping that the discernable scent of smoke didn't betray her. Thanks to that *spratek*, she was a veritable smokestack now.

"Just grab something," she said, reading his infrared signature behind her.

Heatwaves rolled from his skin. Her nostrils flared at his ashy scent mingling with hers.

Twenty seconds later, András made his move. Beta didn't watch. Instead she reached for the SIG Sauer P365 hidden in her ankle holster and came up with it aimed at the head of the man behind the counter.

A fraction of a second before he'd managed to aim his own 9mm.

Beta gestured toward the counter with her head. He hesitated. She shot his shoulder, the one on the arm holding the gun. He placed his 9mm next to her before pressing his palm to the wound. He watched her with wary eyes.

"Greetings," she said in Macedonian while picking up the weapon and pocketing it. "You have something that belongs to me." She paused. "And I want the painting, too."

***

Stasia read the slim volume that she'd taken from Gregori's office while Miró went on reconnaissance around the small French seaside village. Though he'd gotten little sleep the night before, he refused to rest until he could be more certain about the strengths and weaknesses of their position. She would have felt guilty except that he seemed to have a new vitality about him—the bright nimbus had subsided into the earlier warm glow, one that she now seemed to share. Her gaze kept straying to her arm as she read, which added an undeniable element to how she understood the iconoclastic topic of the book.

How else to describe the story of Adam and Eve's expulsion from the Garden of Eden as told by the wily serpent?

Though the title of the book was a little more academic than myth busting: *Divine Mystery: Reimagining the Garden of Eden from the Point of View of the Serpent.*

It would be much more exciting if it was called *Why I Seduced Eve: Confessions of An Angelic Player.*

As Stasia thought these words, the sexual magnetism of Zaccaria Angelli came back to her. Even calling up his image caused her body to react. Her pulse sped, she grew warm, and excitement tickled her groin.

Exasperated, Stasia hummed, drawing on the tightening harmonic bond that she and Miró shared. The warm glow limning her skin pulsed and flared. Then her body quieted.

Thoughtful now, she went and got a notebook from her bag and began taking notes as she read. That's how Miró found her when he returned.

He entered the villa's small living room with his harmonics vibrating faster than the normal human frequency. To Stasia, he should be invisible. But she stirred and looked up, blinking in surprise, and gazing around the room expectantly. Her harmonics resonated with his until she'd matched him. He smiled when she saw him. It would have seemed as though he'd stepped out of thin air to her.

Her responding smile shook him to his core. She'd never looked so genuinely happy and unreserved, except perhaps at Olivia and Mihàil's wedding. That's when Miró realized that Stasia was almost always performing.

Except now.

He bent and kissed her. She met him, her mouth open and her hand coming to hold his jaw. The feel of her soft fingers against his rough stubble, holding him still while she matched his urgency, drove him a little mad. He inhaled sharply. Her perfume with its sweet-smoky notes intoxicated him. For a moment his thoughts swam.

Stasia pulled back a little, panting. He rested his forehead against hers.

"Wow," she whispered.

He exhaled deeply. "Indeed." Then he pulled back and stood upright. He felt bereft as soon as he did. "I have finished checking the perimeter of Saint-Cyr-sur-Mer and set up a minor harmonic barrier. It should be harder for Asmodeus to hone in on us."

Stasia tilted her head. "Is that what Mihàil had around his mansion in Vienna?"

"Partly. It also involved some complex infrared manipulation."

"Infrared?" she sounded intrigued. Her gaze turned inward as she thought out loud. "Angels and their descendants can control the full spectrum of light, including the invisible. That is how you manipulated my temperature after Fagan's goons drugged me."

"Yes," he nodded before sitting next to her on the sofa.

He refrained from pulling her into his lap. Instead he settled for brushing a long strand of hair behind her ear.

"And when *Elioud* battle senses go on high alert, we 'flare.' It is instinctive, but it also serves to shield us from innocent bystanders."

"Does Olivia flare?" She bit her lower lip.

"Not so far, but that may change. We are in uncharted waters. Both András and I came to the awareness of our *Elioud* nature much younger. In fact, András was twelve and had not yet gone through puberty when Mihàil rescued him. Mihàil's combat training developed our *Elioud* abilities."

"He has not known other *Elioud* warriors then?"

Miró shrugged. "Not well. There are very few of us, and we are spread thin as a rule."

"Why?"

"Most people are unaware of their *Elioud* blood. And the ones who are tend to shy away from fighting demons and Dark *Irim* as their vocation." He paused and then asked as casually as he could, "Are you worried about joining such an exclusive group?"

She shook her head. "I am only trying to understand more of the history." She gestured at the book from which she'd been taking notes. "Is there an official account about your–our history beyond the one in the *Book of Genesis* or the discarded *Books of Enoch*?"

"None of which I am aware." He picked up the thin book. "Written by one Z. Angelli, DD." He dropped it again. "What does the good *Doctor of Divinity* have to say about his role in getting the Watcher Angels kicked out of Heaven?"

Throwing her palms up, Stasia tilted her head and shrugged. "He cannot be blamed for his essential nature, which is loving. Nor should he be faulted for loving *Elohim*'s creatures, for they are lovely beyond compare. Lovely *and* lusty, I believe he wrote. Or inspiring lust in any regard."

Miró had watched her while she spoke, her hands dancing gracefully and her eyes bright. He could watch her for hours, he realized, and wished that they had the freedom and the time for him to do so. Instead he reached out and took a silky caramel strand lying over her shoulder and stroked it between his forefinger and thumb. The scent of jasmine and vanilla filled his nose.

"I find myself in agreement."

Stasia dropped her cheek to his hand, her own falling into her lap. After a long moment she sighed and raised her head.

"According to Angelli, *Genesis* and the *First Book of Enoch* tell *the same story* from two different viewpoints, the human and the angelic. *Naturalmente*, the heart of the story is about forbidden sex."

"Naturally," he said, dropping her lock of hair.

He stood and went to get something to drink, wishing that Mihàil's asset had brought something stronger than beer or wine. He settled for an Italian soft drink.

"Would you like one?"

"*No grazie.*" Stasia watched with slightly narrowed eyes as he popped the fizzy orange beverage open.

He sat at the bar, facing her. "*Seraphim* are described as fiery, luminous, winged serpents. Or in some sources as dragons. The talking, reasoning serpent in the Garden of Eden story is clearly a *seraphim.*"

She nodded. "The serpent convinced Eve to eat an apple, an obvious euphemism for procreative sex."

"That is to say," Miró said, "that Yeqon charmed women into having sex with him and his friends. It became a veritable orgy when the men were also seduced."

"Of course, the humans could not be allowed to populate the enclosed Garden of Eden and live forever, so they were expelled. And The Lord Most High punished the serpent by condemning him to 'crawl on his belly' on the dusty ground."

"In other words, the guilty Watcher Angels were kicked out of their Heavenly Choir loft."

"Dr. Angelli says that means Yeqon must grovel now to get laid."

Miró snorted and took a drink. His hand began to warm the can. He set it down with a *think*.

"That simply means that the power of his charisma is limited in the natural world. St. Gabriel could have chained and buried him like some of his co-conspirators."

"He certainly does not sound at all repentant."

She watched him, her expression unreadable, as he picked the San Pelligrino back up and drained it.

She went on. "Dr. Angelli claims that the narrative is separated into two viewpoints to keep humans unaware of the truth. He says that the *Books of Enoch* were deliberately lost for the same reason."

"It makes sense." Miró refrained from crushing the empty can. He stood. "The Creator had a plan for His Creation that the disobedient Watcher Angels stomped all over. As it is, humans like to shift the blame for their sins. 'The Devil made me do it' and all that."

He found that he couldn't sit back down. Instead, he paced from the kitchen to the front of the living area and back.

He went on. "Not all of the *Irim* who came down and interacted with humans did so for love, regardless of what Yeqon's mouthpiece writes." He gestured toward the book on the sofa next to Stasia. "The *First Book of Enoch* describes all of the illicit technology and knowledge that the *Irim* shared with humanity, including weapons and warfare techniques."

Stasia nodded again. "Dr. Angelli writes that Sêmîazâz took over the *Irim* band while Yeqon was making love."

"How convenient," Miró murmured, staring out the kitchen window. "He is a lover, not a fighter. He never meant his actions to have consequences."

Stasia's harmonics buzzed and oscillated. When she spoke, she sounded calm, however.

"Sêmîazâz wanted to use the *Irim*'s celestial knowledge to create a counterfeit religion on Earth devoted to him, one that would harness humanity to satisfy his lust and carnal desires. He also brought along a band of lesser angels like Asmodeus to serve him and his cause."

"And of course Sêmîazâz had the *Nephilim*," Miró added, "the giant half-breeds who rampaged through the world, murdering, eating people, and exploiting humanity. *Elohim* had to send a flood to wipe out the corrupt earthly races."

"Dr. Angelli claims that it is propaganda that only Noah and his family survived."

He felt Stasia behind him. Her harmonics rolled up his back, roiling as they mingled with his.

"The *Anakim*." The race of giants descended from the *Nephilim* who lived in Canaan while Joshua led the Israelites. *After the Flood.* Goliath, a Philistine, came from the *Anakim*.

Stasia turned him. The look on her face said that the next thing out of her mouth would have nothing to do with serpents or giants.

"Is there something you wish to tell me, *amore mio*?"

Eighteen

"That *Doctor* Angelli is full of *drek*," Miró said.

His gaze had iced over and his harmonics were so tightly controlled they sliced through her own, fraying and shredding the blue and gold threads.

Her heart thudded.

Stasia inhaled and hummed, the tip of her tongue pressed against her palate. The hum stayed inside her head. She didn't want to antagonize him. Instead she imagined holding the threads of her harmonics steady, smoothing and weaving until they were whole again. Her heart stopped hammering her ribs.

"As with all such egotistical bastards, *L'Amante* is a child," she said, laying her hand on Miró's forearm.

Uncomfortable heat seeped through the thin cloth of his sleeve and a slight smoky scent burned her nose. She sent a wave of soothing harmonics toward her hand.

He relaxed. A little.

"Understanding that is the key to deciphering the triptych that he 'commissioned' from his *Elioud* masters."

Miró held her gaze. His arm lost its heat.

At last he said, "He wants the lost narrative to be restored and the truth about him told."

"That is my guess." Stasia let her hand drop. Relief washed through her like cool rain on a window pane. "But I do not understand the timing. The *First Book of Enoch* came back into Western scholarship in the eighteenth century. Why were the paintings and book not brought together before now?"

Miró frowned. It was thoughtful, not furious. The last bit of breath that Stasia still held eased from her. Her harmonics returned to normal, though the ruby thread seemed sclerotic.

"For that I do not have any insight," he said. "Dark *Irim* left wandering the Earth have their dark stars to guide them, not the light of the Celestial Realm. One thing is for certain, however. Fagan and Asmodeus, for better or worse, are now playing a part in Yeqon's storytelling."

"Do you think that Asmodeus knows about the triptych? Is that why Fagan stole the first two paintings?"

"How do you know that the Caravaggio is the first painting? Maybe it is the middle painting with the Rembrandt completing the story. It would be in character for Yeqon to show himself in the central role by placing his seduction in the central panel."

Stasia shook her head. "No, that is too easy. Yeqon would not want to remind everyone about the rules binding the Watcher Angels, the ones *he* flouted. Besides I believe that he wants the last word on the story. He wants to be known as *L'Amante*, the one so infatuated with the beauty of human women that he left Heaven for them. It is a subtle seduction. After all that means they are worthy."

Miró nodded. "He also likely gains some power that way. Storytelling is a kind of creative act, a pale reflection of the creative power that belongs to *Elohim*. Angels have no direct creative power, but they can hijack or manipulate a narrative, drawing some reflected power to themselves."

Picking up the San Pelligrino can, he tossed it into the nearby wastebin. Stasia watched the line of his profile. Saw the fine lines at the corner of his eye, the gray hair dusting his temple. A powerful urge to abandon this mission, to let someone else take care of it, surged through her. She wanted to take Miró by the hand and walk through the surf, tuning their joined harmonics to the rhythm of the waves until the past and obligations were all washed away.

He continued. "They can also inspire creativity. Yeqon cleverly inspired powerful *Elioud* painters, who captured angelic power in their brushstrokes. It adds to the authenticity of his tale."

She chewed her lip, thinking. "Perhaps the ending could not be told until *L'Amante* found the right painter. If Asmodeus is aware of the triptych, he may already have the third painting."

Miró shook his head. "I doubt Yeqon would share his plans with Asmodeus."

"So if we are not careful, we may lead Asmodeus to Yeqon's third painting."

"Yes. Asmodeus benefits from having these paintings around even if he has no desire or ability to inspire human creativity. He inspires lust instead. That siphons creative energy." Miró's gaze turned inward as he thought, his fingers tapping on the counter. "They are a kind of angelic battery."

A tingle ran up Stasia's spine at Miró's description. She crossed herself. "That sounds like a bad idea for a Dark *Irim* who has been in an angelic coma and needs a little pep up."

Miró nodded, grim. "For that reason alone, we need to keep the third painting out of his hands and recover the other two."

Stasia tilted her head, studying him. "But you suspect that there is more to the triptych, *è così?*"

He nodded, watching her.

"If one painting is a 'battery' as you call it," she said, thinking aloud, "then three paintings together might have a synergy greater than the individual batteries."

"For all we know Yeqon might have planned using the stored angelic energy for something big. And if we realize that potential—"

"—then so will Asmodeus if he learns of the third painting," Stasia finished. "We have to find it and keep it from him."

"You are now the Dr. Angelli expert on the team. Do you have any ideas about the *Elioud* painter that he would have 'commissioned' as you put it to finish his story?" Miró's predatory gaze pinned her.

Lost, Stasia threw up her hands. *"Mah!* That could be anyone."

"No, no it cannot," he said gently, though his icy gaze burned. "Did you not say that Yeqon wants to spin the narrative of the Watcher Angels? To finish the story so that he can be seen as *L'Amante?"*

"Sì, but I need more than that to go on."

"I rather suspect that whoever he took on as his apprentice had to have some connection with Caravaggio and Rembrandt."

Stasia remembered her meeting with Gregori. *"Sì, sicuro!"* she said, nodding.

She considered what she was about to share and decided that she had no choice. Miró had guessed the connection already. It wouldn't take much for him to learn the rest.

"Which leads us back to Aix-en-Provence. Gregori sketched a story of a possible collaboration between Caravaggio and Rembrandt facilitated by a secret society. It includes a copy of the *First Book of Enoch."*

Miró's gaze sharpened, if possible. "Before the copies brought back to Europe from Ethiopia by the Scottish explorer James Bruce?"

She nodded again.

"That is very interesting." He paused. "How does Aix-en-Provence figure into this delayed collaboration?" He didn't ask her why she hadn't shared this information before now.

She shifted uneasily. She'd forgotten over the last twenty-four hours that Miró's stated goal was to recruit her for the *Elioud* team, and that he'd accompanied her to France as a blatant means of influencing her. He'd also assured her that he had his feelings for her under control, that they wouldn't affect his ability to do his duty.

Since then he'd admitted that both Asmodeus and Yeqon also wanted her.

Stasia clamped down on the sudden unhappiness that pricked her. Now was not the time to digress into her personal issues.

"A Flemish painter and contemporary of Caravaggio went to Aix-en-Provence, where he met with French humanist and intellectual Nicolas-Claude Fabri de Peiresc. Gregori theorized that the Flemish painter gave the *First Book of Enoch* to Peiresc, who then passed it on to Dutch mathematician Christiaan Huygens, who delivered it to Rembrandt."

"So perhaps something similar happened between Rembrandt and the mystery painter."

"It is as good an assumption as any." She left unsaid that she'd already had this thought.

"Then we will try to pick up the trail in Aix-en-Provence."

"*Bene.*"

"We will stay here today. That will give you time to recover and for us to plan our approach and itinerary in Aix-en-Provence where you will have to call on your natural *Elioud* charisma to deflect Fagan from our true mission."

"You want to sell the fiction that we are the mice to his cat. To control the narrative."

Miró smiled for the first time since they'd started discussing Angelli's book and the Watcher Angel triptych. It didn't reach his eyes. "Exactly."

He bent and kissed her, brushing his lips over hers and stepping away before she could react. "I have an errand to run. It will take some time. Please get some rest. If you get hungry, there is a meal keeping warm in the oven."

She watched Miró go, walking past their car and out the front gate. Then she stepped over to the wastebin and looked inside at the aluminum can that he'd discarded.

It was elongated and deformed.

***

András watched as the man behind the counter, his face pale and blood dripping between his fingers as he held his shoulder, came out into the store. He avoided Beta as much as possible, hunching and sliding past the counter to stand near a row of shelves. András grinned. He couldn't blame the man, who wasn't a *bogomili*. The Czech military intelligence officer wore an expression as fierce and dark as any avenging angel.

Beta gestured with her gun toward the back of the market and the door leading to the attached building where her target was. His *Elioud* senses told him that there were only two individuals in the space, though all of the residences around the market had multiple adult infrared signatures. There was no way to know how many belonged to other members of the *bogomili* cell. Regardless, the two guards on watch outside had heard the shot and were about to come through the entrance.

Which is why he stood just inside ready to receive them.

Even so he almost missed the first guard as he watched Beta following the market employee down the main aisle. It was a good thing that neither Mihàil nor Miró were there to catch him ogling her backside. She wore faded jeans and heavy, steel-toed boots that should have been more than her slender legs could manage, but instead she looked strong enough to kick ass with them—which was truth in advertising if he ever saw it.

András had just decided that Beta's slender derriere would fit his palms when the long black muzzle of the first guard broke the plane of the wall next to him. He grabbed it with heated hands, yanking gun and guard into the market. As the *bogomili* stumbled past, András seized the back of his coat and swung him into the shelves next to him. He'd turned back before the guard's deadweight hit the scuffed linoleum.

Only to find the second guard pointing his weapon at him.

András laughed as his adrenaline surged. Hot smoky breath clouded the air between them.

The second guard flinched a half second before squeezing the trigger. In that half second, András surged forward, knocking the muzzle up with one hand while ramming the *bogomili*'s chest with the flat of his other. The bullet went into the ceiling. The guard went into the glass display. Gum and candy and a myriad other impulse buys exploded from the glass counter, which shattered as the *bogomili* hit it.

A large glass shard punctured the *bogomili*'s side. He didn't seem to notice. Instead he raised his weapon again as András fell on him. A moment later András felt the familiar fiery punch of a bullet in his abdomen.

It only infuriated him.

Roaring, he ripped the weapon from the *bogomili*'s hand and flung it away. The superheated metal hit boxes on a shelf, setting them alight, and rebounded into the unconscious *bogomili* on the floor. The man grunted as the molten steel settled on his abdomen and then began writhing and moaning.

András gripped the *bogomili* under him by his jacket and stood, the man's legs dangling. Flames burst around his fisted fingers as the cheap nylon combusted. The man at his feet screamed and thrashed, knocking the glowing lump onto the floor.

The *bogomili* struggled, flailing and striking András hard on the head, neck and shoulders. András growled, ignoring the blows and focusing on the bullet lodged in his flesh. He raised his temperature enough to melt the bullet, forcing the liquid steel out of his body as it cauterized the bleeding.

Unfortunately for the *bogomili* still locked in András's grip, it also scorched the flesh on his upper chest. He shrieked.

András flung him away as if he were nothing more than a crumpled napkin. The *bogomili* landed on top of his partner, who reacted much as a wounded predator would, snapping his jaws and clawing at him.

András shoved the fierce pain in his abdomen out of his thoughts. He kicked the top *bogomili* off his partner. "Enough!"

The two stopped moving at the *Elioud* authority he infused into his voice. András prodded each with his boot, sending a concentrated harmonic jab into their nervous systems. They wouldn't get up again.

Food boxes burned along the shelves next to them, sending hungry flames toward other packages. Scorch marks marred the floor and walls.

András exhaled. He didn't want to burn down the market or the neighborhood. Inhaling deeply, he lowered his body temperature and then walked toward the fire. Passing the burning objects, he slowed their harmonics and lowered their temperature. Seconds later, the fire died. Frost crystals clung to the remnants of the shelves and packaging.

Then he turned and hurried toward the door that Beta and the shopkeeper had gone through.

There had been repeated gunfire since she'd disappeared. She could take care of herself, but the back of his neck had started itching. It only did that when something was wrong.

As soon as he stepped into the next building, he knew what.

There were half a dozen *bogomili* inside. His *Elioud* senses had deceived him.

He didn't have time to puzzle out why, however.

Beta stood with her chain whip wrapped around the neck of a *bogomili* three meters from her. She had her other arm around the shopkeeper, who looked terrified. Two *bogomili* lay unmoving on the floor at her feet. Three more crouched in a semi-circle, one holding a combat knife and the other two handguns. All *bogomili* had multiple gunshot wounds. Two 9mm handguns lay on the floor at Beta's feet. A large flat rectangular box stood in a corner. In the heated air the scent of gunpowder and the smoke of an *Elioud* warrior hung heavy.

As András stepped into the room, the three loose *bogomili* launched at Beta.

He growled. He flared. And then he rampaged.

Two steps and he'd plowed into the nearest *bogomili*. The man staggered and turned, bringing his handgun around. Blinking in the brilliance, he shot wildly until András knocked the weapon from his hand and punched him in the throat. He dropped to the floor, gagging.

András sped his harmonics, his battle senses finely attuned to Beta's infrared signature. He moved behind her, shielding her back from the other *bogomili* with a gun.

Everything slowed down around András.

He felt every single bullet that the second *bogomili* got off. Four in total.

He sensed Beta shove the shopkeeper from her and yank on her chain whip almost simultaneously.

He whirled and stepped forward, gripped the wrist of the second *bogomili*'s gun hand, and snapped it. The man howled and dropped his weapon.

Out of the corner of his eye, he saw Beta release the chain whip's handle, drop her hand, and pull it up again holding the karambit.

He head-butted the second *bogomili* and flung him to the floor.

He swung around as the third *bogomili* reached Beta.

She slashed the wicked hawkbill blade at the man, whose crazed gaze showed no fear.

Bright blood spouted from the man's neck, but he kept coming.

András saw the *bogomili*'s own vicious blade sweep into Beta's now-undefended flank, felt the impact as it plunged into her as if he'd been stabbed himself, heard her grunt and felt her curl and waver while she flipped the karambit around and swung it across the *bogomili*'s neck.

The *bogomili*'s face never lost its feral grin even as his head flopped, blood spraying everywhere.

András caught Beta as she sagged. The dead *bogomili* fell, pushing her into András and soaking them in hot blood.

Roaring, he yanked the body away, his hand now so hot that the *bogomili* spontaneously combusted, falling as ash on the floor. Two steps and they were free of the carnage. The blood evaporated from his skin as he moved, leaving an András-shaped mist hanging where he'd been.

On the other side of the room, a door opened and *bogomili* rushed in, firing at them.

András ignored the shopkeeper, who crawled on all fours at the side of the room. He raced to the door to the market, Beta cradled in his arms. More than one bullet found its target. When he pulled the lever, he found the door locked. He shifted his harmonics to match that of the steel door's molecules, manipulating the unconscious Beta's harmonics at the same time. They stepped through into the market.

He turned and pressed his palm against the steel door. He raised its temperature until the metal glowed and the lock melted. It was unlikely that the door's fire rating would hold against an *Elioud*-induced conflagration.

András strode out, flames blazing as he passed through the destroyed store.

***

Asmodeus sighed and, stretching his arms over his head, wriggled his fingers. The morning sun through the picture window warmed his face and bare chest. When his skin had heated, he dropped his arms down and slouched into the hardback chair. Next to his hand on the dining table was a fresh cup of coffee. Humanity did very little new or interesting, but occasionally he found something that he took without bending or twisting to his own standard. Coffee, even when spectacularly bad, was one of those things.

He sipped the hot brew. This was a moderately good coffee. Hugo, his unwitting host, had a high-end espresso machine and milk frother. The deviant enjoyed indulging his appetites.

It felt so blissful to be fully formed again. That's what happened when *his* appetites had been slaked. And his lust had been satiated. For the time being at least. Too bad it had only been from being a voyeur.

The security system buzzed. Hugo, moving around in the kitchen, let Fagan in.

Asmodeus didn't look toward his acolyte. Nor did he acknowledge Fagan when he came to stand next to him. Hugo delivered a tray of pastries and left them on the table.

Asmodeus ignored the sweets and drank deep of the *café noir*. He relished the spurt of digestive juices that responded to the intense bitter taste and caffeine. He always enjoyed a cup of strong coffee before eating a large meal after he'd regained his full corporal form. It wouldn't last long. *Elohim*—even thinking that name sent a shard of pain through his thoughts—had levied a heavy toll on all the disobedient *Irim* who remained on Earth. The energy required to manifest a physical body meant that most *Irim* couldn't afford to walk indistinguishable from their human targets.

Fagan cleared his throat.

"Speak."

"The Macedonians were hit this morning by two *Elioud*, a male and a female. The compound was destroyed and most of the *bogomili* killed."

"I am aware." Asmodeus let his displeasure at this unnecessary accounting deepen his scratchy voice.

Fagan shuddered next to him. A moment passed before he spoke again. "The painting had already been moved."

Now Asmodeus turned to look at his acolyte, whose manner betrayed no unease at their surroundings. Though he liked that lack of morality about Fagan, he was growing tired of his ineptitude.

"Good."

Asmodeus directed his *Irim* senses far afield on the harmonic plane, seeking more information about the *Elioud* who had tracked the Caravaggio. Recognizing a familiar harmonic signature marred by grave pain sent a tremor of delight through him. For a moment his joy was such that he couldn't speak. His eyes rolled up into their sockets. Gripping the chair's armrests, he thought he might have an orgasm, something he hadn't had in decades.

Fagan continued. "Both *Elioud* were badly wounded, but it doesn't sound as if it was Kastrioti and his bitch wife."

Asmodeus let the wave ride over him before answering. "No, it was not my illustrious former acolyte and your former subordinate, I'm afraid. Pity. You seem to be unable to strike at them."

His gaze showed how he felt about that failure. Fagan had the instinct to look vaguely uneasy.

"No matter. You shall prove yourself by finding the Italian and her *Elioud* bodyguard, before or after they find the third painting makes no difference." He waved the acolyte away before biting into a chocolate-filled croissant.

Fagan gave a curt nod. Then he stepped over the naked, bruised corpse of one of the young women. The other, hanging by her wrists on the wall, he spared a sharply lascivious glance.

Seeing it, Asmodeus took a huge bite of the croissant, laughing with his mouth full.

Nineteen

Fatigue washed over Stasia after Miró left. Though she'd slept during the drive from Viareggio, sleeping in a car wasn't really her idea of refreshing, MDMA or not. Her head ached. She suspected that the tension in Miró's harmonics hadn't helped the lingering dehydration. But she was also running a temperature again despite it being more than twelve hours since Fagan had drugged her. Without Miró to modulate her body's metabolism, she would have to take an over-the-counter medicine.

She grabbed a bottle of water and a clementine and headed back to the bedroom. If she could sleep, she would.

She'd finished reading Angelli's self-serving theological treatise but was no closer to identifying the third artist whom he'd "commissioned" to paint his final painting. Despite studying enough art history to discuss Rembrandt and Renoir with the Dervishi brothers, her knowledge of the subject wasn't nearly deep enough to anticipate who had been an *Elioud* painting under the influence of a Dark *Irim*.

What are you doing here, genia? She sighed and sat on the bed. It didn't take a genius to know that she didn't have any professional reason for driving to France.

She was here because she'd wanted to be alone with Miró, to see if the chemistry between them was more than he could resist. To see, if she were honest, whether he would turn on *his* charm to persuade her to join the *Elioud* team. She suspected that when Miró wanted to be charming he would be forceful.

A memory of him calling her *dušo* sent a shiver through her. That hadn't been charm at all. It had been tender devotion.

No need for charm, chicca, when you got sincerity.

But then what had made him so angry? Stasia suspected that Miró hadn't left to run an errand but to get some space.

She'd finished the bottled water and clementine when her cellphone rang. It was Olivia.

"Ciao. Come va?"

"I'm going to kill Fagan if it's the last thing I do."

Stasia sat up. She felt her harmonics thrum. She tamped them down.

"Beta."

"András just called. He and Beta barely made it out of a Macedonian *bogomili* compound. They're both wounded, Beta gravely. Mihàil flies out later this afternoon with a surgeon."

Stasia's mind blanked. It seemed impossible to comprehend that Beta had been wounded let alone so badly that she needed a surgeon.

"I can be there by nightfall," she said. Running through the logistics cleared her mind. "There are flights from Marseille."

"No, I want you and Miró to keep hunting for clues about the third painting while you distract Fagan. I'm going to Vienna to get the Rembrandt back."

"You cannot do that alone, *cara.*"

"I've asked Miles Baxter to meet me. He's in Zagreb at the moment." Miles was the CIA field officer whom Fagan had tasked with extracting Mihàil the previous summer. Needless to say, Olivia had outmaneuvered Fagan and even won Miles's admiration.

"You think that he will work with you?"

"I'm going to give it the All-American try. If I've read him right, he's more than a little burned out working for guys like Fagan, who have no problem running missions for their own selfish interests. I'm betting Miles won't mind taking a side job for me."

Stasia feared asking the next question. "The Caravaggio?"

"András burned the *bogomili* compound down as they escaped."

L'Amante predicted that she'd keep the Caravaggio safe. He hadn't anticipated András and Beta's disastrous attempt to get it back.

"He is certain that the Caravaggio burned with it?"

There was silence for a moment. "He's sure that the custom VZ packing container burned."

"Ah. Then forgive me, *cara*, if I do not assume that the Caravaggio is gone."

"That's fair, though I don't know how we'll confirm one way or the other." Olivia paused again. When she came back she sounded tentative. "Staz, how are you and Miró?" The words were loaded with meaning.

Stasia's headache sharpened. She slowed her breathing and heartrate until her harmonics smoothed. "*Onestamente*, I do not know." She swallowed as she thought about how he'd carried her from the *bagno* and her degradation there. "What Fagan did to me," she said through a thick voice, swallowing again. "I would not have made it out whole, Liv. But now Miró is gone and angry. And we are no longer simply colleagues, if you take my meaning."

Olivia refrained from commenting on her loaded statement. Instead she said, "Staz, you may not believe this, but angry is good. That man is so tightly controlled that the only time I see anything approaching anger from him is in the sparring ring."

Stasia laughed, tears choking the sound. *Santo cielo!* What was wrong with her? She never cried over a man. "Well, then, we must be doing fine."

"*Ah, mia sorella*," Olivia said, tenderness infusing her voice. "If anyone can handle the demons plaguing Miró, it's you. He may thrash and howl a bit, but the more he does, the more it means that you're winning. Just think of this as the toughest deep-cover op you've ever run. Or an exorcism. Whichever works."

Stasia inhaled deeply and blew her breath out. When she spoke, she'd regained control.

"*Grazie*, but I have never been an independent contractor before. Either I have been on missions for my agency or with you and Beta saving victims involved in sex crimes. If I stay and help find the third Watcher Angel painting, I will be supporting *Elioud* objectives."

"And you're not sure that whatever is happening between you and Miró makes that more or less attractive."

"You must admit that it complicates *your* objectives, *sì*? You say that you want me on your team, but it would be much better for you if Miró and I maintain a professional distance."

"Perhaps. Or perhaps I think that you two would make an invincible duo. You know what the Wise Man said: 'two are better than one ... though one may be overpowered, two can defend themselves.'"

"'A cord of three strands is not quickly broken,'" Stasia finished. It was a bit of Scripture that her beloved grandfather had been fond of saying, urging her to consider love and marriage. For a moment she missed him with a piercing ache.

He would have liked Miró, she thought, though she had no idea how she knew that.

"Is it worth risking the chance to have me on the team if Miró and I–if we...." Stasia stopped. For once she had no idea what to say.

"If you two don't acknowledge that you're in love with each other and choose to be together?" Olivia said. Stasia flinched at her bluntness. "Yes, *cara amica*, I believe it is. In fact, there's nothing more important."

"Then I will do my best to keep Fagan occupied in France."

"And I will get you the Rembrandt so that you have a choice."

***

Miró ran to Marseille.

It was a forty-minute drive via highway A50. Forty-five kilometers as the crow flies over rugged, dry land under bright sun. He could have taken the train, but he needed to burn some energy. He needed to travel so fast over demanding terrain that he couldn't think. He could only keep his focus on his path and his pace.

On his left the brilliant blue Mediterranean sparkled like crushed glass. He was going to have a headache by the time he reached Aix-Marseille University near the harbor in the heart of the city. It didn't matter. He couldn't stop for water now.

It took him forty-five minutes.

When he got to Marseille, he stopped at the Paradise, a fast-food restaurant four kilometers south of the university. There he ducked into the toilet and did his best to neaten his appearance, splashing cold water on his face and combing his hair with his fingers. He'd kept his body temperature low so that he wouldn't sweat (or not much anyway), so his clothes weren't terribly damp. He took the time to dry them a bit, grateful that he'd worn a shirt and pants designed to stay wrinkle-free during travel.

Then he slipped his sunglasses on and went to the counter to order a bottle of water and lunch. It was an Armenian-owned establishment, which meant that along with the American burgers and tacos and the French scallops and *cordon bleu*, kebabs and *beurak* were on the menu. He decided on the platter of Armenian specialties.

He wasn't hungry, but he wanted to stake out a seat facing the window where he could wait for his contact at the *Institut de Sciences des Mouvement*. One of the reasons that he'd accepted Stasia's request to accompany her to Aix-en-Provence was the opportunity to work on a side project, though he would have come regardless.

And therein was the truth at last.

He'd needed to be alone with Stasia. Any other reason for traveling with her was simply unnecessary justification.

Pressing his lips together, he toyed with his fork and squinted toward the street. *Where was Jules?*

Two minutes later Dr. Jules Allard passed the large plate-glass windows. He nodded when he saw Miró and came to dump his backpack onto the booth seat across from Miró before ordering. Miró took a bite and pretended to be absorbed in his food. He could feel his harmonics tightening, tightening the muscles in his neck and shoulders. He sent warmth there.

There was no need to risk being short-tempered with the French nanoroboticist.

After Jules had joined him, shaking his hand, and settling in with his food, Miró said, "Thank you for coming."

Jules nodded as he took a bite from his American cheesesteak sandwich. Chewing, he waited until he'd finished swallowing before saying, "It is always a pleasure to be of service. How is your *signeuer*?" The tone of his voice added a measure of reverence to the title of lord.

"He and his *zonjë* have had a pleasant period settling into married life on his estate. However, the wicked do not rest as you know." Miró pushed his plate to the side, leaving most of his food uneaten. "You have the package?"

Jules slid the backpack from the seat to the floor and nudged it toward Miró. He unzipped the top to reveal a cardboard box that looked like it held a ream of paper. The "paper" was in actuality sheets of graphene, a single layer of graphite that was stronger than steel and thinner than wood-pulp-based paper.

"The surface has been functionalized and the microstructure you specified has been patterned onto the sheets," Jules said before taking a bite and glancing around the restaurant while he chewed.

"What temperature triggers the self-folding behavior?"

"Approximately 45 degrees Celsius." Jules looked at him as he said this. "Can you be so precise in the field?" He asked this delicately. They both knew what he meant.

Miró nodded. "We have calibrated our systems so that we can achieve a level of precision within a degree Celsius."

Jules blinked several times, clearly trying to process that information. Shaking his head after a moment, he turned back to his sandwich. Miró waited. It was necessary that anyone observing them would see two people having lunch rather than guessing that it was a drop of highly experimental technology.

"You will also need to activate the sheets in water."

"That could be limiting."

Jules shook his head and drank from his soda. "So sorry to say, but the water is necessary. The microstructure will also irreversibly bond because the sides touch. If you want to be able to unfold it by lowering the temperature 10 degrees, I can add a rigid polymer layer to the edges to reduce adhesion."

Miró was fascinated at the possibility of unfolding his graphene origami. "What is the drawback of doing so?"

Jules shrugged. "At this scale, what does it matter if your sheet is 20 times thicker? It is still invisible to the naked eye."

"Not to my eye," Miró said.

Jules looked taken aback.

Miró didn't wait for the scientist to recover. "And the sheets can serve as audio transmitters and receivers?"

Jules nodded. "Graphene is ideal for transmitting and receiving sound vibrations up to 100 gigahertz, which you can activate through harmonics and thermodynamics."

"That is much of the angelic spectrum." Miró was intrigued. "So I can daisy chain individual origami in an acoustic telephone?"

"Precisely." Jules looked pleased with his understanding. "Though perhaps it is more accurate to say that you can use them as nodes in a mechanical network. Unlike tin cans linked with string, they are wireless, virtually undetectable, and easily recoverable. However, you will need an interface to capture and record sound. For these I modified a Bluetooth relay. The audio is then sent to the IP address that you specified. But you should know that the Bluetooth specifications for the relay are still in development."

"Which is another way of saying that there are no guarantees that these will work?" Miró was amused. Scientists could sound like politicians when they wanted. "How are the microstructures powered?"

Jules smiled. "You will like this, I think. Each extracts a tiny bit of energy from ambient temperature and motion, on the order of Pico amps of current. Not enough to power your cell phone."

"But enough to transmit audio to the Bluetooth relay or animate the microstructures."

"*Oui.*"

"Brilliant." Miró looked at the backpack. His fingers itched to pull the modified graphene out. "What is the range?"

"Theoretically? A thousand meters. But I would not trust them beyond a hundred unless you are outside without anything between them and the relay. That's for the microstructures. The Bluetooth relay also has a range only between fifty and hundred meters, so you will need a local server if you cannot be in the vicinity with your smartphone."

Jules finished his sandwich, wiped his mouth, and sighed. "I am beyond happy when I have an excuse to come here and eat something that would make my *maman* gasp. But please help me to understand. Why with your considerable gifts"— here he waved his hand across the table—"do you need technology at all?"

Miró held the man's gaze. "As with your cutting-edge devices, I have limits. Think of your high-tech origami as one means of enhancing my gifts." He slid from the booth and stood. "I am intrigued with the potential for unfolding the sheets. I will take delivery of the first set today, but please modify another set with the rigid polymer of which you spoke."

"That will take longer." Jules finished his soda and stood also.

"I understand. Do what you can." Miró zipped the backpack closed and pulled it onto a shoulder. He extended his hand, and when Jules took it, said, "*A la prochaine.*"

"*A bientôt.*"

They cleaned up the remains of their lunch. Miró followed Jules out the door, Jules returning to his bicycle, which he'd left locked on a nearby drainpipe. Miró had already ordered a ride share, which waited for him at the curb. After his earlier need to get away from the villa and Stasia, he felt a much stronger urge to get back to her. His reason told him that she was safe and that Fagan hadn't found her alone, but until he had eyes on her again, he wouldn't feel at ease.

Guilt flooded him. He ignored it and slid into the passenger seat. Removing his sunglasses, he smiled at the man and let his charm loose. "Please, I am in a hurry. There is an extra 50 euros for you if you can reach Saint-Cyr-sur-Mer in thirty minutes."

The driver, a young man who appeared to be an immigrant from North Africa, smiled a wide, white smile. Without waiting for Miró to finish buckling, he took off from the curb and headed south, weaving and moving through traffic as if he had a little bit of *Elioud* sense guiding him. It actually took him thirty-two minutes, but Miró was impressed with his driver's enthusiastic and skillful attempt to do the impossible. He gave him the extra 50 euros with a nod and a promise to rate him highly on the app.

It was now mid-afternoon. The villa appeared quiet. Miró scanned the surroundings for evidence of strange or unusual harmonic activity and found none. No one had visited.

When he entered the villa, he half expected to see Stasia sitting in the front living area on the sofa, one leg bent under her, a pad of paper next to her as she jotted notes. His earlier reaction to seeing her in just that posture upon returning from his perimeter check had shocked him. He'd felt hungry. Hungry to have Stasia waiting for him in *their* living room. Hungry for more than he had a right to expect let alone want.

And then she'd described Yeqon's treatise, his subtle attempt to influence humanity yet again, *ad infinitum* and *nauseum*. Was she influenced as well? Did the Dark *Irim*'s heavy charisma waft from the text and wend its way through her thoughts? She'd deemed *L'Amante* a child, yet her harmonics had sped up and her body heated just at speaking his name. She was not immune to the Dark *Irim*, and the more she pursued his third artist, the more his delicate hooks would set and an irrational desire grow within her.

Miró dropped the backpack on the sofa and went down the short hallway to the master bedroom. Stasia, one arm curled around a pillow and her thigh hiked over it, slept with her back toward the door. She'd taken her clothes off again and now wore a tank and loose shorts. Her harmonics had evened out, no longer strummed and plucked as she reacted to his. She must have trusted his harmonic barrier because every line of her body was relaxed.

Miró took in the creamy flesh of her thighs, the silky strands of her hair tumbling over her shoulder and upper back. Her smoky-sweet scent, warmed by her skin, hung on the still air. He shed his clothes, leaving them in a pile on the floor and moved to climb into the bed next to her.

Only to meet the muzzle of her 9mm.

He froze, half bent, one hand and one knee on the mattress.

Stasia's gaze held his. Miró waited, holding his breath. After a moment, he gently pulled the gun from her with his free hand. There was no external safety on the small semi-automatic pistol.

Even as he placed the gun on the nightstand, he felt the tension in Stasia's harmonics. They crackled and sparked like static electricity. He'd barely set the gun down when she rolled away and sat up, her nostrils flaring and her eyes darkened to a stormy gray-brown. Her sleek hair looked as rough and wild as exploded steel wool.

Miró hummed under his breath, watching through the periphery of his vision as Stasia's harmonics wrestled with his. An instant later, her harmonics undulated and then lashed out toward him. The wave rolled over him like cold seawater. It took his breath away.

For a moment Miró lost control of his own harmonics.

And then the air between them filled with the turmoil of a harmonic storm that shook the bed and thrashed against the walls and furniture.

Miró pressed his arm against the wall and dipped his head, breaking the connection between their gazes. He closed his eyes and reined in his breathing, smoothing his harmonics in the wake of Stasia's turbulent ones as a swimmer swimming against a current. He persisted until he felt her harmonics swing into harmony with his. For a moment he saw shimmering jeweled colors among the vibrations like sunlight on mother of pearl.

When he looked up again, he was panting and sweaty. Stasia's chest rose and fell. A damp sheen covered her cheeks and collarbone.

"I was not sure that you were coming back," she said. Her voice was a rough whisper.

"When I left I was not certain that I would." His own voice came out harsh and uneven. "I do not know if I can bear to go through another betrayal."

Sparks flew from her gaze. "You believe that I will betray you?"

"Can you promise that you will not?"

Something flitted through her gaze, which cooled. Her eyes turned an impassive brown-gray, conveying nothing and everything.

"No, I cannot promise not to betray you."

She looked away, appearing to gather something to herself. When she looked back, her expression was skeptical.

"But neither can you promise to put me above your mission."

It was a statement. An accurate one.

Miró slumped as disappointment crushed him. Stasia's next statement brought him upright again.

"But you did come back. And I did promise Olivia to do my best on this *Elioud* mission. It is enough for me. Is it enough for you?"

He held her gaze. Shadows and clouds swirled there. "Yes."

It would have to be because he couldn't walk away now.

Twenty

Stasia and Miró drove to Aix-en-Provence the next morning in a rented MINI JCW that one of Mihàil's assets had dropped off in the middle of the night. It was Monday, so there was some traffic on A52 north through Aubagne, a small city east of Marseille. Stasia watched the changing landscape outside her window, choosing to let Miró focus on driving.

She'd told him last night about András and Beta's failed mission to Skopje. The ice had descended again over his gaze. He radiated predatory chill. Now she understood. If András needed a surgeon, then fighting alongside Beta had compromised him.

The risks for the *Elioud* were real. They were mortal. They bled.

"I have been thinking about what Yeqon would have wanted painted in the third painting," she said without looking at Miró.

"Himself?" he asked.

She turned to look at him. A pulse beat along his jawline.

"That goes without saying. But he will be central to a group of figures. It will not be a portrait. That is too subtle a story even for him. For him to be known as *L'Amante*, he needs to have a subject or subjects to love in his scene."

Miró appeared to consider what she said. "The first two paintings are dramatic but realistic."

"And, if I am right, painted in progression in time, that is, the first painting is the oldest."

"So the last painter came after Caravaggio. That narrows it down then to the last 350 years."

She ignored his sarcasm. "I think that the third painter is Western European, possibly American or from another country in the British Commonwealth. Some place with the cultural basis for the artist to paint the subject."

"But *L'Amante* narrowed your search to Aix-en-Provence." Miró's jaw had relaxed. He glanced at her. The icy blue gaze remained as opaque as a frozen lake.

Stasia smoothed her harmonics. The tight band of Miró's that was caught in them remained impervious to her effort.

She plowed forward anyway. "Of course. But given that the triptych has remained hidden all these years, I would guess that *L'Amante* was forced to wait some time for the right painter to be born."

"Which means that the painter could be anyone who traveled to Aix-en-Provence like Finson."

"Perhaps." She felt Miró's gaze on her. She waved her hand. "It is too easy to assume that the painter ever spent any time in Aix-en-Provence. *L'Amante* might have easily said Paul Cézanne. He was born and spent his whole life there."

"You are correct. *L'Amante* would not make it so easy."

They'd left Aubagne's northern suburbs behind. In another ten minutes they arrived in Aix-en-Provence and the Musée Granet, which was in the Mazarin Quarter where the Caravaggio had been found in the attic of a mansion. Miró turned down *Rue Cardinale*, the narrow one-way street that passed by the cobbled square in front of the museum's entrance. The street was empty. Museums were closed on Mondays. They planned to survey the exterior before driving through the historic neighborhood.

And troll for the inevitable *bogomili* surveillance. It was time to keep Fagan and his thugs busy.

Miró kept the engine of the small British sports car running. A dark sedan drove by on *Rue d'Italie*, the large cross street behind them. He watched the traffic in the rearview mirror. The sightlines were terrible. At most they would be able to see only two passing vehicles from either direction; one if they passed at the same time. Worse, *Rue Cardinale* jogged around the corner of a building as it exited the square, which obscured all but the first few meters beyond.

Her neck itched. This was not a good place to stay. Bad guys rarely respected street direction regulations.

"Is there something else about Caravaggio and Rembrandt that links them artistically beyond the secret society? Besides the fact that their paintings are dramatic and realistic. Or the fact that Rembrandt likely knew about Caravaggio."

"Of course. I can think of three similarities."

Stasia raised her closed hand and unfolded a finger with each point. "First, their paintings are dramatic because they set scenes and painted people in action. Second, drama and scene suggests theater. Even in Caravaggio's day, there was stage lighting. They were both fascinated with light, and among the first to use it as another medium."

"Third"—she raised the final finger and turned to him—"and this seems like a quirk that Yeqon would exploit, they painted themselves onto the canvas."

Miró pressed his lips together, nodding. "Caravaggio stood behind the Watcher Angel. But Rembrandt did not appear in the *Judgment of the Watcher Angels*."

"*Questo è vero*, but outside of Vincent Van Gogh, he is the most prolific self-portraitist ever. Over 40 years, he painted, drew, and etched almost 100 of them."

"Not a little narcissistic then."

Stasia shrugged, looking at her side mirror. Another dark sedan appeared in the traffic on *Rue d'Italie*, this time heading in the opposite direction. She pulled her full-size Beretta 92FS from her shoulder holster and cradled it in her lap. At almost a kilo, it was heavier than her Kel-Tec P32, but its accuracy at 50 meters and 15-round magazine made it a better tactical choice.

"There was a market for self-portraits, and Rembrandt needed the money. He lived beyond his means and died bankrupt. Beyond that, most historians think that Rembrandt created a visual autobiography."

"You sound as if you are defending him."

"He was a Grey *Elioud*, was he not?" Stasia took her gaze off the mirror to glare at Miró. "Not so simple to condemn him without thinking."

When she looked back, a dark sedan slowed at the intersection of *Rue d'Italie* and *Rue Cardinale*. There were at least three individuals in the car. Even from this distance she could sense the disturbed vibrations going through their harmonics. It was an ugly dark-purple tic.

Bogomili. And they had at least three vehicles.

Merda. A cold thrill of adrenaline surged. Stasia slipped her fingers around the Beretta but kept the safety decocker engaged.

"Time to go," she said, unbuckling her seatbelt.

Even as she spoke, Miró shifted the MINI JCW out of park and accelerated toward the other end of the square. He swung the wheel hard to the left and then immediately to the right, rocketing up the block.

Only to be blocked by another dark sedan entering from the side street on the left.

Miró hit the gas, swerving to the right and missing an iron railing before the MINI mounted the sidewalk. They raced between three parked cars and the building façade as sparks flew from the MINI's sides. Stasia, Beretta gripped in her right hand, got up onto her knees in the jouncing car and looked behind them. The second sedan backed up. Miró swerved off the sidewalk onto the street as it turned and followed them. Behind it came the first sedan.

And somewhere there was a third sedan.

"Turn right!" Stasia shouted as they neared the next intersection.

Miró downshifted and swung the MINI wide and right.

Three blocks up ran *Cours Mirabeau*, the stately avenue for which Aix-en-Provence was known. It was punctuated with fountains and lined with cafés, terraces, and elegant private mansions with wrought-iron balconies. Designed for pedestrians, *Cours Mirabeau* would be far from deserted even on this Monday morning in March.

Fagan wouldn't want to risk the attention.

First one and then the other dark sedan rounded the corner behind them. Miró slowed as he came through the next intersection. Stasia looked left. A white *voiture citadine*—the small car endemic to French cities—had already started to accelerate into the intersection. The car halted and the driver honked and gestured. He'd just started to drive forward again when the lead *bogomili* car smashed into his front bumper, knocking the car sideways as it pushed by the hood.

The front passenger of the lead *bogomili* car leaned out. Stasia saw the muzzle an instant before he fired.

Their rear window shattered.

So much for Fagan not wanting to risk undue attention. A mobile gunfight in a populated tourist district *guaranteed* attention.

Bracing herself on her knees, Stasia took a breath and squeezed off a shot. The *bogomili* shooter slumped from the lead car's window. She followed with rapid-fire shots after that, taking out the windshield. The passengers in the back leaned out and opened fire on them. Bits of glass, leather, and metal churned under the onslaught. Something stung Stasia's cheek, but she continued firing.

They approached another intersection. Miró didn't slow at all. Stasia glanced to the right from which the traffic would come. A French police car a block away drove toward them. At the sight of them blowing through the stop sign, it turned on its lights and siren and sped up.

"Time to lose the mice?" asked Miró.

"Time to lose the mice."

She aimed for the *bogomili* driver and fired again. He collapsed. The car drifted into the intersection.

Miró pounded the car horn, downshifted, and slowed as they came down the final block before *Cours Mirabeau*.

The police car came wailing into the intersection and crashed into the stationary sedan.

The second sedan turned right. That would be a dead-end. Stasia had studied the map of the Mazarin Quarter.

She turned and sat back down, buckling her seatbelt.

Pedestrians scattered as they burst from the side street. A wide cobbled terrace bordered the mansions on either side of them, a double row of tall plane trees lining it. Tented clothing vendors sheltered under the trees on the left. Everywhere there were people, bicycles, motorcycles, cars, and bollards.

Miró eased through this cordon before reaching the avenue and the traffic circle into which the side street spilled. Turning right, he went around the circle to exit east on *Cours Mirabeau*. In the near distance came the sound of sirens.

"Go south on *Rue d'Italie*," Stasia said. "There is a parking garage on the *Boulevard Carnot* under the convention center."

They would leave the MINI in the garage.

Miró grunted and shifted as he came to the light at the end of *Cours Mirabeau*. He took the corner after the light changed to red, earning some angry honking from the car that he'd cut off. They were a block from the *Boulevard Carnot* when Miró spoke.

"We have company."

Stasia saw the third dark sedan as it turned in behind them. She had the uneasy feeling that they'd been herded in the direction that Fagan wanted them to head.

Two minutes later that feeling strengthened when another dark sedan pulled into traffic in front of them a block from the boulevard.

There wasn't much choice here in which direction to drive. Aix-en-Provence, as with many French cities, had narrow one-way streets lined with buildings that shared external walls. Miró's jaw tightened as he downshifted to take the corner right onto the boulevard, which was divided into two-way along the southern border of the Mazarin Quarter. He would be forced to turn and head northeast along with the *bogomili* escort.

"Perhaps a feint onto *Cours Gambetta?*" Stasia asked as they approached the turn.

Miró nodded and, looking over his shoulder at the traffic merging from both *Rue Sallier* and the larger artery of *Boulevard du Roi René*, waited until two cars had gotten between the MINI and the lead *bogomili* sedan. Then he shifted and accelerated, forcing his way in between the two cars on the wide boulevard. Horns blared. The rear *bogomili* sedan tried to follow but was cut off.

"We have more company exiting from *Rue d'Italie*," Stasia said.

A police car with flashing lights and sirens headed east on the *Boulevard Carnot* as well.

Miró downshifted as they came toward *Cours Gambetta*, swerving right onto it. The rear *bogomili* sedan followed. Miró jerked the wheel and reversed course around the pedestrian divider, managing to get into the far right lane and back onto *Boulevard Carnot* before the *bogomili* sedan had stopped and completed a three-point turn. By this time, it was trapped between cars.

Stasia watched as the *bogomili* abandoned their car. A trio of males ran toward *Boulevard Carnot* where they were picked up by the latest sedan. The police car wasn't far behind.

Miró drove in the left lane around a large panel van before swerving back to take the next exit into the underground parking garage. Stasia saw the combined *bogomili* car, the police car trailing, pass them on the boulevard. The *bogomili* clearly saw them, too. They wouldn't have long to leave the recognizable MINI and find another vehicle.

Miró looked for a spot on the first level. They definitely did *not* want to be trapped further underground.

Please, Zophiel, help us.

Stasia had no idea why she asked the guardian angel for help, but at the next turn there was a car pulling out. And next to it sat a silver Audi.

Grazie mille.

And she felt a warm whisper caress her cheek in response.

Miró parked and they got out. As trained operatives, they'd worn leather gloves so that they wouldn't need to wipe down the MINI's interior. Thumbing the safety decocker into place, Stasia holstered her Beretta and grabbed her bag. Miró had already gone to the far side of the Audi. She pulled out her baton.

A moment later Miró punched *through* the driver's window. How he managed that, she'd love to know. There *had* been a sharp disturbance in his harmonics just before his fist hit....

Hurrying to the passenger door, she struck the window in the corner, which shattered the tempered glass.

They got in. Miró opened the center console. To Stasia's surprise a key fob had been left as well as the parking ticket. Miró's smile was fierce as he started the Audi, put it into gear, and then backed out of the space. Seven minutes later they headed south on *Cours Gambetta* headed toward the A8 back to Saint-Cyr-sur-Mer.

"That was a bit more intense than I expected," Stasia said, looking back over her shoulder for a tail.

She pulled her collar up and stuck her hands into her pockets. It was cold in the car with the windows gone.

"Fagan appears to be obsessed." Miró focused on the traffic around them.

Stasia studied him. "You mean with the paintings and not with me."

He nodded. "How else do you explain his aggressive pursuit? An experienced handler such as he is would be very careful not to attract undue attention."

"Agreed. But why do you think that it is the paintings and not me? Is there something that you have not told me?"

"Do you recall what Mihàil said when you asked him whether Asmodeus was out of his angelic coma?"

"He said that you did not believe that was the case."

"If we are correct, Fagan stole the painting without Asmodeus as intermediary. Even if Asmodeus motivated him to steal the painting, Fagan would be vulnerable to Yeqon's angelic emanations."

"Let me guess. Yeqon seduced Fagan *through a painting.*"

"I believe so."

She shivered. "Then Fagan will continue to be reckless."

Miró slipped his hand around hers. It was warm. The warmth radiated up her arm and along the back of her neck, somehow making her less chilled everywhere.

She smiled at him in gratitude.

The next moment a dump truck pulled out of an Esso Express and t-boned them.

When Stasia's awareness returned, she hurt everywhere. For a long time all she could do was focus on breathing.

It was cold. So cold.

She blinked, but her eyes refused to open. And she began to shake.

"Ah, someone is regaining consciousness."

Fagan. *Cielo mi aiuti.*

Stasia struggled to lift her lids. A sharp pain in her side stole her breath. She had at least one broken rib. And a stinging cut over her right eye.

"Prop her up."

Strong hands—male, she guessed—pulled her upright and leaned her against something hard and frigid. Stasia's breath came fast from pain and fear.

"She's going into shock," a male voice said. "And hypothermia. If you want to get anything out of her, we'll need to warm her up."

"Do it." Fagan's curt voice brought her eyelids up.

He stood three meters away next to a large, bare tree whose branches swayed in the breeze. Catching sight of her looking at him, he laughed. His cold, bright eyes never blinked.

"Where is my colleague?" she managed to ask. Her hoarse voice shook, adding to her sense of shock. The large *bogomili* wrapped a thermal blanket around her.

Perfetto.

She engaged her harmonics without the support of breathing. If she was right, harmonics and thermodynamics were interconnected. She just needed to keep Fagan talking while she sped hers up. Where there was friction, there was bound to be heat.

"Someone is tying up loose ends."

What an odd thing to say. It didn't sound as if Miró was dead. She refused to consider anything beyond that. Operatives only survived by compartmentalizing and focusing on the present moment.

"Then you will get nothing from me."

She was definitely getting a little warmer, enough that her shaking had subsided and her hands no longer felt stiff and numb. Unfortunately they'd been zip-tied at the wrists. Soon they'd be numb from loss of circulation. Unless she could warm the plastic of the ties enough to let her break them....

Fagan chortled. "Oh, ho! That's rich from someone in your position."

Stasia shrugged, tilting her head to emphasize the movement. It sent a spike of pain to her injured torso. She managed not to wince.

"Or not. As you may guess, I am not easily manipulated. Or have you forgotten about your little experiment with MDMA?" She saw the speculation in his eyes. "Then again, I am very loyal to my friends. Perhaps you should bring him here." She infused as much charisma as she could into her voice.

Fagan studied her a moment before turning to the *bogomili*. "Clarkson, radio the team. Have them tell the *Elioud* male we have his partner. If he wants to see her, he'll let them take him."

He grinned at her. "We'll do it your way, Ms. Fiore." At her look of surprise, he said, "Yes, it took a while to identify you, but your Italian accent gave me a hint. That and your role in trying to recover the Rembrandt from the Dervishi brothers. How are they, by the way? Enjoying prison?"

Stasia felt the zip-ties sag against her wrists. She kept her face impassive as she looked around her, using her survey to disguise the fact that she'd shook the zip-ties free. They were in a cemetery, and she sat on the rounded granite lid of an above-ground casket-shaped tomb. There was a large cross standing at its head. The graves, like the buildings in the city center, ran in tight rows with no space between plots. The air had gotten noticeably colder as they talked though she was warm enough under the thermal blanket.

"Agron is plotting murder, but Abdyl has made a few friends. He smuggles in drugs and other sundries, like porn."

Fagan chuckled. "All's well that ends well, I see." He saw her looking around. "You should appreciate your perch. It's Cézanne's grave."

Stasia let her eyes widen in surprise. She looked down at the letters engraved in the stone. When she looked up again that's when she saw him.

He was the most terrifyingly beautiful creature she'd ever seen. Taller than Fagan by head and shoulders, perfectly proportioned, with terrible eyes that saw everything, the naked male next to Fagan elicited an urge to run screaming for sanctuary. But no matter how she looked, she couldn't get his form to solidify in a recognizable three dimensions. Instead spectral planes and lines jumped and danced from the nimbus glowing around him as if he had too much energy to be contained in this reality. There was a ghostly knotted cord running between him and Fagan like a tether. Fagan seemed either unaware of the awful being next to him or stupidly unafraid.

She swallowed hard.

Asmodeus.

Voices reached them. A group of *bogomili* escorted Miró, his hands zip-tied in front of him. He stumbled at their pace, but his gaze never left her. She could read his harmonics. They were ready to detonate.

Fagan watched Miró arrive with a smirk on his face.

"Ah, Ms. Fiore," he said turning to her. The smirk had transformed into greedy eagerness. He gestured toward the *bogomili* on Miró's right, who pulled out a combat knife and grabbed Miró's hands.

"Shall we begin? I'll take one of his fingers to start the auction. You'll tell me what you know about the third painting and the secret that Gregori told you about. I'll keep taking fingers until I'm satisfied with your answers. *Capisce?*"

Twenty-One

Mihàil Kastrioti scanned the landscape below as the EC130-T2 Eurocopter rose from the empty field of Železarnica Stadium in east Skopje. He wanted to punch something. Instead he brooded as Daněk, his Czech pilot, maneuvered around the Millennium Cross on top of Vodno Mountain and headed southwest to Albania. The 66-meter tall cross dominated the skyline, but all Mihàil could think about was his injured lieutenant. When had that ever happened before? Never, that's when.

"*Můj pane,*" Daněk said into his headset mic. *My lord.*

It wasn't much, but there was a world of meaning in that address.

Mihàil's attention snapped back to his surroundings. The cabin interior had clouded enough to obscure Daněk's vision. The air filter hadn't been able to keep up with his smoky breath. Closing his eyes for an instant, he forced his harmonics to calm and lowered his body temperature to normal. The air cleared.

"*Mockrát děkuju, můj pane.*"

"You do not have to thank me," Mihàil said. His voice was hoarse and his throat burned. "It is I who should apologize."

Daněk shook his head and said nothing. Mihàil didn't press the issue with his devoted retainer. Instead he returned to watching the mountains below. It was his first mission outside of Albania since he and Olivia had gotten married. He had been too long inside his protective borders. It was time to come out again.

On his right András sat next to Ms. Černá's stretcher, which spanned the space where two seats had been in the seven-seat helicopter. The big man wouldn't leave her side. He'd made it to the Re-Medika Hospital across the Gazi Baba Park from the Čair neighborhood where they'd tracked the *bogomili*, carrying her the entire way. More than a kilometer and suffering from almost a dozen bullet wounds, wounds that normally his heated body healed within moments.

Mihàil could see András's harmonic signature, which was thready and volatile. Even his infrared signature was cooler and more unstable.

What the hell? What did this mean?

He let his senses reach out to assess Ms. Černá, Olivia's lone-wolf friend. She lay motionless and pale on the flat mattress, but he wasn't at all convinced that she was asleep or unconscious, despite being heavily sedated for pain. Her infrared signature had an oddity to it that he couldn't explain. The tight ball of hot white at her core seemed to be riddled with fine black dots as if her internal heat suffered from static. Her harmonics were equally fuzzy.

He shook his head and wished that he could talk to Zophie about these aberrations in Ms. Černá's unique signatures. But Zophie had been noticeably absent since she'd appeared in his gym while Stasia was visiting. It made him uneasy. He hadn't realized how much he anticipated her abrupt visits or enjoyed her indirect, quirky manner. Now that there were two Dark *Irim* disrupting their lives, he'd really appreciate the guardian angel's guidance—especially since he no longer led a team of three hardcore, *unattached* warriors.

According to the emergency-room doctor, who released Ms. Černá into their care only because he understood Mihàil's authority as *drangùe*, András had cauterized the entrance to her stab wound and gotten her to the hospital so quickly that she'd lost very little blood. The knife itself had missed all major organs and blood vessels, thank the Archangel, and she would survive with nothing more than a tiny scar on her right side. A scar unlikely to be seen by anyone save a lover.

Mihàil glanced at András. Was Olivia right when she said that his exuberant, often ridiculously clueless, young lieutenant had more than a friendly interest in the taciturn Czech? If so, perhaps that could explain the Hungarian's oddly unsettled signatures. Perhaps it could even explain the fact that András came to the emergency room with bullets still in his back after decades expelling them from his flesh as molten drops of metal.

It certainly explained the fact that András had ignored his commander's direct order to leave the hospital and Ms. Černá, who needed to remain under medical care for another week. András might be a hothead at times, but he'd never been insubordinate before. He took his duties as an *Elioud* warrior as seriously as any *drangùe* could wish. In the end, Mihàil relented. He'd already intended to oversee Ms. Černá's recuperation and provide her with security at the hospital. Instead, his personal surgeon, sitting next to him in the helicopter, would care for her at his estate.

The flight over the Korab Mountains that defined North Macedonia and Albania took a little more than an hour. Every time he flew over these mountains, Mihàil was transported back in time to the final years of his father's life and the desperate, doomed resistance he'd led against the Ottoman Turks. Ten years after Georgj Kastrioti, the Dragon of Albania honored in that square in the Čair district of Skopje, died of malaria, Sultan Mehmed II's forces—one of the first modern standing armies of Europe—took his fortress at Krujë.

It should not have fallen.

Skanderbeg, as Mihàil's father was known, was never defeated by the Ottomans. Thirteen times he repulsed their invasions. He was a hero throughout Western Europe—the *Athleta Christi*—and an *Elioud* with three-quarters angel blood.

And his son Mihàil, an *Elioud* with even more angel blood, should have made sure that the Ottoman Turks did not subjugate Albania.

Instead, Mihàil had become Asmodeus's acolyte, serving the very sultan his father had held out against. While his brother Gjon managed to get military aid from King Ferdinand of Naples to try to retake his patrimony, Mihàil had ridden with the Ottoman cavalry to conquer Herzegovina. Then he'd gone on to subdue the Tartar khan ruling Crimea and the Safavids rebelling in Asia Minor.

And rather than dying in this despicable cause, Mihàil continued serving first one sultan and then another, eventually rising to the coveted rank of *Silahdar Agha*, the commander of Ahmed I's bodyguard, the Yellow Banners, in 1603. Exactly one-hundred-and-twenty-five years after the great Dragon of Albania died and fourteen years before he bought Miró from a *köçek* troupe. On Gjon Kastrioti II's orders, his name had been erased from memory.

It was better than he deserved.

Mihàil looked again at his lieutenant. András sat hunched next to Ms. Černá.

András had his own troubled history to contend with, but unlike Mihàil and Miró, it didn't include the unique lesson of intimate betrayal. Although Mihàil had betrayed his father by marrying the wrong woman and then going on a decades' long rampage of grief when she'd been killed, Miró had been the one betrayed by the woman he loved.

Uneasiness filled him as he looked at András.

But he kept his doubts to himself as the helicopter set down on his private helipad on the small man-made plateau behind his mansion.

Pjëter met him with a young man, someone new from Fushë-Arrëz who had been vetted personally by his long-time steward. Pjëter was not *Elioud*, and as far as Mihàil could discern, had no *Elioud* blood at all. Yet he had served Mihàil for decades, aging extremely slowly. And his father and grandfather and his grandfather's father and grandfather—

ancestors all the way back to the early 1600s—had all aged slowly in their faithful service to the *drangùe*. Mihàil was grateful. He didn't know what he would do without Pjëter, whose grown son had opted to become Mihàil's chief financial adviser.

The surgeon directed Pjëter and his attendant to move Ms. Černá. But before they could get close enough, András blocked their way.

"No one moves her but me."

Pjëter looked at Mihàil for confirmation.

Mihàil put his hand on András's shoulder. "Let them do their work. You are in no shape to bring her inside."

András looked at him. Hostility filled his dark-blue eyes. Before he could challenge his general directly—and suffer the consequences as a result—Mihàil shook his head. He let his authority show.

"That is an order."

András struggled for a moment with some strong emotion before he nodded. He watched as Pjëter and his attendant got the stretcher out and extended its legs then started to follow as they moved it.

But Mihàil kept his hand on his lieutenant's shoulder. "After the surgeon checks your dressings, go and clean up. Then report to my office."

András nodded again, this time with his gaze down. Mihàil suspected that it was to keep his expression hidden.

"And András? If I have to come looking for you, there is going to be hell to pay. Get yourself under control, understood?"

"Copy that."

This time when András looked at him, his expression had shuttered. Mihàil's unease doubled.

Zophie, where are you?

***

At that moment the guardian angel stood outside the Audi SUV that Olivia had rented upon reaching Vienna. Olivia had been startled when Zophie popped the passenger door open thirty seconds before and held out a travel mug with coffee. She had a printout of various office and industrial rental properties on her lap and hadn't realized that coffee would be welcome in the chill after two hours of touring potential sites for Fagan's personal stash.

"Here."

Nonplussed, Olivia took it.

Zophie next dangled a crinkly pastry bag and then slid in as Olivia grabbed it.

"*Pain au chocolat.* My favorite. Don't tell Michael."

The angel set her own travel mug in the cupholder and turned to Olivia. "Well? If you're not going to eat yours, can I at least have mine?"

Olivia, realizing that her mouth was open, shut it with a snap. She handed the pastry bag back to the angel, who opened it with eager hands and pulled out a flaky, oblong croissant with a heart of chocolate. Its sweet, buttery fragrance filled the cool air inside the SUV. Olivia's heat senses were still weak, but she could tell that the pastry was warm.

Zophie took a bite, closing her eyes and leaning back against the headrest. "Mm. That *is* divine."

Olivia looked at Zophie's serene profile. Some days Zophie appeared as a refined upperclass socialite wearing Cartier and Louboutin. Others she looked like a yoga-practicing ingénue. Today the guardian angel wore a black leather jacket and pants. Her blond hair was long and straight and very pale next to her almost-translucent skin. A small crumb stuck to the bottom of her pale pink lips, which she licked with a delicate tongue, sighing. Of all the things that Olivia had had to get used to after learning that she had angel blood, the hardest had been the nonchalant visits by an actual angel.

"Hm, not always so nonchalant," said Zophie, swiveling her face to look at Olivia. Her shocking blue eyes demanded full attention. "Michael has been a bear lately, if you must know. What with Asmodeus tormenting innocents in France and Yeqon pretending to be misunderstood, he has had his fill of these Dark *Irim* in your purview. Which, of necessity, makes it *my* purview. Hence, not so nonchalant."

She crumpled the pastry bag into a tiny ball and dropped it into the cupholder before sipping her coffee.

Olivia swallowed hard. Zophie was a chatty angel, but this had been a long monologue even for her. A long, *serious* monologue.

"I had no idea that you ever got stressed."

Zophie waved a graceful hand as she took another sip. When she spoke again, the subject appeared to be closed.

"No matter what happens, dear one, remember that I have your back. All of you. The warriors may be my little ducklings to guide or knock up side the head, whatever the situation calls for, but you and your friends are part of my coterie now. Michael may doubt you, but I never will. Plus there is no way I would ever bet on those *angeli infidelibus ponet.*"

The way she said 'unfaithful angels' sounded like an epithet.

"St. Michael doubts us?"

Olivia fingered the small silver medal with his likeness that she wore on a chain around her neck. It was cool to the touch. A slight chill ran down her spine.

Zophie looked at her. "Not you, dear one."

She patted Olivia's hand where it rested on the steering wheel. "You were wise to contact Miles Baxter. I have been nudging him, little duckling that he is, to move away from his current career and toward something more edifying. You are the instrument of his big chance."

She grinned. "But he may not see it that way. Go easy on him. Some of the toughest fighters are the biggest doubters of their self worth."

"He asked me for a little mission support." Olivia couldn't keep the anticipation out of her voice.

She hadn't been on a mission in eight months, and she hadn't realized how much she missed it until she'd decided to get involved in Stasia's efforts to recover the stolen Rembrandt. She may just be helping her best friend to return to her career with Italian foreign intelligence, but that was the right play.

"So I don't know how I'll be able to influence him."

Zophie didn't respond to that. Instead, she tipped her coffee up and seemed to swallow the last of it.

"Well, coffee break is over, I am afraid."

She opened the passenger door and slid out before bending down and saying, "She is going to need something to sleep in. I put it in your trunk."

Before Olivia could ask who the guardian angel referred to, the door shut with a click. Sighing, she finished her coffee and ate her *pain au chocolat*. Zophie might be cryptic and show up unexpectedly, but she gave useful and timely gifts. Right now, Olivia found that the caffeine-and-sugar combination fed her intuition. Circling a listing on her paperwork and jotting down some notes, she dropped the pile into the vacated front seat and started the SUV. It was time to return to her hotel, the Hotel Sacher, in the city center. She must go shopping in order to meet

Miles for lunch as if they were old friends. He would tell her more about his mission and how she could support him.

So at one p.m., she found herself sitting inside the small Trattoria Toscana La No, a five-minute walk from her hotel. It was her favorite restaurant from her time in Vienna, and she'd only shared it with her closest friends. Stasia had proclaimed it a little piece of home when she came to visit. Olivia looked around her, feeling a little nostalgic for her pre-*Elioud* days when she'd donned a *zentai* hood and pretended to be a super hero. She had never brought Mihàil here.

Miles arrived late, wearing sunglasses and a brown suede jacket.

As he came striding toward her, a small smile on his face, Olivia was struck with how handsome the CIA extraction expert was. He didn't have the same magnetic air that Mihàil had, but that was unfair. If she'd never fallen in love with a *drangùe*, she would have found this confident, athletic man both intriguing and compelling.

She wouldn't have recognized the subtle effects of his harmonics, which were more in tune with hers than most of her CIA colleagues were.

Miles had a small shopping bag in his hand, which he set on the table as he bent to kiss her as if they were old friends. Or old lovers.

He took his jacket off, and draping it on his chair, sat across from her at the two-person table. When he pulled the sunglasses away, she saw that his intelligent eyes were an alluring green-blue.

"You're looking exceedingly well." He accepted the glass of Chianti she poured from the half carafe on their table.

She shrugged and sipped her wine. "Being married suits me."

His sharp gaze took in more than she said. "But you miss the game."

"And you tire of it."

Something flickered in his eyes, but he didn't respond. "You have something you need my help with?"

She nodded. From the corner of her eye, she saw the head waiter, the trattoria's owner, lead a couple to a nearby table. It was hard to be secluded in the small space, but she'd made sure that no one would be seated next to them at least.

"Fagan has a certain item that doesn't belong to him in an undisclosed location. I'm betting that he stashed it in Vienna. I need help finding and recovering it."

Miles narrowed his eyes. "That sounds risky."

"Does it help that as far as I can tell he's way off the books on this? As in, this has nothing to do with Company business."

"A little." He toyed with the earpiece of his sunglasses. "But Fagan strikes me as someone who makes little distinction between his business and Company business."

"Agreed." She paused. "Are you in?"

"You and your friends lead my team on a merry chase through Central Europe and you ask me if I'm willing to help you?" There was an edge to his words.

Their waiter arrived. Olivia ordered her favorites, an *insalata mista* and *tagliatelle Bolognese*. Miles chose the gnocchi with pecorino and black truffles. If nothing else, they would both enjoy their meals. As operatives, there were too many times in the field where they were forced to eat protein bars washed down with bottled water. That's why meetings in fine restaurants were popular. And no one ever left without eating well.

"As I said before, don't do me any favors. Do it because I'm helping you with your mission."

He studied her. He was trying to decide if he trusted her. In a flash of insight, she knew that whatever he was doing was a side project, not an official objective for his CIA handlers. Intrigued, she hummed a little, letting her harmonics vibrate on a soothing wavelength. His harmonics responded by relaxing. A moment later Miles made his decision.

He tapped the small shopping bag with light fingertips. "A small present for you."

Olivia peeked inside. A USB device nestled amongst the tissue paper. Next to it was a sparkling crystal star. Delighted, she pulled it from the bag by its white satin ribbon.

"A Swarovski Christmas ornament?"

She was oddly touched even though she knew it was *pocket litter*—a spy's tactic for backing up his identity. Not a personalized gift.

"Every newlywed couple needs one." There was an odd, wistful note in his voice. He cleared his throat. "The elevator pitch for this mission is this: you're going to reprise your role with ABA-Invest Austria when I meet with Zoran Mamic, the head coach for Dinamo Zagreb. He's using fictitious player transfers to embezzle from his club. I'm pretending to represent First Vienna. I'm using Mamic to launder money for an operation and get dirt on him for the Croatian government at the same time."

The waiter returned with Olivia's salad. She ate in silence for a moment. Miles watched her with hooded eyes, but she read the tension in his harmonics. It really mattered to him that she take this job.

At last she said, "There's more to this than conning a greedy and corrupt soccer coach." She held his gaze, letting her *Elioud* authority shine from it.

Miles shifted in his chair and poured himself more wine. His harmonics tightened like cable railing. He fought the pressure she exerted on him. Olivia took pity and placed a gentle hand on his. Her harmonics shifted, easing his. When he lifted his face, there was startled recognition in his gaze.

"Tell me," she said. Her *Elioud* charm was less vibrant than Stasia's charisma but effective nonetheless.

"Mamic has an associate who likes young, inexperienced women. He tells them that he runs an executive training program for foreign companies who plan to invest in Croatia and want local managers."

"He's really grooming candidates for predators, likely businessmen from the Middle East and Asia."

"Yes."

Olivia remembered the sleepwear that Zophie left in the trunk of her SUV.

"And Mamic brought one of these 'candidates' with him to Vienna."

"I told him that I was eager to have an 'assistant' who would help me recruit investors for First Vienna."

"And I'm going to play the naive ABA-Invest intern who will convince this assistant that you're offering her a legitimate position."

"And sweeten the deal for Mamic, who believes that I'll funnel investment funds to him in exchange for her."

Olivia's heat rose. She exuded a bit of smoke.

Miles, twisting in his chair, looked back toward the kitchen. "Are they burning your *Bolognese?*"

Sipping from her water, Olivia dropped her temperature and calmed her breathing. Before she could speak, the waiter came from behind the small counter in front of the cooking area. He carried two white porcelain bowls. The savory scent of their pasta displaced the faint trace of smoke from her momentary loss of control. Setting the dishes in front of them, the waiter grated fresh parmesan over their entrees before leaving them to enjoy their food.

Olivia ignored her *Bolognese*. Instead, she held Miles's gaze. This time she let him see the *drangùe*'s lady in her eyes. His own widened. His pulse raced and his breath sped. A light sheen of sweat on his forehead caught the sunlight from the window.

When she'd judged that Miles truly had some idea of who he was talking to, Olivia said, "Of course, I will help you extract this young woman."

She paused to let the authority in her harmonics swell over his. Then she picked up her fork before taking a bite. He sat speechless.

She chewed and swallowed as if they were having a casual lunch before she said, "And when I've recovered what Fagan has stolen, I'll go to Croatia and convince Mamic and his associates to cancel their training program."

Twenty-Two

At Fagan's announcement, Stasia's heart jumped into her throat.

"Wai—" she said at the same time Fagan gestured.

The *bogomili* holding the combat knife cut Miró's finger off. Miró groaned and swayed. The *bogomili* on his left clamped a hard hand on his upper arm and steadied him.

Stasia's heart jumped around inside her ribcage like a terrified swallow.

Asmodeus watched the drama unfold, a lascivious gleam in his gaze. But he said nothing.

Fagan chuckled. "I know how you field operatives act, Ms. Fiore. And think. I won't be played. Now, you have thirty seconds to tell me what you know about the third painting. Go."

Stasia couldn't think. She couldn't move. If she didn't say something, Miró would lose another finger. Why didn't he flare?

He knows about the third painting….

"I know nothing about the third painting!" Desperation tinged her voice.

Fagan's humor died. He narrowed his eyes and raised his hand to gesture again.

"No!" Stasia shouted.

"You know something," Fagan said. "Why else are you here in Aix-en-Provence?"

"Because Gregori said another painter brought Caravaggio's paintings here. He told me that there is a rumor about a third painting. We came to look for clues."

Stasia had never been so scared on a mission before. She couldn't get her equilibrium, act like a dispassionate professional, *charm* the bastard. Bile rose in her throat.

He'd cut Miró's finger off.

Fagan's hand waited, like the sword of Damocles, over Miró's bleeding hand.

"*What* did he say about the third painting?" His voice had a hard, eager edge.

"Tell him nothing." Pain serrated Miró's voice.

Stasia could have bitten her tongue. She refused to look at Miró. If he hadn't spoken, she could have denied everything. She locked her gaze onto Fagan.

"The rumor is that the paintings form a triptych. They hide a secret about the Watcher Angels."

Fagan waved, irritation showing on his face. "That much I got from him myself." He looked at the *bogomili*. "Cut another one off."

Stasia flared.

For an instant the whole world was flat, bright white as if a giant camera flash had gone off. When she blinked again, the *bogomili* and Fagan stood dazed with tears streaming down their cheeks. Asmodeus stared at her. He looked as if he could eat her soul.

Stasia slid from Cézanne's grave and ran toward Fagan.

Miró raised his hands and the zip ties fell from them. Twisting to the right, he reached for the *bogomili*'s knife hand, grabbing his wrist and yanking his arm up before elbowing the *bogomili* in the chest. Even as the *bogomili* crumpled around the sharp jab, Miró pulled him forward and brought his forearm down on the back of his neck.

That was the last that Stasia saw before she intercepted Fagan, who'd taken a step toward the trio. Grabbing his jacket, she rotated away from the *bogomili* and Miró. Fagan followed her around, his hands coming to grip her arms.

Asmodeus loomed. Terror closed Stasia's throat. She shook.

Harmonics. Miró flashed to her.

Stasia felt a harmonic wave roll toward her from Miró. She let the wave vibrate through her, amplifying it and sending the combined harmonic wave into Fagan. His eyes widened as her harmonics crashed over him, swamping his own harmonics, then rolled into the back of his head. Still he held onto her with a painful claw-like grip even as his knees sagged.

Stasia dropped to her knees under Fagan's weight. She grabbed his forearms and raised her temperature, imagining that Fagan's hands were zip ties. At the same time, she pulled him closer, lowering her head as she did, and smashed the top of it under his chin. Fagan's head snapped back.

The scent of burnt flesh rose.

Fagan began screaming. And thrashing. But Stasia held on, pressing her fingers into the flesh as she imagined it liquefying.

"Stop! Stop! Make it stop, you bitch!" Fagan's face had whitened. He bellowed, ripping his hands from her arms. An instant later he punched Stasia in the face.

She fell back against Cézanne's tomb, catching her cheek on the icy stone edge. Her right eye swelled until she could see only through the left one.

The sound of inhuman laughter stopped all movement.

It ran through Stasia's harmonics like a scraper on an icy windshield. Her flesh crawled as a horde of invisible insects raced over it. She turned and retched against the side of the tomb.

When she turned back, she saw Fagan standing a meter away, his jacket and flesh blackened and torn in ragged chunks, showing white bone beneath. He frothed and snapped like a vicious dog on a chain, but the twisted spectral cord tethered him to Asmodeus, who stood watching her and ignoring his acolyte. The Dark *Irim* looked more solid than he had moments before.

More horrifyingly real.

Just beyond these two abominations stood Miró, panting, near the unmoving forms of both *bogomili*.

Look at me, he flashed.

Stasia tore her gaze from Fagan and Asmodeus and focused on Miró. He was pale and held his ravaged hand under his opposite armpit.

Amore mio. She clung to Miró's harmonic braid as if it were a lifeline. She wanted to go to him but found that she couldn't move.

His face took on a wolfish triumph.

Asmodeus flicked a hand toward his acolyte without looking at him. "Enough." It was a deep, rough growl that ended in a hiss.

Fagan stopped making a sound and stood motionless. His large eyes bugged. Sweat trickled down his temples.

Asmodeus turned and looked toward the *bogomili*, whose corpses had already started to decompose. His gaze honed in on them in a way that made Stasia's stomach hurt in anticipation. He held his hand toward the bodies. And then ghostly forms detached from him and bent over them. High-pitched squeaks and almost inaudible growls chased one another outside Stasia's natural hearing as the ghostly figures devoured the *bogomili*. Within thirty seconds nothing remained of them.

Stasia raised her eyes to Asmodeus, revolted to her core.

"Daughter." His voice modulated as his form had done before, ranging from a low growl to a mellifluous tenor. Its unnatural timbre and cadence made her teeth ache.

"I am not your daughter."

Asmodeus smiled. His knowing gaze assured her that she was.

"My acolyte was too impatient to satisfy his obsession to interrogate you properly." There was a hint of anger in those words. Stasia tucked that insight away. "Mistake me not. I will know what you know."

His *Irim* authority swelled the statement inside her head though the actual volume of sound in her ears was low. It was disorienting, this simultaneous engagement of her *Elioud* and human senses.

Ignore him, Miró flashed. *He cannot make you say anything unless you let him.*

Stasia refrained from looking at Miró to acknowledge his silent message. Her intuition told her that Asmodeus had no idea that they could communicate that way.

He will know what I want him to know, she flashed back.

She gathered her tattered *Elioud* charisma from where it had scattered and spoke, infusing her words with a bare hint. It was best to go softly with this one.

"I told him the truth. We do not know the secret in the triptych."

Asmodeus frowned. Fagan moaned.

Stasia raced to continue, letting her voice shake with the very real nerves that she felt. But they no longer controlled her. *She controlled them.*

"But we have a theory."

Fagan's moan turned into a choking gurgle and then silence.

"Go on." Harsh spectral planes and lines began to flicker along the Dark *Irim*'s periphery.

Stasia licked her lips and swallowed. She fed a little more *Elioud* charisma into her voice. "We think that the third painting is of Yeqon." On impulse she added, "But surely you know this already. Your acolyte works with Yeqon. They stole the Caravaggio painting in Prague together."

The spectral planes and lines disappeared into Asmodeus's solid form. Steam rose from his skin, and the frigid March afternoon heated around them.

Nice, Miró flashed. He not only understood what she was doing, he approved. The warmth of his encouragement trickled into her chest. His harmonics kept hers steady.

She spoke before the Dark *Irim* did. It was time to turn the linchpin toward her, reeling Asmodeus into her net.

"You did not know," said Stasia, twisting her *Elioud* charisma into a semblance of soft compassion while displaying mild shock. "Your acolyte kept that from you."

Fagan's eyes bulged and his throat muscles worked.

"To tell the truth, Fagan most likely did not recognize who Yeqon was. He took on the cover identity of an international art thief named *L'Amante*."

Asmodeus narrowed his eyes. He seemed to grow taller.

"My brother knows that this one"—here Fagan shook as if buffeted by a strong wind—"belongs to me," he growled.

"But the paintings belong to Yeqon," said Stasia. "Perhaps he was simply trying to keep what is his by stealing your acolyte."

There. She'd set the hook.

Asmodeus snarled. "Then my brother will soon discover that his ploy has failed. This human is worthless to me. And I will keep my brother's paintings. *They* are not worthless."

The knotted spectral tether unraveled and dissolved. Suddenly Fagan stood unbound with a mad gleam in his eyes.

Stasia's heartrate sped up. She swallowed.

A blink and Asmodeus stood next to her. His crystalline blue eyes showed no sympathy, only stony curiosity. He lifted her chin with a hard forefinger. She stood rigid and uncomplaining before his exacting scrutiny.

"Perhaps you would care to become my acolyte?" His low, gravelly voice raked her. Invisible warm fingers touched her all over, squeezing her breasts, stroking her between her legs.

Stasia shivered. "No."

Her head was yanked back by her hair. "No? You respond so well, Daughter. Are you certain that you aren't already mine?" She felt the Dark *Irim*'s harmonics play along her skin as he sought to possess her.

A heartbeat later Miró stood behind her. She felt the strength of his harmonics blending with hers until she couldn't tell where hers ended and his began. A soft gleam illuminated their skin, barely visible in the sunlight.

Asmodeus blinked and in a blur of light stood two meters away. His wore a confused, angry expression.

"What is this?" His discordant voice broke into chirps, shrieks, moans, and howls. Every word hurt Stasia's ears.

Miró began to hum, transforming all of the discordant sounds into a pleasing melody on their private wavelength. Stasia's hammering heartrate slowed to normal. She smiled.

Then Asmodeus popped into and out of their sight in a dizzying survey around them before again halting two meters away, no longer solid and towering but shrunken and translucent. His awful beauty had collapsed into wrinkled ugliness around those cruel eyes.

"What have you done?" he hissed. "Your harmonics...your harmonics are dynamic."

"Like an *Irim?*" asked Miró in a voice that rang with *Elioud* authority.

He radiated heat. She felt warm and safe.

Asmodeus studied them as if they were a nasty bug in his soup. Indeed, his nostrils flared and his expression soured.

"No matter, *Elioud.*" He spat the words as if they tasted bad. "I have a better choice, a *much* better choice. In fact, I have dallied here too long for sport. Which, I'm afraid, has lost its appeal. Although it occurs to me that I can redeem this little interlude to my satisfaction."

He laughed. It grated, disrupting the sweetness of the harmonic melody between her and Miró. A hot, rancid wind swept through the cemetery, kicking up leaves.

Fagan chuckled across from them. Stasia's gaze took in the former acolyte. What she saw dropped a cold lump into her gut. There was a decidedly feral look in his eyes and a 9mm Glock in his hand.

And Asmodeus had disappeared.

An instant later Fagan shot Stasia.

Or he would have if she hadn't anticipated the shot and flung herself sideways. Miró sped his harmonics and appeared next to

Fagan, grabbing the gun with his good hand. He immediately struck Fagan's nose with the heel of his injured hand.

Fagan's head snapped back. His head came upright and Stasia noticed two things: blood streaming from his broken nose and froth bubbling from his mouth. He was literally rabid.

The sounds that came from Fagan's mouth were anything but sane. So when he turned toward Miró and attacked, teeth snapping, Stasia wasn't shocked.

Instead she sprung upright and dashed to the other side of him as Miró again sped his harmonics and disappeared from Fagan's line of sight.

Stasia delivered a brutal side kick to the back of Fagan's knee. He staggered as the leg sagged but whirled to face her, oblivious to the pain. Miró appeared behind him, wrapping his forearm around Fagan's neck. Fagan writhed but apparently hadn't forgotten all of his training even in his madness. Sinking down, he kept his chin tucked and stepped back, hooking his foot around Miró's calf. Then he twisted. Though he was too slow and too short to throw Miró, who expected the move, he was able to break free of the headlock.

Hunched over, Fagan head butted Miró in the middle of his chest and kept going. Miró lost a step and then another, throwing up his injured hand to regain his balance. Fagan lunged for the hand as if he scented blood. He caught it.

Excruciating pain rippled through Miró's harmonics and nearly swamped Stasia.

And then Fagan was on top of Miró, teeth snapping and clawed hands scrabbling for purchase as Miró tried to block and defend. Fagan moved like quicksilver. It was all Miró could do to avoid being ripped to shreds. Even so Fagan managed to tear his jacket and bite his arm before Miró rammed a finger in the other man's eye.

Miró delivered a focused harmonic jab that reverberated through Stasia, but Fagan, after a moment of rigidity, shrugged it off. His renewed attack was even wilder than before. There was no way for Miró to use his thermodynamics to spontaneously combust the rabid CIA officer

Stasia watched in horror. She saw no opening in which to help the man she loved.

She'd crept closer hoping to kick Fagan again when an idea hit her.

Incoming harmonics, she flashed.

Copy that.

Humming, she gathered her harmonics in a tight band before exhaling hard. Her harmonics expanded in an explosive wave that dislodged Fagan from Miró for a second. Miró caught the wave as if it were a beach ball and flung it sideways. Fagan flew with it, slamming into the nearest tomb as if shot from a cannon. His body instantly became a rag doll and landed with a dull thud on the ground.

Stasia waited, expecting Fagan to rise and come at them again like the *zombi* she'd once described *bogmili* as. She was sweating and shaking in the chilly air.

Fagan didn't rise.

Miró rolled to his side and used his uninjured hand to steady himself as he got to his knees. Then he stood. His jacket had been shredded. His button-down shirt, previously crisp and clean, was soiled and crumpled with one side pulled free of his waistband. Dirt covered him. It was in the fine lines on his face and the corners of his eyes. There were leaves and sticks in his formerly immaculate hair.

And on everything, blood.

Ignoring the pain in her side from her broken ribs and the throbbing ache in her swollen face, Stasia ran to Miró. He let her slide in next to him and stood while she carefully ran her hands over him, searching for hidden wounds. He made no sound and his expression remained opaque as she lifted his right hand to examine it.

A sharp pang stole Stasia's breath. But she said nothing, simply turning and dropping to her knees.

"What are you doing?" Miró's raspy voice broke the silence.

"Finding your finger." *Please, St. Michael, let me find it.*

"We need to leave. Fagan likely has other *bogomili* teams who will be looking for us even if their master is dead."

Stasia ignored him. The activity had eddied and flowed once Miró had engaged the *bogomili*, but the trio had been standing next to the freestanding sign marking Cézanne's grave. The severed finger couldn't have gone far on the frozen ground.

There! It was lying on a bare patch of earth. She snatched it. Standing, she returned to Cézanne's tomb. The thermal blanket had pooled at its base. She wrapped some of the snow in a corner of the blanket, tying it into a bundle. Then she set the finger next to it before going to Fagan's body. Finding a folding tactical knife in an inside pocket of his jacket, she returned to the thermal blanket and cut the excess from it so that she could tie the finger into its own pocket where it would be kept cool but not damaged from the ice. She slid the tactical knife into her jacket pocket and the package into her other pocket.

She returned to Miró's side. "We are going to the hospital." When she spoke, she eschewed charisma and softness. In fact, she infused her words with finality.

What she heard was *Elioud* authority.

Miró must have heard it too because he nodded curtly. "We can take their vehicle."

Stasia fell into step next to him. Miró's harmonics vibrated oddly as if he were trying to soothe himself. Or maintain his temperature. He was likely in shock. She slipped her hand around the forearm above his injured hand and began humming. She imagined sending warmth into his arm where it would flow up and into his body.

"Thank you." He didn't look down at her, but his posture relaxed somewhat. His lips compressed into a thin line, however. "I closed the wound. It will heal."

"It will also heal once the finger is reattached."

He didn't respond.

They walked around the low stone wall that surrounded the Cimetière Saint-Pierre and crossed the two-lane avenue to the public parking lot where the *bogomili* had parked their black late-model Mercedes. Luck was with them. The *bogomili* hadn't bothered to lock the car. Miró slid into the passenger seat while Stasia got in the driver's side. A cursory search showed that neither luck nor Zophie had left an ignition fob anywhere.

Stasia didn't need either luck or the fob, however.

Pulling Fagan's tactical knife from her pocket, she pried the ignition button cover off and finger started the car.

"I doubt Mercedes would approve of that hack," Miró said drily as she set the navigation system to find the closest hospital.

Stasia looked over her shoulder as she backed out of the parking space. "Then they should fix the design flaw." She stopped and put the car in drive before glancing at him. "Put on your seatbelt."

After that she drove as she'd been trained to drive. The hospital was just over half a kilometer away. She made it in less than three minutes.

ed into a short-term parking spot. Miró waited for her around and together they walked into the emergency entrance of the private hospital. Stasia told the staff what had happened as they helped Miró into a wheelchair. The nurse who accepted the severed finger exclaimed and hustled away to clean and prep it.

Good fortune had been with them again. One of the hospital's specialties, it turned out, was cosmetic and reconstructive surgery.

Miró's eyes closed as soon as he slouched in the wheelchair. He was pale and sweating. His harmonics vibrated in an unsteady pattern. Though Stasia watched as he was wheeled down a corridor away from her, she could sense his rapid breathing. She saw how cool he was. A deep orange-red blossomed in his chest and radiated out in deeper red along his extremities. Suddenly, she realized that she'd seen his thermal signature, and it was abnormal.

For the first time since she'd met him, Stasia understood how mortal Miró was, angel hybrid notwithstanding.

And she was shaken to her core.

Twenty-Three

Olivia waited on a bench at Ressel Park, coffee in one hand and smartphone in the other, for Miles to return from the CIA substation where he'd been scheduled to update the assistant station chief about the operation with Mamic. He'd also used the visit as a means of gathering intelligence on Fagan, who was out of the substation on an unknown objective. Though Miles was known as the Company's best snatch-and-grab operator in Central and Eastern Europe, he'd started as a typical field operative trained in a wide range of means to surveil targets. In this case, he'd learn more about the station chief from his subordinates.

And gain access to Fagan's office.

The access to Fagan's computer and files was priceless. Olivia suspected that Fagan was too paranoid to leave much in his office, but Miles would be able to plant a listening device. And he already had an access card to the station's servers. It would be simple enough for him to use Fagan's computer to log in, and then use Fagan's own hacking toolkit to hack his hard drive. The toolkit would erase any evidence of Miles's access card being used. Fagan would have no idea that his files had been breached.

Olivia smiled to herself. What was that quote? *Oft evil will shall evil mar.*

Fagan deserved everything he got. It was only sweeter that his own tools were being used against him.

Miles arrived, walking from the west side of the park near the Technical University of Vienna. The substation was in Wieden, the fourth district, next to the Vienna city center, in an ultra-modern office tower. She wondered if the offices looked the same with their tan carpets and hard furniture. Her desk had been in a tiny interior room scarcely bigger than a closet. She'd hated the few hours that she'd had to spend there to write up her reports and meet with other analysts. Truth be told, she'd much preferred her cover identity as a grad student working at the much more attractive ABA-Invest offices. It wasn't just the large windows and pleasant coworkers. She'd been good at her cover because she'd been content to pretend that it was who she really was.

"No one seems to know where Fagan is," said Miles as he sat on the bench next to her. "Fagan has been disappearing regularly for the past six months, usually for a few hours here and there. But this time, he's been gone for three days."

"That's because he's in France chasing a friend of mine."

Miles looked over at her. "If I'm risking my career at the Company for you, I'm going to need to know more."

"Are you sure that you want to know more? As I said, this has nothing to do with CIA business. No one will know that you've been involved, least of all Fagan. You've already repaid my work extracting Tadeja, which I would have done regardless."

She glanced at Miles. His profile was hard.

After a moment, he looked at her again. "Yes, I want to know."

"Fagan's been working with someone on the side, someone he met in the Balkans before he came to Vienna. Last fall, he hired two Albanians to steal a Rembrandt painting from an Italian art dealer. The *Carabinieri* sent an operative to get it back from the Albanians, but Fagan got to the painting first."

"Let me guess. The Italian operative is one of your friends." At Olivia's startled look, he said, "I did a little digging into you after our meeting in Budapest. I discovered that you did a joint op in Italy that brought down a Serbian arms dealer. There just happened to be an operative named Anastasia Fiore on the team. Her height and weight match the smaller of the two 'friends' backing you on the bridge."

Olivia felt strangely vulnerable knowing that Miles had sussed out her connection. Then again, he'd known it for some time and not acted on it.

He read her thoughts. "I found myself rather impressed at your team-building skills. It didn't seem necessary to alert anyone at the Company about your extracurriculars."

"It's also why you knew I'd help with Tadeja."

He nodded. "Perhaps you rubbed off on me a little."

Olivia had seen how gently he'd treated the young Croatian woman. She'd had very little to do with his willingness to help Tadeja.

His gaze turned inward for a moment. Olivia suspected that he was thinking about Tadeja, for whom he'd had to find a safe house. She wouldn't be able to return to Croatia until they'd handled Mamic and his partner.

Then Miles looked at Olivia again with his piercing blue-green eyes. "Ms. Fiore came to you when she realized who'd taken the painting."

"She needs to recover the Rembrandt, but she's been put on a leave of absence for helping me out with another project."

"And another Italian operative has been sent to Vienna to deal with Fagan."

"Yes. I've come across traces of this new player, but I haven't run into whoever it is."

"But you have no intention of letting the Italians recover the Rembrandt, is that it?" Miles smiled at her. He really was a handsome man. And too smart for comfort.

She narrowed her eyes.

"The Rembrandt will be returned in due course," she said, letting a hard note bolster her words. "It would certainly help my friend get reinstated, if she chooses. But I'd like a chance to examine the painting first. Fagan wanted it for a reason, and I'd like to know what it was."

Miles studied her for a long moment. Olivia wondered if he was going to ask her why she cared about what Fagan was involved in, but instead he honed in on something else that she'd said.

"What makes you think your friend won't choose to return to Italian foreign intelligence? Are you trying to recruit her long-term for your team?"

It was Olivia's turn to study Miles. She'd known that he was an exceptional operative, but his snatch-and-grab specialty didn't seem as if it would make good use of his ability to read people. Then again, perhaps that was exactly the reason he was so good at locating and exfiling targets, some of whom were hostile to the whole process—often in environments where the local authorities frowned on such extralegal activities.

She decided not to deny that she had a 'team.' She could recruit him, too. Suddenly she understood that this is exactly what Zophie wanted.

"As a matter of fact, I am."

"Let me guess again. Your team helps vulnerable women like Tadeja."

"Among others." She'd leave the details vague for now. But he had enough of an idea about the basic nature of what the *Elioud* did.

Miles didn't say anything. Olivia didn't worry. A germ of an idea had been planted in the last few minutes of their conversation. Now it was up to Miles—likely with Zophie's *nudging* as she put it—to come to the right conclusion. It would be on *his* schedule, however. Today they had to deal with the matter at hand.

"But for now, I need to determine where Fagan has stashed a painting worth fifteen million euros. I suspect that he wanted to keep it close when he was in Vienna."

"So not far from the substation."

"Correct. But not necessarily at his apartment, though I think he'd want to have it near at hand there as well."

"Are you sure that Fagan didn't move it on the black market? He could fund a lot of nasty crap with fifteen million euros, especially if it can't be traced back to him."

Olivia shook her head. "As soon as I knew that Fagan was behind the theft, I put together a dossier on potential buyers. At that price point and given that it's a stolen painting, there aren't many who'd deal with Fagan. I also have reason to believe that his partner has a particular obsession with the painting itself."

"Maybe *he* has it."

No way could Olivia explain why that was unlikely. Time to fall back on her experience working for Fagan.

"Our intelligence says that the partner has been detained, shall we say, for an indefinite time period. My gut tells me that Fagan still has the painting here in Vienna."

"He could return any time. Why is he in France chasing your Italian friend?"

Olivia needed to handle this delicately. She heard an echo of Zophie's earlier admonition: *kiss-kiss*. She smiled to herself.

"Stasia has information that the Rembrandt is part of a series of related paintings that Fagan's partner is interested in. So she headed to France to follow a lead. Fagan had a mole in my household who bugged her when she came to see me. Ergo, he went to find out what she knows."

"And she knows that he's following her, so she's keeping him busy while you get the painting for her." Miles grinned. "I like the way your team works. Anyone that makes a fool of that arrogant asshole has my full and undying admiration."

Olivia felt herself relax and realized that she'd been worried about Miles's interest in their objectives. She also cared that he approved of their methods.

"The mole in my household told me that she'd been asked to deliver a package to Joseph Eagan, Director, Arian Resources, who'd come to Fushë-Arrëz where I live. Arian Resources is a Canadian mineral exploration company, so that much of Fagan's cover checks out. I used my contacts at ABA-Invest to confirm that Arian has a small office in Vienna."

"An office the company strangely is unaware it opened and has only one employee. Maybe someone to answer the phone."

"That would be a phone service. And a rented mailbox. I have gone through office and industrial rental listings in a three-kilometer radius from the substation, however, and I identified which space Fagan rented for his fake office. I'm doing recon this afternoon. Are you in?"

Olivia waited, sipping her coffee, while Miles mulled the details that she'd just shared.

She didn't have to wait long.

He stood. "Let's do this."

***

Olivia Kastrioti had parked at the Karlsplatz Garage next to the park and a five-minute walk from Ressel Park. They'd gotten only as far as Karlskirche on the southeast corner of the plaza when Miles realized that they had a tail. Olivia walked next to him, graceful and elegant, and exuding an arresting authority that disturbed him on some level. She'd been captivating before she left the Company. Now she was undeniable. Forceful in a way he'd rarely encountered. Marriage had certainly been good for her.

He slipped his hand around hers. Smiling at her when she looked askance, he escorted her up the steps to the large Baroque church, gesturing toward the bas-relief columns on either side of the Greek-style portico.

"Those are based on Trajan's Column in Rome," he said loudly. In a lower voice, he added, "We've got a tail."

Olivia didn't falter or look around. Instead, she smiled back at him.

"This is the oddest-looking church I've ever seen." While she spoke in a normal voice, it carried. Then she added in a voice directed into his ear, "Northeast side, near the museum, tan overcoat and black tote bag?"

"Yes. She's good, but my neck hairs are tingling."

"The operative the Italians sent." She sounded certain.

Miles had no reason to doubt her.

Olivia threw her empty coffee cup into a wastebin, and they walked around to the right side of Karlskirche to the entrance. She glanced to either side where angels flanked the doorway, fingering the small medallion at her neck as she did. Once inside, they stopped to pay the entrance fee, which gave them access to the Museo Borromeo in one of the side chapels as well as the elevator and stairs to the 70-meter dome. Miles accepted the printed brochure describing features in the church. He studied it a moment.

"I suggest that we take the elevator. The dome is supposed to be incredible up close."

Olivia caught his eye and grinned. Good operative. She understood what he intended to do. They headed into the interior, turning right toward the glass elevator built as a temporary structure more than a decade ago. Despite its ugliness, the church had kept it as well as a narrow flight of metal stairs integrated into its scaffold for intrepid tourists. It was a welcome and reliable source of income to the parish for renovations to the magnificent structure.

As expected, the Italian operative followed them inside. It was the only way that she could be sure to keep track of their whereabouts. Although there were other exterior doors, they were typically locked from the outside and inaccessible to the general public. Not something that would stop two operatives seeking to ditch a tail, however.

But first they would need to slow her down.

She tried to hang back, but Miles made a show of holding the elevator door for her. So she graciously accepted the chance to ride up with them.

Time to seed some misdirection. If they did it right, she'd believe that they'd let real information slip before they realized her motives.

Miles turned in toward Olivia.

"I spoke to Fagan. He plans to move soon on a deal." He spoke in English in a normal voice.

Another misdirection. He was betting that the Italian operative understood them. By speaking so freely, he'd encourage her to assume that he had no idea that she could.

She pulled her smartphone from her tote bag and began swiping. A casual observer wouldn't recognize that she listened very intently.

He wasn't a casual observer. Neither was Olivia.

"Kastrioti says word on the street points to Macedonia." Olivia sounded very convincing. She winked. "For this package, he'd use Fuchs to go overland via truck. I have a contact with them from my time at ABA. I'm headed there after we meet."

Subtle tension energized the Italian operative's posture. It confirmed for Miles that she'd been following Olivia and found the information credible.

The elevator stopped with a slight jar and its door opened. They stepped out onto a wobbly viewing platform. The Italian operative stepped out behind them. Across from them cherubs, angels, and saints floated in fluffy serenity. Above them a single dove ringed by cherubs crowned the elliptical dome. A white-haired but athletic-looking couple descended the narrow metal stairs that led to the top of the dome.

By unspoken accord, Olivia followed him toward the stairs. Their footsteps were loud on the gently swaying treads as they began to climb. Just as they approached the same flight as the couple descending, Miles touched the back of Olivia's hand.

She took three steps up the flight before pausing to grip the railing and look back at him. "I'm getting dizzy."

"Let's leave then."

He took Olivia's hand, and they turned on the stairs, which swayed at their movement, ahead of the couple.

"So sorry," he said over his shoulder to them.

The Italian operative hesitated. For her to turn around at this moment would be to alert them that they'd been made, something that she couldn't risk. Plus the couple was now between them.

The operative continued up the stairs as they crossed the platform. Miles knew that she would abort the climb as soon as the elevator door closed. They weren't going down in the elevator, however. They took the metal stairs alongside it instead, moving briskly. He estimated that they'd get a thirty-second head start.

More than enough time to lose her.

"She's on the stairs now," Olivia said. She looked exhilarated.

Miles twisted as he looked back and up the open framework. He glimpsed tan overcoat three flights above them. Olivia's gut must be especially sensitive.

They bounded from the stairs, turning around toward the exterior wall where their progress would be momentarily hidden, and sprinted up the side toward the sacristy. They'd reached the marble steps leading up to the altar when the elevator door opened behind them, letting the white-haired couple off just as the Italian operative stepped from the stairs. Neither Miles nor Olivia paused to look as sounds from the trio's interaction echoed in the superior acoustics.

Instead, they mounted the steps. Miles led Olivia to the set of double doors on the right beside the ambo. One door was open.

They ducked into the small hallway leading to the back vestibule and sacristy door. A minute later they were outside in the crisp March afternoon. They ran down the steps to the sidewalk and headed east. The Karlsplatz Garage was just past the church, and Olivia's Audi was on the second level. By the time they reached it, Miles had gotten sweaty. Olivia hadn't. If anything, he got the sense that she'd been holding herself back in some way so that *he* could keep up.

What an odd thought.

Two minutes later, Olivia exited from the opposite end of the garage that they'd entered. If the Italian operative had seen them enter it, she hadn't managed to see them leave.

Olivia looked at him with shining eyes. "That was fun."

"I take it Albania isn't so fast paced?" he asked drily.

"Nope, not even close." She grinned.

Miles grinned back at her. He couldn't remember the last time he'd enjoyed himself so much on a mission. He realized that he'd been disappointed when Olivia hadn't contacted him again. She'd caught him off guard last summer and caused him to fail—for the first and only time in his ten years with the Company—to grab a target. When he'd met Tadeja, his gut prompted him to contact Olivia. It had been an incredible coincidence that she'd called him for help on her mission first.

He didn't believe in coincidences. But in this case, he wasn't sure what to believe in.

Olivia drove south to Favoriten, Vienna's tenth district. Fifteen minutes later they were parked at another garage, this time across from what was known as the Vienna Twin Towers in the Wienerberg Business Park. Olivia had located an office rented to Arian Resources on Level 19 in Tower A. The towers were connected on the ground floor by a popular shopping mall.

Olivia gave him a sly look. What was she thinking?

"How would you like to pretend to be my husband?"

Ah. That's what she was thinking. For a moment Miles allowed himself to be drawn into that stunning blue-gray gaze. His heart beat a little more quickly. He grew warm. But when he began to imagine kissing her, another expressive face superimposed itself on Olivia's.

"I'm not sure that I can pull off The Dragon of Albania," he said, smiling.

"You'll do just fine. Just follow my lead." She sat up and peered at herself in the rearview mirror, running her fingers through her hair. Amazingly, when she looked back at him, her skin glowed. "Ready?"

Two minutes later, they entered the main doors of the shopping mall. Olivia headed toward the offices, walking with clear confidence. She led him toward a large desk through an open lounge where businesspeople worked at small tables. There were fresh flowers on the counter and a colorful pink lampshade on a nearby floor lamp. Two attractive women sat at workstations. One looked up and smiled.

"May I help you?" she asked in German.

"Yes, I'm here to activate my membership," Olivia said back in German.

"Of course. You must be Olivia Kastrioti. May I see an ID, please?"

Olivia handed her a passport. She put her hand on his arm, smiling and cordial. "This is my husband, Mihàil."

Miles felt an odd vibrating sensation. The receptionist blinked, looking a little dazed.

"Of course," she said again. "Welcome, Herr Kastrioti. Here is your membership card, Frau Kastrioti. If you have any questions, please feel free to call the community manager."

"I will. Thank you so much."

Olivia led Miles toward a hallway painted with cheerful splotches of color and lined with rows of white and blue tenant mailboxes.

"Is this shared office space?" he asked as she pressed her access card at the security turnstile.

"Yes. Fagan leased several rooms in an office suite. I also rented a room on the same floor."

"Of course." He mimicked the receptionist's tone.

They laughed.

"See, you're a perfect Herr Kastrioti," she said.

Miles looked at her as they walked toward the elevator. "About that. What happened back there?"

She didn't pretend to misunderstand. Instead, her face got very serious. "Now isn't the time to explain, I'm afraid. Let's just say that there's more to the name 'The Dragon of Albania' than you might be ready to wrap your mind around."

Frowning, Miles held the door to the Tower A elevator for Olivia.

That didn't sound ominous at all.

"Later then over drinks. I'm buying."

"Deal."

Something changed between them after that. They rode in silence to Level 19. Miles wondered if she regretted bringing him along, exhilarating escape notwithstanding. He followed her through the glass-lined hallway. Around them the offices were filled with stern, busy worker drones. He had no idea what it would feel like to be trapped inside this pretty terrarium all day. But halfway down the hall the wall panels were frosted.

Olivia stopped in front of the door for Arian Resources. She looked up at him, a small smile playing around the corner of her mouth. Then she pulled out a small electronic device with a braided cable attached to a smaller square, which she held up to the RFID card reader on the wall. Clearly she'd managed to hack the access card that she'd just picked up at the reception desk. It was a slick hack that not even the Company had the ability to pull off. Yet.

She pushed the door open, stepped inside, and halted. Miles, who'd followed, bumped into her.

When he stepped to the side to see what had stopped her in her tracks, he blinked in surprise. There was a Rembrandt hanging on the wall in front of them if he wasn't mistaken. And another painting.

"Is that a Caravaggio?" he asked.

Olivia looked at him, her eyes wide. "Yes. *The Infatuation of the Watcher Angels.* We thought it had been destroyed in a fire."

Twenty-Four

Despite his shock, Miró sensed Stasia as the ER staff wheeled him away from her. Her infrared signature showed elevated heat around her torso—she'd likely been injured when the truck slammed into them—and her harmonics had an uneven, frightened quality. He wanted to flash a message to her, but his thoughts were all jumbled and out of control. It had been a long time since he'd been injured so badly that he'd needed surgical care.

Since World War II and the assault on Monte Cassino at the Winter Line.

A team of scrub-clad men and women bustled around him. First they cut the arms off of his coat and shirt, exposing his right arm. Then a nurse drew blood before an attendant wheeled him to get an x-ray of his hand. After he was brought to the operating room, someone hooked him up to a heart monitor while another inserted an IV into his uninjured left hand and attached a pulse oximeter. Finally someone gave him a shot that must have had a sedative, probably something for tetanus as well.

Miró relaxed enough to stabilize his core temperature and to stop the nurse anesthetist when she came to administer a nerve block. He allowed her to clean his arm and hand, but when she used a hand-held machine to stimulate his nerves in order to find the right one to numb, he pulled his arm away.

"No." He shook his head.

"But, *monsieur*," she said, "it is necessary to numb your hand before the surgeon reattaches the finger."

"I will do that myself." Miró held her gaze, letting her see and hear his *Elioud* authority.

She blanched.

A nurse next to her spoke. "His temperature has risen to 37.4, but blood oxygen and pressure remain steady."

The surgeon, his dark eyes severe over his mask, approached.

"*Monsieur*, please, no games. I cannot operate unless your hand is numb. I must remove damaged tissue and attach the finger using metal wires and pins. Then I have to reconnect tendons. The final step means repairing arteries, veins, and nerves. It will take hours and be very painful unless your hand is numb."

"It *is* numb," said Miró. It was a flat, granite statement. He was tired and wanted nothing more than to make sure that Stasia was safe and being taken care of. He didn't have time to cajole, *Elioud* charm or no. "Do what you need to do."

Unfortunately for him, his surgeon didn't accept his assurances. Then again, Miró thought sourly, that was actually a fortunate sign. He didn't think that he'd want a surgeon who'd trust him on sight. Besides the amputated finger, he'd clearly been involved in a vicious altercation.

"Either let her block your nerve or I will order general anesthesia medicine for your IV."

"Try it."

"*J'abandonne.*" The surgeon turned away, taking his mask off as he did. "I note that you refuse to consent to treatment."

"I consent to treatment without the nerve block."

Now the surgeon spun around. His eyes flashed. Until he caught a look at Miró's own eyes. Swallowing hard, he took a step back.

Miró, his head pounding with the effort, sent a targeted harmonic wave behind the man, blocking his exit. He closed his eyes and began tapping on the surgeon's back, lightly at first, moving around the man's body until he tapped him on the forehead. When he opened them, the surgeon wavered, his dark eyes wide.

In response, Miró sent soothing harmonic fingers down the man's back. Only once. He was too tired to placate the stubborn fool any longer. He closed his eyes again.

"If you numb my hand, it will make it harder for *me* to do *my* part in healing. I assure you that I have numbed the median nerve. In fact, I blocked it almost as soon as the finger was severed. I cannot, however, reattach the finger."

Still the man hesitated.

Miró looked at him. "Please. You must know that nerve blocks are not without risk and sometimes fail. My metabolism is such that it will not last for the entire surgery regardless." He sighed. "If I could alter your memory beforehand so that you think my median nerve is blocked, I would."

The surgeon blinked at that. Then he looked at the anesthetist, who'd sat watching them wide-eyed and motionless, and motioned for her to leave.

Miró closed his eyes and listened to the activity around him, wondering where Stasia was and how badly hurt she was. When he'd come to after the dump truck hit their Mercedes, it was to see her being carried by a large male. He'd flared then.

A lot of good that did him.

They'd left behind a strike team of five well-armed mercenaries.

His flare had allowed him to extricate himself from the crumpled Mercedes and speed his harmonics so that he'd made it to the car in which Stasia had been dumped. Just in time to hit an acoustic jammer that knocked him down. It was like running into an invisible brick wall. In the next moment, the extraction car sped off and he was being shot at by mercenaries who could slow him down if he tried a straight harmonics jump. He was left using his unique syncopated style of harmonics leaping to avoid being hit.

It kept him alive. It also kept him from breaking free of the team, which had him pinned down within its frequency band. Until Fagan chose to let him go.

At that moment the nurse anesthetist said, "He is in tachycardia." There was a hint of judgment to her tone.

"Then it is time to use the Bupivacaine, *monsieur*," said the surgeon.

"That will not be necessary," said Miró, calling on long years of self-control to bring his resting heartrate back to 50 beats per minute.

After that, the surgical team moved around him to begin the taxing work of reattaching his finger. He felt them debriding the damaged tissue that he'd sealed to stop the bleeding. Low whispers told him that they were amazed and shocked to see that it had been closed up so cleanly. Another few minutes passed in which the team seemed to have forgotten that Miró had never gotten the anesthetic injection.

Five hours later, he emerged from surgery, tired, bruised, and achy. And desperate to see Stasia.

When at last she walked into his room, it felt as though his world had been set right and shaken all at once.

Her face was swollen and purplish-blue on one side with a stitched cut over her right eyebrow. She walked stiffly and her normally creamy complexion was sallow. Her hair, a burnished caramel that usually flowed in long waves around her face, hung limp against her shoulders. She was still wearing the clothes that she'd worn that morning when they'd set out from Aix-en-Provence. They were creased and dirty. The left knee of her slacks was torn. Beyond the surface evidence that she'd been in a fight for her life, her infrared signature showed an elevated hot spot along one of her ribs. Though she didn't yet know how to use thermogenesis consciously to heal herself, she'd intuitively raised her temperature where her body needed it most.

She came to his bedside.

"*Ehi*," she said, touching his face with gentle fingers. "They told me that you will be released shortly. The local police want a statement about what happened at the cemetery, but I promised that you would give it to them tomorrow. By that time, you will be long gone, of course."

She let her fingers drop. Miró wanted her to kiss him, but she stood there, her hazel eyes wary and watchful.

Miró shut his eyes, sighing. He opened them again. She still stood where she'd been standing a moment earlier, but somehow she appeared farther away. Her harmonics, though entwined with his, hummed in a low, tight range. She was both heartachingly beautiful and unnervingly distant. This was a side of Stasia that he'd never seen.

"I imagine that they would like to know what took place at the cemetery, and before, when the dump truck hit us."

"I explained the basics. I readily told them who Fagan is and who I am. I also told them the truth, that Fagan followed me to France. I left the details as to why on a need-to-know basis related to our secret clearances."

"Who am I in this scenario?" he asked.

He watched Stasia closely. The convenient narrative that she'd crafted would be useful for writing her report to her superiors in Italian foreign intelligence. He saw in her gaze that he'd drawn the right conclusion. The muscles in his upper back and jaw tightened. His mind, only moments before fogged from exhaustion, cleared. His newly reattached finger throbbed painfully.

"You are an unfortunate civilian with whom I shared a ride from Italy."

"And you conveniently provided them with the details of the ride share."

She shrugged. "Enough that they were able to verify that we crossed the border into France early yesterday morning."

"Did they wonder why I was still in your company?"

"Not really. I insinuated that we had a sexual encounter before I asked you to drive me to Aix-en-Provence."

Miró had to clamp his mouth shut. Despite his tight control on his core temperature, the temperature around them rose several degrees. He smelled a whiff of smoke. If Stasia could read his infrared signature, she would see that at the center of his chest there was a curious dark space, exactly like the blackbody radiation of a star.

"And your *Elioud* charisma scarcely had to work to sell that half-truth." It was a statement. He heard the raw anger and hurt in it, even with his heroic effort to contain it.

Stasia's gaze shuttered. *"Sì, facile come bere un bicchiere d'acqua."*

Miró recoiled from the insult.

Yes, as easy as drinking a little bit of water. That's what making love with him had translated to in her narrative spinning.

"And, of course, you have already contacted your superior about what happened with Fagan. Claim to kill him alone, did you?" he asked. Ice ran through his words, but his core had become a white star. "So when do you return to Rome and your career, Ms. Fiore?"

Now she had the grace to flinch. But her face remained impassive. She straightened her shoulders, and a blink later she stood across the room next to the door.

Oh, very good!

A part of him wanted to acknowledge that she'd mastered an *Elioud* skill, but he shoved that knowledge into the back of his mind. It wasn't the time or place to celebrate.

"I fly back later this evening." Again her demeanor was uncharacteristically reserved and opaque. Her mind was closed to him as well. It was almost as if they were strangers.

Miró was stunned. He hadn't actually thought that Stasia would return to Rome. Not yet, anyway. He still had time to win her. To him. To the *Elioud* cause.

"Without the stolen Rembrandt painting that you set out to recover in order to redeem your reputation as an operative?"

He heard the note of desperation in his voice. It made him angrier.

"In addition to telling Major Costa about what transpired with Fagan, I was also able to tell him that I have recovered the Rembrandt."

Miró tilted his head. He narrowed his eyes. Stasia wasn't lying.

"Indeed." The coldness in his voice directly belied the burning in his chest. "Do tell."

"Olivia went to Vienna while we were distracting Fagan. She located the Rembrandt." She paused as if reluctant to admit the next piece of information. "And the Caravaggio, too."

"And gave you the exit that you needed." It wasn't a question. Of course, the *zonjë* would prioritize her friendship over the good of the *Elioud* team. *Over you*, a little voice whispered at the back of his thoughts.

She shrugged a single shoulder. It was quite a haughty gesture. Anastasia Fiore could play a *drangùe*'s lady if she needed.

"We still need to work out some details regarding the paintings. Now that Fagan is dead, Olivia believes that it will be harder for Asmodeus to locate them. Unless you disagree?"

Miró took a moment to answer. He didn't want to be guilty of letting his emotions drive his thinking. Though he hadn't heard Mihàil's name in this revelation yet, he doubted that Olivia would operate without her husband's tacit blessing. And once he turned over the news and looked at it from every visible angle, he knew that it was true. Without an inside mole to aid him, Asmodeus wouldn't be coming for the paintings any time soon. Once again, the Dark *Irim* had chosen his own expediency over the more careful stratagem necessary to succeed.

Yes, Olivia had found a way to deliver Stasia, but truthfully she'd also delivered the *Elioud* team, too.

He shook his head. "No, not at all. What we have been calling *bogomili* for your sake is simply the latest incarnation of Asmodeus's typical minion. They will not have the capacity to penetrate our defenses."

"Mihàil thinks that Asmodeus will go on a lust-driven spree now that he has freed himself from the anchor of an acolyte."

"That would be in keeping with his *modus operandi*." Though forced to agree, Miró wasn't sure that he liked the conclusion.

Perhaps he was looking for a way to object.

Before Stasia could say anything else, he asked, "What about *L'Amante*?" He deliberately softened his tone, sliding the question inside her harmonic defenses.

She shifted, crossing her arms over her waist. "What about him?"

There! Her harmonics thrummed in guilty recognition.

He'd guessed correctly. She'd been able to harden her harmonics against anger, hostility, even iciness. But warm, vulnerable tenderness had pried her open. Inside her tightly controlled hum, he saw a chaotic mix of desire, need, doubt, regret, and resolution.

Now he knew how to manipulate her if he needed to do so.

"You intend to go after the third painting." He fed a little more subtle *Elioud* empathy into his words. "Without me."

"No." Her harmonics registered a funny ping that suggested that her answer wasn't quite true.

What was she hiding?

"What reason would *I* have to pursue a third painting?" she asked, interrupting his silent analysis. Her tone was confident, and her stance had eased so that she appeared to be leaning against the doorframe.

Miró shook his head. Something was off in her harmonics, but he couldn't pinpoint what. That in and of itself shocked him to his core. It was as if the past few days had never happened.

He'd let his guard down, and now she was manipulating *him*.

He kept his voice even. "As you say, what reason would an Italian spy have with an *Elioud* painting?" He paused. Then, gripping his harmonics with a firm hand, he said, "I gather we are saying our farewells."

Stasia nodded. He saw nothing in her expression to show that it mattered at all to her, let alone that it hurt.

"I am going to the villa to gather my things now. Olivia will send someone to drive you once you are released. She wanted me to tell you that Daněk will be waiting at the private airstrip. She said that you would know where." She paused, though she looked like she was going to say something else.

Before she could speak, Miró said, "Then I wish you well, Ms. Fiore. And I hope that you manage to stay within the Grey spectrum, although I fear that *L'Amante* will find you a tempting target. When he has won you to his cause, I will show you no quarter."

Stasia held his gaze. A warm harmonic caress traced his cheek and jaw followed by a featherlight touch across his lips that made him think of a delicate kiss. His eyelids dropped of their own volition.

Allora rimarrai con un pugno di mosche. Then you will be left empty handed.

When he raised his eyelids again, the room was empty.

***

The villa in Saint-Cyr-sur-Mer was dark when Miró and his driver arrived late that evening. His harmonic defenses showed that no one had crossed them except Stasia, who'd left the key to the front door in the potted plant at the base of the front steps. Olivia had relayed the message of its location when she called earlier while he was still at the hospital. Miró had said as little as possible to the *zonjë*, who seemed not to notice his lack of enthusiasm for the recovery of both the Rembrandt and the Caravaggio. He did, however, ask about András.

"He is on light duty on Mihàil's orders. The surgeon was able to remove the remnants of the bullets, and his metabolism has taken over. It will take a little longer than usual for him to heal, but he's definitely out of the woods. He's taken to eating everything in the pantry, including all of the baked goods I froze to try to get ahead of his gargantuan appetite."

Miró thanked his lady for the information and promised to head straight for the Kastrioti estate where Mihàil's personal surgeon would check on his finger and where the staff had been instructed to cater to his every need.

"Miró, Mihàil thinks there's every reason to hope that your finger will regain its mobility and feeling." She sounded like she was trying to convince him that the second-place finish in the race of his life wasn't such a bad ending. "It's just a matter of resting and letting your *Elioud* metabolism do its healing work."

He mumbled something that he hoped sounded appropriately grateful and acquiescent. He had no intention of going back to the Kastrioti estate once he arrived in Albania, however. He preferred to hole up in his apartment in Fushë-Arrëz and lick his wounds. His finger may heal, but he wasn't sure that the howling rent in his heart would.

He was in the villa's bedroom where Stasia's smoky sweet perfume hung in the air, packing his duffel, when he realized that Zophiel lay on the bed watching him. He paused with his splinted and bandaged hand on the cardboard box that held the graphene sheets for his invisible origami surveillance.

"Ah, my blackbird. Is it so hard to have faith in love?" Her eyes were sad.

Miró swallowed hard. His throat was so thick he almost choked.

Zophiel moved to a kneeling position. She gently took his injured hand between hers and blew a soft, warm breath on it. The deep ache that had been there since he'd left the operating room eased and then disappeared. He saw the localized heat radiating as the bone knit. The titanium pins and wires melted, dripping harmlessly into her cupped palm without burning him.

She sat back and looked at him.

He inhaled and let it out as carefully as he could. When he thought that he could speak reasonably calmly, he said, "Forgive me. I want to believe in love, but Stasia has chosen a different path. I seem to have chosen wrongly yet again."

"You don't trust your own heart." She placed her hand on his chest above that willful and obtuse organ. "Then you must trust *me*, Miró, and not the mistakes of the past."

"What would you have me do?"

"Don't be so sure that you know what path it is that your little flower has chosen. Perhaps she too must have a little faith. Can you give her a reason to trust love when the time comes?"

"Does that mean that you know what she is going to do?" Miró couldn't help it; hope lifted his voice and buoyed his heart.

Zophiel shook her head, her face solemn. "No, dear one, I don't. Just as I never know exactly what you, my beloved wards, are going to do. But I trust that you merit my faith in you, as I have faith in all those who can still be redeemed. I have no other choice."

Miró understood. He looked down at his finger, still swollen and sore, but whole once more.

"Then I will trust you, Zophiel, and not the mistakes that I have made in the past."

Zophiel smiled a brilliant smile then, and, leaning in, kissed him on the forehead.

Twenty-Five

Olivia watched as Mihàil, dressed in designer slacks, silk shirt, and suede loafers, made his way through the crowd inside Restaurant 360 in Dubrovnik, Croatia. The swanky establishment, located inside the medieval Fortress of St. John, had been rented for the evening by Mamic's associate, businessman Joško Celik. Inside the stone walls and on the terrace outside, 50 of the world's elite mingled with actors from the British TV show Game of Thrones, which had filmed scenes for the mythical King's Landing in the surrounding walled Old Town. Moving among them were beautiful young women wearing designer dresses and serving cocktails.

Olivia wasn't at Mihàil's side as his lovely bride, however. For this operation, she was part of the wait staff. Her husband had returned to his role as European playboy, this time not as one of the continent's most eligible bachelors. It didn't seem to matter. If anything, the heated looks that the women gave him—the guests, not the staff, who were unaware that they were on the auction block—suggested that they found his married state something of an aphrodisiac.

It disgusted Olivia.

She didn't worry that Mihàil would be tempted to stray. Even if she couldn't read the strength of his harmonic bond with hers, she got so many flashed jokes from her husband attempting to set her at ease that she feared she'd flub her cover.

For instance, when a tall, gaunt woman wearing a pink sequined dress with a single shoulder strap leaned into him as he stopped to chat, he said aloud, "Pardon," but he flashed *those implants could bruise someone* as he smiled at the woman. Her wide smile in return did nothing to hide the speculation in her gaze. Or the white-hot temperature radiating in her groin as she watched Mihàil walk away.

Olivia rolled her eyes. She herself had dressed in a white cocktail dress with a sheer full skirt and a demure lace bodice with sleeves and a high neckline. She'd also sped her harmonics a half step so that she would always appear just outside of the periphery of a typical human's eyesight. If anyone did manage to catch a glimpse of her, they would likely find her a pale attraction next to the glittery, heavily made up young women vying for attention in the private party.

Eyes on the prize, she flashed.

Yes, ma'am. She heard the humor in his response.

They'd come to this private event at the Michelin-rated restaurant to grab Celik, who was closely guarded. Miles had already been in touch with Croatian authorities to help set up an investigation into Mamic's fraudulent player transfers. But the slippery Celik had left little evidence anywhere of his illegitimate "executive training program." As far as they'd been able to ascertain in the two months since Miles had come to Olivia for help, only Tadeja had been rescued from the "placement process." All of the other young women (and some men) had disappeared and become a statistic.

So of course they would do what needed to be done. They would convince the "businessman" to move into other markets.

Besides moving on Celik, they needed to find out where he kept the victims when they weren't socializing with their future abusers. Most were there of their own free will, but they were too inexperienced to recognize the armed guards at all the exits. Or the minders who kept an eye on everyone to ensure that the guests didn't try to sample the wares before purchasing.

"Celik is heading toward the restroom." Miró's voice came over the team's earwigs. They were using the audio technology for Miles, who waited outside the fortress in a dark sedan.

"Copy that." Mihàil adjusted his route to take him toward the restrooms.

Olivia eased around to the side, threading her way through the throng. As she passed a small group, she overheard a woman say in German, "I can't believe he's married. No one seems to know who the fortunate woman is."

Olivia couldn't help herself. She tuned in on that conversation and listened even as she got closer to the restroom where she would distract the security guards when the time came.

"What does it matter?" This time the German was accented. A Brit, if Olivia wasn't mistaken. "He's here now, isn't he?"

"But not for one of *us*. See? He's talking to Celik."

That was her cue. Olivia approached Mihàil and Celik with a tray of drinks. A security guard stepped to meet her just as she shifted the tray off center and into his path. The entire tray flew up, aided with a harmonic shove, launching drinks in a cascade of glassware and alcohol. Celik was showered.

In the resulting confusion, Mihàil stepped closer to the shorter, pudgier man and led him to the restroom while Olivia made a show of cleaning up the mess. They each directed a subtle barrage of *Elioud* charm in the form of running commentary, confusing and encouraging their targets so that none knew exactly what was happening. In the midst of this chaos, Miró sped his harmonics and slipped into the restroom behind Mihàil and Celik.

From there it was only moments before the trio returned. This time no one but Olivia saw them. Mihàil and Miró stood on either side of the drooping Celik, whose toes dragged as they carried him from the restaurant.

After dancing around the guards, Olivia left the tray and shattered glasses and hurried after her teammates. The guards, prompted by her *Elioud* charm, stood wiping their jackets and pants. It would be several minutes before either of them thought to check the restroom for Celik. By then, he would be far from the Old Town.

They reached the car moments later. Miles, standing outside the rear passenger door, opened it for their captive, who'd started to revive from the harmonic jab that Miró had delivered.

"Celik." His voice was pleasant, but his gaze was hard. "Let's visit the trainees, shall we?" He looked up at Olivia as he shut the door.

"Welcome to the team, Miles," she said.

***

Zaccaria Angelli knew as soon as the most compelling woman he'd met in a hundred years walked into the charity event at the Museum of Contemporary Art in Rome.

A delicious frisson flashed through the harmonic veil around the guests. Like the tinkle of angelic glass bells. It reminded him very much of that winsome singer he'd loved, the one with the *Elioud* blood and the name of an angel. *Serafina*.

And there she was: a lithe vision in a full-length black gown with her hair swept into a dramatic chignon. Tiny crystals, sprinkled throughout the warm strands, winked in the overhead lighting. She walked through the crowd as Cleopatra had walked, exuding confidence and mysterious allure. She'd called herself *Signorina Crea—Miss Creates—*when they met in Prague. It was a false name, like a domino worn at a masque. She wore it lightly and well.

He was delighted, of course.

He hadn't been himself since he'd left Signorina Crea his gift. She'd been so tempting among those downy white sheets, her glorious hair spread about her on the pillow. But he'd restrained himself. She would come to him.

She'd been his from the moment she'd looked at him with those large hazel eyes.

So he'd returned to Rome where she lived, booking public events as a sommelier at museums. And his patience had been rewarded at last. Although Signorina Crea as yet seemed unaware of his presence here among the glittering crowd of wealthy benefactors, he knew that it was only a matter of moments before their dance of seduction began again.

It was hardly a problem to wait in the ancient city of romance. Angelli adored Rome. As he should. He'd been instrumental in its founding three millennia ago, although he'd been known then by a different name: Romulus. *That* had been a glorious time for romantic conquest, raw and untamed. History knew that Romulus, as king, had engineered the marriage of Sabine women to Romans. Unfortunately, that situation had been twisted into a false tale of mass *rape*.

Why did everyone believe that he'd taken innocent women against their will when it was King Titus of the Sabines who brought 30 virgins to an ancient orgy? Well, essentially an orgy: the Neptune Equester festival that his brother Araqael had urged him to hold. Why should *he* be blamed when the king's married daughter, Hersilia, left her husband for him?

Angelli tamped down his irritation at this pejorative spin.

Of course his other brother, the Father of Lies, often interfered in Angelli's seduction efforts simply for sport.

But that was ancient history. Ancient women had different prerogatives. Mostly they refused to be seduced because of the consequences, fatherless children being a burden more than a blessing. Possibly also because they recalled in their DNA what had happened to the first women, the ones who'd been so sexually innocent that it had been like drinking new wine to show them all the pleasures that the body had been made for.

The pleasures that Signorina Crea's body had been made for.

The target of his desires eased into the side of a tall man, who slipped his arm around her waist possessively.

Angelli's core temperature spiked. Harmonic discordance shuddered in the air around him in an unseen blast. Guests moved uneasily. Someone dropped a wineglass. There was a nervous titter and low murmurs.

He'd been in the midst of pouring an Extra Brut Prosecco to a small cluster of adoring female tourists while explaining the six sweetness levels of Veneto's famous sparkling wine and sharing little anecdotes that kept them rapt. But he almost walked away when he saw Signorina Crea's escort. He would have if he hadn't caught a glimpse of the human male's face.

And then he nearly spoiled his wine diplomacy by laughing.

It was that Roman actor, the one who looked so much like him.

Ah, let her defer her desire for the moment. It was all too understandable. She had no idea how to find him. Yet.

This modern business of seduction took far more time and thought than ever before. How could it not? The rules were much murkier now that sexual congress could—and did— occur at the drop of a hat as the Americans said.

Angelli felt affectionate indulgence for humanity. He imagined that it was exactly what a father would feel toward his grown children, who'd taken his great lessons to heart and then made them fully their own. What matter if they chose to pursue desire more directly with little thought of finesse and patience?

It was his great pleasure—his great duty, as he saw it, as a connoisseur of *Elohim*'s Creation—to adulate and woo women.

In the midst of lifting a fresh bottle of Prosecco to pour a new round of drinks, Angelli realized that Signorina Crea no longer stood near him. Scowling, he thrust the bottle at his assistant.

When the unaware young man nearly dropped it, Angelli said, "Continue the tasting." *Irim* authority gave his voice a hard crystalline edge along its mellifluous notes. "I must mingle."

It was but a moment's effort to locate the tantalizing Signorina Crea. Angelli was rather surprised and, even better, intrigued that she'd managed to move away from him without setting off his angelic radar. He focused on her, trying to get a better read on her harmonics.

Just then she turned and her gaze caught on his. For a moment Angelli felt his heart race. She raised her wineglass in a slight salute and smiled. Her smile dazzled him. She sipped from the glass, turning away as if their nonverbal *tête-à-tête* across a crowded room hadn't been anything more than an accidental meeting of wandering attention.

Angelli blinked. What had just happened? He could find nothing untoward in her harmonic signature, nothing that showed more than a trace of *Elioud* heritage. And yet, for the second time since he'd met Signorina Crea, he'd been taken by surprise at the magnetism in her smile.

Perhaps that was why that *Elioud,* the cool one whose core had blazed as white as a whole heavenly host, had been stalking her in Prague. She'd looked at that male *Elioud* and the resulting harmonic detonation had been more than Angelli had ever witnessed on Earth between those with human blood. Clearly the *Elioud* was smitten.

Angelli straightened his cuffs, unable to hold back a slight sneer.

Fool. As if a mere *Elioud* had a chance when an *Irim*, the Master Seducer himself, had targeted a woman, regardless of her bloodline. As witnessed by the fact that she was here now in Angelli's orbit with a placeholder who resembled him, if poorly.

Angelli took a step toward Signorina Crea. It was time to move this along.

"*Signore, signore*! You must come! A case of Prosecco has sprung a leak."

Angelli whipped his gaze toward another of his assistants who approached from the direction of the staging area where they'd stocked several cases of Prosecco. He speared the importunate young man with an icy glare.

"Can you not handle this looming disaster yourself?"

The young man paled at Angelli's sharp tone. "But, *signore*, the museum director sent me to find you."

Angelli sighed and shut his eyes, slowing down the harmonics around him so that time seemed to stop at the event. He was *this* close to flaring, for Heaven's sake! Violence wasn't his forte, but that didn't mean he couldn't wreak havoc when pushed beyond his limits. He reminded himself that he wasn't Sêmîazâz, who thrived on engendering discord and violence in human relations.

Angelli opened his eyes again. Around him humans stood as still as wax figures. He looked toward the spot that Signorina Crea had stood only moments before. She wasn't there. Neither was his human twin.

They were behind him, outside the main event area.

He turned on his heel and strode over to them. Signorina Crea stood looking up at her escort, adoration in her eyes and her delicate hand on his forearm. The actor looked down at her, familiar desire shining in his eyes. It was an intimate embrace.

These two were lovers.

Angelli stopped within touching distance, tilting his head as he studied them.

Or they had been lovers. Not anymore.

He walked all the way around the couple, studying them from every angle. The actor wanted to make love to Signorina Crea. She was a cipher, however.

Angelli was tempted to send his rival away, to shift harmonics so that he and Signorina Crea were the ones in an embrace while the actor was left alone, blinking and stunned, somewhere in the middle of Rome. But the *Irim* didn't want to give in to his desire. Yet. He wanted to savor it.

He leaned closer to Signorina Crea, inhaling deeply of her perfume. In a previous life, he'd been instrumental to the development of the art of fragrance design. Who better than an *Irim* with his angelic senses and his passion for seduction to teach humanity how best to use scent to attract? And Signorina Crea definitely knew how to captivate with her fragrance. The warmth of her skin sent delicate hints of sweet vanilla and anise over rich iris with the smoky touch of benzoin. And beneath these scents the spicy aroma of musk and patchouli.

Ah. He recognized this perfume. It was called *Café Chantant*. A modern fragrance, it nevertheless called to mind the Parisian cafés where female singers beguiled the men in the audience. Serafina had been just such a *chantant*, or *la sciantosa* in Italian.

I wonder, he thought, reaching out to trace a fingertip over her brow.

The intrigue deepened. This young woman looked nothing like Serafina, but there was something familiar in that trace of *Elioud* blood that he'd already detected. Angelli smiled then and angled his head so that he could kiss her full lips. His heart danced. His loins tightened.

"I know you," he said in a low voice, watching as her harmonics effervesced in corresponding joy. Her own groin radiated white heat. He could take her now with him, and she'd melt in his arms.

Instead Angelli returned to the staging area to find a large puddle on the floor and his incompetent assistants in media res, one frozen kneeling to wipe up the wine while the other stood nearby holding a mop. He paused for a moment, frowning. There was something in the harmonics that niggled, some echo of a disturbance. The faint ringing quality reminded him of that meddling *seraphim*, Zophiel. The one Michael often sent to disrupt his plans.

Well, if Michael thought to stop him from wooing this human woman, he was sadly mistaken.

Ignoring his two assistants, Angelli searched for an undamaged case and an unopened bottle. After popping the cork on the Prosecco, he grabbed two wineglasses and returned to the couple, still embracing. The pathos of the scene moved him. It was bittersweet indeed, knowing that at this moment they were on the cusp where desire swirled between them and future romance gleamed on the horizon. Angelli took a moment to memorize it. He wanted to recall it later when at last he made love to Signorina Crea, Serafina's great-granddaughter.

He returned the harmonics of the event back to the normal plodding human rate.

"May I pour you both a glass of Prosecco?" he asked.

Both of them tilted their faces toward him, astonishment showing on the actor's face at the sudden appearance of the sommelier at his elbow. Signorina Crea held his gaze, however, her smile wide and warm and filled with recognition. Angelli's heart thudded in his chest.

"I would be delighted," she said, her voice low and mellifluous like an angel's.

Angelli was besotted.

***

Zophiel watched as a cloud of nano-origami, invisible to the human eye, floated around the tableau below, circling almost lazily around Stasia's head before riding a harmonic current toward Zaccaria Angelli. Their lack of motor meant that even Angelli, who could see them, wouldn't suspect them of any purpose. If he'd take a moment to consider his surroundings—highly unlikely given his self-absorption—he'd wonder at the blackbird form of the microscopic dust motes.

After a moment the tiny origami flapped their wings and alighted in Stasia's hair and along her bare neck. Her harmonics vibrated in response, but they recognized Miró's harmonics and quieted. Stasia's aura flared slightly and then steadied into a brighter glow as Miró's own aura bolstered it. Even if Stasia was unaware of the nanoblackbirds now settled on her, she would benefit from their presence.

"Oh, well done, my blackbird," she said from her perch near the skylight.

Of her three wards, Miró Kos was the one she worried about the most. His anger and his wounds made her heart ache. Miró wasn't meant to be alone. She so wanted him to find the peace and healing that only came from romantic love.

More than that, Archangel Michael's plan depended upon it.

Zophiel looked down at the Bluetooth relay in her hand.

Of course, she was going to have to follow Stasia around for a while to make sure that Miró's tiny microphones transmitted the audio that they picked up.

Twenty-Six

B eta had never remained in one location more than a few days in a row until now, not even at her own apartment in Prague. Then again, she'd never had a knife with a 10cm blade jammed into her before. It was a good thing that the *bogomili* hadn't had any training. He missed everything important in her abdomen. The result was some lacerated muscle and adipose tissue as well as a bruised rib where the tip of the blade had been deflected. Not fun to deal with, but she'd recover with only a scar—not her first and certainly not her last.

She pulled the waist of her shirt up and looked at the thick white bandage clinging to her right side. Though Kastrioti's surgeon said that she was healing astonishingly fast and well, she still hurt. She walked like an old woman, slowly and gingerly, favoring her side. And sometimes, when András startled her from her frequent reveries, she flinched and pulled her arm in tight in an instinctive defense that set her teeth on edge.

András set her on edge.

He scarcely left her alone when there was no possible way that she could be ambushed in Kastrioti's secure mansion. Today she'd hidden in the euphemistically named 'media room.' He'd find her anyway, but for a moment she masked her thermal signature by sitting pressed against the server.

It didn't help that András had been deemed unfit to return to the field. He seemed fit enough to her. She suspected that Kastrioti was humoring the big Hungarian. She didn't blame the *drangùe* to some extent. It was better to leave a distracted team member at home than let his distraction endanger the whole team.

Across from her, live video streamed in multiple smaller windows from the security cameras around the estate. She watched them for a while. Miró had set the system to send alerts to him and Olivia, but in the two days that the *Elioud* team had been gone nothing unexpected had happened on the perimeter. If anything did happen, she wasn't sure who would respond besides the recovering *Elioud* tracker. Not the sweet-natured Pjëter surely.

Perhaps that was the real reason that András had remained behind. To defend the estate if necessary. But if that was the case, why hadn't they just told her that? Why the pretense that András wasn't combat ready?

Because they don't trust you.

Swift on the heels of that thought rode another: if she were Asmodeus, now would be the perfect time to penetrate Kastrioti's defenses. And she wouldn't use any angelic weapons. Just a car driven by an ordinary human wearing a bomb vest with an IED in the trunk. An ordinary human that no one suspected because she'd been on the grounds before.

Beta shivered.

Her desire to face just such an assault scared her because when she envisioned it she could see through the eyes of the bomber.

Standing, she rubbed her palms over the back of her arms. What was wrong with her? Was she thinking morbid thoughts because she'd come so close to being dead?

She missed her rope dart. It had likely melted in the storage room in the Čair neighborhood where she'd been stabbed. But she'd never know because she'd been unable to return to the scene. Her karambit had also been lost in the chaos, but that was easier to replace. Or would be once she was free to replace it.

She shook her head. What was her problem? She *was* free. She could leave if she wanted to.

Why did she feel so ambivalent? She'd never been ambivalent in her entire life before. She hardly even knew that what she was feeling was uncertainty. It had only dawned on her what was making her so edgy earlier today when she couldn't decide whether to eat an omelet or a pastry for breakfast. She never used to think about food one way or another before she was wounded. She ate only to keep her energy up. Whatever was put on a plate in front of her, she ate in quick, efficient bites. Lately, however, she either played with her food or wolfed it down.

Sighing in irritation, she walked through the double doors into Kastrioti's private office. Behind his desk were French doors to a balcony that ran the length of the second story. She crossed the office and opened the doors wide to the warm May afternoon before stepping outside. In the distance she could see the cultivators that Kastrioti had hired to transform the mountains around his mansion into terraces of medicinal and herbal plants.

Albania exported a lot of sage, thyme, and lavender, but most of those were wild harvested, leading to unsustainable harvesting and shortages. Cultivation would replace the wild botanicals, leading to more reliable crops and farming jobs. Olivia planned to get their herbs certified as organic and, after hiring locals in Fushë-Arrëz to process and package them, distribute them directly in the United States.

It was a brilliant scheme to aid the local economy and boost Albania's reputation internationally. Given that most Albanian sage was imported by wholesalers and food service companies (who marked it up four times what it cost them to procure), cutting out the middlemen meant a lot more money for Albanians. Olivia had taken to her role as the *drangùe*'s lady with a passion and had already started transforming lives without using her *bō* or 9mm.

Beta scowled and crossed her arms at her waist where the bandage under her shirt reminded her that she was an invalid incapable of helping others in the only way that she knew how.

Maybe that's why she was so restless. She felt powerless.

She pivoted to exit Kastrioti's office when her gaze slid across the easel standing to the right of his desk. She halted, holding her breath in shocked astonishment as she faced the

Watcher Angel painting. It ensnared her in a way that nothing material had ever done. Even if she'd wanted to look away, she couldn't. And that made her uneasy. She was used to controlling her interests and her emotions, not the other way around.

The canvas glowed with an unearthly light.

Beta took a step forward with her hand raised. The glow leapt toward her fingertips. She recognized it. It matched something in her *Elioud* blood. Wild joy danced inside her as the celestial energy raced up her arm and toward her chest where it filled a hollow space she hadn't recognized until now.

And then something dark and ugly opened its maw and swallowed the angelic manna streaming from the paintings.

Horror clawed at Beta. She felt choked for air. Tears sprang from her eyes. She wanted to flee but was rooted to the spot.

"What are you doing in here, Gomba?"

Mushroom. He called her mushroom. As nicknames went, it wasn't very endearing. But maybe accurate. She was hardly a showy flower that needed sunlight and rain.

Whatever gripped her let her go. She turned to look at András, who stood just inside the doorway to the media room. The memory of him bursting into the storage room in Skopje flooded her. He'd looked like a conquering titan, his eyes fierce and so dark they looked black instead of blue. As she fought for her life, she'd felt him behind her, covering her back in the onslaught from the *bogomili*.

He'd taken bullets for her. Nine to be exact. And not including the bullet he'd taken in the market before coming to her rescue. Wounded as he was, he'd carried her to safety and medical care. She owed him a debt she could never repay.

"Hiding from you, *spratek*." Hoarseness made her voice rough. She swiped at the wetness clinging to the corners of her eyes.

A heartbeat later András stood next to her. He didn't touch her, yet invisible fingers stroked her spine just as they had before their doomed mission to rescue the painting behind her.

"Are you all right, Gomba?" he asked softly. There was tenderness in his eyes.

She scowled and gestured toward the Caravaggio. "Why did Fagan want this painting?" she asked instead of answering.

He looked at her a moment longer. The stroking settled into a firm pressure at the small of her back. She straightened her spine in response but didn't move away.

András glanced at the painting. His body radiated heat and his own heady cologne that made her think of the terraced fields and mountains outside. Not shady, damp places with rotting logs where mushrooms grew.

"For the same reason you were standing here with your hand outstretched just now."

Guilt threaded through her. Beta stepped away from András, disrupting the invisible pressure on her back. It didn't return.

She forced herself to hold his gaze. "I have nothing in common with that man." Even as she said it, she knew it wasn't true. She switched topics. "I need to burn some energy in the gym."

He tilted his head to study her. He was reading her infrared signature. She didn't like it.

"Your wound is still healing," he said in a tone that suggested that she was borderline crazy. "It wouldn't be wise to push yourself too soon even if you are an *Elioud*."

Narrowing her eyes, Beta stepped closer to András despite her gut screaming a warning. Aggression, familiar as her heartbeat, felt like a warm blanket right now.

"Get me a karambit, and I will show you how wise I am."

***

"*L'Amante* made contact?" Major Costa's sharp gaze held Stasia's across his desk.

She nodded. "Last night at the Museum of Contemporary Art."

Costa leaned forward. "You are certain that he will lead you to a third painting? A painting no one else knows about?"

"That is not entirely true, *signore*. As I said in my report, Emilio Gregori at the Borghese Institute said that there is a legend about the Watcher Angel triptych." She paused. "And yes, I believe that *L'Amante* will lead me to this third painting. He wants very much for me to know about it."

"Because he knows that you are a member of the Art Squad?" Costa frowned. "That makes no sense."

"Because he is vain." She shrugged a shoulder. "And because he wants to seduce me."

"Ah." Costa leaned back and steepled his fingers. "So his moniker refers to more than art?"

"*Sì. Senza tentazioni, senza onore.*" *Without temptation, without honor.* "*L'Amante* has made me an obstacle to overcome on his way to infamy."

"You believe that you can use that against him, to pull information out of him about the American, Fagan, and his plans."

"I believe that it is possible that we have their relationship backwards, *signore.*"

"Fagan worked for *L'Amante?*" Costa sounded skeptical.

"More likely that *L'Amante* was using Fagan in some way." Stasia took a deep breath, gathering her *Elioud* charisma and feeding it into her next words. "Now that Fagan is dead, we have run out of leads."

"Hm."

Costa sat silent for a long moment. Stasia sent soothing harmonic waves into the tense air as she waited. After an uncomfortable time, he seemed to come to a decision.

"The operative I sent to Vienna found an office space that Fagan rented under an assumed name."

That set off an alarm in Stasia. She kept her harmonics steady as she asked, "Was there any evidence of Fagan's plans for the paintings?"

"No, there was nothing there except paperwork for a sham business. Fagan apparently used it for personal reasons." He paused. "But there was another odd thing, Fiore. Do you know who the last person was to visit this office?"

Stasia shook her head.

"Olivia Kastrioti, the disavowed CIA operative that you visited before meeting *L'Amante*."

Stasia held herself still. She had to tread carefully now. "What are you suggesting?"

"I am not suggesting anything. It is not my job to speculate. It is my job to get results." His dark eyes glittered. "That said, I want your assurance that the Rembrandt is secure."

"It is."

"See that it stays that way." He studied her. "The Art Squad may be anxious to get the Rembrandt back, but I tell you that I intend to discover whether any of this has a bearing on Italian foreign security."

"I understand." Stasia eased a little charisma under the words, not daring to smile. She paused. When he said nothing, she went on. "I have agreed to meet *L'Amante* for dinner this evening. Do I have your permission to continue working him as a hostile source?"

Costa studied her before waving her away. "I expect frequent status updates, Fiore. I do not want to be the last to know that we are funding international terrorism because one of my officers let a handsome man distract her from her job."

Stasia stood with her chin up and shoulders back. "That, I assure you, *signore*, I will never do."

***

Six hours later Stasia sat at a small table in La Campana, the oldest restaurant in Rome, waiting for the Dark *Irim* who called himself The Lover. She tasted her red wine as she glanced around the dining room, the fingertips of her other hand touching the fine gold chain around her neck. The antique bronze medal that hung from it stayed hidden between her breasts.

Nonno had given her the St. Michael medal for her fifteenth birthday. He'd known he was dying. She'd refused to wear it.

She heard her grandfather's voice in memory. "*Amante non sia chi non ha coraggio.*" A lover is not the one without courage.

For the first time in her career as an intelligence officer, she understood what he'd meant.

Tonight she would put her courage to the test.

The door to the restaurant opened, and the air pressure dropped. Around her the harmonics slowed until the other diners paused, their forks and wineglasses raised and their eyes wide. *L'Amante* had arrested the activity at the fundraiser the same way. She'd been expecting him to make a grand entrance. If he expected to find her frozen in her chair, dazzled to see him appear in the seat across from her as if materializing out of thin air, he was going to be sadly disappointed.

She sipped her wine nonchalantly.

L'Amante sauntered toward her table, a smirk on his handsome face. It was a small dining room, and the tables were close. As he walked, they and their occupants slid sideways to give him more room.

He paused next to the empty chair at her table.

Stasia adjusted the harmonics around her to give the chair a gentle push. It moved enough to allow the Dark *Irim* to sit.

It was the Dark *Irim*'s turn to look astonished. Stasia kept a tight leash on her harmonics as she felt his probing their edges. She gestured toward the chair, letting a slight smile curl the corner of her mouth.

"Please join me."

L'Amante sat down before signaling the owner, who raced to fill a carafe with red wine. Around them the diners began murmuring again. Their tables had slid silently back in place.

"I was going to apologize for keeping you waiting," he said, his own smile flirting with his full mouth, "but I see that you have already started." He nodded toward her wineglass.

Stasia lifted a shoulder, tracing her fingertip around its rim. There was no need yet to prove that she did things on her own schedule and not his. Let him think that he could dominate her with a little effort. She would bring him to the right conclusion.

She'd start by running the subject of their conversation.

"It would be better if you apologized for wasting my time." She smiled to take the sting from her words. She saw when her charisma hit him, followed a moment later by the realization of what she'd said.

A brief angry glint lit his gaze, but he shunted it aside. The restaurant owner arrived at that moment. *L'Amante* ignored the anxious man, who had trouble pouring his wine. Stasia, keeping her gaze on *L'Amante*, steadied the man's hand with a gentle harmonic hold.

"Leave us," *L'Amante* said when his glass was filled.

He drank his wine, closing his eyes and sighing. When he opened them, they were a bright cerulean, mesmerizing and dangerous. Stasia felt a chill shiver down her back and an excited tingle in her core. She tamped down the urge to lean forward and inhale his scent.

"Do you know how old La Campana is?" When Stasia would have spoken, he rode over her words. "Five hundred years.

Many, many famous people have dined here. Caravaggio's favorite was the *artichoke alla giudia.*"

He picked up the carafe and poured wine to the top of her glass. She accepted it from him with a nod.

"You must be something of an expert on Caravaggio," she said, easing a breath of *Elioud* charisma into her voice. "As you are on the Garden of Eden mythology."

The harmonics tightened around them. Stasia found it harder to breathe. *L'Amante* watched her with the predatory focus of a cobra. In response, the St. Michael medal burned against her tender skin.

L'Amante grinned. In the low light of the restaurant, he transformed from poisonous snake to charming wolf. His glossy black hair gleamed with gold highlights where it tumbled over his brow. An image of his naked chest leaning against snowy white linens wavered before her.

Stasia realized with a shock that he projected it.

"Indeed I am. I see that you visited my good friend Emilio Gregori, who has a copy of my book on his shelf."

Stasia cocked her head, studying him. "You do not look like a wizened doctor of divinity." She hummed, caressing his jaw with harmonics. It felt as though she stroked a live wire.

The air around them grew thick with harmonic tension.

He took her free hand and began playing with her fingers, tracing an intricate, invisible design with harmonics on its palm and back. It felt as though he were weaving a spell around her. Languid warmth spread up her arm and through her torso like hot honey, pooling in her lower abdomen. Her breasts grew full and heavy, her nipples tightening. Although she'd been sparing in drinking red wine despite her ploy, her thoughts grew sleepy and unfocused.

She panted a little.

L'Amante raised her hand to his lips. When he kissed it, harmonic lightning struck her core.

"Oh," she said, breathing out.

He tilted his head, his smile soft and hungry. "No, I am not wizened. And my divinity is far from academic. But you knew that."

Stasia swallowed. She struggled to control her harmonics. It was like she was a fly trapped in a sticky web. The more she flailed, the more she was caught.

So she drove forward. "Yet you wasted my time sending me on a hopeless hunt for a third painting."

L'Amante sat up, narrowing his eyes and dropping her hand. The harmonics crackled around them. "I did not waste your time. You gave up too easily."

"I was pursued by someone else who wanted to know where the third painting is."

L'Amante lifted his wineglass and drank, studying her over its rim. After a moment, he lowered the glass and dipped his chin in acknowledgment. "You tell the truth." Then he shrugged. It seemed petulant to her. "But it is no matter."

Now she had her opening.

Leaning forward, Stasia took the Dark *Irim*'s hand. "Ah, but it *does* matter to you, does it not?" she asked, slipping a little more *Elioud* charisma into her voice.

The fly might be caught, but the spider would also find himself stuck.

She went on before he could answer. "It is the painting that corrects the story, *your* story. You have waited so long for the time to be right to share it with humanity, am I right?"

At his nod, she said, "Then let me be the one to reveal it."

L'Amante's eyes took on a ravenous gleam. Tilting his head, he leaned forward, so close that she could feel his breath on her lips. "That, my dear, is exactly what I intend you to do. And then we will consummate this desire between us."

He kissed her. It was a soft, promise-filled caress that stopped all thought.

This time when the Dark *Irim* disappeared in a flash of white, Stasia's harmonics remained firmly in normal human oscillation. On the tablecloth below her palm was an invitation on heavy white card stock.

Stasia lifted her water glass to her lips with a shaking hand. Taking a sip, she waited until she'd regained control over her harmonics and her heartrate.

The opening play had succeeded. Why did she feel lost then?

Twenty-Seven

Miró watched across the street as Stasia approached her apartment building alone. She'd just reached to unlock the exterior door when he jumped harmonics to stand next to her.

She didn't startle. Instead she turned cool eyes to assess him.

"Waiting long?" she asked, turning back to twist the key. A loud click signaled that the tumblers in the lock had shifted. She opened the door and walked in without staying for his answer.

He followed her up the stairs to her small studio. Her stiff back gave him no sign that she was happy to see him.

She led him inside, holding the door until he'd slipped past her into the cool dark room. When she turned the light on, he took in the space with a quick glance as she dropped her keys and purse on a side table before shuffling her low heels off. It looked much the same as it had in February when he'd let himself in.

The redbrick wall next to him lent the room a rustic feel, but the furniture was modern and unadorned. A large vintage black-and-white photograph of a woman standing near a streetlight with an Italian cathedral in the background dominated the redbrick wall. There was something about the jaunty thrust of her hip and her pursed lips that made him think of Stasia. She looked lonely.

Stasia stepped into the tiny kitchen and stepped back, waving a bottle of wine. "A drink before you smite me?"

He sighed and sat at the small table next to the kitchen, which was half covered in mail and bills.

"Do I have a reason to smite you?" he asked, letting dry humor temper his tone.

She brought out two wineglasses and set them down. After she'd poured them each some of the deep red Nero d'Avola wine, she handed his glass to him. Her fingers brushed his, sending a tingle through him. Her hazel eyes had deepened to a lovely green, the outer rims of her irises a smoky gray. He caught the scent of her perfume, and it pierced his reserve. He wanted more than anything to take her in his arms, brush the hair from her tired eyes, and kiss her.

"Why did you not tell me that you and Olivia had decided to run a honeypot on *L'Amante*?" he asked at last.

Stasia looked at him, an eyebrow raised. "It seemed best to keep it from you at the time."

She took a drink and leaned tiredly in her chair. Miró set his own wineglass down and then, leaning over, picked her feet up and put them in his lap. He began massaging them, gently tugging the toes and rubbing the pad of his thumbs on her soles. He hummed, stroking her feet with light harmonics. She sighed and, digging her heels into his thighs, stretched her feet farther into his lap.

"Because you needed to be able to control your harmonics without me amplifying or distorting them as I did at the National Gallery Prague."

Stasia opened her eyes again. "Yes."

Miró could see Stasia's harmonics now, shimmering gold and navy above her skin. He saw a ruby band there, interwoven tightly within the vibrations. Where his hands touched her skin, their auras flared and merged until he couldn't tell where his ended and hers began. They had stopped being two completely separate individuals long ago. No matter what happened now, they were bound together on another plane.

If Stasia was hurt or lost to him as she played her dangerous game with the Dark *Irim*, he would feel it in his soul. He would never be whole again without her.

"Your finger seems to have healed fully," she said, her voice husky. When he looked up at her, he could see tears shimmering in her eyes. "I am sorry, *amore mio*, so sorry that you were hurt because of me." Her voice caught on the apology.

Miró dropped her feet to the floor and, leaning forward, grasped her face in both hands. He kissed her with everything he felt, the desolation and hurt when she'd left him, the hope, the understanding that had come at last when he'd gotten the audio from his nanoblackbirds. It wasn't the play he would have made, but he would do everything in his power now to keep her safe and ensure that what she did wasn't for nothing.

They had to find the third painting. No matter what it depicted, it was best for the world if the *Elioud* team recovered the final painting in the Watcher Angel triptych. Nothing that a Dark *Irim* wanted to share with humanity had ever led to anything beyond misery, strife, and discord. In many ways, the gross violations that Asmodeus perpetrated were much less insidious.

Yet he suspected that *L'Amante* had a darker purpose in mind. After all, Stasia had seen herself in the Caravaggio painting. It was both arrogant hint and subtle seduction. The Dark *Irim* wanted to make her a new Eve to his new Adam in direct contradiction to *Elohim's* redemption story. And its poison had been working on Stasia for months.

If Stasia fell to *L'Amante's* invidious charisma, the world would be plunged back into the murderous, violent chaos that characterized the time before the Flood. *Nephilim* and *Anakim* would be replaced with all the horrible technology that humans had devised for themselves.

Miró rested his forehead on Stasia's.

"You have no reason to be sorry, *dušo*. My injury is not your fault." He pulled back and looked at her. "And I would lose my finger all over again if it gave you the chance to fight and live."

She swiped a finger under first one eye and then another, laughing a little. As she moved, something glinted in the overhead light. Miró slipped a fingertip under the delicate chain around her neck, lifting up the St. Michael medal that had been stored in a velvet pouch the last time he'd seen it. It glowed softly with blessing.

The blessing that the Archangel had given it after Stasia's grandfather had saved Miró at the Battle of Monte Cassino.

"You have decided to wear this," he said, gently lowering the medal back to her chest.

She lifted a shoulder. "I need all possible help, earthly and divine."

His relationship with her great-grandmother hung heavy in the air.

He sat back. As he began speaking, he found he couldn't look at Stasia.

"Beatrix truly deserved her stage name 'Serafina.' She sang with a crystalline purity that I recognized as an *Elioud* gift."

He stopped, remembering. The modern studio apartment faded around him, and he sat at a small side table in the Café degli Specchi. A young woman sang near a grand piano in front of red-draped windows while men at a dozen tables listened, rapt.

"Beatrix came to Trieste only a few months before I arrived in October 1914," he said finally. "By then, the Habsburg authorities had started cracking down on the Italian political activists. Not long after that the naval blockade began, though it would be a few more months before famine and conscription halted the café concerts."

"My great-grandmother came from the country. She wanted to go to Vienna and make a career in opera, but the assassination of the archduke changed everything."

Now Miró did look at Stasia.

"She was very young," he said gently. "Eighteen. And beautiful. Even if World War One had never happened, your great-grandmother was unlikely to end up in Vienna singing professionally without a reputable singing master taking her under his wing."

Her eyes had shifted in color to a murkier gray. It was as if a shutter had covered them. Her scent had deepened to an earthy musk entwined with patchouli.

He went on anyway.

"Instead she found herself singing in cafés as one of many *sciantosas* vying for the attention of the men in the audience. Meanwhile other women mimicked her dress and her mannerisms. For a brief time, Serafina was the epitome of flirtatious femininity."

"In other words it went to her head." Stasia pulled her arms back and tucked them around her waist. "She believed that the men she beguiled loved her."

He gripped the stem of his wineglass, his fingers heating until the glass softened and bent. "I wanted to protect her."

"Then why did you abandon her when she was pregnant?" The soft question sunk a barb into Miró's chest.

"What?" he asked. He was too stunned to understand. The sorrow in Stasia's voice barely registered.

"When my great-grandmother nursed my great-grandfather in Treviso after he was wounded at the front line, she was five months' pregnant with my grandfather. He fell in love and married her anyway." Stasia paused to let the words take effect. "She spoke of the Croatian officer who had courted her in Trieste before Italy joined the war against Austria-Hungary. She said that she wished that he had never left her."

Miró shook his head to clear it. His harmonics buzzed.

"I had no idea that she was pregnant," he said. Five months … Sweet *Elohim*, Beatrix's child could be his. He raised his eyes and met Stasia's flat gaze.

"But you do not deny that you and she had been lovers." There was no accusation in her even tone. Why didn't she rail at him? Throw her hands around in extravagant gesture?

What did it mean that Stasia, the woman that he loved more than he'd ever thought he'd loved Beatrix, might be his descendant?

He held her gaze. "I loved Beatrix. I wanted to marry her. But she broke it off." Despite himself, bitterness crept into his voice. "She had found another lover."

Stasia sighed, closing her eyes. When she opened them, they were no longer flat. Just weary looking.

"So there is no way to know who the father of Beatrix's child was."

Miró shook his head. "I doubt that DNA testing would rule me out." All at once he felt the chasm that had opened up between them. A chasm that could never be bridged.

Stasia apparently agreed.

"Then we are at an impasse, you and I," she said at last.

Miró nodded. "Understood."

Stasia stood and went to the side table next to the apartment door. She pulled out a large white card from her purse and, returning, dropped it onto the table in front of him.

"*L'Amante* has invited me to a private showing of his art collection."

Miró picked up the heavy card. It was formal and expensive.

"This is near Todi in Perugia." He frowned. "I would never have guessed that *L'Amante* would make his home in Umbria. There are no large cities. It is filled with medieval hill towns, olive groves, and rolling vineyards."

"*Sì*, the 'Green Heart of Italy.' No coastlines or borders with other countries." She shrugged. "But Perugia is known as one of the great art cities. And the wines are as good as or better than those in Tuscany."

"I confess that I am quite curious as to what kind of home *L'Amante* would live in."

"Well, you will soon know." She picked the invitation up again. "Although I admit that *I* am not looking forward to being alone with Zaccaria Angelli."

"Olivia and Mihàil are here in Rome," he said quietly. When she turned a sharp gaze on him, he went on. "We wrapped up the operation in Dubrovnik just before you sent your message. I came to tell you that we are here to support you."

Stasia sighed. It sounded a bit shaky. She ran a hand through her hair before picking up the bottle of wine and pouring more in her glass and taking a sip.

"I would prefer not to go into the lion's den alone."

Now was the time to tell her about his nanoblackbirds.

"As to that, you already have more support than you are aware."

When Stasia looked at him in surprise, Miró shifted the harmonics around her until the individual nanoblackbirds nesting along her hairline and down her neck had gathered into a recognizable mass. To further aid her, he adjusted the nanogeometry of the graphene by gently heating the air until the mass reflected the overhead light.

And then there was a fist-sized bird fluttering in iridescent particles like suspended glitter before Stasia.

"What are these?" she asked in a low voice, raising a tentative finger towards them. The nanoblackbirds scattered as she did, only to alight on her fingertip and the back of her hand to her wrist. Her skin shimmered from their subtle cosmetics.

"My optimized origami design. They will go with you wherever you are and be invisible to everyone but you."

He couldn't touch Stasia now, but he sent the nanoblackbirds on a warm caress over her lips. She closed her eyes as he moved them slowly up her face and into her hair.

"I can hear their harmonics." Stasia tilted her head back and the nanoblackbirds rose in a cloud over her. "They sound like us." There was wonder in her voice.

"They are keyed to our conjoined harmonic signature," he said. "No other *Elioud* or *Irim* can readily sense our harmonics and not at all if we do not wish it."

"Because our signature is dynamic. Like an *Irim*." She held his gaze. "That is why I was able to maneuver around *L'Amante* when he made contact."

He nodded. "I control these blackbirds by manipulating heat and harmonic vibrations near them. You can also learn to control them."

He held out his hand and called the nano-origami to him. Stasia watched with an eager expression on her face. He thought about how quickly she'd mastered several harmonic skills and knew that she'd be able to make the blackbirds work for her. It wasn't much, but it made him feel better knowing that he'd given her another tool that not even a Dark *Irim* would anticipate. He felt a grim spike of humor at that thought. It was the *Irim*, after all, who'd disobeyed the Creator's wishes and brought technology to humanity.

Though once deployed, it wouldn't take much to overwhelm the nanoblackbirds with a harmonic wind or thermal shift if the Dark *Irim* recognized what they were.

"For now, I can track you with these blackbirds. Even better, they function as tiny listening devices that cannot be picked up by bug detectors. The only drawback is that you need to carry a Bluetooth relay to forward the sound that they gather to your cellphone."

"As long as you can disguise it in either a piece of jewelry or some other item that I can keep with me that should not be a problem. But what if there is no cell tower nearby? We will be in Umbria after all."

"We can work out the details now that we have an address. Mihàil, Olivia, and I will go ahead and scout Todi while *L'Amante* is distracted with you here in Rome. The invitation is for two days from now. That should give us enough time to make sure that we can get audio from you."

"That all sounds reasonable." Stasia sat down at the table again. "But what if our dynamics fail? What if our harmonics become unstable or *L'Amante* is able to pinpoint our conjoined harmonic signature and can trap me?" Her hands danced around her face in agitated urgency.

Miró knelt before her, putting his hands on either arm of her chair. He held her gaze until she shifted, sitting up straight, and settled her hands on her thighs. Then he ran warm harmonic caresses over her face and shoulders until she relaxed. It wasn't as good as touching her, but it was all that he *could* do. It would have to do.

"Hear me, *dušo*. And listen well. We are bound together. No matter what happens, we will always be in tune. Our dynamic signature will not fail."

"But *L'Amante* overwhelms me a little more each time I see him. What if I let him trap me?"

Fear knifed Miró. Stasia had gone straight to the heart of the matter.

He slowly nodded. "That is a real possibility. He is The Seducer, after all. Your guess that he manipulated Fagan was likely on target. You must not stay in his presence any longer than necessary."

Stasia searched his face. "I have never been so unsure of myself on an operation before."

"If you think you are in danger of submitting to his will, you can use a code word. I will come for you. Mihàil and Olivia are quite capable of creating a distraction worthy of a Dark *Irim*."

"Code word?" Stasia blinked in surprise. It was as if she'd forgotten that they were teammates on this mission. "Such as 'Sagrantino?'"

He cocked his head. "Your favorite red wine?"

"*Sì.*"

"Very well." Miró stood reluctantly. "Then I will say goodnight. I will contact you once we have surveyed the Todi site, and we will go over plans before you leave. I will also bring you a Bluetooth relay." He paused and then added, "And *dušo*, remember to be a *bushtër*. A dragoness. Understand?"

"*L'ho capito.*" Stasia nodded and followed him to the door to lock the deadbolt once he left.

As he heard it slide home against the strikeplate, Miró had a sense of foreboding. He hadn't told Stasia everything about Beatrix. In Prague he'd recognized the lover for whom she'd broken Miró's heart.

It had been Zaccaria Angelli.

***

Angelli slipped in behind the *Elioud* male who exited the apartment building where Signorina Crea lived. He had followed her after she left La Campana, toying with the idea of speeding along his seduction—after all, she was his one way or another.

Now he chided himself for almost spoiling his meal by eating dessert first.

He had been so intent on Signorina Crea in Prague that he hadn't gotten a good look at the *Elioud* male there. He should have anticipated that the lovestruck hybrid would find Signorina Crea and press his suit.

It's what he'd almost done, so no blame there really. Knowing that he had a rival whetted Angelli's appetite like nothing else could—especially a rival who radiated sexual frustration in his tightly constrained harmonics. The visit had been a disappointment for him.

But Angelli didn't want to be guilty of giving Signorina Crea too much leverage. The wise always understood who the competition was. And planned for contingencies.

He would show Signorina Crea that she, too, had rivals for the third Watcher Angel painting.

Angelli trailed the *Elioud* through the Pigneto neighborhood. It was a warm night and numerous people were out on Via del Pigneto, a route dedicated to pedestrian traffic with restaurants and bars that had outdoor seating. Many people were still eating dinner. The *Elioud* walked beyond the entrance to the metro station and stopped at a restaurant several blocks down. Angelli waited until the *Elioud* had been seated and was engrossed looking at a menu before he let himself be seated.

There was nothing unusual about the hybrid's actions. Nothing to indicate that he knew he was being watched. He ordered a leisurely meal and a half carafe of red wine.

The house wine.

Angelli sniffed. That said something about the mysterious *Elioud* but didn't provide much beyond his poor tastes.

Unless....

Angelli sent tentative harmonic fingers toward the hybrid, careful not to touch him. Even if he didn't know that Angelli was there, he would certainly feel the actual harmonic contact.

But if Angelli was right, the *Elioud* was Wild and would have no idea what that touch meant. That's what the hybrid descendants who knew what they were—and had some control of their *Irim*-derived abilities—called the strays no side had claimed or trained.

There was no other answer to the *Elioud*'s inferior taste buds. No *Elioud* with more than a smidgen of *Irim* blood would willingly drink house swill. Or sit so calmly with an *Irim* at the next table.

Angelli sat through an entire meal, scarcely tasting his food or wine as he kept track of the *Elioud*'s every move. He studied the hybrid's infrared signature and prodded again at his harmonics, which were deeply resistant to any harmonic turbulence. Though that didn't confirm or deny the amount of *Irim* blood he had; some humans were so closed to the supernatural that their harmonics had all the flexibility of a chair.

After the meal, which almost closed down the restaurant, the *Elioud* went to the metro station and took the last metro to the Vittorio Emanuele stop. Then he walked a few blocks north to an apartment building. Angelli stayed outside as the *Elioud* entered.

Was the *Elioud* as unaware of Angelli as he appeared to be? Or could he be trying to mislead Angelli?

He would need to devise appropriate tests to determine the truth.

Which would be almost as much fun as making Signorina Crea the prize in his cloister.

Twenty-Eight

The massive campaign to win Stasia began the next morning.

She'd had a terrible night with little sleep until the early hours of the morning when her loft bedroom began to lighten in the dawn. In the wan halflight she'd recalled the nanoblackbirds nesting along her skin and in her hair. And then she became fixated on sensing them.

It was a welcome distraction.

She had to slow her harmonics and her breathing, entering an alert, calm state that was neither awake or asleep. She saw the gentle golden aura around her and the braided colors of her harmonics as they vibrated. She imagined plucking and strumming them as she would a harp or a guitar. At first the music that she heard with her *Elioud* senses sounded tense and twangy, but as she kept her breathing steady her harmonics grew pliable and resonant.

She relaxed on the verge of drifting off, but she told herself to think about the nanoblackbirds, to imagine them nesting within the bands of her harmonics. After a few moments searching, she remembered that Miró had increased the temperature around them and then the nanoblackbirds had winked into visibility.

How much had Miró heated the air? Just on the edge of uncomfortable.

She closed her eyes and envisioned raising the temperature by extending the redder band of her infrared signature a meter above her body.

That's when she saw them with her *Elioud* senses. The origami clung like bright seed pearls to the cooler outer band of her signature.

She opened her eyes and saw tiny reflective particles like brightening makeup on her skin.

"There you are," she said.

She hummed and waved her fingers, visualizing as she conducted the harmonic vibrations rising from her. The minute nanoblackbirds rose from her and slowly coalesced into an unformed lump. She continued conducting harmonic changes as she varied her own humming until she'd directed the blackbirds into a more recognizable form. Overhead a small bird hovered, sparkling in the sunlight now streaming through her window. Their harmonics tinkled in a distinctive rhythm with her own.

Stasia spent the next twenty minutes playing with the nanoblackbirds, making them wink out of visibility and back, and sending them hovering, flying, and landing, until she could move them without audibly humming. It would take some more time to make her actions less conscious and more natural, but she knew that at some point these little nanobots would become second nature to her, like her 9mm or her *surugin*.

Though without the Bluetooth relay, they would be nothing more than an excellent harmonic training tool.

She'd just gotten up to make an espresso before showering when there was a knock on her door. When she answered it, all she could see was a bouquet of pale pink roses interspersed with white calla lilies and baby's breath that filled the doorway. But when she allowed the delivery man to bring it inside her apartment, he was followed by four other people all carrying equally large and equally extravagant bouquets with hundreds of expensive flowers.

Uneasiness set in. How had *L'Amante* learned her address? She was extremely careful to leave as small a footprint online as possible. She owned no property for tax records. Even her mail was directed to a rented mailbox. And he didn't know her true name.

Stasia had scarcely found a place to set all of the bouquets when her cellphone rang.

"*Buongiorno, bellissima*," said *L'Amante*. "I hope my delivery did not wake you."

And she hadn't given him her cellphone number.

"No. But it did keep me from making my espresso," she said, letting her irritation show.

"Hm," he said, "then perhaps it is a good thing that I am outside your door with breakfast."

Cold sweat started on Stasia's neck. An ice cube lodged in her throat. She touched the St. Michael medal where it nestled under her sleep shirt. It was warm. She took a steadying breath. Lifting her chin and pulling her shoulders back, she began to walk to the apartment door.

"Well, I suppose that I can forgive you then," she said, this time forcing warmth into her voice.

In bocca al luppo.

The familiar jaunty idiom bolstered her resolve. That and imagining *L'Amante* wearing a red clown nose.

Pulling her door open, she took in the sight of Zaccaria Angelli holding a takeaway container and smiling. Over the other arm he'd slung his suit jacket. His white button-down shirt was open to mid-chest, where sunglasses draped against the cloth. Tailored wool slacks clung to well-built thighs. If she had to guess, his leather belt and shoes had been made for him. He smelled indescribably good—a combination of the still warm croissant in the container and his masculine cologne that projected musk, leather, and honey.

His sexual magnetism hit her. Hard. Now she understood the word "swoon."

She gulped.

L'Amante stepped in before she could greet him, leaning in to kiss her.

"You look like you only this moment came from bed." His velvety voice filled her ears and sent a shiver straight to her core.

Stasia took a shaky breath and shut the door behind him. She wished that she had on more clothes. That her 9mm was strapped to one thigh and her BC-41 on the other.

And a garrote hidden in a bracelet around her wrist. Even then she would feel vulnerable. Because there was no killing an angel, was there?

Already the heavy scent of roses perfumed the air. It wasn't her scent. Too floral, too romantic, and too innocent. Olivia wore a perfume that had rose notes, a perfume that had been created for her using her very own cultivar, The Harlequin. A cultivar that Mihàil's mother, an *Irim*, had developed for her daughter-in-law.

It didn't suit Zaccaria Angelli either.

He'd disappeared into her tiny kitchen. Stasia trailed after him and watched in horrified fascination as the Dark *Irim* set about making her espresso. A memory of Miró making her scrambled eggs the morning after she'd been grabbed and drugged almost overwhelmed her.

It cleared her head of the cloying rose fragrance and pierced her heart with yearning. Miró looked better in bare feet and untucked shirt than *L'Amante* did in his elegant, bespoke wardrobe.

He turned and saw her watching him. Smiling, he handed her an espresso before carrying his back to her small table. He sat, crossing his legs.

Taking a sip of his espresso, he gestured toward the other chair. "Do sit and enjoy your croissant, *tesoro mio*. It is still warm, naturally." He smirked.

Stasia sat and picked up the croissant. As promised, it was as warm as if it had come from the oven only moments before. She took a bite. It melted on her tongue.

L'Amante looked around her apartment as he drank his espresso. His gaze stopped on the large print across from them.

"Not a very inspiring photograph," he said, tipping his head toward it. "Though I do admire the repetition of the geometric stripes."

Stasia shrugged without looking over her shoulder. "I liked the contrast with the red brick."

"What did your *Elioud* think of it?" *L'Amante* looked at her with a sly sidewards glance.

Stasia's heart thumped against her ribcage. She gripped her nerves hard, keeping her breathing and her harmonics steady. He'd obviously seen Miró in Prague and again last night outside her apartment building. She was now behind in this *tête-à-tête* and scrabbling to stay balanced. She must be careful not to disclose more than he already knew.

"He did not say." She paused. "But I doubt that he liked it any more than you do."

"Oh, I did not say that I did not like it." *L'Amante* spoke quickly. Too quickly. Then he paused. "An interesting answer, *tesoro mio*. You, at least, know what the word 'Elioud' means."

Stasia's heart beat so hard that she couldn't hear her thoughts. He'd trapped her into admitting knowledge about angelic descendants. It was the first major stumble that she'd made in an operation since her early years as an intelligence officer.

Then her brain snagged on the tiny little verbal reveal in the words 'at least' modifying the subject 'you.'

Could *L'Amante* be unsure of Miró's status as an *Elioud*?

It seemed unlikely, but perhaps the Dark *Irim* had no other evidence than the phosphorous flare that András had mentioned during the Prague operation. Miró had made that seem instinctive based on his attraction to her.

She tried to read *L'Amante*'s harmonics, but they were steady and gave nothing away of his inner state. His gaze, however, had stayed fixated on her, waiting for an answer.

Stasia could read what was there.

She smiled, engaging her *Elioud* charisma and channeling her nerves into it. *L'Amante* blinked as it wrapped around him.

"My"—she gave a subtle emphasis to this possessive pronoun—"*Elioud* has a certain amount of, shall I say, appeal?"

Sending harmonic caresses over *L'Amante*'s face and down the front of his chest, she continued in a throaty voice. "I find that he is often overcome in my presence."

Let the Dark *Irim* think that he needed to best *her*, not go after Miró.

***

"What in St. Michael's name is she doing?" Mihàil asked. "She is baiting a Dark *Irim*. Does she actually believe that she can seduce the original Seducer?"

They were listening to the live audio feed from the bug that Miró had planted in Stasia's apartment in February. He'd actually forgotten that it existed and never accessed its feed before. But he couldn't sleep much after he'd left the restaurant last night, especially knowing that *L'Amante* had followed him from Stasia's apartment. Followed and tried to test his harmonics. That's when he remembered the listening device on the frame of the print.

Any guilt Miró felt about its existence had been wiped when the listening device picked up the knock on her apartment door. He'd quickly brought his general and his lady in to monitor the situation.

Miró looked at his general now. He said nothing. He wasn't sure that he *could* speak.

Olivia answered her husband. "That's what she needs to do, my love. It keeps his focus on her. I take it that you *Elioud*'— Miró noticed that she used this term as if she weren't one of them—"don't go for intrigue and infiltrating the enemy's operation, do you?" She sounded exasperated.

Mihàil looked at her with a furrow between his brows. "No, not that of a Dark *Irim*. Even if I could conceal my identity, it would be challenging not to slip into Grey status. Or attempt to beat him to a pulp, which would likely not end well for me."

"You managed to work me for a while," she said, "without losing sight of who you are. At least for a few days, anyway."

"You were a Wild *Elioud*, my lady," said Miró. His tongue had unglued itself from his palate, but his harmonics were so tight that a sharp ache pierced his right eye. "Mihàil knew that you posed no danger to his moral compass."

Olivia looked at him. Her blue-gray eyes saw more than he wanted to reveal.

Before she could ask him if he was afraid that Stasia would succumb to *L'Amante*, the Dark *Irim* spoke.

"Indeed." His tone sounded silky even through their earwigs. "I find that engaging the uninitiated is a heady experience. Almost orgiastic. But that is nothing, *amore mio*, with the pleasures to be attained with those fully aware of their...gifts."

There was a pause. Miró held his breath.

And then Stasia laughed. Miró saw Mihàil blink. His general looked a little dazed.

His own thoughts were cold and crystal.

Olivia scowled and hit her husband on the shoulder. Hard. Mihàil looked first sheepish and then astounded.

"Sweet *seraphim*," said the *drangùe*. "Stasia may indeed be able to hold her own against *L'Amante*."

After that Stasia spoke. Her voice was low. "Who said that I am fully aware of my...gifts?" She paused to emphasize the word exactly the way that Angelli had.

Miró imagined that she'd leaned closer to the Dark *Irim* as she did, wrapping a hand around his holding his espresso. He closed his eyes. The image was so real it burned the back of his eyelids.

He would swear that the sensitive listening device picked up Angelli's hard swallow.

"You two. I could knock your heads together." Olivia threw pointed glances at Mihàil and Miró. "I don't know exactly how *Elioud* charisma works, but if I had to guess, I'd say that Stasia has found a way to rebound *L'Amante*'s desire onto himself."

Mihàil gave her a sharp look. "If that is true, then she would not be the first of your team to find a Dark *Irim*'s weak spot."

He referred to Olivia sending Asmodeus into an angelic coma that took him out of play for six months.

Miró felt hope stir. But imagery floated through his vision as if he sat in the same room with his beloved. Stasia lifted Angelli's espresso and sipped. In response, the Dark *Irim*'s eyes glowed with an unearthly light. His groin radiated a white heat. He leaned closer to Stasia and, placing his hand on her bare knee, nuzzled her neck. White heat flared in her groin in response.

Miró's hope faded.

"But perhaps you would be willing to teach me about them?" Allure vibrated through Stasia's silky voice, matching Angelli's earlier tone.

It was a tone that promised that educating her would be a gift all its own.

"Nice," Mihàil said. "She has appealed to his vanity."

"And his previous success as a teacher," Miró added in a strained voice.

"What is it, Miró?" Olivia asked.

He felt her hand on his arm. He turned unseeing eyes toward her. "I can see her. Them."

Mihàil's quiet voice came from behind him. "It happens."

Before Miró could ask what Mihàil meant, Angelli spoke.

"Something tells me that you know more than you realize." He paused. In the silence, Miró saw him study Stasia. "Or I may be mistaken. You may know perfectly well what your gifts are, though I doubt you truly know their worth."

Then Angelli stood up. "Come. It is time to pack your things. I am taking you to my estate today."

Stasia sat up. She looked startled. And a little uneasy. "Your invitation said tomorrow."

Alarm jolted through Olivia and Mihàil's harmonics. Miró ignored them.

He imagined bolstering Stasia instead. But the distance between them was too great for his harmonics to affect hers.

"I changed my mind." Angelli waved his hand nonchalantly about his face as he spoke, pivoting and heading toward the stairs to her loft. "The prerogative of an art thief."

He turned back to look at her before he started to climb. "I have a surprise waiting for you."

"But I have to go to work." Stasia's voice had a sharp edge. She followed the Dark *Irim* to the bottom of the stairs. "And your wonderful flowers. They only just arrived. Besides, I have not yet showered and dressed."

Angelli was already halfway up the stairs to her sleeping area. He spoke without turning around. "I understand perfectly, though you must not go to great lengths with your hair and makeup. I live a simple life in the country. Two hours should be more than enough to get ready. The flowers will come with us, of course. The florists are still waiting in their vans outside."

Angelli's head appeared over the top railing of her loft space. "Would you like me to speak with your boss? I can be very persuasive."

Miró expected Stasia to work 'Sagrantino' into the conversation. She couldn't go to Todi yet. They hadn't had time to scout Angelli's property or prepare an extraction plan. If she got into a car with Angelli, she'd be walking into the unknown without a support team.

She didn't say the name of her favorite wine.

Instead she said, "*Molto bene.* But I can pack for myself."

Miró exploded. "Say it, Stasia. Say the code word. Do *not* let Angelli move up the timeline."

Mihàil and Olivia said nothing.

Miró's unexpected visual connection disappeared. He didn't have time to understand what any of that meant. He stood up. He had to do something to keep Stasia out of *L'Amante*'s lair.

Lair. As if the Dark *Irim* was a wild animal.

Or a dragon whispered a small voice. Dragons liked to keep their treasure close in a secure space. And *L'Amante* had called her *tesoro mio.* My treasure.

"As you wish." *L'Amante*'s voice sounded closer to the bug than before. He must have descended from Stasia's loft.

Olivia coughed. "No need to asphyxiate us," she said, waving her hand under her nose to make her point.

Miró clamped his jaw and lowered his temperature. The smoky scent lingered around them, however.

Too bad *he* wasn't a dragon. He'd love to breathe fire on Angelli's estate and his stolen art collection.

"But, *per favore*, Signorina Crea, no more than two hours. I have been a very patient man until now. However I see no reason to delay getting acquainted any longer."

"*Naturalmente*," Stasia said. "I will be ready in two hours."

"More than enough time to deliver the GPS relay," Olivia said cheerfully next to Miró.

He looked at her without turning his head.

"What?" She asked, all innocence. "Oh, I know. I forgot to tell you that Mihàil's asset delivered it last night while you were out stalking Stasia."

From the audio feed came the sound of a door latch and Stasia's apartment door swinging.

Good. The bastard was leaving.

"Oh, yes, one final thing: I will be very hurt if your *Elioud* admirer should delay your packing. I should hate to leave without you." Warning sharpened Angelli's tone.

Miró clenched his fists. He opened his mouth to speak.

Frowning, Mihàil shook his head. His battle senses were right. The Dark *Irim* had more to say.

"But I will. Because I am no longer as certain as I was, Signorina Crea, that you are the right one to make the last

Watcher Angel painting known to the world. There are others on whom I can rely."

There was a long silence, and then the sound of Stasia's apartment door shutting.

Miró shut the feed down. There was no need to listen in to Stasia alone. He wanted to go to her, but he knew that he couldn't. Not without risking the Watcher Angel painting. And she hadn't said 'Sagrantino.'

"It sounds as if The Lover doesn't want to share Stasia." Olivia looked at him and Mihàil. "He's the jealous type. That's good. We can use that."

"But how am I going to get the GPS relay to her now?" Miró asked.

Olivia shrugged. "I'll deliver it."

Mihàil growled. "It isn't safe."

She looked at him. Her gaze was steady. "When has it ever been safe on a mission? Besides, you would risk your life for your lieutenants. Would you ask less of me?"

The *drangùe* looked uncomfortable. "Keep your harmonics steady and your radio open."

Olivia laid her fingertips briefly on his jaw. Miró imagined that she sought to reassure her husband with a light harmonic touch.

448 | L I A N E   Z A N E

"*L'Amante* won't know that I'm an *Elioud*, I promise. And if for some reason he kidnaps both me and Stasia, I know you'll track me down to the ends of the earth. I'll be fine. He's not going to hurt me. He's not Asmodeus."

Mihàil didn't look mollified, but he didn't argue. Instead he said, "Show Miró what the piece looks like before you deliver it."

She smiled and kissed him. Then, turning to Miró, she said, "It's absolutely beautiful, Miró. She's going to love it."

They waited while Olivia went to her large leather totebag and pulled out a small flat jewelry box. She brought it back to Miró and watched with an eager expression as he opened it. Inside lay a sterling silver charm bracelet. Custom silver beads in the shape of blackbirds and flowers studded with blue-green crystals alternated with other beads in the shape of hearts. In the center of the rope-like bracelet sat an oblong glass bead about a centimeter wide. It was handpainted with a blue flower nestling a blackbird.

Blackbird and flower. *Kos* in Croat and *Fiore* in Italian. Their *Elioud* codenames.

It was not, however, the first time that he'd been known as The Blackbird.

Miró fingered the custom glass bead. That was where the electronics for the Bluetooth relay were stored. The hollow silver bracelet hid pin-shaped rechargeable lithium-ion batteries. The blue-green crystals were sensors that measured temperature, light, and humidity.

Clever. This just might work. He squelched the dark foreboding that nagged him.

"I'll have to test it before you leave." Miró looked up at his general and his lady. "Tell Stasia...." His throat closed. He cleared it. "Tell Stasia I'll be waiting for her in Todi."

Twenty-Nine

Two hours later Stasia and Angelli sat in the backseat of a chauffeured Mercedes S-Guard sedan—a special armored version of the German luxury car. The rear windows were tinted midnight black, and the hand-sewn leather interior a dramatic red. Despite the tinting, the interior of the car was bright from the open sunroof. Atonal jazz played from the Burmester speakers.

Stasia hated it.

The center console between them held a bottle of Torgiano Rosso Riserva, an exceptional Umbrian red wine whose grapes grew only in elevated vineyards. She held her wineglass—made of real glass—in a relaxed grip. Angelli left his on the console. There was absolutely no danger that either of their glasses would spill on the fine Nappa leather. The Mercedes drove silently and smoothly, gliding over the highway.

On Stasia's left wrist glinted the charm bracelet that Olivia had brought earlier. She wanted to touch it but dare not.

"You are unusually quiet, *tesoro mio*."

Stasia looked at Angelli without turning her head. "I am just trying to imagine your art collection. Is it as large as your"— she paused suggestively—"wine collection?"

Angelli smiled. The air around them heated, mixing with his honeyed musk and the scent of leather. Stasia carefully matched his temperature. It wasn't much, but it kept hers from becoming swamped in his. Unfortunately, she'd also caught a glimpse of his infrared signature. There were unhealthy bands of yellow-green and black that sickened her.

"My art collection spans centuries and is rather eclectic. Although I have found that the period following the Impressionists offers the most interesting variety for paintings. And the most malleable artists with which to work."

Stasia rotated the wineglass in her hand but didn't drink. She needed to keep her wits about her. She cocked her head as she looked at Angelli. His glossy dark hair slipped over his forehead and dark stubble roughed his jaw. That and the open shirt said that the rules didn't apply to him. He could wear classic tailored clothes and groom himself any way that he liked.

"I take it that you collect more than paintings?"

He nodded, watching her. "Much more." The words held innuendo that she couldn't decipher. It made her uneasy.

Miró had predicted that *L'Amante* wanted to seduce her not only sexually but spiritually. To make her his acolyte.

She needed to keep the conversation going. To make it about him, not her. That shouldn't be too hard with someone whose vanity was all encompassing.

"What is your favorite piece of art?"

Angelli inhaled. "Hm. I have not thought of that." His gaze fixed on her. "There are so many worthy pieces. It is hard to choose just one."

His words definitely meant something more than art. Stasia quelled the instinct to swallow. She couldn't give anything away. Predators like Angelli scented the smallest weakness. She must do all that she could to find out about the competition without appearing too eager. But she'd seen his desire to tell her about a piece only an instant before he'd withheld the information. She could use that.

"Surely you have something in mind?" She laced the question with a breath of *Elioud* charisma, smiling widely as it hooked into his desire.

His desire was no match for her mission. *Yet*, she admitted to herself.

Angelli shifted in his seat, but no awareness lifted his features. Instead he waved his hand and said, "I am rather partial to an ivory sculpture of Adam and Eve done by Georg Petel in 1627."

"I know that piece," Stasia said sharply. "It was stolen from the Rubens House in Antwerp."

"What can I say? I had to take it. Sleep eluded me for two weeks after I first laid eyes upon it until I could find the time to return and collect it. Of course, I also needed to recruit an assistant."

Stasia snorted. She didn't care if Angelli heard her derision. "As you recruited me in Prague?"

"More or less." He smirked. "Although I did require this assistant to prove her—ah, mettle—prior to joining me. Even though she is not an *Elioud* as you are, she is still one of my most cherished staff. You will meet her along with the others."

Stasia filed that information away. Of course, Angelli had referred to his property as an estate, so there would be a staff. Without any time for surveillance or reconnaissance, however, she had no idea how many others were there. Or what their status and capabilities were. He was a Dark *Irim*. Surely he had some *Elioud* on his staff. Or even an acolyte. He seemed like the type to get bored and move on when his attention was captured elsewhere.

As she had captured his attention.

She shivered.

"Is she one of those that you can rely upon?"

"Undoubtedly." Angelli finished his wine and poured another glass. "I must confess that when I realized you had a suitor, I was overcome with jealousy. And then I thought, 'Why be jealous? If she has someone vying for her affection, perhaps you should play the field a bit, hm?'

"So I have decided not to limit myself. That has never been my approach for good reason. You see, competition brings out the best in everybody."

Stasia ran a thumb around the rim of her wineglass. She wished that she had a nice potted plant nearby to dump it into. Soon she would have to drink it.

"What does that mean?" she asked when he wasn't more forthcoming. "More competitors than those who are already loyal to you?"

Angelli, who was staring out the side window at the Umbrian countryside, started. "Hm? Oh, yes. In this case, it means an art auction." His tone was fraught with meaning.

"Art auction? You are going to sell the Watcher Angel painting to the highest bidder?" She paused, frowning as she thought. "That means it is at your estate. I thought you said it was in Aix-en-Provence."

"I did not." Now he sounded irritated. "Do keep up, *tesoro mio*. I told you to go to Aix-en-Provence. I did not tell you that the painting was there. Why would I make it so easy for you?"

"And yet you are taking me to it."

"True, but now you will have to earn it. You have missed your chance to find the painting following the breadcrumbs that I left you. Now you will have to outbid a number of uncommitted *Elioud*, who will want the painting and may be swayed to join my little group to get it."

Uncommitted *Elioud*? Is that what Miró called Grey *Elioud*, those who had chosen neither side in the ongoing angelic battle between the forces of light and dark? Had *L'Amante* turned his personal quest for glory into a recruiting mission?

And in order for her to take the painting out of play, she would have to convince him that she was the perfect *Elioud* to become his acolyte.

Stasia fingered the beads on the bracelet. Maybe it was time to ask if there was any Sagrantino in the estate cellars....

"That is a lovely trinket," Angelli said in her ear.

Stasia startled. Looking up she saw that he was no closer, but his bright blue eyes gleamed in a way that frightened her. For a moment she was transfixed as a hare is transfixed by a cobra. He smiled. It was a slow, sensuous smile. Her heart raced. Her nipples hardened. And desire tightened her core. She wanted to be devoured by him.

"Is it from your *Elioud*?"

She nodded dumbly.

"May I?" Angelli held out his hand expectantly.

Stasia set her wineglass down on the console and undid the barrel latch on the rope bracelet. She handed it obediently to her host.

His fingers brushed hers as he accepted the heavy silver beads strung together. A sharp bolt of pleasure arced to her groin. She gasped involuntarily.

Angelli ignored her to study the bracelet. "What a queer little design. Birds and flowers. Almost Victorian except at how exquisitely carved each of the beads are."

He ran an elegant finger along the beads. Stasia felt it run along her skin. It was almost painful in its pleasure. Her thoughts scattered. She squirmed, flushed and dazed.

Now Angelli looked at her. His gaze pinned her to the Nappa leather. Harmonic fingers began stroking her everywhere while she couldn't move. Stasia felt naked and completely at his mercy.

"*Per favore*," she managed to whisper.

"Does your *Elioud* know that you are staying with me?"

She nodded. Tears pricked the corners of her eyes. She would *not* let him bring her to orgasm.

Angelli dropped his gaze to the bracelet again. He hefted it in his hand for a moment. At last he sighed and handed it back to her at the same time releasing her from his infernal assault on her body. Stasia sank in relief against the welcome comfort of the seat. She squelched the sudden urge to open her door and fling herself out of the speeding car. That would be like putting fire out with gasoline.

"It is a cheap piece of jewelry," he said sniffing, "albeit harmless. You may continue to wear it, even though it offends my sensibilities."

Stasia dangled the bracelet around her wrist and struggled to engage the clasp with shaky fingers. Angelli made no effort to help her. Instead he drank his wine. After she managed to connect the two halves of the bracelet, she picked her wineglass up and drank deeply.

He hadn't discerned the secret in the bracelet.

That's because the two small lithium batteries wouldn't power the Bluetooth transmitter unless she pressed a small button on the side of the clasp. And the transmission would read as just another cellphone to anyone scanning for it. As long as she was near a cellphone—any cellphone—he shouldn't be able to isolate the wavelengths for her bracelet. Olivia had told her that the relay had been coded to force pair with any Bluetooth device within 10 meters. While it meant that data transmission would be spotty, it also meant that if she didn't have her cellphone with her for some reason, she could still be ears for the *Elioud*. Even if she was unconscious or dead.

They arrived at Angelli's estate outside Todi in the early afternoon. Several buildings, including a church, clustered around courtyards and terraces, and all were enclosed by a stone wall. The main villa had tangerine stuccoed walls, wrought-iron balconies, and arched columns. The church and cloister were mixed gray-and-tan stone. Besides the main villa, there was another villa and three apartments. Although Stasia couldn't take everything in as they parked in the large lot behind the main building, she saw ornamental trees and hedges, olive groves, and vegetable gardens. All the buildings were connected. Angelli assured her that all had independent access and could be separated from the main villa by closing doors.

Stasia scarcely wondered why that would be necessary before it became apparent.

As they strolled along the outside of the church under a grapevine-covered arbor toward the main villa, a group of women approached. It was a narrow walkway, so Stasia couldn't be entirely sure how many infrared signatures she read, but it was more than half a dozen. Then she recalled Angelli's "staff," those upon whom he could "rely."

What a covert-operation nightmare.

Even if Miró, Olivia, and Mihàil had managed to get here to survey the grounds and buildings, there were too many variables to track and control: entrances, people, and places to gather inside and out. And tonight more people arrived for the art auction.

And of course, that didn't account for any angelic or human security measures. She might be able to get a sense for the number of guards and their training and weapons as well as the cameras being used, but she didn't trust herself to identify the harmonic barrier let alone any other angelic methods to which she'd never been exposed or taught.

Stasia didn't have time to note more than a few relevant features for the map that she would sketch later in her room before the group of women reached them. She stopped at Angelli's side and studied them. They were dressed in simple long gowns in colors of white, tan, and peach and wore their hair long with no makeup on their radiant faces. A tall blonde stood at the head of the group. She had large, smooth features and high cheekbones. Her intelligent eyes gave an impression of serenity, but Stasia knew that this woman saw everything. Around her waist she wore a belt upon which dangled a heavy ring of keys.

She held out her hand. "Your purse, *per favore*." Her accent was difficult to identify. Perhaps Dutch.

Stasia kept her purse on her shoulder. It was all a show. She'd expected this and hadn't left anything in it or her luggage that would raise any flags. But deflection and misdirection served covert operatives almost as well as lock picks and RFID micro trackers.

She narrowed her eyes. "Why?"

"It is just a precaution, Stasia," said Angelli.

She started. She hadn't told him her name and had convinced herself—naively, it seemed—that he'd tracked her apartment as András tracked his quarry: by following faint traces of her infrared signature. Instead he knew who she was.

"We would not want your bosses at the Command for the Protection of Cultural Heritage to learn about the art auction or the rather vast collection of stolen artwork that resides inside my home."

Stasia laughed, using her anxiety to give it energy. It was an old trick, leaning into her nerves. She widened her eyes and lifted her shoulders. "Of course, Signor Angelli. You have nothing to fear from the Carabinieri, I assure you. They have no idea that I am here."

The truth also gave power to her words.

Now it was Angelli who laughed. "Ah, *tesoro mio*, you are a continual surprise. But of course you are here for yourself. Then

460 | L I A N E Z A N E

you really should have no qualms about letting Eva review what you carry with you." He paused. "And she will keep your cellphone with her until we can be certain that it is clean."

Stasia had no choice then. She slipped the purse from her shoulder and handed it to Eva, whose gaze sharpened. She clearly suspected that Stasia held something back.

Afterwards Angelli drew Stasia into his side, wrapping his arm around her waist and leaning in to kiss her in front of the assembled staff. Stasia felt a dozen eyes looking at her. Their harmonic signatures, all strangely aligned, buzzed and flared. Worse, there was something feral and suspicious about the group's harmonics. Stasia, her eyes closed to accept Angelli's kiss, saw more clearly with her *Elioud* vision how the women's harmonics moved and shifted within his harmonic sphere.

Only her harmonics remained free of his malign harmonic gravity.

For now.

Yet she could already see how Miró's harmonics, interwoven into her own harmonic threads, had begun to fray and weaken.

Angelli turned to his staff. When he spoke, his voice carried clear command. "Ms. Fiore's flowers and luggage must be taken to her suite. Eva, we will dine in the main dining room as soon as Ms. Fiore has had a chance to freshen up. Have you heard from our other guests?"

"Yes, lord." She glanced at Stasia, clearly not wanting to speak in front of her. "They will start to arrive this afternoon, and all except Willem will be here for the cocktail reception on the terrace."

"Excellent!" Angelli said. He'd kept his arm around Stasia's waist, pinning her to his side. "I expect everyone to be dressed accordingly."

"Yes, lord," the women responded in unison. Their voices, variously sharp, flat, raspy, and gravelly, broke in odd places, however.

Angelli smiled down at Stasia as his harmonics caressed her. "Come. Let me show you where you will be staying tonight."

Stasia shivered. She feared that she would be staying in his bed.

***

"Insufferable bastard."

Miró, who watched the video feed from the small drone he operated near Angelli's estate, started at the vehement tone. He turned to look at Zophiel, who now sat beside him in their surveillance van. The guardian angel wore a hard expression that he'd never seen on her face before. She was also dressed in camouflage in a pattern that uncannily matched the colors of the landscape around them. The camouflage didn't hide her imposing physique or muscles, however. Zophiel embodied as a warrior angel. This was also a first for Miró.

"I take it you do not approve of Angelli living in a former convent," he said dryly.

Zophiel looked at him. Her frozen gaze burned. "I am so going to enjoy this."

Miró looked back at the screen. Although the drone flew autonomously, he didn't trust it to stay out of the airspace over the grounds. Angelli's harmonic perimeter extended six kilometers into the air—well above where most helicopters flew. Mihàil and Olivia intended to fly their origami eagle into the grounds once the cocktail reception started. But until Stasia's nanoblackbirds picked up more information about that event, they were holding off. It wouldn't do to give their presence away. In the meantime, the couple traced the perimeter of the estate, which was double the size of the walled and landscaped grounds surrounding the house and obscured by dense woods.

"You sound more certain than I feel about our chances," he said.

The drone banked and came around the front of the main villa where dense shrubs and stone walls enclosed a rectangular green lawn. A small swimming pool and a covered patio could be seen next to a flight of stairs from the main house. On the lawn, several women wearing cocktail dresses moved around tables covered with snowy-white cloths and sparkling place settings.

While they watched, Stasia left the villa and descended the stairs before strolling toward the pool. She wore a pale sand-colored evening gown that hugged her like a second skin except where it was split up to her thigh. Her long, dark-caramel hair cascaded in thick waves over her shoulders. Miró's gut clenched. She was so beautiful. Yet the sensors in the bracelet read a high body temperature. He would be unable to rely on the nanoblackbirds if she lost control.

Stasia, my love, he flashed before he could stop himself even though he knew they were too far apart.

She turned toward him.

An instant later, Angelli appeared at her shoulder in a burst of white. Next to him stood an older woman with hair the color of steel wool and a dark-haired man. All wore evening clothes.

"Insufferable bastard is right," Miró murmured.

"You should go to her." When Miró looked at Zophiel with wide eyes, she said, "What? Do you need an invitation?"

"Yes." At her narrowed eyes, he went on, "If she says the code word, we will extract her."

Zophiel shook her head. Sadness softened her features so that she was no longer an avenging angel.

"That would be far too late." She nodded toward the screen. "And Ms. Fiore is as stubborn as you are, I am afraid, my blackbird. She will not call for help to save herself if it means failing the mission, but she will fail the mission on her own."

Her words sent an arrow of fear into his gut.

"What do you propose? Angelli will know as soon as I cross his harmonic barrier."

Zophiel cocked her head. "True, but is that a bad thing?"

Miró's heart sped up. There was a slight ringing in his ears. Zophiel waited while he thought through the implications.

The third Watcher Angel painting was *here*. And more Grey *Elioud* had already arrived to bid on it.

Zophiel laid a gentle hand on his forearm. "If you want it to be better, make it better."

Miró knew that she wasn't speaking of the mission now.

Standing, he tapped the call button for Mihàil and Olivia's radios. "My lord, my lady." He paused, took a breath, and stiffened his spine. "I am going for Stasia."

Thirty

When Miró crossed Angelli's perimeter, the resulting phosphorous flare engulfed the entire 10 hectares of the private grounds. Its brilliance brought the light of midday to the people of Todi almost three kilometers away. Reminded about the nature of the residents living in the converted convent, some crossed themselves while most went inside. Tourists, bewildered by this behavior, nevertheless couldn't shake a sense of unease and reconsidered their evening plans. At the estate itself, the simultaneous harmonic feedback from Miró's breach created angelic white noise on a massive scale, stunning everyone for several minutes.

More than long enough for Mihàil and Olivia, wearing harmonic-dampening gear and braced for disruption, to sneak inside undetected. It would be up to Miró to keep Angelli distracted so that he didn't realize that the *drangùe* and his lady had penetrated his secure location.

Miró would find out soon enough whether he could manage that.

He'd disabled the electronic security system at the ornate gates in front of the main villa and climbed the stairs, reaching the inner courtyard before Angelli appeared with Stasia. The angel's eyes gleamed, whether in anger or amusement Miró couldn't be sure. He suspected it was both.

He ignored the Dark *Irim* to study Stasia, whose arm was threaded through Angelli's. Flushed and unsteady, her glazed eyes shocked him. Worse, her thermal signature radiated white heat throughout her torso. It was as if Angelli had drugged her with MDMA. Her expression certainly suggested the drug's other effects.

Her expression and her behavior.

She pressed against Angelli, her breasts brushing his sleeve in a suggestive manner while her free hand stroked Angelli's bicep.

Miró shunted his rising heat carefully through his soles and into the ground. No need to antagonize the Dark *Irim* just yet. Still, he needed to clench his jaw to remain silent.

Are you all right? he flashed.

Stasia didn't respond, but a slight tremor echoed in her harmonics.

"Ah, the suitor." Angelli sounded indulgent.

Guards, dressed in black and wearing sunglasses against the early evening sun, jogged into the courtyard and took up positions at the exits. They carried AK-47s, the ubiquitous assault rifle favored by dictators and terrorists.

Therefore human and capable of being subdued or killed by trained operatives.

Six guards in the courtyard carrying semi-automatics, he flashed to Mihàil and Olivia, who would be busy mapping heat signatures for all the individuals on the estate grounds.

A moment later and Angelli hit him with a targeted harmonic blast.

Miró fell to his knees clutching his head. It felt like a church bell had been dropped over it and then hit with a mallet.

The vibrations stopped abruptly, leaving him with a massive headache. Angelli lifted him to his feet, staring at him with a hard gaze. Miró refrained from doing anything except keeping his own gaze steady on the Dark *Irim*'s face.

Around them others gathered in the courtyard, avid curiosity twisting their features. The handsome older woman and the dark-haired man who had been speaking to Angelli on the front lawn stood with another couple on the steps to the church. They all held filled wineglasses and looked like they were enjoying this unexpected entertainment.

Grey *Elioud*. Descendants of angels and humans who had answered the invitation of a Dark *Irim*. The third Watcher Angel painting must be very valuable indeed.

Miró schooled his expression into impassivity. He was a master at not showing disgust. He'd learned how to do it in the *köçek* troupe when adult men had watched him dance with open lust.

The women wearing cocktail dresses waited on the crushed stone path behind Stasia. One, a tall blonde a half step in front of the others, appeared to be their leader. Her ravenous gaze took the three of them in. Everything in her posture said that she barely restrained herself from coming closer. The harmonics for all of the women had been keyed into Angelli's, forming a foul Dark angelic chorus. They jangled Miró's harmonics, sharpening his headache.

Angelli gestured over his shoulder with a languid hand. A guard trotted up and wrenched Miró's arms behind his back before ziptieing them together. He yanked Miró to his feet.

The next moment Angelli ran harmonic fingers over Miró, prodding and invading. Miró hadn't felt this violated since he was a boy. His temperature rose involuntarily, and smoke filled the air around them.

Angelli laughed in delight and dispersed the smoke with a swift harmonic wind.

"Now, now," he said, chuckling. But the harmonic assault stopped.

The Grey *Elioud* on the church steps smiled. The dark-haired man lifted his wineglass in silent toast.

Stasia's lips opened in a passionate pout. She undulated next to Angelli in a manner that suggested that he was stroking her with harmonic fingers. Miró caught her nearly inaudible sigh of pleasure. This time he managed to keep his temperature in check. Barely.

"Do you know what you are?" The indulgence was back in Angelli's voice.

Miró blinked, bringing his gaze back to the Dark *Irim*, who watched him as if he were an alien. "What?"

Inside the perimeter, flashed Mihàil.

Make that two of us, flashed Olivia. *I'm in the structure outside the lawn. One guard patrolling along the stone wall.*

Angelli seemed to be enjoying himself. "Tell me you have never noticed that lovely *eau d'ash* you exude when you are angry? Or am I mistaken? You enjoyed my caresses, hm?"

The Dark *Irim* withdrew his arm from Stasia, who stumbled. He either didn't notice or didn't care. He circled Miró, who felt his penetrating gaze as a physical touch. Miró's jaw and upper back began to ache, but it was a human response, the only one that he'd allow himself. He'd never been in the presence of a full-blooded angel for so long. His gut told him to be very careful about everything that he said and did.

He kept his gaze focused on Angelli, who'd finished his tour and once again stood in front of him. The Dark *Irim*, manifested in a tall, muscular body, wore a tailored tuxedo, and carried a cocktail. He exuded the kind of sexuality that attracted everyone within ten meters.

"Not particularly," Miró said, irritated. He kept his voice even, however. "But to answer your question, I rarely get angry." He deliberately didn't answer Angelli's real question.

That question confirmed the suspicion he'd had since this afternoon after listening to the audio from the nanoblackbirds. That and the fact that only plastic zip ties and armed guards were used to secure him.

The Dark *Irim* thought that he was Wild. Untrained, untaught, and using his *Elioud* gifts instinctively. Miró needed all the advantage that he could get against the angel, and

Angelli's misunderstanding was a significant error on his part. Then again, hubris had been the Dark *Irim*'s downfall. That and his inability to control his lust for that which was forbidden to him.

Miró's anger and irritation died completely. Cold logic and rigid control dominated him now.

Angelli sipped his drink, nodding. "I can see that." He looked over his shoulder at Stasia, whose eyelids drooped in banked desire. "His eyes are rather extraordinary, *tesoro mio*. Like fiery ice."

Miró saw Stasia's harmonics waver as Angelli spoke. His ruby thread had become a thin, tattered filament.

She came closer, leaning in to him and holding his jaw steady as she stared at his eyes. Although she wore heels, she only reached his chin. Her fingers were warm and gentle. "They are his most attractive feature."

Angelli made a face. Sparks flew from his gaze. "If you say so."

"What should we do with him?" Stasia asked, studying Miró as if she'd never seen him up close before.

As if they'd never made love.

Miró narrowed his eyes. *Mihàil and Olivia are here.*

Stasia didn't acknowledge his message. Instead, she let his chin go and stepped away from him.

"Hm." Angelli pretended to consider Stasia's question. "Whatever *we* do with him, I should keep an eye on you. I can see that your harmonics are entwined with his." He sounded disapproving. "If I did not see it for myself, I would not believe it."

Stasia tossed her hair. "Harmonics?" she asked as if she didn't know what he was talking about.

She didn't wait for Angelli to answer. "I told you that this *Elioud* appeals to me. I enjoy how he responds to my...charms."

Her answer gave the impression that she was a vain woman with little understanding of her angelic gifts. Miró was suddenly reminded of her great-grandmother Beatrix.

Angelli laughed. "Tell me, what is your name?"

Thick angelic charisma draped over Miró in an invisible blanket.

Miró blinked as if dazed. He wasn't though. He was immune to Angelli's lure. Nevertheless, he answered. "Miró Kos."

Angelli, tilting his head, said, "There is something familiar about that name...."

Stasia stepped closer to Angelli. Miró saw her harmonics bend and meld around the Dark *Irim*'s own harmonics. She rose up on her toes, pressed herself against him, and reached around his neck in a sinuous movement before kissing him. For a moment the Dark *Irim* looked besotted. Miró narrowed his eyes, wondering.

A moment later the blonde who'd been standing with the other women appeared at his side. "Lord?" she asked as if he'd called her, and Angelli turned to her, his musing apparently forgotten.

"When does Willem arrive?"

"His flight lands in Rome around five-thirty. He alerted me that he would be here around eight-thirty this evening."

"Excellent." Angelli took Stasia by the elbow and began to steer her back toward the lawn and the cocktail reception. "Escort our guest into the church then, Eva. He can wait there until Willem arrives."

Eva smirked at his announcement. Miró's gut gave a twinge of unease.

Stasia, fingering the beads of the bracelet, asked Angelli, "What is so special about this Willem?" Her voice was pitched so that Miró could hear her.

Miró felt her charisma from where he stood even though she moved away from him. Hers *did* affect him. He swallowed his smoky breath and sent even more heat into the ground.

Eva came up next to him and took him by the upper arm. Her eyes gleamed in feral excitement. Her thermal signature verified that desire heated her core, whether for him or for the events unfolding around him, Miró couldn't tell. When she touched him, her disordered harmonics jarred him as if he'd suffered whiplash. He gritted his teeth and calmed the wild vibrations. He needed to be able to concentrate, to act on a moment's notice.

As Eva took a step, he heard Angelli answer. "Ah, Willem is challenging. He has been uncommitted to my cause for decades. I think I may finally have a way to tempt him to join my little coterie. He absolutely adores fighting yet can never find anyone worthy of his skill. I think he would enjoy testing this one's angelic reflexes."

I've taken care of the guard near me. Olivia's voice in Miró's thoughts brought him back to the mission. *He's wearing my gear, so his thermal signature won't show up on Angelli's radar.*

One step behind you, flashed Mihàil.

Stasia hasn't responded to my flashes. Out of the corner of his eye, Miró saw two charred footprints where he'd been standing. The soles of his shoes had been entirely burned through.

Stasia and Angelli disappeared through a covered archway on the other side of the church. The four Grey *Elioud* followed them, chatting and throwing looks over their shoulders at him.

"Where are they going?" Miró asked Eva, feeding a little *Elioud* charm into his voice. He already knew the answer but used the opportunity to modulate his harmonics in an effort to influence hers.

"There is no need for you to worry," she said, squeezing his arm. She brought her other hand around and gripped his bicep. "Mm. You are quite muscular under that jacket, are you not?"

She smiled over at the other women wearing cocktail dresses as they passed the group. The women fell into step behind them. Miró's thoughts became fuzzy as their strident harmonics pushed against his. Eva led him inside the small church which was decorated in gold marble and white woodwork. The floor was warm terracotta tile while glazed floral medallions lined the organ loft and the arches of side chapels. A beautiful gold chandelier hung just before the steps to the altar. The confessional booths, pews, front rail, doors, and stands were all made of plain dark wood. Beautiful oil paintings hung everywhere, including a huge painting over the altar.

Miró struggled to steady his harmonics. Though difficult, all he needed to do was close his eyes for a moment, take a deep breath, and imagine Stasia's harmonics strengthening his. A moment later he felt them surge into his harmonics as if she'd sent them toward him on an invisible wave.

His thoughts now clarified, he glanced at the painting over the altar. It was a dark garden scene with a somber, kneeling figure. Not a painting that showed the Seducer in a better light…except, wait, the kneeling figure looked a lot like Angelli.

Miró's ire rose when he realized that all of the paintings in the church, when looked at more closely, featured the arrogant Dark *Irim* in the main role. But none of them were the third Watcher Angel painting. None of them had been painted by a Grey *Elioud*. No angelic power had been captured in their workmanlike brushstrokes.

Eva walked to one of the confessional booths, and pulling the red velvet drapes aside, said, "Sit." She pressed a hand against his chest.

Miró sat.

She bent over, pretending to examine his zip ties. She pulled back a little and ran a fingertip over his jaw. Miró forced himself to remain steady, matching her gaze when her fingertip met his lips. She smiled and then leaned in to kiss him. Her lips were unpleasantly cool. She smelled off, a little sour with an underlying rank scent. He inhaled sharply but didn't flinch.

"When you lose, we will be here to console you," she said before standing and gesturing to the other women. "We will show you how your *Elioud* gifts are best put to use."

Laughing knowingly, the women turned and left. Miró caught a glimpse of the single guard who stood inside the church door—the only door—with an AK-47 before Eva pulled the drapes closed, leaving him in the dark.

Where did they take you? Mihàil asked Miró.

To the church. Or what used to be the church. There is nothing sacred left. The painting is not here.

Are you guarded? Olivia asked. *I counted twenty-five thermal signatures on the grounds, not including ours.*

A sole guard. Angelli seems to be under the misapprehension that I am Wild.

Ah, Olivia said. *Between that and his jealousy, he sadly underestimates you.*

Let us hope so. But I gather you have not heard from the nanoblackbirds since Stasia arrived here.

No. Does she still wear the bracelet?

Yes. He must have taken her cellphone.

We will have to move forward blind then, said Mihàil.

Another Grey Elioud *arrives at eight-thirty. I am to fight him as some sort of recruiting technique for Angelli.*

I will come to the church and take the place of your guard. Olivia will scout for the painting.

Copy that.

Miró, blocked by the curtain from seeing the interior of the church, nevertheless read the guard's infrared and harmonic signatures well enough that he could monitor what happened when his general arrived.

A minute later and Mihàil knocked on the church door. The guard stepped to the side and, opening the door, let him in. Obviously the man had only been told to ensure that Miró didn't escape, not to worry about intruders.

That was too bad for him.

Mihàil, dressed as one of Angelli's other guards, grabbed the end of the AK-47 before the guard realized what was happening, and yanked the barrel. The guard had remarkable presence of mind, managing to keep his grip on the gun, which was strapped around his body. As the guard stumbled toward him, Mihàil brought his right elbow up and struck him in the head. The man collapsed into Mihàil's arms.

Mihàil sent a harmonic jab into the guard to keep him unconscious. Then he dragged him to the other confessional booth and hid him inside. The barrel of the AK-47 he melted before stuffing the inoperable weapon next to the guard.

A moment later he stood looking at Miró, who'd freed his hands from the zip ties and sat rubbing his wrists. His destroyed shoes lay on the floor next to his bare feet.

"Stasia has not responded to your flashes?" Mihàil didn't waste any time asking the critical question. "You may have to accept that we are too late."

"No." Miró shook his head and stood. He held his general's gaze, letting him see his conviction. "She indicated that she was not entirely under Angelli's sway."

"Indicated how?"

"She distracted him when he was about to remember who I am."

"Ah." Mihàil was silent a moment.

They'd both known that was a risk after Miró recognized *L'Amante* as his old rival in Prague. The Dark *Irim* should have recognized him immediately. It took Olivia, the newest member of their group, to realize why he hadn't. Miró's harmonics had been altered since he'd met Stasia. It was as if he'd gotten a new *Elioud* identity.

But he hadn't been entirely remade. If he spent enough time in Angelli's presence, the Dark *Irim* would know him. Which would take away any advantage they might have.

"She knows that Beatrix left you for Angelli?"

"No." Miró inhaled before admitting, "I suspect that she was just acting on her instincts as an intelligence officer to keep a teammate's cover intact."

Mihàil nodded. "Do you have any idea about the Grey *Elioud* you are slated to fight?"

Miró shrugged. "Not much. His name is Willem."

Olivia appeared next to Mihàil. "I found it." Excitement threaded her voice. "It's in the chapter house."

The chapter house was the room that the convent had used for daily Scripture readings and other meetings for their order.

Mihàil and Miró stared at her.

"It's really large. It's going to be tricky to move without getting caught." She held out her smartphone. "Take a look."

On the screen was a painting that had the same figures and composition of Caravaggio's *Infatuation of the Watcher Angels*. Unlike his, which had vivid contrast between dark shadows and bright illumination, this new painting had large brushstrokes and brighter, almost primary, colors.

"It's a Van Gogh," Olivia said. "The plaque on the frame says 'Infatuation of the Watcher Angels (after Caravaggio).'"

"Of course," Mihàil said. "What better way to control the narrative than to show his fault in a different light?"

"There are subtle changes," Miró said, studying the image. "More than a change in color and style."

He stood upright. "But it does not matter. I am here for Stasia." He held their gazes.

Mihàil nodded slowly, understanding in his eyes. Olivia placed a hand on his forearm but said nothing. There was nothing to say.

Mihàil straightened, looking alert. "Your time has come. A group is climbing the stairs from the front lawn. It appears that Willem has arrived."

Olivia disappeared. Mihàil moved to the door where he took up a stance as guard.

Miró would need to keep Angelli's attention on him, however, to prevent the Dark *Irim* from realizing that there were too many infrared signatures in the church, one of which belonged to the *drangúe*.

Perhaps a little misdirection....

A Wild Elioud loses control sometimes, he flashed Mihàil in warning.

Mihàil grinned and nodded.

Turning, Miró grabbed the edges of the confessional booth and raised his temperature. A moment later the dark wood combusted. The heavy velvet drapes caught fire as he sent a harmonic gust toward the flames.

When the church door opened, Miró looked over his shoulder to see Angelli and Stasia standing at the head of a group of people that included the Grey *Elioud* and the women of Angelli's household. A lone man, his arms folded across his waist, stood to the side watching Miró with hawklike intensity.

Miró spoke into the stunned silence.

"Is setting things on fire one of my *Elioud* gifts?" he asked.

Thirty-One

Stasia blinked and blinked and blinked, but she couldn't focus. Her eyes felt as if they had lotion in them. Somewhere in the recesses of her psyche a tiny version of herself, locked inside a clear booth, banged and screamed to be let out. She couldn't think coherently even though she'd barely sipped her wine at the reception. She clutched Angelli's arm, swaying as her body rebelled against her control. She felt too much for her own skin. Everything was too much. She wanted to tear off her clothes and rub against him.

She didn't know where they were. Somewhere inside. Her unfocused eyes saw only bright overhead light and golden-white surroundings. The others clustered behind them in a mass that exuded body odor, perfume, and excitement. She inhaled, and the excessive scents made her stomach churn.

How much time had passed since Miró had been taken? Where was he? Why had he come?

More importantly, how was she going to help him?

In front of them red-and-orange light flared around a blurry figure. The acrid scent of smoke burned her sensitive nostrils.

"Is setting things on fire one of my *Elioud* gifts?"

Her heart soared at the sound of Miró's voice. She fixated on it and his harmonics. Her vision cleared. Her harmonics, which had grown more and more sluggish, steadied.

Next to her Angelli snorted. A moment later he clapped his hands. The resulting air current caressed her overheated skin, raising goosebumps.

The leaping red-and-orange light, which came from a blaze behind Miró, disappeared.

"Something tells me, Miró Kos, that you know full well that one of your abilities is thermogenesis."

The dark current in Angelli's voice penetrated the unnatural euphoria that still dominated her. She shifted, fingering her bracelet.

She wished now that she hadn't taken off her grandfather's medal when she'd dressed for the reception. It hadn't gone with her attire, but ever since then she'd struggled against the dampening influence of the Dark *Irim*, whose outsized presence weighed on the gathering.

Miró shrugged. It was a nonchalant gesture, but his expression was anything except easygoing. She recognized the predatory look in his eyes, and a premonition shot through her like icy water.

He had come for *her*. He was going to challenge Angelli for her.

He looked at her, and the intensity of his gaze softened. He held out his hand. "Stasia, *dušo*, please come here."

Everything was suddenly clear.

Stasia stepped away from Angelli on unsteady legs.

Only to be pulled back by Eva. Stasia turned into Eva, stepping back into the larger woman's stance, and rolled her over her shoulder. Eva landed on her back on the floor, stunned. The other women clustered around her, helping her sit and checking her for injuries. Willem, who'd taken a step toward Eva, halted.

Before anyone else decided to act, Stasia continued toward Miró. With each step her harmonics grew stronger and her thoughts more lucid.

Angelli stopped her when he said, "Interesting. It appears that he is not the plaything that you made him out to be."

Stasia turned around and faced the Dark *Irim* fully. "No, he is not. Miró Kos is nobody's plaything."

The Dark *Irim* looked thunderstruck. "You would choose this—this *hybrid*—over me?"

Stasia, again walking toward Miró, answered over her shoulder. "Yes."

As she reached him, he drew her into his side. Immediately she felt right again. He steadied her harmonics and siphoned the excessive heat in her blood. She reached up to caress his jaw, remembering the terror that she'd felt earlier when Angelli hit him with a harmonic blast. Seeing him fall to his knees, clutching his head, had made her heart stop for one awful moment. All she could think to do at the time was to distract Angelli, to give Miró a chance to escape.

"I wonder if you would still choose him if you knew him as I do," said Angelli.

Stasia saw recognition and fear wrest control over Miró's features. His harmonics, steady a moment before, tensed.

She wrenched her gaze back to Angelli, who studied them. Seeing that he'd gotten their attention, he strolled over to a wooden bench and sat. As he did so, Stasia realized with a start that they were gathered in the church. Or what had been a church. Something told her—perhaps the paintings of the Dark *Irim* as heroic figure all around them—that Angelli's "cloister" celebrated in ways that would shock the previous owners.

The others, including Eva, followed him and sat among the hard pews. Willem, the Grey *Elioud* who'd shown up just before they'd left the reception, trailed behind and remained standing. She noticed that he kept his eyes on Eva although he didn't approach her. For her part, Eva sat on the edge of her pew, her avid gaze locked on the drama unfolding in front of her.

Swallowing hard, Stasia asked, "What do you mean?"

Angelli shrugged. "I met him in Trieste before the start of World War I. Did he tell you that?"

Stasia's heart thumped. Next to her, Miró shifted. She glanced aside at him, but all she saw was the side of his face and his shuttered gaze.

"No." She kept her voice calm, steadying her own harmonics, which eased Miró's.

She slipped her hand into his before sending soothing waves through him. No matter what Angelli said, they would face this together. He looked at her with surprise but didn't pull away.

"Of course, he was an uncommitted *Elioud*. Like these others." Angelli swept a hand toward the group of Grey *Elioud* sitting across from him.

"And Willem, over there." He nodded toward the last Grey *Elioud*, who stood not far from the door.

That's when Stasia saw Mihàil standing guard. He wore the black shirt and pants of Angelli's security team and held an AK-47. But unlike those humans, his gaze held hers.

My lord, she flashed.

Stasia. He sounded shocked at her use of mental messaging. He recovered instantly. *His words sound true. Use caution.*

Sempre. Always.

Stasia turned back to Angelli, who remained unaware that a *drangúe* had taken the place of his guard. Olivia must be somewhere on the estate grounds.

Aloud, she said, "He said that he was there infiltrating the Italian irredentists."

Even as she said it, she remembered that Miró had told her that he'd wanted to prevent Croatia from changing one foreign master for another.... He hadn't mentioned Mihàil. Or an *Elioud* mission.

Or Angelli for that matter.

Angelli smiled a slow, wicked smile. "Is that what he called it? 'Infiltrating'?"

His gaze traveled to Miró, whose expression was blank. "Is that how you would describe your activities, Blackbird?"

Something in the way that he said that word sent a shiver down Stasia's spine.

Miró's lips tightened. His grip remained loose around her hand, but his harmonics had grown so rigid that Stasia's head began to ache.

Angelli laughed. "This is so delicious! Your harmonics are so entwined that Stasia looks like a spike has been driven through her left eye. It seems as if you have some details to clear up between you given how close you have grown."

Miró immediately relaxed, but now his guilty expression had only deepened with worry. He spoke to Stasia, ignoring the rest of the room.

"I was in Trieste on my own," he said. His strained voice came out low and harsh. "I thought that my gift as an *Elioud* truthseeker would allow me to identify the most dangerous agitators—"

"What he means to say," Angelli interrupted, "is that he chose to assassinate a number of Italian patriots. Receiving a visit from The Blackbird of Trieste meant sure death. You may want to reconsider the blackbirds on your bracelet, Stasia— they *are* blackbirds, are they not?" He smirked as he said this.

Nausea and doubt agitated Stasia. She pulled her hand free of Miró's. He didn't stop her.

Out of the corner of her eye she saw Willem easing toward the side of the church. And Mihàil shadowing him. The harmonics around the group thickened as anticipation vibrated from the assembled guests. She half expected to see roiling thunderclouds obscuring the high ceiling. Instead the group emited a low, excited buzz. The shrewd-looking older woman and the fussy dark-haired man, sitting together in a side section, leaned close and whispered.

What was Angelli's endgame? He might be a Dark *Irim*, but she still had her training and her experience. And her *Elioud* charisma. She couldn't let him control the narrative.

And that was exactly what Angelli wanted. He wanted her to tell *his* story, glorifying the role that he played in the downfall of the Watcher Angels and the corruption of humanity.

If Asmodeus couldn't control her, then neither could Angelli.

In addition Olivia had told her that *Irim* couldn't kill humans. It was one reason they had decided that a honeypot operation—deliberately enticing *L'Amante* with her as the prize—would lead them to the third Watcher Angel painting. That and the fact that he saw himself as a lover, not a fighter.

But what about his unholy sisters? Or the other Grey *Elioud* here for the painting?

She looked back at the group. Willem now stood near the outside wall of the church about three meters from them. Mihàil stood beyond the peripheral view of the group, but his alert posture told her that he was ready for anything. Stasia wondered how this was all going to end. What could they do to a Dark *Irim*? How could she and Miró and Mihàil and Olivia get away?

Perhaps it was time to take the offensive.

Stepping toward Angelli, she modified her harmonics in a way that made her voice carry in the space. "He did not tell me about you because he did not want me to know that you had seduced my great-grandmother."

Silence descended.

Miró looked stunned. If she hadn't been certain before, his anguish confirmed her guess.

Angelli's gaze snapped. Stasia's heartrate sped, but she slowed her harmonics. She wasn't overwhelmed by him anymore.

"And that you might be my great-grandfather."

In a flash of white, Angelli loomed over her, his spectral form shifting and leaping outside of the hard planes of his manifested body. He stared at her through narrow eyes. Stasia felt terror in her soul. This creature before her only wore the aspect of a beautiful human male on Earth. In reality he was a terrifying being who belonged in a spiritual realm.

This time when he touched her chin, it took all of her willpower to keep her gaze on his.

"Perhaps, Daughter," he said in a silky voice. "But then all of your kind are my descendants."

"All?" Miró asked, stepping closer to Stasia. She felt his harmonics engage and sustain hers. "You will take all of the credit for the *Elioud* race? How about all of the blame, too?"

A blink and Angelli stood now in front of Miró, whose eyes glittered dangerously.

What are you doing? she flashed. But she knew.

He was drawing Angelli away from her.

Angelli's lips pulled back in an ugly sneer. Stasia didn't know how she'd ever thought him irresistible.

"Without me, you would not exist, *Elioud*," he said. His once mellifluous voice had grown harsh. "And neither would Serafina, no matter where her *Irim* blood originated."

He pressed toward Miró, leaning so close Stasia was sure that Miró would be forced to step back.

Miró didn't.

If anything, he appeared to grow larger. His face hardened.

Stasia gulped. What would happen to Miró if he engaged a Dark *Irim* hand-to-hand?

To her shock, Angelli stood back instead.

"You seduced a young woman too naïve to know better," Miró said through clenched teeth.

Angelli looked sulky. "The same can be said of you, *Elioud*."

"Yes." Miró choked out the word. Yet he went on. "But I admit my fault. And Michael assigned me penance, which I did. Can you say the same?"

Angelli hissed when Miró spoke the name of his angelic judge. He took another step back. His spectral form had disappeared inside his body.

"There is nothing to admit." He waved his hand dismissively. "She was not with me long, preferring the company of another."

"Translation: you tired of her and foisted her on someone else," Miró said.

"Regardless, it would be impossible to say who the father of her child was."

"Impossible? Or you refuse to say?" asked Miró with narrowed, icy-looking eyes.

The others watching shuffled their feet and shifted uneasily. Stasia looked between the rivals, trying to discern the truth.

Angelli studied Miró for a moment. He lifted a shoulder. "I cannot say. She had not yet decided to decline your marriage proposal when she and I became lovers. It is all too complicated to sort—a gray situation as you *Elioud* like to say."

Miró scoffed. Before he could respond, Angelli tipped his chin. A moment later, Willem attacked.

Miró managed to step to the side, deflecting some of the force directed at him. Stasia moved out of the way, hurrying closer to Mihàil. The rest of the women and Grey *Elioud* scattered to the far side of the church where they watched with clear avarice.

Miró turned to face Willem, who'd slid into the confessional booth with a resounding boom and pivoted to come at Miró again. But he'd lost his surprise edge, and now Miró had his hands up in a defensive pose guarding his face. Willem, his eyes coldly assessing, moved his hands up too. Like Miró he moved with a fluid grace.

Stasia slipped her heels off. She bent and ripped the seam of her cocktail gown up to the thigh before tying the ends into a high skirt.

I will keep an eye on the others, Mihàil flashed them. *You and Miró are in charge of getting us out of here with the painting. Show this faithless Irim bastard what you can do.*

All you had to do was ask, Stasia flashed.

Zophiel called him an insufferable bastard, said Miró as he circled Willem.

The Grey *Elioud*'s gaze never strayed from his opponent as he moved in tandem.

I can think of a few other words to describe him, Stasia said. To Miró she added, *I am with you*.

Then I cannot lose.

Willem exploded with a vicious left jab followed by a right punch. Miró took the first blow before getting his hands up in time to block the second, but Willem continued to circle and test his defenses. Miró, for his part, settled into a slower pace as he read the patterns of Willem's moves and adjusted accordingly. He used a front *teep* and quick reflexes to keep Willem from connecting with any power. Given enough time, Miró's cooler head and exceptional training would dominate.

But Stasia saw with a sinking heart that Willem had more fury in his blows.

Or rather desperation.

If she was right, he'd come to win Eva, not the Watcher Angel painting. And he'd spent the past ten minutes watching Miró like a deadly predator. He intended to win the fight almost as soon as it began.

Almost as soon as she recognized this, Willem struck like a cobra, landing a vicious blow to Miró's unprotected head, opening up a cut along his hairline. Blood sheeted his forehead as he righted himself. A moment later, and it rose in steam around him and dissipated.

Stasia, so focused on watching for an opening—any opening—to lend actual tactical support, winced as stinging pain cut across her forehead. She touched a fingertip to the spot. It came away wet with fresh blood.

Willem renewed his attack on Miró, who moved around the church as the other man drove him backwards, landing multiple blows for every one of Miró's. Wooden pews were knocked over until Angelli, laughing, waved an arm and sent them into a tumbled heap near the steps to the altar. Eva had joined him. Stasia wondered what her relationship with Willem had been before she'd come within Angelli's orbit. And what Angelli had promised Willem if he defeated Miró.

She was about to hum on the private wavelength that she shared with Miró when the woman with the steel-gray hair appeared at her elbow. Stasia saw that Mihàil had gone toward the group of Grey *Elioud* where the dark-haired man had pulled out a handgun and waved it around in a careless manner.

It was just her and this stranger. A Grey *Elioud*, she reminded herself.

"Ms. Fiore," said the woman. Her accent said that she was from Subiaco, a smaller town within the Rome metro area.

Stasia, distracted, looked at her. The woman's dark hazel eyes reflected nothing, but her knowing expression sent a warning tingle through Stasia.

She hadn't been introduced to this woman as Ms. Fiore.

"Do I know you?" she asked, looking back at the fight between Miró and Willem.

"No, but I know you." The woman's words were freighted with meaning. "I am Gina Orlandi. I am employeed with the Command for the Protection of Cultural Heritage."

As she spoke, Stasia felt a whisper of something along her skin. It ruffled her harmonics and then dissolved into them with a hint of warmth.

She turned to give Gina her full attention.

"You were the one who told *L'Amante* about me?" she asked, horrified.

Gina shrugged. "I did. I needed something useful to give him so that he would invite me to the art auction."

Stasia heard a grunt. Stealing a glance at Miró, she saw that he drove Willem, now covered in sweat, back toward the altar with a series of knee and elbow strikes. Mihàil had disarmed the gunman and stood watching over Angelli's staff and guests. As far as Stasia could tell, no one yet suspected that he wasn't the guard that Angelli had sent into the church with Miró.

She turned back to Gina, who didn't seem at all concerned with the explosive hand-to-hand combat going on behind them. "Then you and I are not on the same side, regardless of your position with the Art Squad."

"Oh, but I think we are," said Gina as she leaned closer, and warmth spread over Stasia's skin again, soothing her. "You see, I did not tell our host about your true mission for AISE."

Stasia's focus sharpened at her companion's revelation.

"So Angelli is using a little divide and conquer?" she murmured, aware that Gina directed *Elioud* charm at her. It made her a little angry. "Tell me, Signora Orlandi, has the auction started then?"

Gina laughed, tossing her head back. Her heavy gray hair remained perfectly coiffed despite the movement. "*Naturalmente!* You are very green for a Grey *Elioud*." She laughed again at her pun. "He is evaluating all of us even now. He wants us to fight over his legacy. But I would rather not join his cloister. Perhaps we can work something out?"

Stasia tilted her head. "You think that we can work together to steal the painting from the Dark *Irim* who commissioned it? How would that work?"

Gina lifted a shoulder, pressing her mouth together in a noncommittal manner. "Do not think of it as stealing. It is more a way to earn Angelli's admiration and forebearance."

"I can do that without you," Stasia said, turning back to watch Miró, who had started to dominate Willem, though Willem's heart wouldn't let him quit. She almost felt sorry for him.

"I am sure that you can," Gina said. "But are you prepared to give up your position with AISE?" She too had turned and pretended to watch the fight. It didn't lessen the sting of her implied threat. "This way you can remain uncommitted, if you take my meaning."

Stasia understood. If she and Gina slipped away with the third Watcher Angel painting, she could remain an Italian foreign operative, unencumbered by ties with either Miró or Angelli. She would become a star among her shadowy intelligence colleagues while Gina basked in the glory earned from bringing a priceless art treasure to Italy.

She would just have to give Miró up forever.

Thirty-Two

Despite reading Willem's harmonics quite accurately after battling for more than ten minutes, Miró knew that there were only two outcomes to this match. Either he convinced the Grey *Elioud* to give up or he'd have to deliver an incapacitating blow to his determined opponent. And the way it was looking, 'incapacitiating' meant that he'd have to kill him.

Miró rarely fought anyone these days who displayed such single-minded devotion. Certainly no one who wanted to prove himself as part of an initiation ritual. Because frankly that's what this was—a desperate attempt to join Angelli's merry band of degenerates. Not something Grey *Elioud* did as a rule. They kept their own counsel.

And yet here he faced a man whose eyes had grown wilder in direct inverse to the strength of his blows as they'd moved around the church. Willem no longer had the *Elioud* energy to evaporate the blood and sweat sheeting his face and bruised knuckles. He could hardly stay upright for the love of St. Michael.

Miró, who'd seen Willem's gaze fixated on Eva, Angelli's lead sister, recognized that wildness for what it was.

It was the same wildness he kept at bay when he thought he might lose Stasia to Angelli.

"Give it up!" he said as he got inside Willem's defense and clinched his torso, preventing Willem from striking him. "You cannot win."

As he gripped the other man, he used thermogenesis, boosting Willem's temperature until his face steamed clear of blood and sweat. Willem, by way of thanks, head butted Miró in return. He broke Miró's hold and shoved him, hard.

Miró, caught off guard and head hurting as if he'd been hit with a hammer, took two steps and caught his balance.

Incoming flare, he flashed Mihàil and Stasia.

And then his battle senses flared.

Willem never stood a chance after that.

As a Grey *Elioud*, the Dutchman had never been trained in angelic fighting tactics. Miró's flaring white light acted like a cool phosphorous grenade, blinding everyone unprepared in the church for five seconds. Miró, however, moved. He jumped next to Willem, jabbing the other *Elioud* in the chest with targeted harmonics. Willem fell, unconscious, before the white light cleared.

Miró pivoted, searching for Stasia's infrared signature among the signatures on the other side of the church.

It wasn't there.

Mihàil? he flashed.

Here. Mihàil's infrared signataure blazed red like a beacon.

At the *drangúe's* feet two infrared signatures marked the unconscious bodies of the Grey *Elioud* that he'd subdued. In the pews in front of him were half a dozen infrared signatures of the women from the cloister. They writhed and moaned, their hands covering their ears and eyes. None of those included Eva, however.

And Angelli was gone.

Miró jumped harmonics to stand next to the *drangúe* as his flare subsided.

They looked around them. Angelli's sisters scattered, terror blanking their expressions. Their unmoored harmonics left them erratic and volatile. They'd been keyed to Angelli's harmonics for a long time. Without him, they would eventually go mad.

"The chapter house," Mihàil said. "He took Stasia and Eva."

"And one of the Grey *Elioud*. This one's partner." Miró nudged the dark-haired man lying on the floor with his toe.

The Grey *Elioud* didn't respond.

"Olivia has not responded to my flash. But we cannot rush in there. Besides the security guards that he has called, he can likely count on Eva and the Grey *Elioud* to get in our way." He paused. "And maybe Stasia."

"And maybe Stasia," said Miró through stiff lips.

"Whatever you do, you will do it with me."

Mihàil and Miró turned in astonishment toward Willem, who swayed two meters from them. The Grey *Elioud*'s eyes had nearly swollen shut from Miró's numerous elbow strikes. He obviously didn't know how to regulate his body temperature to keep that from happening.

Miró studied him. Willem meant what he said.

"You may not get Eva back," he said.

"I must try."

Mihàil shifted next to him. "So that is the way of it?" he asked the Grey *Elioud* in a sympathetic voice.

"Yes." The Dutchman's hard voice left no room for doubt.

"Then now is the time to choose, brother," Mihàil said. *His* hard voice also left no room for doubt. "Either you are with us or you will have to go through us to save her."

He paused before adding, "And I guarantee you that you will not succeed."

Willem wavered as if in answer to that ultimatum. Holding himself upright with apparent willpower, he tilted his head. Even obscured in puffy flesh, his keen gaze assessed them.

"You will show me how to protect Eva? To emit blinding light and heat my skin?"

"That and more," Mihàil assured him. "We fight together."

Willem hesitated.

A moment later an almost invisible cloud of nanoblackbirds swirled around Miró's face. He lifted a hand, and they began settling along his index finger.

Stasia had sent them to him.

He looked at Mihàil. "Does Olivia have her cellphone on her?"

"Yes." Mihàil frowned and then smiled when he saw the nanoblackbirds on Miró's finger. "Stasia has found a way to give us audio. And you should be able to see into the chapter house with your connection to Stasia."

Miró nodded. He'd already recognized faint ghostly outlines of another space hovering in his peripheral vision. He raised his hand and sent the nanoblackbirds, keyed to Stasia's harmonic signature, back to her.

He and Mihàil both turned to pin Willem with hard stares.

"Well?" Mihàil asked.

"You do not try to persuade me? To use *Elioud* wiles on me?" Willem seemed astounded. "You are offering for me to join you with no hidden strings attached?"

Mihàil made an impatient sound, but Miró put his hand on the other *Elioud*'s shoulder.

"We are Light *Elioud*," he said. "You will have to have faith in that."

At last Willem nodded. "What do I do?"

Mihàil flashed a fierce grin. "First allow me to take care of your eyes."

Willem stood while Mihàil held his head in his hands and ran warm thumbs over the former Grey *Elioud*'s forehead and cheeks. After a few seconds, the swelling receded. Though he still looked like he'd been in a fight, his bruises and cuts would heal much faster.

Mihàil turned to his lieutenant. He held out a cellphone. "It will work best with your angelic sonar."

Miró accepted his *drangúe's* cellphone, which had the app for the nanoblackbirds open. He paired his earwig with the phone before looking up at Mihàil.

"Thank you, my lord." His voice betrayed him.

They shared a look.

Turning to Willem, Mihàil said, "Miró leads this mission. We take orders from him."

Miró listened to the streaming audio with his eyes closed so that he could locate and map the chapter house, which lay across the inner courtyard from the church.

"There are two armed guards on the covered walkway outside the entrance. Two more are inside the lower level on either end of the hall connecting it to the old convent. The final guard is inside the chapter house next to the entrance into the hallway. Inside I count six infrared signatures, including Olivia's."

Miró looked at Mihàil. "She is crouching next to one of the benches nearest the hallway. Everyone else is either in the center of the room or along the sides."

"But it is only a matter of time before someone spots her," Mihàil said grimly.

Miró nodded. Neither of them knew what Angelli would do if he found Olivia. It was unlikely that he would order her killed, but he could attempt to dominate her *Elioud* senses. Olivia was exceptionally strong willed and wouldn't be easy to overcome, but it wouldn't be pleasant for her. She would eventually break.

Mihàil would never let that happen. The whole situation could spiral out of control pretty quickly if the *drangúe* went after his wife. Stasia could take care of herself, but Miró didn't like the uncertainty. There were just too many unknowns with a Dark *Irim*, a Grey *Elioud*, and thugs with semi-automatic weapons.

And a painting with stored angelic manna.

"Angelli, Stasia, Eva, and the female Grey *Elioud* are standing in the middle of the chapter house next to the painting. The Grey *Elioud* is describing her plans for the painting."

"That is Gina Orlandi."

Miró and Mihàil turned to Willem, who watched them closely. His face had already healed so well that only faint traces of his earlier beating remained. Either he'd learned to do that before now or he was an extremely fast learner.

"She works for the *Carabinieri*. Angelli uses her for inside information."

That made Miró uneasy. Could she know something about Stasia that would make her more vulnerable?

Mihàil looked at Miró. "I saw her talking to Stasia just before you flared."

Miró thought about that. "Does she know how to speed up her harmonics?" he asked Willem.

Willem shrugged. "Probably. She is also very persuasive. Eva used to be a curator at the Van Gogh Museum in Amsterdam until Gina Orlandi introduced her to Angelli."

Miró considered their options. If they tried to leave the church, the guards in the cloister outside would see them as soon as they opened the door. It wouldn't matter in terms of being fired upon. He and Mihàil could manage to avoid being seriously wounded long enough to disable the guards, but it would alert Angelli.

Then again, Angelli would be expecting something.

Miró considered Willem. "Angelli expects one of us to win our fight." He waved a negligent hand. "I suggest that it is you."

"But he saw you winning," Willem said.

"He left before your friend"—here Miró clapped Mihàil on the shoulder—"aided you."

Willem narrowed his eyes at them. "Are you suggesting that I would fight dirty?"

"I am suggesting that Angelli believes that you would do whatever it takes to free Eva."

"He would not be wrong."

"In this case, that means deceiving Angelli." Miró paused. "Are you willing? Because it is go time. His wife, Olivia, has been found."

Willem grinned. It transformed his face. "Of course. I would *love* to deceive that bastard Angelli."

"Between the two of you, I think that you can distract the guards long enough for me to get to the convent. I am going to have to make a door into the chapter house."

Mihàil, his mouth set in a hard line, said, "You have one minute before I storm the entrance."

So much for him being in charge. "Copy that."

"How will we know when you have breached the wall?" Willem asked.

Now it was Miró's turn to grin. "When you hear a great *boom*."

***

Stasia, swaying and blinking rapidly as if blinded, continued to pretend that she hadn't recovered from Miró's battle flare as Gina spoke to Angelli about her plans for revealing the third

Watcher Angel painting to the world. The Grey *Elioud* had worked all the angles like a true con artist, and Stasia was pretty sure that she was trying to con Angelli, who by the looks of it, enjoyed indulging the brazen woman. Gina, for her part, had approached Eva as well as Stasia to buttress her efforts. Eva, pressed against the Dark *Irim's* side, glowed at the prospect of validating Angelli's Watcher Angel painting, which as it turned out was a Van Gogh—her area of expertise.

So the dark horse candidate for the role of Angelli's mouthpiece seemed to be edging ahead of the other candidates.

And in the middle of the chapter house stood a large canvas radiating enough angelic energy to drive even the sane mad. Even if she hadn't learned what this painting was and had nightmares about how its power could be used to manipulate and hurt people, Stasia would have been afraid of it. Now she was terrified.

And she could only speculate on what Angelli's plans were for the angelic energy.

Stasia tried to run scenarios through her mind, but she had no idea what had happened to the other *Elioud* team members. She would just have to stay alert.

And then the guard inside the chapter house spotted something on the interior of the enclosed wooden bench at the far end of the chapter house.

Even before he leaned down, Stasia knew that he'd discovered Olivia hiding.

Gina fell silent as the guard leaned down behind the half wall. Olivia, however, refused to accommodate him. Stepping gracefully out of his reach as she stood, she kept her gaze on Angelli. For her part, Stasia hid recognition of her friend. It wasn't a good sign that Olivia had been caught inside alone. But they knew each other very well, and Stasia trusted Olivia to follow whatever play she made.

She also prayed that Olivia still had her cellphone. Their escape might depend upon it.

Angelli's gaze flared with interest. "Well, my dear, this is a surprise. Not an unwelcome one as I see that you are an *Elioud*, a beautiful *Elioud*."

A wave of charisma flared out from Angelli like the hidden shock wave from a nuclear bomb. It washed over Stasia, making her woozy and weak for real.

It broke on Olivia, who stood firm with a little smile.

Angelli frowned. He did *not* like being thwarted.

"What is this then?" he said in a voice that rang around the chapter house with *Irim* authority. "Who are you to rebuff my advances?"

"Olivia Kastrioti," said Olivia, her voice ringing with the authority of a *zonjë*, one married to an almost full-blooded *Elioud*. "And your enticements are less than useless against me."

Angelli's *Irim* form flared as he discarded his manifested body. Where he'd stood well over two meters before, now he was closer to five, and his nimbus glowed against the shadowy ceiling of the chapter house. As with Asmodeus, spectral planes and lines danced from him. Instead of the violent, erratic movements of his brother Dark *Irim*'s form, Angelli's approximated music—the music of someone whose timing was off a couple of beats. Around him a fine harmonic web pulsed, occasionally leaping beyond its boundaries.

His harmonics dominated the inside of the chapter house and touched everyone inside.

Eva, like a spider's prey, was wrapped tight within his harmonic web. She couldn't have left Angelli's side without a major spiritual wound. Gina's harmonics had a ragged edge caught within a fine mist of Angelli's harmonics; every time the Dark *Irim*'s harmonics pulsed, more of this mist surrounded her. The longer the compromised Art Squad member interacted with the Dark *Irim*, the more she fell under his influence.

To her horror, Stasia saw that Angelli's harmonic mist had infiltrated her own harmonics.

"Are they? Are they indeed?" Angelli asked as he sent another, softer wave of charisma at Olivia.

His voice, free of his manifested body, had a shifting, mellifluous quality that mesmerized like a dark forest pool touched by a light breeze. Stasia felt its deceptive, alluring pull.

So too did Olivia. She blinked and moved. Her harmonics wavered. Then she straightened her back and lifted her shoulders as if adjusting to an invisible weight. Her harmonics steadied, and she smiled.

It didn't reach her eyes.

"I can do this all day," she said.

Stasia wasn't so sure. She slid toward the Van Gogh painting while everyone else's gaze remained fixated on Angelli and Olivia. Its energy throbbed from the canvas, almost repulsing her as she came within a meter. Stasia forced herself to ease closer, finding that an oblique approach allowed her to step inside the invisible perimeter around the painting. When she did the luminous glow blazed brighter for a moment as the golden aura around her skin met it.

"Is that so, my dear?" Angelli asked in a low voice that resonated around the room.

In a blink he stood holding Olivia in one arm while he raised the other arm to brush her long blond hair from her face.

Olivia shivered but stared defiantly at the Dark *Irim*. The harmonics tightened in the room, making Stasia's head ache.

And then the sound of raised voices outside sliced through the tension.

Angelli looked toward the closed double doors before the guard, clearly responding to a silent command, moved to open them. The guard swung the doors wide to reveal another guard aiming his AK-47 at Willem and Mihàil, who looked like they'd been arguing with him. In the brief instant before he clamped down on his reaction, Stasia recognized the fury that lit Mihàil's face when he saw Angelli holding Olivia.

Miró wasn't with them.

Bitter disappointment and fear pierced Stasia. Just before flaring, he'd forced Willem back toward the altar. She was sure that he would win the fight.

She'd been counting on it.

And then her mind noted that Mihàil was with Willem.

Angelli turned, still holding Olivia against his side. Eva came to join them, but Gina crept backwards toward the interior door leading into the convent. She seemed to have excellent instincts for when the situation called for a response that she was ill suited to give. No wonder she'd managed to live this long as a Grey *Elioud*.

Angelli studied the pair for a long moment. So long that Stasia began to get the creeping feeling that he could see through Mihàil's exterior disguise as one of the non-descript human security guards that he employed on his estate.

But then the Dark *Irim* manifested his human form again, looking somehow more sinister than dashing in his evening wear.

"I take it that you found an ally to help you overcome Stasia's suitor?" he asked Willem. Even his urbane diction had taken on a disturbing tone, setting Stasia's nerves on edge.

Willem smiled through his bruises. "You know that I will stop at nothing to get Eva back."

Angelli inclined his head. "As promised then, you may have her."

Eva stumbled forward as if pushed. She gasped and twisted as if trying to return to Angelli, but he shook his head. She began to walk toward Willem and Mihàil with an unhappy expression on her face. It was excruciating to watch as she took two steps forward, caught herself, picked up her foot as if to set it behind her, and then lurched two more steps forward.

Stasia was watching this halting progress when her nanoblackbirds rose from her skin in a glittering cloud around her face. And then her harmonics pealed as if they'd been struck and began to vibrate at a higher and higher frequency.

Tension rose in her. She looked toward the others in the chapter house, but no one seemed to notice that she now resonated at a different frequency than the rest of them. Higher and higher her frequency rose until she thought that she might disappear from sight. Or explode. She closed her eyes. When she did a ghostly outline of the room and its occupants filled her mind's eye. And then her new sight saw beyond the walls of the chapter house as if she'd developed x-ray vision.

That's when she saw Miró. He pressed his hands against the other side of the wall in front of her. His harmonics vibrated in time with hers. All at once she understood that he'd keyed in on her.

She opened her eyes as Eva reached Willem, who pulled her into his arms.

And then the wall detonated.

***

Thick gray dust clouded Miró's view into the chapter house. His harmonics surged through the rough opening that he'd blasted only moments before, sending the dust farther into the space beyond. He stepped through as the particles swirled into a milky column where they met a harmonic barrier invisible to human eyes. And then a microscopic swarm broke through the dust, drawing miniature vapor trails in the air as they flew toward him.

Miró held up his hand, and the nanoblackbirds landed on it.

A moment later a tumult of shouting and the sounds of gunfire and fighting eviscerated the silence of the chapter house.

Miró rushed toward Stasia, who wore only a very fine sprinkling of dust in her hair and on her skin. As he passed through the harmonic barrier surrounding her, his aura leapt in joy, and his harmonics sang. And then she was in his arms kissing him back. For a moment that reality was the only thing that he could take in.

As the dust and debris settled around them, however, it revealed a chaotic and ghastly tableau. The guard lay on the floor covered in a layer of fine powder, his head at an odd angle. Eva leaned against a side wall, an arm wrapped around her waist where a spreading bloodstain matched other bloodstains on her thigh and shoulder. Willem had collapsed like the damaged wall, blood pooling under him. Gina, her perfect coif pulled into messy puffs, glared at the guard from the hallway gripping her upper arm. Her harmonic signature revealed her terror.

But the worst part of the scene was the sight of the *drangúe* locked in a sizzling harmonic battle with the Dark *Irim* while the *zonjë* lay unconscious at his feet, out of reach of her frantic and furious husband. Angelli's darkened face, intense gaze, and the spectral sparks surging from his angelic form added a demonic dimension to the struggle.

Stasia, who'd been staring at Miró as if she could devour him whole, turned and took in the state of the conflict.

Then she did something that shocked him to his core.

"Stop." Her clarion voice rang with authority. *Irim* authority.

A moment later Miró felt her harmonics draw on his, steadying their conjoined signature. Then Angelli and Mihàil broke apart as if magnetically repulsed from one another.

Angelli snarled and whirled toward them, shedding his manifested body as easily as a dog sheds rainwater from its coat. Whatever celestial beauty he'd formerly displayed, it had been wiped from his visage by blazing fury. His spectral body, no longer engaged with Mihàil's and no longer constrained by his vanity, soared and spiked, the planes and lines no longer clearly delineated but a terrible rush of discordant harmonic energy that shrieked and wailed around them.

"How did you do that?" he demanded in an awful voice that filled the chapter house.

Miró kept Stasia at his side, her hand in his. He was acutely aware of her, her warm smoky vanilla scent, her breathing. Her heartbeat fluttered. She was so beautiful, and she fit perfectly at his side.

He deliberately ignored Angelli and said, "I love you, Anastasia Fiore."

She turned her wide hazel eyes towards him. Their changeable hue settled on smoky-green.

"As I love you, Miró Kos, my beautiful blackbird." She raised a hand to touch his jaw with light fingertips.

Their harmonics, already in tune, chimed.

An instant later Angelli stood next to them, again manifesting a body.

A magnificent, *naked* body to rival the most perfectly sculpted male form with broad shoulders, heavily muscled abs, and powerful thighs. He radiated strength, grace, and sexual magnetism—and sported an enormous erection. Heavy pheromones underscored his honeyed musk in the suddenly heated air. He was primeval sex personified.

The swiftness of the Dark *Irim*'s change rattled Miró. He felt dirty, small, and weak in comparison.

Next to him, Stasia shifted restlessly, her own temperature rising. A white-hot spike in her core signaled her body's response to the lure of sheer physical pleasure.

It was Angelli's turn to ignore Miró. He studied Stasia before smiling, his eyes gleaming unearthly blue and his teeth vivid white in the darkening room.

"Tell me, Daughter, what is it you truly desire?"

Charisma draped over Stasia as thick as heated caramel. Harmonic fingers stroked down her back and along her flanks. They squeezed her breasts, teased her nipples until they tightened in painful pleasure, and then they dipped into the space between her legs. She widened her stance and swayed toward Angelli, her face flushed. Her harmonics wavered as if being swamped in the wake of a larger vessel.

For a moment the unique sound she made on the spectral plane—her individual harmonic signature—disappeared.

Miró felt *everything* that Stasia felt. He clenched his jaw. Angelli made love to Stasia in front of him. He would win her body. And then her soul

Not if he had anything to do with it.

He cannot have you. You are mine, he flashed to Stasia, siphoning some of her excess heat and steadying her harmonics.

As you are mine, she answered, raising her chin and locking her gaze on Angelli's.

"I desire you," she said, charisma and sexual need thickening her voice.

Angelli blinked.

Angelli circled them, pressing against Stasia and stroking her with his long, elegant fingers. Miró almost flared when the Dark *Irim* cupped her breast and bent to kiss her. Stasia moaned even as she clutched at Miró's hand.

Trust me, she flashed. *Trust me to be a* bushtër. *A dragoness.*

I trust you.

"And I desire you, *bellissima*," Angelli said in an equally thick voice.

"*Sì?*" she pressed, leaning into the Dark *Irim's* chest and capturing his hand between them. She kissed him, holding his jaw as she explored his mouth with her tongue.

"*Sì*," Angelli choked, his eyelids drooping. He reached a finger to hook into the top of her gown.

Miró tensed himself. He was about to break his promise. And then he felt a surge of energy that bolstered his and Stasia's harmonics before she gathered it into her core.

"I may desire you, but I do not want you, Yeqon the Seducer," Stasia said, her voice ringng with conviction.

And power: the power of naming and the power of the manna from the painting behind them.

Stasia had used Angelli's charisma and desire against him.

Angelli roared. The sound shook the walls and ceiling now grazing his head. But the heavy thickness of his angelic presence had lifted. They recognized it for what it was: a petulant storm of impotent rage.

Delighted laughter chased the shadows out of the room. On the half wall enclosing the bench nearest the windows sat Zophiel, still wearing her angelic warrior form. A luminous sword rested on the half wall next to her.

Angelli fell silent, his harmonic energies exhausted and suppressed.

Zophiel wiped at her eyes and gave a loud, satisfied sigh. She beamed at Miró and Stasia.

"Well done, my flower and blackbird. Well done."

Then she turned to Angelli and narrowed her eyes. "Be gone. Your 'sword' is no match for mine."

He winked out of view, but not before they saw him shrunken in all meanings of the word, ugly and malformed.

The Infatuation of the Watcher Angels (after Caravaggio) remained, depleted of its angelic manna.

Thirty-Three

Pain stung her bare feet, and a dark wave of exhaustion rolled down Stasia. She swayed before Miró caught her elbow. She gripped his arm to steady herself.

"You should sit," he said.

Stasia shook her head, blinking to clear her vision. Her gaze had fallen as she'd moved, and she saw the matching blood and dust on Miró's feet.

"What happened to *your* shoes?" she asked, puzzled.

He shrugged and smiled wryly. "Steel-toed combat boots cannot withstand high heat as it turns out."

Stasia was about to question Miró further when movement behind them preceded his sudden disappearance. She pivoted, sucking in a quick breath at the sharp bite of the shredded skin on her ankles and toes, and saw Gina backing into the chapter house ahead of Miró, whose narrow gaze threatened violence. The *Carabinieri* officer stopped at Stasia's side, her harmonics moving in an unsteady rhythm. Miró also halted.

"No one leaves until we say so," he told the *Grey* Elioud. "And I know when you are lying, so save your explanations for someone else."

Gina watched Miró go and kneel next to Eva, who'd slid to the floor as they watched. "That one is not going to live."

Stasia didn't respond. But the cooling of Eva's infrared signature to a dull red confirmed Gina's assessment. Miró touched Eva's neck and then laid a palm on her chest. He looked back at her, shaking his head. Then he laid the dead woman gently on the floor next to Willem, who despite the large pool of blood spreading under him, still radiated a strong white core in his infared signature.

Mihàil joined Miró over Willem. They conferred in low voices about the newest member of their team as Miró used a utility knife that Mihàil gave him to cut Willem's tuxedo jacket and white shirt open.

Gina looked at Stasia out of the corner of her eye. "You can have no use for me. You do not need me to recover the Van Gogh." She gestured deprecatingly.

Stasia, about to go to Olivia, turned to her "colleague." She bit back the spurt of anger at Gina's sly hint of charm. Even now the woman hoped to turn the situation to her advantage.

"You are wrong. I do have a use for you."

She left that tantalizing bit there knowing that the other woman wouldn't be able to leave without satisfying her curiosity and made her way to the end of the chapter house where Olivia had taken a seat on the bench next to her earlier hiding spot. She sat down next to the *zonjë*, who'd already recovered her composure and her 9mm, which she'd left on the floor when the guard disarmed her.

Olivia looked at Stasia. Her changeable blue eyes, which often conveyed her emotions when her face didn't, had a steely cast to them.

"We good?" she asked Stasia.

Stasia didn't pretend to misunderstand the American idiom. "*Molto bene*," she said, nodding.

Olivia smiled. It radiated from her whole face. Her eyes had changed to the variable blue of a sunny Tuscan sky. She touched the bead bracelet on Stasia's wrist.

"That was very helpful. Your guy has some pretty ingenious ideas at times. You *are* keeping him, aren't you?"

Stasia swallowed. It was certainly one thing to tell Miró that she loved him and to use that declaration to ground her in the face of the most powerfully sexual being she'd ever met. Quite another thing to tell her best friend Olivia that she had no intentions of letting Miró go after all that they'd managed to handle together. Because that made her decision about more than her and Miró: it also made it about the *Elioud* team that she would became a part of.

The team that Olivia and Mihàil led together as The Dragon of Albania and his lady....

In bocca al lupo took on a whole different shade of meaning now.

She glanced over to Miró, who'd stepped back to let Mihàil lift the still-unconscious Willem in his arms. A heavy layer of drywall dust and debris coated Miró's normally immaculate hair and clothes. An image of him in the hospital bed in Aix-en-Provence came to her, and an earlier one at the cemetary where Fagan's *bogomili* had cut off his finger followed on its heels.

Feeling her gaze on him, Miró looked over his shoulder and smiled.

Stasia's heart leapt. Strange fluttering tickled her stomach as if she'd gotten her first field mission. It was both excitement and trepidation, she realized, and not a little heady infatuation—a great surprise to her after all this time. She'd believed she was too mature, too cynical, for such an idealistic state.

"*Sì*. I am never letting him go," she said, surprised at the huskiness in her usually confident voice. She blinked and cleared her throat.

"Fantastic," Olivia said, pulling her smartphone from a side pocket on her tactical pants. "Miró deserves to be happy."

She looked down to swipe through a few screens before pressing her earwig to switch to phone calls.

"And me? Do I deserve to be happy?" asked Stasia.

"*Naturalmente, cara*, which is why Mihàil and I want you to know that there is no hard boundary on the team's location. Miró has always had a thing for Italy. Now he has someone to watch over him here."

Olivia's gaze shifted as whoever she'd called answered. "Beta! Tell András and Danek to get the helo in the air. We're mopping up here, and we need your help. Bring a surgeon." She paused. "No, it's for a new teammate we picked up on the mission."

Pressing her earwig, she sighed and looked up before speaking again.

"Of course you must come. We wanted you and András closer, but he has been like an old mother hen where you're concerned ever since you got stabbed. He told Mihàil he wasn't up to going on the op, but we suspect he really wanted to stay to watch over you."

Stasia, who'd watched as Miró picked up Eva's lifeless body before he and Mihàil left the chapter house, turned at that. It didn't seem like a good idea to her to draw Beta's notice to András's interest, but Olivia knew the standoffish Czech better than she did. They'd met months before she and Olivia worked on the Venetian operation, though Stasia gathered that their initial interaction had been a lot more turbulent and not clearly destined for close friendship. She wondered if she'd ever learn the details of what happened between the two women, who were in many ways polar opposites.

Except when it came to being strong-willed and tough as steel.

"No, not Stasia. Someone that *L'Amante* had been trying to recruit." Olivia paused and looked at her. She winked. "Stasia and Miró have a few things to work out, but they've declared their love for one another in front of all and sundry, including a Dark *Irim* who didn't take it too kindly. And yes, we have the third Watcher Angel painting. Oh, okay then. See you in a couple of hours."

"Beta is coming?" Stasia asked as soon as Olivia pressed the 'hang up' icon.

She suddenly found herself anxious about the laconic Czech's reaction to the news about her and Miró. After all Beta had had a lot more insight into their romance than she'd had—and that was rather disturbing, all things considered.

Olivia nodded. "We were still negotiating with András about how to use them when the timeline got moved up, making the point moot. Meanwhile Beta has been even less forthcoming than usual. It's been a trial having her stay with us to be honest."

"She is semi-feral, *cara*. Being cooped up, even in a mansion, has made her even more eager to escape. Perhaps you should not have left her freedom to András, who has as much tact as a sheepdog."

Olivia laughed at the comparison. "That explains why she jumped at the chance to get on a helo and help us deal with a few mercs, some unhinged women, and a group of untrustworthy Grey *Elioud.*"

She put her arm around Stasia. "I'm so glad the worst part of this operation is over, Staz, and you're sharing your mind with me again. No more secrets, promise?"

Stasia sensed Miró's harmonics before she saw him. As she looked up at the *Elioud* whose intense gaze now guaranteed more heat than icy hostility, she smiled and said, "I promise."

Miró stopped next to them, his hand descending to rest on Stasia's shoulder. "Mihàil carried Willem into Todi to get him stabilized. He has lost a lot of blood."

He glanced back the way he'd come. When he looked at them again, he'd grown somber. "He woke up long enough to ask for Eva. Mihàil told him. It has been a long time since I have seen such grief."

"Will he lose the will to live?" Olivia asked. All playfulness had left her. Instead sympathy made the changeable hue of her eyes bluer.

Miró shook his head. "I do not know." He looked down at Stasia. "But I would be more dead than alive if I lost you."

Stasia turned her face and pressed a kiss on the back of his hand. It was the one whose finger had been severed. *That* had been almost more than she could bear. It had driven her to do everything she could to recover the painting. She needed to keep Miró safe.

"And I you," she assured him.

Olivia sighed and stood up. "Okay, I'm recovered enough to go get the van. Also I'm the only one with shoes on. Miró, I'd love to hear how you lost your combat boots once we're able to debrief, but for now, I'd like you two to watch over the painting and Signora Orlandi. What's the status of the remaining guards and the non-combatants?"

"All of the guards are unconscious and zip tied. The other Grey *Elioud* have fled, but we can send Andràs after them when he gets here. It would be best to give them a little amnesia and a different narrative memory about the third Watcher Angel painting and Angelli's 'art auction.'"

"And the women?" Olivia asked. The strain in her voice belied its quietness.

"They have been synced with Angelli so long that they have no ability to function on their own without him. They will be secure enough in the church until Mihàil and I can stabilize their harmonics. Then we will need to arrange transport to a safe house. We may be able to help them, at least some of them, with music therapy."

Olivia nodded. "That leaves the painting to deal with. Maybe she can help." She gestured with her chin toward Gina. "We hadn't had time to arrange suitable packaging and secure transportation with our local assets when the situation changed. I'll leave that to you, Stasia, to work out."

"*Naturalmente,*" Stasia said, nodding.

Olivia gripped Miró on the upper arm in wordless gratitude as she passed him. He murmured *my lady*. And then she was gone. Gina slumped over the half wall in front of her, her hands clasped on its shelf-like edge. She could be praying, but somehow Stasia doubted the woman believed in anything but herself. She would have to deal with her soon but not yet.

Instead, she turned to Miró, who'd rested his head against the wall behind him and closed his eyes. He looked tired. Dust had turned to a thin mud in his sweaty temples and the fine lines at the corners of his eyes. His bare feet, covered in fine powder and cuts, had started to mottle with purple bruising. He wasn't as viscerally attractive as Angelli, but his physical beauty had no compare for her.

He felt her gaze. Opening his eyes he said, "Not as handsome as some."

Stasia, instead of answering, crawled into his lap. He brought his arm up to anchor her. Nothing had ever felt more right and good. She avoided his gaze as she brushed hair off his forehead, her thumbs smoothing the lines there. Next she stared at him so that he would make no mistake about her intent or her feelings.

Teasing, she said, "*Vero, ma i gusti non si discutono.*" *True, but there's no accounting for taste.* She kissed him then, a sweet, soft kiss that shook her to her foundation.

When she sat up, he smiled. "No, I suppose not." Then he turned serious. "I am not your great-grandfather, Stasia."

"I know." She began to swipe at the drywall crumbles on his shoulders.

He tilted his head and studied her. "How do you know? Angelli was telling the truth when he said that it is impossible to know who fathered Beatrix's child."

She shrugged and gestured. "I think that Angelli is impotent."

"The Dark *Irim* lost most of their generative power post-Flood, but it is not unheard of for a child to be born of their unions with human women even if it is unlikely."

"But Angelli took credit for the entire *Elioud* race. He also wanted us to believe that he could have sired Beatrix's child." She shrugged again. "I cannot say for sure how I know, but my intuition tells me that he cannot sire children anymore."

"That does not rule me out," he said.

"No, not directly, no. But I think he would have been happy to tell us the truth in that case. Leaving it ambiguous was a way to have it both ways. You could both be responsible."

"Or neither," Miró said, brushing a lock of her hair out of her eyes and behind an ear. "Since he did not lie, I cannot be sure either. But he was certainly not telling the full truth."

"Whatever Angelli said or did not say makes no matter."

"Why?"

"Because of two things, *bello*: one, our harmonics would give the relationship away, would they not?" At his nod she hurried on before he could speak. "But more importantly I do not think that Zophiel would condone our romance let alone encourage it."

"No," Miró said, shaking his head slowly and smiling. "That is true. She would not. So I suppose that we spent the past few months miserable for no good reason?"

Stasia toyed with the collar of his shirt now. "I would not say that. I think that we needed some time to realize how important this relationship is and to commit to it."

If you want it to be right, make it right, Zophiel's voice came in Miró's memory.

He nodded. Taking Stasia's hand he looked at her until she brought her gaze to his. Her lovely eyes had darkened to a muddy gray, rich and promising.

"I can think of nothing else that I would rather do. My love, will you marry me?"

A moment passed in which Miró feared that Stasia was too shocked to answer. Or too terrified to say yes.

And then she smiled a large, warm smile, and her charisma wrapped him in heavy velvet. "As quickly as possible, *mi amor.*"

***

Three days later András awoke to total darkness, though that didn't matter because his *Elioud* vision saw a wider light spectrum than the normal human one. He just had to focus on the infrared range when it was this dark in his room. That meant his bedroom, one of the smaller rooms on the second floor at the Kastriotis' Albanian estate, presented as a cobalt blue canvas with a few organic shapes in lighter blue, green, and yellow from the residual heat from sunlight. In other words, his room resembled a Van Gogh painting.

He didn't know what woke him. The room was silent except for the underlying hum that came from the *musica universalis* and the electronic hum of his smartphone on the nightstand. Then he heard the *snick* of his bedroom door as it opened and the *click* as it closed. The figure that stood before his door had a distinct infrared signature, one that he'd come to know as well as his own. White-hot light burned in a thin band at its core, but its recent strange graininess had grown across all the color bands, and her harmonics had a shadowy edge. The sensuous and exotic scents of orchid and incense wafted to him, distracting him from his constant concern.

"Gomba?" he asked softly, hardly believing that she was, in fact, in his bedroom, and that this wasn't a dream.

She didn't answer. Instead she came on soft feet to him. Despite the evidence of his thermal vision, he didn't realize that she was entirely naked until she pulled back the sheet and slipped into bed next to him, her silky skin sliding against his. She was hot, much hotter than she should be, but she felt so unbelievably good lying pressed up against his entire length. The tight buds of her small, high breasts pushed against his chest while her long, slender legs tangled with his. He knew that he was a big male, but for the first time in his life he actually felt like the giant indicated by his surname, Nagy. He wanted to protect her, to wrap himself around her and keep her safe forever.

Still he would have questioned her, but she put a long, thin finger on his lips when he started to speak.

"Sh, *spratek*," she whispered and, removing her finger, she kissed him.

András barely wondered why she called him "brat" before his thoughts swam from the drugging effect of her lips and her tongue. He had never kissed a woman so deeply, and he'd wanted to kiss Beta for so long that he had no hope of recalling his rational brain to question why now, why this intimately, when it was all that he'd ever wanted and more.

She moved him to his back and, straddling his waist, thrust her hands into his hair and ran her lips over his forehead, his eyelids, his cheekbones, and his jaw before coming back again to his mouth. András caressed her as he'd dreamed of doing for months, his large hands tender and slow, his touch filled with awe and gratitude. When his fingers came to the threadlike, raised scar along her side where the knife had lacerated her skin, hot tears pricked his eyes.

After that his thoughts dissolved into a kaleidoscope of sensory overload as she moved above him and he in her. When they reached their fulfillment together, he cried out her name.

And when he drifted to sleep afterwards, curled around her back, his arm possessively cradling her, he told her that he loved her.

The next morning she was gone from his bed and gone from his life with no explanation and no trace.